Frankensteins and Foreign Devils

by
Walter Jon Williams

Edited by Timothy P. Szczesuil

NESFA Press
PO Box 809
Framingham, MA 01701
1998

FIRST TRADE PAPERBACK EDITION
First Printing, December 2000

Library of Congress Catalog Number. 97-75646

International Standard Book Number: 1-886778-30-2

This is a reprint of a limited hardcover editon of 1200 copies, published
February 1998.

Copyright Acknowledgments

Contents

Introduction
by Gardner Dozois

If the Many Worlds theory of cosmology is correct, then there must be many alternate probability worlds in which the book that you are holding in your hand doesn't exist—because in those worlds, Walter Jon Williams's first career as a writer of sea-adventure novels—he wrote and published five such novels before selling his first science fiction novel—took off rather than fizzling out as it did in this continuum, and Walter went on to occupy the slot on the bestseller lists currently occupied by Patrick O'Brian ... and so, although he does have a palatial estate in the hills above Malibu in that universe, he's too busy churning out Hornblower-like sea adventures to have time to write science fiction and fantasy stories.

That universe's loss is our universe's gain. And I suspect that our Walter is happier than that alternate-world Walter as well, even if the Alternate Walter is considerably richer—because the truth is, Walter has never been happy writing the same kind of thing for long, and I suspect that a steady diet of churning out nothing but sea stories would quickly bore him. The fact is, one Walter Jon Williams story is rarely much like any other Walter Jon Williams story, often differing widely in tone and mood, subject matter and style of attack, to the point where you could easily believe that any half-dozen Walter Jon Williams stories picked at random had been written by half-a-dozen different authors altogether.

To mention Walter's encyclopedic knowledge of history (Walter seems to know something about every historical period I've ever heard mentioned in his presence, and often he knows about them in intricate and exhaustive detail, including the behind-the-scenes-who-really-did-what-to-whom stuff that most historians don't know) and his love of obscure and little-known

9

historical milieus and odd corners of history (the more obscure and quirky the better), can make him sound like the New Howard Waldrop—and indeed, Walter has produced some of the best Alternate History stories ever written, including the deeply moving Alternate Civil War novella (following Edgar Allan Poe's career as a Confederate general) "No Spot of Ground" and the compassionate and melancholy look at the alternate and alternately entangled lives that might have been led by Mary Wollstonecraft Shelley, Percy Bysshe Shelley, and Lord Byron, "Wall, Stone, Craft." He has also managed to make believable and convincing some oddball scenarios quirky enough to rank with the most off-the-wall Waldropian scenarios, including, in "Red Elvis," the idea of Elvis Presley growing up to become an inspirational Socialist leader whose influence changes the course of modern history—an idea that Walter somehow manages to make seem actually possible as you're turning the pages.

But when you factor in Walter's wide range of other interests—including, but not limited to, the martial arts (Walter is a black belt and occasionally teaches martial arts classes himself), Eastern philosophy and religion, scuba diving, sailing (Walter loves the sea, but lives in the desert in Albuquerque, New Mexico. Go figure.), economics, Hong Kong action movies (especially those featuring Jackie Chan—about whose oeuvre Walter must rank as a world expert), military history and tactics, Regency dancing, birdwatching, gourmet cooking, political systems, and Native American culture—somehow the mix comes out differently.

There's far more to Walter's range than just Alternate History stories, even gonzo Alternate History stories. Walter has also written gritty Mean Streets hard-as-nails cyberpunk, in stories such as "Wolf Time" and "Video Star" and "Flatline," and in novels such as the influential *Hardwired* and *Voice of the Whirlwind;* he's written some of the most inventive, Wide Screen, and most gorgeously colored Space Opera of modern times, including the evocative and unforgettable "Prayers on the Wind," as well as the monumental novel *Aristoi,* one of the most vivid far-future adventures I know (it's no accident that Walter was selected by Roger Zelazny himself to write a sequel to Zelazny's famous story "The Graveyard Heart," and ended up producing by far the most successful Zelazny hommage I've ever read, the complex and eloquent novella "Elegy For Angels and Dogs"); he's written with depth and real ingenuity about the interaction of humankind with aliens, in the brilliant "Surfacing," as well as in novels such as *Angel Station;* he's written light-hearted, wryly amusing, socially satirical novels of manners, featuring the adventures of a Raffles-like thief in a future society, in *The Crown Jewels* and *House of Shards;* he's written dark, moody, intricate, involuted studies of Realpolitik in action, full of betrayals and counter-betrayals and counter-counter betrayals, such as "Solip:System" and "Erogenoscape" (Walter is one of the few SF writers, in fact, who is really interested in and knowledgeable about the day-to-day workings of practical politics, something that can also be seen in *Metropolitan* and *City on Fire,* and it's tempting to picture him as a boy, sitting at the dinner table, reading Machiavelli while shoveling in the Tuna Hot Dish during those long Minnesota winters. Considering his familiarity with political Dirty Tricks and entrapment schemes and intricate double-crosses of all possible stripes, perhaps it's lucky for Albuquerque politicians that he never went into local politics ...); he's written near-future stories such as "Side Effects" and "Days of Atonement"; he's written far-future stories such as "Dinosaurs" and "Lethe"—you name it, it's a good bet that Walter has written a superior example of it.

Not satisfied with a wide enough range of material to fuel five or six separate careers, Walter also mixes genres with audacity and daring, mixing fantasy with technologically oriented "hard" science fiction in books such as *Metropolitan* and *City on Fire* successfully enough to be counted as one of the progenitors of an as-yet nascent subgenre sometimes called "Hard Fantasy," mixing classical Chinese mythology with the chop-sockey fantasy of Hong Kong martial arts movies in the droll and extremely entertaining "Broadway Johnny," mixing sword & sorcery with (aha!) the sea story in "Consequences," having costumed superheroes grilled by the House Committee on Un-American Activities in the McCarthy-era America of the 1950s in "Witness," and sending H. G. Wells's invading Martians striding into the bizarre, ritualized, and mannered world of the Forbidden City in 19th century China in "Foreign Devils."

In a society where the most easily pigeonholed authors are often the ones who perform the most successfully on the nationwide bestseller charts, perhaps Walter's versatility and fluidity and his playful genre-mixing are a financial liability. Perhaps the publishers would be more comfortable with him if he was more easily classifiable, if everyone knew in advance what a "Walter Jon Williams story" was going to be like ... but nobody can ever know that. I don't think that even Walter knows that, from story to story—and I think he likes it that way.

No doubt that Alternate Walter, the one who churns out volume after volume of best-selling sea stories and nothing else, consoles himself with the finest Napoleon brandy and his own private catamaran—but our Walter has the consolation of being able to let his restless intelligence roam as far and as freely as he likes ... which, as we've shown, is pretty damn far, and pretty damn free.

As for us, the other inhabitants of this particular Probability World, we're clearly the winners in this contest between continuums—because we get to read the stories in this book, and others like them by Walter elsewhere, and those poor deprived alternate world folk do not!

Poor bastards. Lucky us!

Gardner Dozois

Frankensteins
and
Foreign Devils

Solip:System

Somewhere a voice is screaming. Reno is moving at the speed of light, and around him the universe cries in pain. Brightness dazzles his eyes. Odors sting his nostrils. Above him swim the stars, and their soft glow is blurred by tears.

He is lying on his back. Something under him makes a crumpling noise. The stars are staring with gleaming pupils of light.

Reno moves his arm. A simple thing, but he had forgotten how to do it. He wants to wipe the tears from his face, but he touches his temple by mistake and feels something different, a wire thrust into his head. His coordination has badly deteriorated. The body seems wrong. His throat aches. His mouth tastes foul.

He remembers where he is, what he intends here.

He remembers the screams were his own.

The room is large, high, all swooping curves without a single straight line. Orbital fashion, brought to Earth. Reno realizes the stars above him are holograms, hanging below the cold night ceiling.

He is lying on a bed, on a tumbled stack of computer printout. The room smells of sweat. He tries to sit up. The stars spin overhead, in his mind. He drags in air.

"Reno? Reno?" A voice in his mind. His own voice.

"I did it," Reno says. "I'm in."

"It works, then."

"It works. Leave me alone now. I'll talk later."

Something smells bad in here.

He turns his head, scans the room. There is a computer console, chairs, video monitors, a desk piled high with dirty dishes. A half-open door leads to a bathroom. His bed has burgundy silk sheets, a yellow comforter. He is dressed in white cotton drawstring trousers and nothing else. Reno pulls the wires from his head and tries to stand. He fails. The soft carpet absorbs him. He crawls toward the bathroom. The prickle of the carpet against his feet and arms feels like nails being hammered in. Inside the bathroom, the wallpaper is made of full-size photographs of refugee children, all dirty faces, bare feet, torn clothes, huge dark eyes.

Reno reaches for the marble countertop and pulls himself upright, then to his feet. He sways as he stares into the mirror and sees a face he's never seen before. The eyes of dirty children echo his amazement.

He remembers what his friends asked him to do, in return for certain favors.

He remembers what it was like to die.

Once he had been a pilot flying contraband, then later a speculator, riding the face market up and down and making money on every financial wave. Reno's body died weeks before, the result of a fiery accident, but before the body failed entirely a pattern of Reno's mind survived in analog form, sitting in a vat of liquid crystal in Havana, in the Florida Free Zone. Reno's friends are growing a clone body for him. His mind will be read into the clone, and Reno will live again.

Reno's friends, who are paying for all of this, are not precisely disinterested. Because something called Black Mind has been uncovered, a project prepared as a secret weapon by the United States just prior to their loss in the Rock War. A project that would use neuronic interface technology against itself, would not simply make information available to the mind, but overwrite the mind with invading data.

After the U.S. lost the war the developers shut down the project, perhaps because they were unimaginative and had no orders, perhaps because they were afraid of the technology, the power it represented.

Reno's friends are not unimaginative. And they are not afraid.

And now Reno is an Orbital power himself, his brain-analog read, courtesy of Black Mind, over the forebrain of man named Albrecht Roon, an architect of the Rock War, a war criminal according to many—and a man who is, thanks to a proxy fight and considerable stock fraud, the new chairman of Tempel Pharmaceuticals Interessengemeinschaft, and about to fly from his private home in the Cordillera Oriental to his giant drug factory in the sky.
. . .

Reno looks at himself in the mirror, sees a beardless, thirtyish man with a scalp lock, kohl-rimmed eyes, corroded teeth. There are dark ceramic interface sockets on his temples and over his ears, each decorated with diamond chips. His muscles are lax, and the pale flesh sags on his chest and around his middle.

Reno's not himself any more: he's died, come through the fire, been reborn.

Earth's savior.

He can't help laughing.

Albrecht Roon was an old man in his eighties, transferred nine years ago, via crystal analog, into a younger body. Brain transfer is an inexact science, and sometimes leads to problems of adjustment, incomplete transfer, personality changes. Until Roon could demonstrate his mind was unimpaired, he was demoted and dropped down the gravity well to prove himself again before rising on high to his former place of eminence. Dropped down to where Reno and his friends could get at him.

Where Black Mind could do its work.

It all seems insane now. Reno has no confidence in his ability to bring off the impersonation. A few minutes ago, when his consciousness consisted of a fractal analog of his original neural net, the choice had seemed simple—take over Roon's mind, take over his company, use it to benefit the planet. Now the notion is merely preposterous.

Reno runs his hand over his face. There is a sharp stink in his nostrils, and he realizes it's his own cologne. He hasn't smelled anything in so long that the sensation is oppressive. There is something horrid in his mouth. Probably his sense of taste is awakening as well.

He tries to walk. Vertigo tugs at his belly. His feet keep melting out from under him. The body is *wrong*. The arms and legs are too short. The center of gravity is off.

Reno perseveres. An appalling taste stabs his tongue like a knife. After an hour, he can walk fairly well, has begun, tentatively, to use Roon's reflexes. He returns to the bed, takes one of the phone studs and puts it in a temple socket. The phone line is still open.

"Anyone home?" he asks.

The voice that answers is his own.

Suddenly a memory comes back, returning with such force that Reno staggers. It isn't taste that he's regained, it's thirst. His tongue grates on the roof of his mouth. Now that he recognizes the sensation, the discomfort doubles.

Reno steps out of the room and into the corridor outside. Against the wall, the hologram of a refugee girl-child burns with cold laser fire. The hall curves to the left, falls slightly. He has a hard time walking. His balance isn't working properly yet, and he has difficulty coping with the way the floor keeps dropping out from under him.

Another child appears. Reno thinks she's another hologram, but then realizes that this one isn't dirty or round-bellied, that she wears a white dress and has interface sockets on her head. Her hair is clipped short and parted on the right. He thinks she is about ten. She stops her movement as he appears, moves to stand with her back to the wall, like a soldier making way for a general. She stands with her eyes down, waiting. Panic throbs in Reno's chest.

"I need a drink," Reno says. He tries to sound like a man used to giving orders, but his voice grates like an old file on steel and his tongue feels like a dry sponge. "Come with me."

"*Sí, tío,*" the girl says. Her eyes are still downcast, as if she doesn't want to look at him. She turns and leads Reno down the corridor. In a cold sweat, Reno tries to remember what he knows about Roon, whether he has any family on Earth. He doesn't think so; so far as he knows, the Roon family is all in orbit.

Another child appears in the corridor. This one is a boy, dressed in dark slacks and a white shirt. His hair is short, his face sockets dark on his temples. He carries a little schoolboy satchel. Like the girl, he steps aside and stands with his back to the wall as Reno walks by.

A few steps beyond, the girl walks into another room. It's a lounge with a wet bar. Rare petroleum-plastic bottles stand ranked beneath its long mirror. Reno hurries behind the bar, almost taking a fall in his eagerness, and fills a glass with water from the tap. He drinks it eagerly.

It's the first drink in months. Water pours from the corners of his mouth, splashes on his bare chest.

He fills the glass again, drinks half of it. He puts the glass down and sees a holographic model of Jupiter hanging below the ceiling, complete with slowly orbiting moons.

The little girl is still waiting, her eyes downcast. Reno holds out the glass.

"Want some water?"

"Thank you, uncle." The reply is barely audible. She takes the glass, sips from it, stands with the glass in her hand. She never looks at him. Reno takes the glass.

"You can go," he says.

"Thank you, uncle." Moving quickly, she takes his free hand and kisses it.

As the chill wet lips touch his skin, Reno realizes what Roon has been using the children for. His flesh turns to ice. He stares at her in shock.

Above his head, frozen moons circle a planet that failed in its effort to become a sun.

By evening he has almost got used to talking to himself. The crystal analog of his mind is still in the vat in Cuba and is happy to talk to him on the phone, knowing his clone is still growing in a white, sterile room next door. It's only

the Reno in Roon's body that's on a suicide mission; the other will live happily ever after on Earth.

Reno wonders which of them is the real Reno.

Then he realizes. The real Reno is dead. His brain boiled and exploded
from his skull when his house caught fire. ...

The two ghosts talk long into the night.

Movies of Albrecht Roon flicker on the monitors. A Western American voice
sounds in Reno's aural centers, someone who'd met Roon and knew him, talking to Reno through a scrambled channel.

"He talked in aphorisms. Almost as if he was white-brained, but not
quite."

"A face case."

"He had his head in the interface all the time. Trying to keep track of
things. He didn't have access to the big AIs in orbit, and he had to do it all
himself. His rivals in orbit would have torpedoed him if they could, and he
had to keep informed."

Reno watches the way Roon moved, as if he were still in orbit, drifting
from place to place. Listens to the way he talked. *The architecture of the future
is implied by the architecture of crystal intelligence. ... We can integrate our consciousness with the incorruptible perfection of data. ... Crystal recognizes only
reality, only necessity.*

Roon, Reno realizes, was crazy. He's invaded the mind of a madman.

The recording ends. White noise fills the room.

"You didn't tell me about the children," Reno says.

There is a moment's silence. "Yes, I did." The voice is surprised. "That
was the first thing I told you. We wouldn't have sent you in there without that."

Cold talons touch Reno's nerves as he realizes that the memory failed to
implant.

He's in the head of a crazy man, and he doesn't have everything he needs
to survive there.

Roon's closet is full of orbital-style clothes, shoes with velcro strips, light sleeve-
less cotton jackets tailored to the body so they won't billow out in freefall. No
ties, since ties can catch on things. The latest cuts, the latest styles; some of
the best North African designers. All the clothes fit perfectly. Roon had been
planning his return to orbit for some time.

Reno pensions off the children, puts them onto a shuttle for the Florida
Free Zone, where they'll be put into boarding school in Mobile. He does it by
remote control; he doesn't think he can face them.

Roon's slate for the Tempel Board of Directors was confirmed before
Black Mind took him. Reno absorbs everything he can find on them before

he takes his private plane to the Gran Sabana port. His own knowledge may be faulty: he has to crosscheck everything.

People are waiting for him at the wide personnel lock, a long, round tube padded in white chamois brought up from Earth. He scans the faces, recognizes members of the board of directors. There's a man right in front of him, hand stuck out, and Reno recognizes him as someone named Jackson van Allen, an old crony of Roon's, head of the Orbital Freeport Control Commission before Roon's demotion, now back in his old slot. He looks older than the photographs in his dossier, more jowly. His blond hair is light as down, and his handshake is firm, dry.

"Herzlich Wilkommen, Albrecht," the man says.

"Jackson," Reno says, and freezes. He knows what's expected, and that what's expected is German, and he doesn't know the language.

His heart lurches. He's been here two seconds, and already it's over.

"Viele Grüssen, Kamerad," he says, the words just coming out, and somehow he knows not only the phrase, but the fact that it's more a Bavarian saying than a northern … how the hell did he know that?

The corporate anthem begins to blare out of speakers. People straighten a bit, look more respectful. Reno tries to calm his panicked heart, slow his breathing.

He notes that van Allen has sockets on his head, old-fashioned metal ones. Reno makes note of that. He might have to make use of it.

The other members of the board wait behind van Allen in the airlock. Reno progresses along the chamois-lined tube and greets them all, manages to remember their names and shift the conversation to English. He's weightless here, and the board members pass him from hand to hand. Security people drift in the background, weightless, their heads turning left and right, scanning like radar receivers for things out of place. They're all mercenaries from Earth: Reno isn't about to trust people belonging to the previous administration.

Cold surges up his spine. These are some of the people, he realizes, who planned the Rock War, who schemed not only for independence for the Orbital habitats — an independence which might have some point — but who had planned to seize control of the Earth as well. The men and women who had drowned Earth's hopes in a barrage of falling stars, artificial asteroids that crushed cities, crushed dreams. …

"Ladies and gentlemen, there will be a full board meeting tomorrow," Reno says. "For today, I want only to get my reflexes back. And celebrate being in space again, and among my friends." They applaud politely: their grip shoes hold them at all angles, upside-down, rightside-up, cockbill. Reno smiles, his lips tight over corroded teeth. "Tomorrow," he says, "we'll start putting our affairs back in orbit."

Van Allen follows him out of the airlock. Reno flails for a moment, and van Allen grabs him by the sleeve. With van Allen's help, Reno manages to plant his grip shoes on velcro strips by the airlock door.

"Reflexes gone, eh?" van Allen asks. In English, thank God.

"I'll get them back." Reno's heart is thundering. He has the impression that he's staring wildly: he tries to calm himself.

Van Allen leans closer. His eyes are hard.

"What happens now, Albrecht?"

Reno looks at him. "We take the next step," he says. It seems to be the answer van Allen wants.

"Our stock has risen by three hundred percent following the actions of the Orbital Soviet and my announcement of a policy of retrenchment," Reno says. "In a few more days or weeks, after the common stock ceases to be the subject of such widespread speculation, we can expect it to return to pre-crash levels. And retrenchment *is* our policy for the present. But I want us to be looking beyond retrenchment, beyond merely maintaining our position."

Reno is happy to be in gravity again, in the huge rotating cylinder that is Tempel Habitat One. The long Tempel boardroom table is a half-inch laser-sliced ovoid, asteroid material, coated in smooth gas-planet plastic and gleaming softly with flecks of silicon and nickel. Placed around the table are nine of the fourteen board members. The rest, in the Ukraine or South Africa or the Belt, watch through coded communications links. Reno can see their faces on video monitors inset into the ceiling, all except the woman in the Belt, who is so far away that she can't effectively participate and is recording the meeting for viewing later.

"We're still weak in aerospace," Reno says. "Almost forty percent of our cargoes are moved in carriers belonging to other companies. Although we can begin to build our own fleet, it will have to be done almost from scratch, and will prove an unacceptable drain on our now-scarce capital. The board should contemplate a takeover attempt."

Board members cast surreptitious glances at one another. On the video monitors, heads appear to be consulting their control switches.

"Albrecht," says Viola Ling, the head of the Pharmaceutical Division. Her eyes are uneasy. "Your predecessor ..."

"My predecessor failed in just such an attempt at takeover," Reno says. "Yes. That is correct." He looks at each of the members in turn and sees them full of doubt. He tries to think of Roon sitting in his alloy house in the Cordillera Oriental, alone in the dark with his phantom stars. Tries to think of the mind that built the place, the flowing corridors, arching ceilings, swollen-bellied holographic reminders of squalor and death. Tries to remember the incantatory, evocative way he spoke, as if delivering his monologues to the stars themselves. "My predecessor was unsubtle. He had a military back-ground: his actions were direct and easy to counter. Stock manipulation, di-rect action, sabotage ... inelegant. Inefficient." He looks at each again, turn-ing at the last to van Allen, seeing the answering resonance in van Allen's ex-pectant eyes. "We must learn to be more subtle than Mr. Couceiro," he says. "More careful in our movements. We have some time before we move into the next stage. And when we do, we must be ready."

Reno turns to Viola Ling and smiles. "Don't worry, Viola. Your Research Division is our mainstay. You won't lose your funding. Not this time."

"Thank you, Mr. Roon," she says. He senses something wrong in the way she reacts to him, as if she finds him distasteful. She has turned her head away, and Reno wonders if Roon used his corroded teeth as a weapon, smil-ing when he wished to intimidate, make people give way. Yet Viola Ling has always been one of Roon's allies, had been exiled to a research lab in central Russia after she backed one of his attempts to return to power.

Perhaps, he thinks, she's heard about the children.

Reno rates a room with an actual window to the outdoors, one at the far end of the Orbital habitat, insulated from his employees by a screen of Japanese security and from Earth by vacuum and radiation. The room is paneled in teak. A Miró and a Velázquez watch each other from opposite walls; a giant holo-gram-simulation of the station, slowly rotating, faces his desk. He plants his bare feet on Navajo rugs worth tens of thousands of dollars and watches Earth, the startlingly pure blue and white, brown and silver snakes that are rivers filled with erosion, the fragmented coastlines where the rising seas are eating the land, just as Earth's remaining resources are being eaten by the population. Soon the population may be the only resource left. The Orbitals were once their hope, a gateway to new resources. Now the Orbitals stand like a wall between Earth and its broken dreams, claiming the future for their own.

Reno can't change that, not even with Black Mind. The Orbitals hold the high ground, and the Earth hasn't anything left with which to take it.

All Reno can do is try to give Earth some relief. "I want a private comm link set up between my office and this address in Havana," he says. He holds out a data cube.

"Yes, sir." Akinari is one of his Japanese mercenaries. Reno likes the Japa-nese for their stylish sense of loyalty: if they ever betray him, it will be in a big way, no sniveling half measures but a true apocalypse, death and mad excess and a rain of blood. ...

"Please tell Mr. van Allen he can come in."

"Sir. Thank you, sir."

Akinari leaves, taking with him Reno's private link with his ghost self. He needs a way to communicate with his friends on the ground.

Van Allen enters and takes the drink and the chair that Reno offers him. He looks clumsier in gravity than in freefall, and paunchier.

"You've settled in?" van Allen asks.

Reno nods. "I want to tour everything in my first week," he says. "Every lab, every office. Let everyone know I'm here and responsive."

"I'm sure they'll be reassured to know you're among us."

"I hope so." That really isn't the reason for his intended tours: in reality Reno's trying to find reasons to delay making any major decisions until he feels more confident.

He can't delay this, however. Van Allen and Roon had been close; van Allen is obviously expecting something from him.

"Jackie," Reno says. His voice is tentative, his nerves hum in fear. That's what van Allen's dossier said his friends called him.

"Al." Reno feels his tension ease. That wasn't the wrong opening.

"I wanted to have a talk with you about how I see things," Reno says.

"I'm flattered. Thank you."

"You've earned my confidence. I wouldn't be here if it weren't for you." Which is probably not true, but seems a good opening.

Van Allen looks at his drink. "Thank you, Al."

Reno perches on the edge of his desk. Earthlight burns on van Allen's face, showing the broken veins, the pouched cheeks, the puffiness around the eyes of someone who spends a lot of time in freefall. "I'm trying to look at the long term, Jackie," Reno says. "I've been into the deep crystal here, and I've seen some things that bother me."

Van Allen seems surprised. "Projections are up."

"Short-term projections, yes. But the primary market for pharmaceuticals is on Earth, and Earth is running out of the resources to pay for them. A large percentage of our profits has been from the manipulation of the market, and the Earth people have been getting smarter in ways of circumventing our manipulations. No, Jackie, we've got to look outward."

Van Allen looks up involuntarily, past Reno and the rotating globe to the cold glitter of the stars beyond. "We're not suited for that."

"We've got to be ready for the next step. We—the Orbital blocs—have been diverting too much of our attention, and too many of our resources, to keeping the Earth under our domination. There's no reason for that. The Earth is finished anyway. We've got to be ready for the next fight, and that's going to be waged beyond Earth orbit, for the resources that lie out there."

Van Allen nods slowly. "So that's why you want transportation."

"We've got what we want from Earth, Jackie," Reno says. "We've got our freedom. But what have we done with it?"

Van Allen considers. He hasn't resisted the idea at all: he's already considering how to implement it. "Ling isn't going to like this. It will mean degrading the Pharmaceutical Division."

"The PD's vital. But it's not the future."

Van Allen's tongue, a washed-out pink in Earthlight, touches his lips. "We could give her a directorship of another division. One that will be emphasized under your program. Promise her that in return for a few more years' good work with Pharmaceuticals."

Reno feels relief turn to triumph. "Very good, Jackie." Van Allen looks up at him. "I think we're going to make this transition work." Reno looks into van Allen's eyes, seeing the Earthlight shining there. He puts a hand on van Allen's shoulder. "I want you to help me manage it. No one can do it better."

"Thank you, Al. You know, it sounds strange speaking to someone who looks as young as you—" He grins uncertainly. "But you've always been a father to me."

"Welcome to the top," Reno says, and answers the grin. "My son."

The little man smiles at the sight of two women engaged in mutual foreplay. One is black, the other blonde. "I like the blonde," says the little man.

Reno smiles back. "She can be yours," he says.

The little man raises an inhaler of snapcoke to his nose and fires a pair of torpedoes to his brain. "I'll take my time," he says.

The black woman has just produced a little crystal dildo attached with laseroptic wire to her head studs. She begins to copulate with the blonde via computer interface. Reno has to admit a certain imagination is present in the staging, on the blue and red spotlights that highlight the action, that gleam off the little dildo.

The little man's name is Lippman, and he is Reno's guest at Tempel's executive brothel. Lippman is a major figure in transport in South America west of the Andes, his firm moving Tempel's product from the Gran Sabana spaceport. He's just come up the well to sign a new contract that should allow him to finance an expansion of his company and provide him with a lot of Tempel's business, in return for which Lippman and his family will forfeit most of their control and receive their ticket off the dead zone of Earth and into the Orbital ruling class. It's a perfectly sensible arrangement, one that Albrecht Roon had been trying to make previous to his re-ascension, and that his enemies had blocked for reasons more political than economic.

Now all that's needed is the appropriate thumbprints and an appropriate South American bonding ritual, in this case a visit to the whorehouse. The whorehouse itself is a private club catering to high-level executives and their guests, the walls black, the floor and ceiling mirrored. There are floor shows and a very good litejack band. The hostesses mix dangerous martinis and also sleep with you. They're on salary and are ordered to refuse all tips.

The official reason for the place is that unlicensed sex is a security risk. It's better to get laid in a place where hygiene is taken care of and blackmail is an impossibility—unless of course it's Tempel I.G. doing the blackmailing with recordings made through two-way mirrors and concealed audio pick-ups.

But that's the official reason. The real reason for the place has to do with power. The Orbitals embrace a wide variety of passions, but the greatest is the need for strength, for potence. Weakness is forbidden; the Orbitals are winners in war and everything else, and as powerful a passion as sex can threaten the illusion of omnipotence. Here, sex is removed from anything real, anything threatening. The parody of sex exhibited in the floor show is intended as an exorcism of the real thing and the passions it implies. Passion is to be made harmless here, turned into something hygienic, sterile, acceptable. Anyone foolish enough to do something genuine, anything worth getting black-mailed over, deserves only what he gets.

Reno's ordered a clean room for Lippman. Tempel already owns him: the company doesn't need to gather compromising data on a loyal subject.

The drum synthesizer beats seven against sixteen. Lippman leans closer to get a better view of the action. Reno reaches into his pocket and takes out an envelope. He pushes it across the table to Lippman.

"A year's complimentary membership," he says.

Lippman laughs and buys Reno a drink. Shortly thereafter he's got the black girl and the little blonde bouncing on his knees. Reno decides it's time to make his own choice.

He finds a hostess who approximates his type: tall, rangy, young enough not to seem too jaded. She has a wicked laugh that he finds attractive. The sex is technically perfect; but somehow it doesn't interest Reno very much. Too hygienic, he concludes.

He returns to the brothel in the next few weeks, visits the tall hostess again, then others. The sex grows more imaginative, but the experience doesn't change much.

Strange. They were all his type.

He stares at the rolling planet and listens to his own voice clanging in his head, vibrating his implant crystal. He's worked out security procedures with his ghost brother: the scrambler code will be changed daily, and the codes generated on Earth, a week's worth of codes brought up at a time, straight from Havana to Reno's office.

"I have a few ideas," Reno says. "I've been into the deep crystal here. I've got access to everything: I think there are things here that no one knows about. But I can't deal with it all. I'm working twelve, sixteen hours per day. I've got the access, but I don't have the time."

The other Reno, the crystal ghost, burbles his answer. "Send it to me. I can sift the data faster than you."

"Good. I'll do that." He flexes a shoulder. He's been working out, trying to tone Roon's slack muscles, and his frame is full of minor aches these days.

"One thing more," he says. "We've got to guard Black Mind."

"Yes."

"How many people know about it?"

"Cowboy and Sarah, among our own people."

"They can be trusted."

"Outside of our group, a dozen or so. All CIA or computer jocks."

"That's too many," Reno says.

The ghost's answer is prompt. "That is correct."

It's the right decision, but Reno wonders at the calm way the ghost can condemn a dozen people to death. Reno thinks of the pattern in its crystal matrix, its lightspeed thought. He thinks of all the things he had to relearn—walking, smelling, what it meant to be thirsty. The ghost, he thinks, is growing more and more remote from those memories, growing away from them. Losing all humanity as it waits in its tank.

The clone is almost ready. Reno wishes his brother well, but he needs to make use of the ghost before he transfers.

Little movements are made on the planet, propelled by a minuscule fraction of Tempel's muscle. Eighteen people die in various ways: bullets, poison, accidents. A few others are permitted to live under house arrest in the Tempel compound in Orlando. The lab in Havana becomes a subdivision of Tempel Pharmaceuticals I.G. Akinari's mercenaries stand guard around the building. Black Mind is secured.

No one, barring some local police making pro forma inquiries, seems interested at all. Few people on the planet want to inquire into why the Orbitals want to do what they do.

It's obviously not healthy.

"Mr. Roon." She doesn't look at him, this waif; her vision is focused on his belt buckle. She's twenty-two and painfully thin; her brown eyes are large, heavy with mascara; her dark hair is short and swept back in wings over her ears. There are face sockets in her head. She holds her briefcase in front of her with both hands.

Reno sits down in his chair. The Earth spins behind him. "Sit down, Miss Calderon."

He finds himself staring at her, and wonders why.

There's a problem in the SPS division, Reno has discovered: necessary data hasn't been arriving on time, or has arrived garbled. It's difficult to find out what's happening out on the power satellites. There's no one out there charged with the responsibility of reporting to Tempel HQ; the managers report when they get around to it, or not at all. Reno concludes he needs a liaison with the bureaucracy in the satellites, a personal representative free to take a tug to the stations and gather the data herself. The job isn't critical— the future of the company won't depend on it—and no one in a senior position would be interested. Reno's had Personnel send five people his way, and Mercedes Calderon is one of them, the last he's seen.

A refugee, he knows, from the rock that fell on Panama City; she got a scholarship to the Krupp College of Engineering in Bogotá and has a first-class degree. She knows solar power systems inside-out, she's familiar with computers and statistics, and has been getting outstanding reports from her superiors.

There's something about her, some whisper of memory, like déjà vu. Reno doesn't know what it is. He's certain he's never seen her before.

"I realize this position is well outside the normal track," Reno says, "but it isn't permanent. This job will last a few years at most, and then, assuming all is satisfactory, a promotion will be coming your way. To a supervisory post, if you want it."

Her eyes come up, but not to him; she looks at Earth. He can see its crescent reflected in her pupils, a little mad wink of white light. For some reason Reno shivers. "I'd like that, sir," she says. Her voice is almost inaudible.

He wonders if she's got enough drive to confront the SPS people when she needs to, to demand the data they've been sitting on. She's qualified in all other respects.

She glances nervously at him, then looks down again. Reno feels himself shift uncomfortably in his chair. He keeps looking at her. Wondering.

"Tell me about yourself," he says.

Her eyes turn to his in stunned amazement. He can't understand why. Even after he chooses her for the post, she stays on his mind.

Thirteen board members face him across the asteroid-slice table: the fourteenth is still in transit from the Belt. She is not made a party to this session: the contents are too sensitive to transmit even by code.

"I have looked at the profiles for the transportation companies that have been submitted," Reno says. He holds a data cube in his hands; he tosses it from one hand to the other. "I think that Osmanian A.G. will suit our needs best. A merger would suit both our interests."

Reno can see people exchanging glances. "Mr. Roon." It's Herschel, the man who conducted the study. He seems to be struggling rather hard to conceal his annoyance. "Osmanian is ostensibly a public company, but in fact its actual ownership is very private. Abdallah Sabah is a very independent man; he has a controlling interest, and the rest of the stock is divided along clan lines. No non-Somali has a substantial interest. And they stick together."

"I am aware of that." Roon looks at him coolly. "There is stiff competition in aerospace, and they can benefit from our financial muscle power. Their orbital assembly plant is new, produces state-of-the-art equipment, and can easily be expanded to meet our increased needs. They have a fifty-year lease on the African Horn launching site. Our marketing division can be put at their disposal. They can teach our own transport division a great deal. The logic," he smiles, "the logic of the numbers compels our union."

That, Reno thinks, and the logic of Black Mind.

"Sabah isn't precisely a logical man," Herschel objects.

"Perhaps he only has to be approached the right way," Reno says, and smiles with his decaying teeth. Herschel looks away.

"Let us prepare an offer," Reno says. "If it is a good one, if it has the right logic, the answer will be inevitable."

"Your offer is kind," says Abdallah Sabah. "I regret we must refuse." Reno can see Sabah through his video connection. The old patriarch is in his eighties and is dressed in an old-fashioned Savile Row suit, striped tie and all. He speaks English with an Italian accent, and is drinking tea from a silver cup. The wall behind him is covered in silk wallpaper with a pink flower design. Patterned sockets stand out on his bald skull.

"I am sorry to hear this, sir." Reno has called Sabah on a private conference line; he's made his offer, showed how it would benefit Osmanian Source. The old man has remained polite, but has steadily refused.

"There is one other thing, sir," Reno says. He lifts an interface stud. "One last offer. Would you humor me and face in? I would prefer not to speak this aloud."

Sabah frowns, then agrees. "If you like, Mr. Roon," he says. "Though it won't change my mind."

"Give me this one chance." He studs into the face, then smiles as he pulses a mental signal to Havana.

The ghost rises, a whine of data transmitted by crystal, by optic wire and radio link, a rising wave of darkness invading Sabah's mind. Reno sees the old man slump in his chair, try to raise a hand to his forehead to yank the stud away, sees the hand fall. Tremors move over the old man's face. Saliva glistens on his lower lip. Reno turns away, unable to watch. Black Mind shrieks over the radio link.

The transmission ends. The cold hiss of space fills the radio link. Reno looks at his video again, sees that nothing has changed. The old man continues to stare blankly at the camera.

Reno terminates the transmission. Black Mind worked or it didn't. If it worked, the ghost will call him back.

He waits, watching Earth tumble against the black velvet night. There is no call.

Black Mind has failed.

Word comes, through private sources, that Abdallah Sabah has had a breakdown. Reno calls to express his concern, speaks to other members of the family. The old man had driven the strongest members away, and used the weakest ruthlessly: there's no one left with the founder's inner power, or his vision. The inevitability of Reno's logic becomes clear.

The merger is voted on, and passed.

The board offers their congratulations. Three expressionless Somali faces look at him from behind the round meteor table. *My praetorians,* Reno thinks.

Reno wonders about the old man in his weightless padded cell, two personalities warring in his head, raging at one another, struggling for control. The strong old Somali, and the ghost that has tried to possess him.

Reno looks at the board and smiles. His power is secure: they don't know how he brought it off, but he's lucky and they won't betray him as long as his luck holds.

"The next step," he says. "Always the next step."

Mercedes Calderon is back from her first trip, sitting across from his desk, wearing a navy jacket over a blue pinstripe shirt. The holo image of Habitat One rotates ponderously behind her. With her briefcase clasped in her two hands, she looks like a starving schoolgirl. She's got her information, and she projects raw figures into the vid set on his desk. She talks rapidly about methods of analyzing the data and raises a hand to brush her hair back over her ear. Her wrist is knobbed, the arm sticklike. She looks more emaciated than the last time he'd seen her. She won't return his glance.

She's not Reno's type. He doesn't know why he can't stop looking at her.

She falls silent. He glances at the vid set and sees she's come to the end of her presentation.

"Thank you, Mercedes," Reno says. He stands up. "I'll review the data again later. You've done very well."

"Thank you, sir," she says, almost voicelessly. He stands up to show her to the door.

"Are you well?" he asks. "You don't look as if you've been eating."

"It's just the strain of travel. I only need some rest." It's the same toneless voice.

He puts his hand on her shoulder, feels the skin drawn taut over sharp bone. She doesn't react to his touch, just stops and stares at the door he hasn't yet opened. Her cheeks are dead pale. Behind her the holo habitat rolls on, oblivious.

Reno realizes that she won't react no matter what, that she's as inert as the cotton fabric beneath his fingers. He touches her chin, turns her head, kisses her. Her lips are cool. Her eyes avoid his. He can see the pulse beating in her throat.

Flame licks Reno's nerves. She isn't his type, he thinks.

He leads her to his adjoining apartments, takes off her clothes, pushes her down on the bed. The roof tents over her in a series of smooth interlocking non-Euclidean curves. She doesn't speak. He can count the hollows between each rib. He touches her, strokes her skin lightly. No matter what he does, she doesn't react. He takes her chin in his hand, turns her toward him.

"Look at me," he says. She obeys. In the half-light her shadowed eyes seem as large as staring craters of the moon.

Suddenly there is fire. Somehow he knows how to touch her, make her react, give her pleasure. She clings to him, her hipbones sharp against his skin. Little cries arise from her throat, are absorbed by the room's perfect architecture.

She isn't his type, Reno thinks.

Afterwards Reno has a meeting, and it's too important to cancel. She lies like a broken stick-figure in the bed while he dresses in silence. He feels her eyes on him. He doesn't know what to say.

She says it for him. She sits on the edge of the bed as he is about to leave and takes his hand. He is surprised by the cool touch of her lips on his knuckle.

His blood freezes in the knowledge of what Mercedes is about to say.

"Gracias, tío."

Thank you, uncle.

Reno is sweating as he scans through her file. Where can it have happened?

There. Roon's path might have crossed with Mercedes' eight years before, just after he'd received his demotion and dropped to South America. She was at some kind of refugee school in Panama City. Roon would have had a lot of business at the Panama spaceport.

The name of Albrecht Roon is not to be found on her records, but a surprising number of high-ranking Tempel officials seem to have written recommendations for her. That's the evidence, then, the smoking gun. Perhaps Roon was being more careful about his passions then, but he'd still pulled strings for his protégée, got her into college and then into orbit. Being kind, by his lights. Maybe, before he'd gone insane in his little Cordillera paradise, he'd had a conscience, and tried to pay it off.

Reno can't stop thinking about her, the sharp angles of her body, the mad deep craters of her eyes. He spends most of the night in a fever, working, clearing his computer of all open files. Then he heads for the executive brothel. It's late and the floor show is over, the band gone home. He finds a woman, someone his type, yawning over a cordial at the mirrored bar. With her he tries to fuck Mercedes out of his mind. He is desperate to need this woman, find in her something he actually wants. He spends the night there, the tired whore wrapped in his arms. In the morning he takes her again, bulling her in a thunderous display of vigorous lust, hoping to find in her somnolent, sterile flesh an antidote to the acid that is searing a path through his veins. The passion remains his alone.

The next day he wanders through his schedule in a frantic display of failed concentration. Mercedes is continually floating through his thoughts. He decides he has to speak to her, explain things somehow.

She appears in his office carrying her briefcase in her knobby hands. Her eyes are rimmed with red, her cheeks are hollow. She doesn't look as if she's slept, either.

Reno has planned to say all manner of things, make all manner of apologies. "Miss Calderon," he begins, and then she takes his hand and kisses it, and at the brush of her lips on his knuckle Albrecht Roon's madness rises, all the animal lunacy that Reno had thought was buried beneath the coded onslaught of Black Mind. Reno lifts her in his arms and the briefcase tumbles to the office floor. He carries her to his apartments. She is weightless as a wand.

This time she isn't passive; she clutches his body with her hands, her legs, demands the pleasure he gives her. There is surprising strength in her spidery frame.

After their spasm the strength fades, and suddenly Mercedes seems a desolate fawn, all knees and elbows and sharpened bone, an angular contrast to the smooth polymer curves of the room. Reno gathers her in his arms. Her eyes avoid his.

"Thank you, uncle," she says.

"Don't call me that." Reno's answer is instant and sharp.

Mercedes doesn't seem surprised. Perhaps it's what she expects from him. "Yes, Mr. Roon," she says.

Vague bits of his planned speech resurface in his consciousness. "You're not the girl you were," he says. "I'm not the man I was." True as this last statement is, his words sound heavy, leaden. He isn't convinced himself.

"We should start something new," he says. "Don't kiss my hand any more. You're my lover, not my pet."

"Yes. If you like." He can't tell if she's absorbed any of this. She's become passive again, a reflection of him.

"Call me Reno." he says. And for the first time. she seems surprised.

The ghost brother's voice sounds as if it's drowning in a tank of liquid glass, transformed but ringing with clarity. Little inflection is left, little to indicate personality. Little that is human.

"The transfer failed. The clone wouldn't take the program and went into seizure instead."

"I'm sorry. I will order another clone prepared."

"That's already been done. I suspect it won't work."

Reno is surprised. "Why not?"

"I believe our original program was damaged in transfer to the tank. It was done under emergency circumstances, when we were trapped by the fire, and it may not have all come across."

Reno gazes into the black velvet coldness beyond his window. "Why did Black Mind work for me, then?" he asked.

"Because Black Mind wrote over a mind already inhabited by a personality. Roon's personality was already there to fill the gaps in the program."

A tremor runs along Reno's nerves. "I've wondered about some things," he says. "How easily I've got along here. How I've always seemed to know what to do." He casts a glance toward the door that leads to his private apartments, where Mercedes had been only a few hours before. "Some feelings I've had," he says, "that I didn't have before."

"That's not unusual with mind transfer. Personality change is a hazard."

"I'll get you into a body," Reno says. "I have a plan."

"Don't rush things. I can wait."

"Perhaps not."

There is a short pause. "What did you mean by that?"

"We've talked too long on this channel. I'll send a coded package with the next messenger." Reno switches off.

He looks toward the door to his apartments and thinks of Mercedes. Now he knows why he wants a woman who isn't his type.

Roon is living inside him, in the gaps between his own program.

And Roon is mad.

"My father is still ... not well," says Mohammad.

"I'm sorry. He is a great man."

"He talks strangely. Of things he has never seen, people he has not met." He sips his little gold-rimmed cup of tea. Behind him, the holo habitat gleams in sunlight. "There are those in the family who believe he is possessed by a devil. There have been ..." He gives a wry smile. "... attempts at exorcism."

"I can understand the family's concern, particularly when conventional modes of treatment fail. More tea?"

"Thank you, sir."

There are other ways of knowing people besides bringing them to brothels. Mohammad is a strict Muslim, and in his case the executive brothel would not be a good idea. But even in a Puritan there is always a key.

Mohammad hates his father.

Mohammad is one of Abdallah's sons, one of the most capable and one of those the old man drove into semi-exile. When Reno called him to the Tempel board, Mohammad was running an insignificant transport operation in the Ogaden. He's tall, hawk-nosed, probably brilliant. Reno needs someone to negotiate the labyrinth of Osmanian, the strange network of kinship systems and obligation that serves the transport company in place of a formal structure. He needs someone smart enough to manipulate that complex system, and for that wants someone more loyal to him than to the company, to the cousins who were promoted ahead of him.

And Mohammad hates his father. Maybe he's looking for another father-figure, a man who lives in the sky and has his best interests at heart. Someone like Albrecht Roon.

"Your reports have been outstanding," Reno says.

"Thank you, Mr. Roon."

"I'm prepared to go to the board with the proposal for the new Century Series of fast frigates. We need to move quickly on that matter if the public is to believe that Osmanian's efficiency won't be hampered by the acquisition."

"Sir. I'm very pleased."

"I suspect your abilities are a little constricted in your present circumstance. Perhaps your talents can be better utilized in another direction."

Mohammad sips his tea. "Yes?"

"Acquisitions."

Earthlight glimmers in Mohammad's deep eyes. "I'm interested, sir."

Mercedes lies with her eyes closed, her head partly turned away. She is passive again, a straw doll in Reno's bed. Her passivity drives him into frenzy: he uses her fiercely, desperate to force some reaction from her. Her breath quickens; she bites her lip to stifle a sound. That suppressed cry is enough to trigger his climax.

Afterward Mercedes lies motionless on the dull maroon sheets, still the straw doll. He thinks of the clone dying, its brain an erupting electrical storm, and of what fills the gaps in his own pattern. Albrecht Roon, the architect of the Rock War, with the blood of millions on his hands. Despoiler of children, and of the straw doll lying in Reno's bed.

A wave of disgust washes over Reno's mind. He is compounding Roon's crime, victimizing a woman who has already been victimized more than anyone could possibly deserve.

With a shock he realizes that she hates him. Hates him so much that she can't even move when he touches her.

"You don't have to do this," he says.

Her eyes open slowly, as if she is arising from a dream. She takes a breath. "Do what?" she asks.

"Have sex with me. Not if it's just because I'm your boss. That's not … what I want from you."

"What *do* you want from me, then?"

"What do *you* want? That's my question."

Mercedes gazes at the ceiling. Reno watches the pulse beat in the shadowed hollow above the sharp relief of her clavicle.

"I know you like me to be still and not move," she says. She seems to be talking to the ceiling. "I try to do that for you. But sometimes I want you so much that I have to bite my cheeks and tongue to keep from crying out. Sometimes I want to scream with what I feel for you."

Reno feels blood rush to his skin. He reaches a hand to her, turns her face to his. "You don't have to lie still," he says. "You can do what you want. This is something we can share."

Her expression is faintly puzzled. He doesn't know whether he's been understood. He doesn't want her on Roon's terms. He doesn't know how else to explain it to her.

Mercedes leans forward, brushes her lips against his. He strokes the back of her neck. Her fingertips slide over his body. He can feel the touch of her breath on his neck. His skin seems aflame.

There is a peculiar intent look on her face. She is exploring the relationship between them, her movements still tentative, her mind investigating possibilities.

He closes his eyes and lies back while she caresses him. By now he is perfectly engorged. She throws a leg over him, rides him astride.

Reno looks up at her angular body, the flesh stretched over her ribs into ridges and valleys, the skin drawn so tight over her sharp shoulders that he wonders how it isn't worn through. She looks as though she's been living in a refugee camp for years.

Roon has done this, he thinks. Twisted her, driven her, probably come close to breaking her. But he also taught her to love. Even if that love is for a monster, it's still something Reno wants to cherish.

But it's not for him. As she rides him to climax, she cries out not for Reno, but for *Tío*.

Uncle. A monster. And, in the U.S., a term of surrender.

Mercedes has left Habitat One on another data-collection job to the power satellites. Reno is free to purge her from his blood, extend the work he has begun.

He takes van Allen to the executive whorehouse. A new stage show features a man with a grafted artificial penis, black and preposterously large, studded with metal and cruel barbed hooks. With this apparatus he gives apparent satisfaction to several willing partners. Jarring feedback wails from the amps. Reno wonders what manner of genitalia have been implanted in these women for them to be able to affect enjoyment of this. No doubt he's intended to wonder.

Van Allen enjoys the show. His eyes sparkle, his pouched cheeks glow with excitement.

The bugged rooms here, Reno decides, are crude, inelegant. And unnecessary when people hand you keys to their minds just by watching stage shows. Not when they show you, just from what they stare at, that they want power and potency so exaggerated as to seem ridiculous.

"Jackie," Reno says, "I wanted to talk to you about the next step."

Van Allen looks up, interest in his eyes. "Yes, Al?" he asks.

"I don't like the projections," Reno says. "In the short term our current rate of profit will continue, but in the long term—even with the acquisition of Osmanian, we're still going to encounter a shortfall." He looks at van Allen and smiles. "I want to be here for the long term, Jackie. I'm sure you do, as well."

"With Osmanian," van Allen says, "we have the basic tools for expansion. We haven't employed them yet. Haven't had time, really."

"I want to reach for self-sufficiency," says Reno. "Acquiring Osmanian has strained our energy resources. Their plants take a lot of power, and mostly they're buying it."

Van Allen purses his lips. "I don't know if we can smoothly absorb another company. Our structure isn't …"

"I didn't mean another takeover attempt," Reno says. "I agree, there's danger in expanding too fast. But there's danger if we continue our dependency." He leans close to van Allen, forces intimacy. Van Allen has to strain to hear him over the litejack band.

"I think the days of the United Orbital Soviet are numbered, Jackie," he says.

Van Allen is disturbed. He looks at the stage show, frowns, thinks about it for a long moment.

"Consider what I'm saying, Jackie," says Reno. "I saw the need for the Orbital Soviet twenty years ago; I helped create it. The Soviet was set up to fight for our independence, then to control Earth once we'd won the fight. Earth is beaten. Now we can't *help* but control the planet: the Orbital economies are too critical, too huge. The Orbital Soviet is losing its reason to exist."

Van Allen doesn't seem to want to commit himself to this idea just yet. "Perhaps," he says. "But what does that mean for us?"

"We've been controlling distribution of our product on Earth by subsidizing some operations at a loss to drive Earth competition under, or by forming cartels with other companies to exploit a given market. We've been selling to the black market in order to have a measure of control over their operations. One thing we really *don't* do is compete." Reno shakes his head as screams of feedback accompany a simulated orgasm. "We're not set up for competition. We're not efficient enough, not streamlined enough. We don't command enough resources to be able to compete effectively. And too many of our resources are siphoned off into trying to control Earth."

Van Allen's face is solemn. The stage show appears to have lost his interest. "What you're saying is very dangerous," he says.

"Reality," says Reno, "is dangerous." He gazes coldly into van Allen's eyes. "Power," he says, "is dangerous." Van Allen considers this. Reno puts a hand on his shoulder. "We live in dangerous times, Jackie. That's why we need to be self-sufficient in power. I don't want our new factories hostage to someone throwing a switch."

Van Allen draws back, putting room between them. Litejack crashes from the speakers set in the ceiling. "You obviously have something in mind."

"General Power Systems Satellite Number Four. Their latest. The Singapore bloc mortgaged themselves to the hilt to build it."

"That would serve our present and future needs very well." Objectively. "It's the biggest GPS has built."

"We'll need the help of someone in the Pharmaceutical Research Division. Someone who isn't Viola Ling. I don't want to involve her in this."

"I think I know what you want," van Allen says. His eyes have a familiar light in them, the same light Reno saw when van Allen was watching the man wielding his lethal phallus.

"Then I won't have to say it," Reno says. "And that's all the better in a place like this."

Later, after van Allen disappears with his partner for the evening, Reno steps to the bar and watches the bar mirror, the images of the hostesses as they move from place to place, their walk studied, their smiles bright, their eyes dead. He can't seem to get interested in any of them.

They're not his type any more.

Later that week he has his rotten teeth pulled, replaced with strong ceramic-over-alloy implants.

When the emergency signal goes out from GPS Four, the nearest ship is the prototype Century Series frigate. Mohammad is aboard, supervising the new warship on its trials. He orders the trials aborted, and the frigate diverts on a rescue mission.

Mohammad arrives five hours after the distress call. He finds the eighteen man crew dead of some unknown disease. He enters the station alone and seals himself in.

Using the station radio, Mohammad files a claim for salvage with the High Court of the United Orbital Soviet. General Power Systems protests.

GPS is in debt, and everyone knows it. Without Satellite Four, they have no hope of making their payment schedule. Within the ten minutes following release of the news to the screamsheets, GPS stock has lost forty percent of its value on the Chicago and Singapore exchanges. From his office on Habitat One, Reno announces an attempt on behalf of Tempel Pharmaceuticals to acquire a majority of GPS stock. Tempel seems uniquely placed to take advantage of GPS's problems, having on hand a large amount of liquid capital from a recent bond issue, and Tempel moves with surprising speed and efficiency.

Reno, his jaw throbbing, waits in his office for the call he knows is coming.

"Albrecht."

"Mr. Korsunsky."

Pain hammers through Reno's skull. Knowing this was coming, he's avoided painkillers, not wanting to dull his perceptions.

"Would you mind if we use the face?" he asks. "I've just had oral surgery."

"If you like."

Reno studs into the face and looks into the vid. His pulse rises. For years he has looked at this man as an enemy, as an accomplice to the destruction of Earth's cities and the slaughter of its population. Now that he can deal with Korsunsky as a near-equal, he has to keep reminding himself they're supposed to be friends.

Korsunsky is President of the United Orbital Soviet. He is the handpicked successor to Grechko, its first and most brutal president, who has been going quietly senile in a Tupolev sanitarium for the last ten years, successive attempts at brain transfer having failed.

Korsunsky's red, elderly face seems kindly, but his eyes are a window into a blue Siberian winter. Reno knows he can depend on nothing from this man.

"GPS has filed suit in the High Court." Korsunsky's voice roars in Reno's head. He winces and turns down the volume. "They are claiming an unprovoked attack, a violation of the Orbital Pact."

Reno shrugged. "They will be proven incorrect. My man's action was precipitous, but not illegal."

"GPS is alleging a biological attack."

"Absurd."

A pause. "You are in a dangerous position, Albrecht."

Reno gazed back into Korsunsky's baleful eyes. "Dangerous in what way? I would welcome any objective investigation."

"Would you? The questions raised in any investigation would alone be enough to damage you."

"What questions?"

"There is a pattern forming. What are we to make of it? Abdallah Sabah suffers a breakdown and Tempel I.G. absorbs his company. A mysterious plague afflicts GPS Four, and a Tempel ship is on hand to take advantage of it. Your move on GPS has been very fast: do not insult my intelligence by telling me it wasn't planned in advance. Not when your rescue ship contains Abdallah Sabah's son, whom Tempel has rehabilitated and advanced. Were I GPS, I would advance the claim that this Mohammad is your personal assassin, first having disposed of his father and then the crew of GPS Four."

"That claim would be nonsense."

Korsunsky's face is intent. His voice rings through the interface, the relentless sound echoing in Reno's head in time to the painful throb of his jaw. "The claim alone would damage you. After what your predecessor attempted in the failed Korolev takeover, the Orbital Soviet could not afford to support you." Korsunsky raises his index finger to make a point. "There is a way out. You have made a profit by buying GPS stock after its decline. You can announce the salvage claim was unauthorized and drop it—you didn't make it yourself, after all. You can claim you made the stock purchases only to stabilize the situation. You can withdraw from this attempt with honor and profit intact."

"If I don't do this?"

"I will instruct the High Court to rule in favor of GPS. The Orbital Soviet will also call in the loans it made to Tempel following the failed Korolev bid. That would put Tempel in an extremely precarious financial position— Tempel itself may become the subject of a takeover attempt."

Reno shrugged. "Anatoly Victorievich—I don't understand why you are threatening me this way."

Korsunsky's look softens slightly. "The Orbitals are still in a delicate situation, Albrecht. We are not free of our dependence on Earth, and we are the object of vast hatred. You yourself were re-elevated to the chairmanship as a result of stock manipulation by people on Earth. That proves we are dependent on them, that they still have power. We must remain united, Albrecht. We can't afford to fight each other. We can't afford recklessness. If Tempel must be dismembered as a lesson to others, then so be it."

Reno struggled to keep his face neutral as his heart leaped. He knows he should argue more, try to soften Korsunsky's position, but the chance to destroy this enemy is too great.

"Anatoly Victorievich," he says. "There is an overriding reason for Tempel's actions, of which you are perhaps not aware. Are you alone in your office?"

"No." Korsunsky's eyes track off camera. "But I can be."

"If you will indulge me. This is for you alone."

Korsunsky studs out of the face, then withdraws from vid range. Reno can hear sotto voce discussion. Then Korsunsky returns, puts the studs in his sockets.

"Yes, Albrecht? I'm alone."

Reno leans forward toward his camera and smiles with his bright new teeth. "Die," he says, aware of a certain melodramatic intent here, and triggers Black Mind.

Korsunsky jerks and pitches forward, falling onto the camera lens. Reno peers anxiously into the vid as the screen turns dark. He can hear the whine of data, Korsunsky's hoarse grunts.

Black Mind fades. Reno hears a long moan.

Korsunsky leans back. Blood is running freely from a gash on his forehead. He must have cut himself when he fell on the vid unit. There are tears in his eyes.

"Yes," he says, his lips not moving, the words pulsing through the interface in a voice that is Reno's own. "Black Mind worked." Korsunaky blinks blood from his eyes. "The Orbital Soviet will remain neutral."

In the end, Tempel needs help in dismembering GPS: Mikoyan-Gurevich buys twenty percent, comes away with a new power satellite and some facilities in Asia. The Orbital Court, under Korsunsky's prodding, rules the takeover legal. The disease that killed the crew of GPS Four turns out to be a mutated meningitis virus that has in the past been responsible for several small, deadly epidemics in various parts of the world, including GPS's home base of Singapore. The precise means by which the disease was introduced into the satellite remains unknown. Contaminated food or water is suspected.

There are screamsheet analyses about the "new, predatory era" in corporate relations. Reno receives the congratulations of the board. Abdallah Sabah and Grechko die in their respective padded cells. Tempel is one of the five largest corporations in history.

"The next step," Reno says. "Think of the next step."

Mercedes Calderon returns from her journey to the power satellites. That night, in Reno's bed, she falls limp beneath him and Reno thinks she's gone passive again. It isn't until later he realizes that Mercedes is unconscious. His attempts to revive her fail.

Mercedes is committed to the hospital for treatment of malnutrition.
She's been starving herself to death.

Reno wonders why he never really noticed.

It would seem he isn't the only one on a suicide mission.

Her eyes are rimmed with black. It isn't makeup, Reno knows. Her arms lie
atop the pale green sheets, and he can circle each with his thumb and forefinger.

He stands by her bed and watches her breathe. She is in partial weightlessness here, easing organs strained by malnutrition. Above the bed, on a crystal
display, her vital signs glow a subdued blue in the semidarkness. He reaches
out to touch her hand. There is a rough bandage on the back from where a
needle was taped to a vein.

Suddenly her hand seizes his. Her eyes come open. A crazy, jagged gleam
of blue, the crystal display is reflected in the darkness of her pupils.

"*Tío,*" she says. Her grip is fierce.

He tries to smile. "Call me Reno."

"*Tío.*"

"You're going to be okay. We'll put you on leave till you get better. Then
you'll have another job, a promotion. Where you won't have to travel so much."

"*Tío.*" A desperate, imploring whisper.

"Stop trying to surrender." There is an ache in Reno's chest. With his
free hand he strokes her hair. It's as light and dry as dust.

"*Tío.*" She pulls his hand to her mouth, kisses it. Reno wants to cry.

"Call me Reno," he insists.

She goes to sleep again, her dry lips pressed to the back of his hand.
Reno stands over her bed like a sentry, and knows the enemy he guards her
from is himself.

Mercedes is put on medical leave, moved into a spare room in Reno's suite,
guarded by his prowling samurai bodyguards. A nurse visits regularly, and so
does a dietician. Mercedes puts on a little weight, takes her vitamins. She still
looks like a refugee. She is withdrawn, unsmiling, hesitant. Intravenous
feedings tattoo her arms with bright splotches of blue and yellow.

Reno, unable to stop himself, spends every night in her bed, his vital
signs leaping with hers in the cold lights of the hospital bed's crystal display.
Only then does Mercedes show signs of passion: she clutches at him, cries
out, weeps in terror. He doesn't know what she's afraid of.

Below, on the hammered Earth, war between Estonia and Muscovy
comes to a negotiated end. The demand for medicine declines. Tupolev sees
its chance and tries for Pointsman Pharmaceuticals A.G., winning control
after a long fight that weakens both.

Black Mind wasn't even necessary, Reno thinks. The changed climate was enough.

Mikoyan-Gurevich, its appetite whetted by its easy consumption of GPS, lunges into action against its old rival, buying up enormous quantities of Tupolev stock.

Korsunsky and the Orbital Court again decline to intervene. A Mikoyan-Gurevich messenger queries Reno about another shared takeover. Reno puts out feelers to the Tempel board, finds them unwilling to step into the fight on either side. He doesn't feel it wise to press them, and offers the MiG envoy his regrets.

Mikoyan-Gurevich has a power-sharing directorate, an old-style Russian collective. They aren't vulnerable to Black Mind, but Tupolev is. Reno gives their chairman a call. Black Mind takes him, then the CEO, then drives the vice-chairman raving and into a padded room.

Within days, Tupolev cutters and frigates strike MiG targets. Silent lights blossom in the night sky, lasers cut the darkness. Mass drivers are turned on orbital habitats; power satellites cut loose with slow-cooking microwaves. Pressurized atmosphere boils out into vacuum, crystallizes, drifts slowly to dust the frozen faces of corpses. The preemptive strike is almost entirely successful: Mikoyan-Gurevich is laid bare. Mercenaries in the pay of Tupolev roar into orbit from launchpads in California, Malaya, and Kenya to occupy MiG facilities.

This time the Orbital Soviet acts against the atrocity. Reno offers the Soviet his forces, and the new Century Series frigates fight alongside Korolev cutters, Toshiba marines, Pfizer mercenaries. The Tupolev forces are crushed. Their directors die in the fighting. Remaining assets are divided among the victors.

During the emergency Reno has a lot of conferences with his peers. Black Mind strikes again and again, driving mad those it cannot overcome.

The stunned members of the Orbital Soviet regroup. Stock prices for members of the weapons bloc rise and keep rising. Everyone is nervous, and everyone is arming.

"The next step," says the ghost brother, his voice the sigh of wind through distant trees. "Always the next step."

Less human every day.

"Who are you?" A voice screams in his ear. Reno flounders out of sleep. *"Who are you?"*

Mercedes is in the bed, grappling him, clutching his wrists. Her spittle flies in his face. *"Who are you?"* she demands.

He battles her, fights her onto her back. He can see the tears on her face. Mercedes tries to knee him in the groin, fails. "What's going *on?*" he yells.

Her claws draw blood from his face. "Wake up!" Reno shouts.

Her resistance collapses suddenly. She is sobbing. In a spill of yellow light from the hallway he can see her emaciated breasts trembling with each wracking sob. Lust surges through him, and he is appalled.

He lies by her side and puts his arms around her. His blood is warm on his face. "What happened?"

"Un ensueño," she says. "Un ensueño malvado." An evil dream. He kisses the tears from her eyes. "I dreamed Uncle was killed," she babbles, still in Spanish. "And you had taken his body."

A sliver of frozen ammonia lodges in Reno's heart. He can't say a word. She looks at him and her eyes widen. Reno knows that she knows. "Dios mío," she says. Reno can't think of anything to do but admit the truth.

"My name is Reno," he says.

"My God," she says, English this time. She pulls away from him and he lets her go. She gets out of the bed and backs away slowly, all shadows and fawnlike eyes and sharp angles that Reno can no longer figure. She runs a hand through her cropped hair, hesitates, then turns and disappears into the hallway. He can hear her bare feet on the soft Chinese carpet.

Reno stands and walks back and forth and wonders what to do. She knows too much, he thinks, she knows too much. A song. Knows too much, knows too much.

Knows too much.

He knows what the ghost brother would tell him, and he doesn't want to hear it.

He hears water running. Mercedes is in the bathroom. Reno begins to feel silly standing naked in the dark room with blood trailing down his face. He puts on a dressing gown and steps into the hallway. Mid-twentieth-century paintings hang in shadow on the wall. The bathroom door is closed. He raises a hand to knock. "Mercedes?" he says.

The door opens before he can knock. In the cold fluorescent bathroom light he can see things gleaming: the knife, blood, teeth and eyes. Mercedes is screaming in Spanish. He tries to protect himself with his raised hand and the Razorware kitchen knife slices his palm. Reno stumbles back and Mercedes is right on top of him. He can feel himself being cut. He strikes out with an open hand, catches her on the side of the head. She reels. Reno goes for the knife, fights her for it. She claws at him with her free hand. He slams her knife hand against the wall. The knife falls and so does a Mondrian, its silver frame ringing as glass shatters. He slaps Mercedes again, sends her stumbling back. She goes down on a sharp-edged hip, jarring. Her eyes fill with tears. He picks up the knife and wonders what to do next.

There is blood all over the place. Most of it, he realizes, is hers. She cut her wrists with the knife before using it on him.

Mercedes has collapsed, all fight gone. He throws the knife away and puts his arms around her.

"Don't die yet," he says.

"I have betrayed you."

He picks her up. She is light as a child. Her blood is slick on his hands, trails on the Chinese carpet as he carries her to bed. "I've been working for Viola Ling," she says. "She wants to destroy you. She thinks you're dangerous."

"She's right," says Reno.

"I don't know how she found out about me and Uncle. But she knew everything. She told me about the other children. I wanted to kill you then."

He puts her on the bed. Call Akinari, he thinks. Have him get the Japanese medic in here. No one else he can trust.

She looks at him. "Is Uncle really dead?"

He strokes her cheek, leaves a trail of blood. "Yes." He hates himself for a liar.

She closes her eyes. He can sense her slipping away.

"Don't die yet," he says. "I've got things to do first."

Matted lashes flutter against her red-streaked cheek. Desperation surges through Reno.

"I'm here to destroy them all," he says. "After that, we can both die. Together."

Her lids open slightly. Reno looks down into twin crescents of glittering darkness.

In them, he can read assent.

"She is a danger."

"Viola Ling is the danger."

"Viola Ling is predictable. Her actions follow a pattern. Your Mercedes Calderon is a wild card."

"I can deal with it."

"I am not inclined to believe you."

Reno represses a shiver. The ghost brother's voice is like the sigh of wind through naked trees. There is nothing human left at all.

"Let's talk about Ling," he says.

The purpose of the executive brothel, he knows, is to exorcise passion, on the theory that passion is weakness, and an unwholesome passion can be used against you as a weapon. With Roon, with Reno, the prophylactic failed; Viola Ling has a weapon to use against both of them.

She has not chosen to use it yet, and Reno knows why. He's been too successful, and her attempt would miscarry—she'll wait for one of his gambles to fail, then try to disgrace him.

The ghost brother's thoughts, beyond agreement in the matter of Ling, are not further stated. But Reno knows what they are.

He tells Mercedes never to use the face. He doesn't have to tell her why; it's clear she already knows.

Viola Ling dies over the Pacific Ocean, in a transport headed for Singapore, en route to address a meeting of several affiliates. The pilot's final transmission indicates an explosion, possibly a missile.

Just a few months ago the Orbitals would have assumed that saboteurs from Earth were responsible. Now nobody seems to be sure. Is someone gunning for Tempel? Was it an Orbital frigate?

Reno speaks the eulogy. He praises Ling and promises that anyone responsible will pay for their actions.

After which there's a directors' meeting. Another two squadrons of the Century Series are voted, and there's not a dissenting word.

Things are looking too frightening.

A protege of van Allen becomes the new head of the Pharmaceutical Division. Mercedes is made assistant to the head of the Biochem Warfare group, which is substantially reinforced, and ordered to report all progress to Reno. Vaccines are developed against known biological agents. Means of delivery are contemplated and developed.

Reno stands by the door to his apartments as Mercedes prepares to leave for her job. It's the first time she's left the apartment in months, and Reno insists on two of Akinari's bodyguards accompanying her at all times. He can't be sure what the ghost brother is up to.

She is in her grey suit, her blue pinstripe shirt. He takes her hands and kisses the silver scars on each wrist.

"Don't worry," she says.

"I need you. I can't do any of this without you."

"I'll live," she says. "For you. For now."

She brushes her lips against his and is gone. A matter of months, he thinks.

A matter of months before Roon can die. Die for good and all.

"Why are you doing this?" the President of ARAMCO screams into the interface. "We didn't have anything to do with Ling's death and you know it. If this goes on we're all going to destroy each other!" Her face is anguished. *"Why are you doing this?"*

"I'll tell you," Reno says, and triggers Black Mind.

Because, he thinks as Black Mind sings across the face, if the Orbitals turn their aggression against one another they'll need the Earth again. They won't have the strength to just take what they want; they'll have to deal with the Earth on near-equal terms.

Because maybe the Earth governments can't run things forever, but an Orbital self-destruction will give Earth a breathing space, allow the shattered planet to renew itself.

Because, Reno thinks, the Orbitals deserve what is going to happen to them.

"Get the message?" he says.

In the eyes of the woman from ARAMCO Reno can read a Yes.

This one is the last. The last for Black Mind. Everyone can die now.

The assassin is small, a little woman not even five feet tall, her chest crushed by the impact of a dozen hollowpoints. She lies in a pool of congealed blood on a polished floor of Genoan marble. Mercedes stands with her face to the wall, not wanting to watch, her frame trembling, her face pale. Akinari's men shot the assassin even as she was lifting her pistol.

Reno's pulse speeds, slows, speeds up again. He's run all the way here, burst out of his office like a madman. It's lucky there wasn't a second gun waiting for him.

Sweat slicks his eye sockets and he keeps wiping it away with the backs of his hands. He's more terrified than Mercedes.

Who is this? Reno wonders. Who is so fanatic a killer as to walk into this suicide situation? She must have known the guards would kill her, kill her even if she succeeded in killing her target.

A thought strikes him like an arrow. Maybe she didn't care if she died, he thinks, because there's another of her. In a tank of liquid crystal in Havana, he thinks.

Right next to the ghost brother.

He looks at Mercedes. How can I tell her, he wonders, that I—that another Myself—just tried to kill her?

He takes Mercedes off the job. In the month she's been supervising the Biochem division her tasks have almost been completed anyway. She lives with him now, behind a wall of guards and biosensors, in his apartment, beneath the curved sound-absorbent ceiling, among the looted paintings.

She is more alone than anyone, Reno thinks, more alone than any of the children in the Cordillera Oriental. More alone even than the ghost brother, who has Black Mind brethren to talk to.

She seems not to mind. She is waiting, and Reno knows for what.

Reno tries to remember how the world appears to the ghost brother, existence perceived as pure data, the numbers raining down, each data-droplet with its own velocity, its own impact, its own inevitability.

And far above, arching across the sky, the Solipsystem, bodies moving in orbit about the primary. A reflected rainbow of monsters, alternate points of view, the creatures of Black Mind. Fragments—Reno superimposed imperfectly on the others—the ghost brother augmented, crippled, by alien desires, alien thoughts and abilities.

Freaks. Creatures created for the single purpose of atrocity, of self-destruction.

Let it happen, Reno thought. But let it start with the greatest monster of all.

He speaks to his military commanders. One of the mass-drivers is programmed to drop a ten-thousand-ton rock on Havana, atop the ghost brother's crystal tank. If self-destruction is the end, let all the selves be destroyed.

Perhaps Black Mind exists in a backup somewhere, Reno thinks. Perhaps the ghost brother is backed up, too. But he owes it to humankind to try to destroy a thing that can write itself over humanity itself.

It will be the first shot of the war.

Thirty hours from now, unless someone else fires first.

"I can try to get you out," Reno says. "It's not too late."

Mercedes' gamine limbs sprawl over the cream-colored sheets. Her head is turned away from him and her voice is muffled by the pillow.

"The aerosols are emplaced in the ARAMCO and Korolev main habitats," she says. "The mutated aseptic meningitis virus, different from the one we used last time, will be triggered at H-Hour minus twelve. Symptoms should begin appearing a few hours before the war begins. One-fifth to one-third the population should be incapacitated by the time the shooting starts. Military installations will receive a dusting of the new Anthrax-XVII spores, which should render them uninhabitable for a period of years."

She turns to him. Her eyes gleam with identical chips of cold, brittle lunar light. "Most of the people who will die aren't our enemies. They're not executives, they're just people. They'll be just as dead as Rock War casualties, and I'm responsible for that. I didn't turn away from it." She throws her head back and gives a mad little laugh. He can see the vibrations in her throat. "I don't deserve to live. I don't *want* to live, knowing how many thousands I'll kill." She reaches out to caress him, a touch like the paws of a small, desperate animal on his chest. "I don't want to live without you anyway. So let it happen." She is weeping now. "Let it happen," she says.

His arousal is profound. He reaches for her, despising himself.

He won't have to live in Roon's head for much longer.

Hand in hand, like children at a fireworks show, Reno and Mercedes sit in the near-dark and watch the apocalypse from his office window. Lights flare in the night, brief, silent, and shattering. Orbital squadrons flicker like fireflies and are gone, become tumbling wreckage. Power stations take hits from kinetic kill weapons and fly apart in awesome slow motion—spinning, crumpled dragonflies. Mass drivers slam rocks into the big stations, producing great Roman fountains of fire, but the results, if any, are difficult to evaluate. The big habitats are well-shielded—it's the biological weapons that will do the damage there.

On the Earth's night side, Reno can see Havana burning. The ghost brother, returned to the fire from which he was born.

There is a shudder, a tremor so deep, so low in frequency, that Reno can feel his insides clench. There is a fountain of light from the outside. A 10,000-ton mass-driven meteor has struck the station.

Reno waits, suspense ticking through his mind. There are no depressurization alarms, no warnings. No fluctuation in the gravity. A glancing blow, or one that failed to penetrate the station's massive radiation shielding.

The dimmed lights burn brighter, then dim down again. A laser had tracked across some of the station's solar cells.

There's a hammering on the door. Reno activates his comm unit.

"Who is it?"

"Mr. van Allen, sir." Akinari's voice.

"Let him come in."

There is an oily sheen on van Allen's face. His eyes are yellow, dazed. "We've lost!" he shouts. "Mohammad's squadron smashed the Tupolevs, but the Orbital Soviet's stepped in on the other side—I thought they'd *promised* us they'd stay neutral! We've been wiped out!" He wrings his hands, the first time Reno has actually seen a human being use such a gesture. "They've declared us war criminals! They're going to occupy our habitat!" He leans on the desk for support. "We've got to run for it," he gasps. "It's all over!"

It's all part of the plan, Reno wants to tell him. The United Orbital Soviet will not survive its intervention by forty-eight hours.

Instead Reno presses the button that summons Akinari. The mercenary arrives with two of his men. All are ready for combat: biochem suit, armor, automatic gauss rifles.

"Give me a grenade," Reno says.

Akinari unclips a grenade from his harness, hands it to Reno. Reno feels the weight of it in his hand, heavier than expected. He points at van Allen with his other hand.

Reno feels in that moment an electric contact between himself and the mercenary, that he and Akinari understand one another very well. His impression is that Akinari knows what he is going to say before he says it.

"This man is a defeatist," he says. "Take him into the hallway and shoot him."

"Very good, sir," says Akinari.

Van Allen screams as hands fall on him. He tries to break away, to beg for his life, and has to be dragged out of the room, his heels tearing at the Navajo rugs. Akinari is visibly embarrassed by the man's loss of control. The execution, the silent gauss bullet through the head, comes as a relief.

The first body, Reno thinks, outside his door. When the occupying troops come, there will be more. Akinari will not surrender. In his moment of understanding Reno knew that.

He puts the grenade on the desk and turns to Mercedes. An explosion, very close, lights her face momentarily. There is a joy there, that and a wild fulfillment. How many others can claim an apocalypse as accompaniment to a suicide? She opens her arms.

"I'm ready," she says.

Had he died when he was supposed to, Reno thinks, he would not have found her. He has been a monstrosity all these months, but she has transformed his existence, made the monster serve love.

"We have a little time yet," he says.

He takes her in his arms, kisses her, lowers her gently to the soft carpet. Lights flare and flicker outside.

The end, not of the world, but of heaven.

He remembers his birth into this life, on a bed alone, with holo planets moving in cold silence overhead. Now the planets are afire, and he can see their flames flashing on Mercedes' face as she clings to him.

There is the sound of running feet outside, then cries. Bullets, fired in silence, thud audibly into the steel bulkhead. The Velázquez bounces to the impacts.

It is time. In silence Reno reaches for the grenade. Mercedes looks dreamily out the window, Earthlight and distant violence glowing on her body.

How many times, he wonders, has he killed himself today? The ghost brother, the other Black Mind victims, all engaged in a frenzy of mutual suicide.

Mercedes takes his hand, the one with the grenade, and brings it to her lips. He can feel her lips on the back of his hand and his nerves go chill. He pulls the pin, lets the lever go.

"Call me Reno," he says. She looks at him, surprised, and then her lips, at the very beginning of a hoped-for affirmation, start to form the word.

People have always bugged me to write a sequel to my novel *Hardwired*. What they don't realize is that the book has two sequels already.

The first, and accidental, sequel is the novel *Voice of the Whirlwind*. I had written the novel intending it to be a stand-alone work. When I finished it, my editor asked if I could make it a sequel to *Hardwired*.

"Why?" I asked.

"Sequels sell better," I was told.

This struck me as a morally justifiable reason for altering the work, so I made a few minor changes and an awestruck world was subsequently informed that *Voice of the Whirlwind* was set in the same future as *Hardwired,* only 100 years later. It had no characters or situations from the earlier work, just a few references here and there. Just enough to sell it as a sequel.

Voice of the Whirlwind was, I think, a successful novel. But it was only marginally a sequel, and the world it described was different from that of *Hardwired. Hardwired* began with the notion, not precisely unknown in science fiction, that the Earth's space colonies had staged a revolution in order to gain independence from Earth. But in contrast to other books using this idea, *Hardwired's* colonies were not after mere political independence: once they had destroyed Earth's defenses, they found the vision of a helpless planet too tempting to resist. They dominated their home planet and were united, under a loose government called the Orbital Soviet, chiefly by the desire to exploit Earth's remaining resources in order to build their own economies.

In *Voice of the Whirlwind,* humanity and its economies were still dominated by space colonies, but Earth had become not so much oppressed as nearly irrelevant. The Orbital Soviet was gone, and tensions between Earth and its children had diminished.

How did one future lead into the other? In *Hardwired,* a clue had been given in the form of the character Reno, who at the very end of the novel had been transplanted, via the Black Mind program, into the mind of the Orbital boss Roon. In contemplating the gap in my future chronology, I decided to write a story about Reno.

"Solip:System" was originally published, with what is perhaps the ugliest cover ever seen on a professional publication, as a limited-edition chapbook from Axolotl Press, and reprinted in *Asimov's* magazine for September 1990.

It hasn't stopped people bugging me about a sequel to *Hardwired,* though.

Broadway Johnny

The joint was jumping as I strolled in from Lockhart Road. The band was jazzing away on "Skid-Dat-De-Dat," the clientele was expending world-class quantities of vim in dancing the black bottom, and the bar seemed to be doing enough business to suggest there had been a twelve-year drought ended only just that afternoon.

I doffed my silk topper and ambled up to the bar, seeing in its wavy deco mirror a picture—all modesty brushed firmly to the side—of soigné elegance. I was in evening dress, my tie a perfect butterfly shape, my white silk scarf floating casually off my shoulders. In one impeccably white-gloved hand was a silver-topped cane. One had to admit that my shoulders were rather broader than the proper Vernon Castle ideal, and my neck thicker; but on the whole Art substituted rather well for what Nature had not provided. I removed one glove, draped it elegantly over the rim of my topper, and signaled with a faultlessly manicured hand to Old Nails, the bartender.

"What ho, o son of toil," I said. "My customary grasshopper, if you please."

"Right, boss."

I lit a cigaret and inhaled. All, I couldn't help but feel, was well with the world. The horizon seemed cloudless. No cares were reflected in my countenance.

Then I glanced down the bar and saw an immortal, and the heart's blood ran chill.

Probably no one else observed that this prune-faced geezer sitting at the bar was anyone out of the ordinary. But if you've been around immortals enough, you recognize the signs at first glance.

Old Nails swanned up with my cocktail, and as I sipped it I found myself wishing I'd ordered a double bourbon.

"Who's the undertaker down the bar?" I asked.

"He's been sitting there all night," Nails said. "He said he wanted to talk to you."

"I'll just bet he did," I muttered, and took another swig.

"Only bought one drink," Nails said. "No tip."

I tugged on my cuffs to cover the profusion of hair on my wrists—my worst feature, I've always thought. Then I put on my best smile, summoned such bonhomie as remained, and sauntered toward my visitor.

"I understand you wanted to see me?" I said.

The prune raised an eyebrow and looked at me. "I do if you're Chan Kung-hao," he said.

"Call me Johnny if you like."

"I'll call you Mr. Chan, if it's all the same."

I adjusted my silk scarf. "Suits me," I said.

"My name is Ho. I'm one of the Ho Ho Erh Hsien."

You may have heard of the Ho Ho Erh Hsien, known otherwise as the Two Gods Named Ho. If you haven't, I imagine they'll serve well enough as an introduction to the intricacies of Chinese legend.

One of the immortals in question is a fellow named Ho Ho, famous for having traveled ten thousand *li* in a single day to pay a call on his brother. Another of the twain is a disreputable monk named Han Shan, who made rude noises during meditation, cursed and kicked the abbot, and eventually got biffed out of the monastery to live as a hermit. And a third is a chappie named Shih-teh, who worked in the kitchen of this selfsame monastery and fed Han Shan on kitchen scraps. Because Ho means Harmony in Chinese, they're all celebrated as immortals of compatible union.

If you've been paying strict attention here, you may note a discrepancy or two in the accounting. Firstly—*bereshith,* as it were—the Two Gods Named Ho are actually three. Secondly, only one of them is actually named Ho, and he's named Ho twice. Nextly, one of these immortals celebrated for his utter and sublime mateyness was, by all accounts, an utter misanthrope, incapable of holding civil converse with man or beast.

These sad contradictions, I'm sorry to report, are perfectly in accord with Chinese cosmology. The inhabitants of the Middle Kingdom appear to have taken to heart Emerson's dictum that consistency is the hobgoblin of little minds—taken the dictum, that is, flogged it within an inch of its life, and then booted the remainder right through the goalposts. Nothing in Chinese legend makes any kind of sense, especially once you've met a few of the principals involved. Take my word for it.

This particular Ho was a tall, spare, disdainful bird, dressed in a long silk Chinese gown and skullcap—elegant enough, but not often the sort of thing seen in my nightclub. His pinky fingernails were about five inches long and protected by silver caps. He carried a two-foot-long iron tobacco pipe with which he probably clouted disrespectful pedicab drivers and unruly children. His expression suggested he'd just choked on a plum pit.

As I eyed him I wondered which of the chummy threesome he represented. Ho Ho, the one who traveled ten thousand *li,* seemed a useful sort of bimbo to have around, particularly if you fancied a quick vacation or needed a fast trip out of town. Shih-teh, the cook, seemed pretty goopy, but at least he might have picked up a few recipes in his years m the kitchens. But knowing the way that Fate has of flinging me in the soup, I was certainly prepared for the worst, which meant Han Shan.

"Do you actually *like* this hideous din?" the immortal demanded. "I've been sitting here for hours!"

"I take it," I replied, "that you aren't a jazz baby conversant with the syncopated rhythm and the hot-cha-cha?" I gazed with pride at my house band, Chinese made up in blackface to help provide the proper *Vieux Carré* atmosphere. "The Ace Rhythm Kings provide the heppest sound this side of Basin Street," I said.

"The Ace Rhythm Kings can retire at once to Bad Dog Village in the Infernal Regions," my guest griped. A pretty crude thing to say, which only confirmed my worst surmise.

"Han Shan, I take it?" I said.

"Correct."

"Would you like to go to my private office?"

"And get out of this hell of imitation foreigners?" he said. "Lead the way!"

As I took the prune-faced god of concord aside I cast a wistful glance in the direction of the band singer, Betsy Wong, who was about to launch into her rendition of "I'm a Little Blackbird Looking for a Bluebird," my personal favorite among her repertoire.

I led Han Shan into my office and put my hat and cane on their respective racks.

"Can I get you something to drink?" I asked.

He gave a sniff. "Do you have anything Chinese in this place?"

"Will mao tai do? I have a particularly potent vintage in my possession."

"If it's the real thing."

Ignoring this slur on my oeniphilic discrimination, I unlocked my private cabinet and poured my guest a drink. "I think you'll find it possesses a fine bouquet," I remarked, "hearty and challenging but without pretension." I offered it to him, then picked up my grasshopper. "Skin off your nose."

We drank. He looked suspicious as he raised his glass, perhaps worried that for mischief's sake I'd try to slip him a Château Latour '03 or some other inferior vintage. But after the first sip came another, and then he tossed down the whole glass, and by the time I'd refilled it he looked somewhat less the twenty-minute egg. He actually managed a thin smile.

"Thank you, Mr. Chan. I see you haven't been completely contaminated by foreign tastes."

"Sorry to have kept you waiting," I remarked. "I was at the Lyceum for the Asian Road Company premiere of *Music Box Review,* the new Irving Berlin musical. Then I went out to the clubs with some of my pals and the girls from the show."

Han Shan looked as if he wanted to retract his last appraisal. I smiled at him.

"Seeing as it's late and I've kept you waiting," I went on, "perhaps we should play the last waltz, as it were, and see the cotillion to its conclusion."

"If I take your meaning, which is difficult due to your insistence on marring good Cantonese with bizarre foreign idiom, then I find your suggestion agreeable. I have a condition, however: what I tell you may not go past these doors."

"Of course," I said, "I have no desire to attract attention to myself by exposing my dealings with immortals."

"Very good." He knocked down his third drink and poured himself a fourth. "Are you familiar with the golden swords Kan Chiang and Mo Yeh?"

"I believe I've heard a legend or two."

Kan Chiang and Mo Yeh are swords named after the smiths who made them, a chummy married couple who owned their own swordsmithing shop on Shih Ming Mountain. They died on the job, as it were, by chucking themselves into their own furnace in order to provide the necessary *matériel* for turning a couple of magic gold nuggets into swords. Perhaps, I have thought, their charcoal delivery was late.

"The two golden swords," the Ho said, "are mighty items of great power. They contain nothing less than the martial fortune of the Chinese people."

"They don't seem to have done us much good the last few centuries, what?" I said.

Han Shan looked sore as a gumboil. "That's because of a certain immortal named Wu Meng."

"Wu Meng? The filial piety chap?"

"Yes. The same."

"Hmm."

Chinese, as you may know, are very big on a quality called *hsiao,* which gets translated into English as "filial piety," though on reflection I could think of a few other words for it. Wu Meng was an immortal famous for being filled to the bunghole with *hsiao,* which probably meant that he probably spent his days giving the old oil to his grandparents in hopes of getting an extra slice of inheritance. Maybe he got it and maybe he didn't, but he got immortality, which in the long run is probably better.

As you may have gathered by now, I'm about the least filial Chinese you'll ever meet. You may consider this is a great sin, but then you haven't met my family. Try having your doting parents sell you into slavery at the age of eight, and see if it doesn't provide a whole new perspective on this *hsiao* business.

If Wu Meng's family had sold him into slavery, he probably would have sent them half his gruel.

"So what did Wu Meng do?" I asked. "Did he let the swords get rusty or something?"

"No. Wu Meng had nothing to do with the swords. He was the guardian of another great token of power, the Five Tiger Fan. The nation that possessed the Five Tiger Pan was guaranteed to have a great spirit of enterprise, originality, and genius. Due to our possession of the fan, China became the greatest nation in the world, the envy of all. But during the Ming dynasty, Wu Meng lost the fan in a dice game with a Portuguese merchant named Pires de Andrade."

"I see. And as a result, the spirit of enterprise has fled the Middle Kingdom?"

"Correct. Our decline as a nation can be traced to that unfortunate dice game. We can't originate anymore: we can only repeat the patterns of the past. And the martial valor guaranteed by possession of the golden swords is of much less value without a spirit of genius and enterprise among the soldiers."

Well, that was two strikes against Wu Meng as far as I was concerned. First the filial piety business, then losing the spirit of originality for the whole bally country. And the Five Tiger Fan strife affected me personally—as fine musicians as the Ace Rhythm Kings may be, they never sound any different from the recordings I play for them on my gramophone. "Improvisation," I keep telling them, "is the keystone of jazz." But all they do is nod and agree and then play "Dippermouth Blues" exactly the way King Oliver's band did five years ago.

"And how did the Portuguese do?" I asked.

"He got rich trading and went home to Portugal."

"Which," I mused, "judging from history, lost the fan shortly thereafter."

"If you say so. You're the expert on foreigners."

"And how about Wu Meng? How did the Jade Emperor and the other gods feel about him losing the fan? I imagine they dished him good and proper."

"I'm not here about the fan!" Han Shan snarled, and banged on my desk with his glass. "To hell with the Five Tiger Fan!"

I reflected the mao tai seemed to be hitting him pretty hard. He was the one who brought the fan up, after all.

"Right ho," I said. "All thoughts of the Five Tiger Fan are hereby consigned to perdition." I took a last puff on my cigaret, then stubbed it out in my Baccarat ashtray. "Why did you say you were here, exactly?"

The immortal banged down another round of mao tai. "It is my honor to be the appointed guardian of the golden swords."

I considered that if I gave him a bit of the old soft soap, he'd get to the point a little quicker. "They couldn't have been entrusted to a better fellow," I said.

"The swords lie concealed beneath the waters of a fountain."

"So your lodgings have a water view, I take it? Couldn't be better. But don't the swords rust?"

"They do not rust," he said, "because they are so sharp they cut the water in half."

"Excellent swords, then," I said.

"The finest swords in all history!" he shouted, banging his glass once more. And then, to my amazement, he began to weep. "And they're gone!" he sobbed. "I lost them!"

I leaned across the desk and handed Han Shan my handkerchief with one hand while I refilled his glass with the other. Baleful harbingers of dread were beginning to cloud my personal horizon. My part in all this was becoming ominously clear.

"Perhaps you remember where you were that day?" I suggested. "Have you checked the left luggage office?"

"I know precisely where I was!" he wept.

"Well, jolly good," I said. "That should make finding them easier, what?"

"I was gambling with a kami and I lost them!"

"You were gambling with a communist?" I asked.

He glared at me. "Not a commie, a kami! A Japanese god."

"Ah."

Gambling, I might observe, is the curse of the immortal class. They get bored, I suppose, hanging out on their mountains, meditating endlessly in their shrines, or standing guard over their treasure troves—to name three favorite immortal occupations—and they don't have the prospect of death to focus the mind and quicken the pulse the way it does for the rest of us, so after a few centuries of glassy-eyed boredom they take themselves to the city and risk everything on a throw or two of the dice. Entire empires have been known to change hands as a result of a couple immortals wanting to relieve their ennui with a few brisk rounds of mah-jongg.

It's the sort of thing that results in disillusionment, once you discover how these things really work. Results, in fact, in chaps like me.

"Some sort of immortals' convention, was it?" I said. "Best dry your eyes and tell me the whole story."

He dabbed his cheeks, then honked his beezer and went on. "Well, we were playing fan-tan at a club in Shanghai, and I kept losing—oh, it was really unfair! You shouldn't be able to lose *that much* at fan-tan—not with a fifty-fifty chance at every throw!" He snarled. "It's all Wu Meng's fault!" he snapped.

"How so?"

"If there were any reward for enterprise left in this benighted country, I would have won."

"Not necessarily. The game was probably rigged."

He stared at me. "How do you mean?"

I lit a cigaret. "Well, you put the beans in a dish, right? And then bet even or odd—all you have to do to change the outcome is palm a bean, you know. Easiest thing in the world. And if you want to make absolutely certain, you can carry loads of beans up your sleeve, and then add the palmed bean or not, depending on how people are betting."

Han Shan's eyes widened with belated understanding. He howled and stamped on the floor. "That rat! That fixer! That's how he must have won!"

"Indubitably. Now who was this Japanese bimbo exactly?"

"His name was Teruo Shokan No Kami Minamoto No Tadaoki." His face contorted with anger. "'Call me Teruo,' he said. 'Come into the club, have a drink, have a little fun. Meet some girls. We immortals should get together more often!'" His expression darkened. "I should have known he was after something."

Indeed. It was obvious enough that anyone who actually invited a wet smack like Han Shan to share some raucous good fun was in pursuit of something other than a jolly fine time.

"So I gather," I said, "you would like to commission me to gaff this Teruo bloke and chuck him off your lakeside property."

He looked a little crafty. "Well," he said, "in a manner of speaking."

"Why? Where's the fountain?"

"It's in Tsingtao."

I frowned. "Tsingtao is under Japanese occupation."

"Well," he admitted, "yes."

"So how am I going to kick Teruo off the land if he can just call in the marines and jump your claim all over again?"

"It's not as bad as all that," he said hastily. "The fountain is actually in an amulet."

I must have looked a little blank. "The fountain's inscribed on an amulet?"

"No, it's *in* an amulet."

I took a firmer grip on my cocktail glass. "I understand how swords can be in a fountain, I suppose, but how can a fountain be in an amulet?"

"It's a metaphysical fountain," he said simply. "It can be anywhere it likes."

I suppose this made as much sense as anything else immortals ever get up to. "Fine," I said. "Spifferino. What's the amulet look like?"

"It's made of two colors of gold, red and white back-to-back. It's about the size of a copper *cash*, it's covered with writing on one side and a picture of the Door Gods on the other."

"So why don't the Door Gods guard the fountain?"

"I don't know. I don't make the rules."

"And where in Tsingtao is the amulet?"

"Around the pirate's neck, I imagine. I wore it around mine."

I tapped cigaret ash into the Baccarat ashtray. "And where in Tsingtao is this Teruo geezer?"

"I don't know where he lives, but I've done a little discreet checking, and I've discovered that he's the personal kami of the 142nd Military Police Battalion based in Tsingtao, so I imagine he can be found in the vicinity of the barracks."

"Yipes!" I took a swig of my grasshopper and wished, not for the last time, that I'd thought to order bourbon.

"Well," I said, "it was a pleasure meeting you. I believe you know the way out."

His face fell about fourteen inches. "You're not going to help me?" he whimpered.

"It's bad enough you want me to take on an immortal," I said. "Immortals have long memories—not that they can help it, I suppose. But an immortal with his own private battalion of Imperial Japanese plug-uglies—now that takes the cake!"

"But, Mr. Chan—it's your patriotic duty—you owe it to your homeland!"

"Tell it to the marines," I said. "If you have a hang about patriotism and the homeland, you wouldn't have wagered the amulet in the first place."

Han Shan turned haughty. "Your maternal grandfather would have undertaken this quest at once."

I self-consciously tugged my cuffs back over my hairy wrists. The grandfather in question is an unpredictable egomaniac with a big stick, and in my estimation stands about as high as the rest of my family, concerning whom I believe you have already been informed.

"Fine," I said. "You can approach him, then, if you like."

"But—where is he to be found?"

I shrugged and took a puff off my gasper. "I'm afraid I don't know. We seem to have lost touch."

Which, I'm pleased to report, was perfectly true.

Tears came to the Ho's eyes once again. "Please, Mr. Chan! You must help! If I don't get the swords back before long, the other immortals will find out!"

"And then you'll really be in the cart, eh?"

He sobbed and took another swig of mao tai. "If only I hadn't been so hard on Wu Meng during his trial!"

"Ah? Really?"

Tears were beginning to stain his gown. "Yes!" he moaned. "I insisted he be punished severely for the betrayal of his trust."

I was beginning to sense why he'd insisted on changing the subject when the matter of Wu Meng's fate had come up. "How do you punish an immortal, anyway?" I asked. "You can't kill him."

"No." He gulped. "But you can chain him for four hundred years in the Hell of Having Your Entrails Eaten by Dogs and Wild Pigs."

"Sounds gruesome, all right," I said. "But I guess old Wu Meng should be getting out of stir anytime now." I grinned at my guest. "Perhaps he'll be out soon enough to sit on *your* jury."

Han Shan began to wail. "Won't you get the swords back, Mr. Chan? I don't know what to do—I'm not a fighter or a thief!"

"Neither am I," I said, "if I can help it." I waved a hand. "It's true that in my wayward youth, I undertook various commissions on behalf of certain prominent personalities. But I've given it up, and I've opened Broadway Johnny's here and commenced a very successful career as a man-about-town. Surely an upright person such as yourself will appreciate the values of my reformation."

He snarled at me. "I'll curse you!" he said. "I'm an immortal! I can make your life a misery!"

I tugged at my cuffs again. I was onto his curves by now. "Oh, come now," I said. "If you do, I'll know who did it. A little word in the right celestial ear, and it's Entrail Heaven for the hogs."

He began to tremble. He took a swig of mao tai from the bottle. "I'll give you money!" he said.

"Didn't you gamble it all away?"

"I lost everything I had with me. But I'm an immortal, and I've been around a long time—I know where there are hidden treasure troves."

I examined my nails while I considered my finances. Though the club was doing well enough, it could always stand a few improvements. A band composed of genuine jazz artists, say, imported from Basin Street. A line of chorus girls in sequined flapper garb and Josephine Baker bobs. Perhaps a talented mixologist imported from the States—since Prohibition started over there, bartenders were probably easy enough to come by.

And if I could wring enough of the ready out of this bozo, perhaps I could even embark on a career I'd only dreamed of, that of theater impresario. With a trip to New York and London every year, to see the new shows and decide which to bring back to the East.

"Treasure troves?" I said. "Probably just old strings of cash buried by frugal peasants."

"No! Real treasure! Silver ingots! Ancient bronze and porcelain! Gold! Gems!"

"It better be a lot," I said. "If I do this for you, I'll need a bankroll before I ever set out."

"Why? I can pay you when you're done, after you steal the—"

"I'm *not* going to steal the swords back," I said, and before the old monk's chin began to tremble I added, "That would be foolish in the extreme, with the target surrounded by a battalion of cops. I'm going to get the amulet the same way Teruo did—I'll win it gambling. And for that, I'll need a stake."

He looked at me eagerly. "You'll do it, then, Mr. Chan?"

I frowned deliberately. "Possibly," I said, "but you'll have to make it really worth my while."

I'll spare you the details of the agreement, save that, as I ushered Han Shan out of the club, there was a smile on my face and a puzzled frown on his. He really ought to stick to minding his fountain and leave money matters alone. Finance is not, as the saying goes, his forte.

Still, my smile faded the second I turned and walked back into the club, and not even Betsy Wong's rendition of "Cakewalking Babies From Home" could set me right. So I sat in with the band and tickled the ivories for a couple sets, hoping that "Texas Moaner Blues" might set things right; but it didn't, so I went to the bar and ordered another grasshopper and brooded.

Grasshoppers aren't precisely the sort of drink that traditionally accompanies brooding; but I've always felt that, with sufficient dedication and attention to detail, these sorts of handicaps can be overcome.

After the club closed I collected the receipts and had the Hispano Suiza brought round to the Lockhart Road entrance. Betsy Wong looked at me expectantly, probably wondering if I'd ask her over for a nightcap, but the blues had set in good and proper, and I just kissed her good night, hopped in the Hispano, and buzzed off into the night.

I was cautious on approaching the bank night depository. There was a general dock strike in progress up and down the Chinese coasts, and people had been thrown out of work. Some of them were desperate enough to turn to robbery. But there were no suspicious lurkers around the bank, and I dropped off the receipts and buzzed off home.

I'd got my apartment cheap because it was haunted. Ghosts, I've found, daunt most people, but after my life of dealing with immortals and my crazy grandfather, a collection of spirits was a trivial annoyance at best. The ghosts were busy as I arrived, sitting at a corner table and making a lot of racket playing mah-jongg. A rough lot they looked, too, with their scars and tattoos—they were gangsters who had been sitting at the table gambling when an acquaintance paid a call. Unfortunately for the gamblers, their acquaintance had first thought to provide himself with a Browning automatic rifle.

If you looked closely at the wall, you could see the patches in the plasterwork where the bullet holes used to be.

I wasn't in the mood for the company of surly dead people, so I walked straight up to their table and began to spit at them. The ghosts looked at me resentfully for a few baleful seconds, then faded, along with their mah-jongg tiles.

Most Chinese hold the belief that human saliva is somehow toxic to ghosts. This may be true, but I'm inclined to the belief that ghosts leave because they're annoyed they can't spit back.

I poured myself a snifter of brandy and sat in my easy chair and continued my pout. Immortals were entering my life once more, like thunderclouds on a beautiful springtime day, and it hardly seemed fair. I had built a pleasant life away from all of that, and I disliked being dragged back into my past. I felt, as the poet said, like a "jazzbo looking for a rainbow."

Oh well. At least there was hard cash involved.

Fate, I decided, was at least furnishing a few compensations.

After Han Shan provided the promised funds I took a ferry across the bay and from thence a cab to the Kowloon Walled City. The Walled City is a part of Kowloon which, through a technicality, still belongs to China rather than the British Crown. Since the Chinese government pays no attention to the place, and as the British can't enter, the Walled City has become a den of criminals, fugitives, political extremists, and refugees from the mainland. It is a decidedly unsafe place to be at the best of times, and these were not the best of times, with the dock strike increasing the city's population of desperate people—indeed, I could not get my cab driver to drive through the crumbling gate.

I paid him off and walked through, my cane tapping the ground at every other step. My pockets were laden with jingling coin, a certain temptation to the wicked inhabitants of the place, but I wasn't worried about robbery. I knew that the luck I had temporarily acquired would not permit accidents.

And indeed it didn't. A pickpocket who moved in my direction stumbled on a heretofore unseen crack in the street and went down with a crash, breaking his nose on the curb. A hatchet man let fly from a dark alley, only to bury his hatchet in the skull of his partner, who had just lunged at me from behind a barrel. A gang of surly youths in red turbans, swaggering toward me with the obvious intention of exacting a heavy toll for my trespass on their territory, suddenly found themselves the objects of profound attention on the part of another surly gang of youths, these in yellow turbans, who charged out of an alley, knives and hatchets gleaming bright as the homicidal glint I believe I detected in their eyes.

In each case, I was able to amble on unmolested, smoking my cigaret and enjoying the sights.

I knew this would be the case, for I was about to visit the luckiest man in the world.

His name was Ping, though he was also known as the Great Sage of the Chinese City, as the Walled City is also called. Since I was about to give Ping money, I knew that his luck, or joss as it's called here, would not permit me to suffer any indignities while I was en route to his dwelling.

It was what would happen to me after the visit that concerned me. Once I'd given the Great Sage his coin, he'd have no further use for me, and getting out of the Walled City was going to be less easy than getting in.

Ping's house was an eccentric place, a three-story structure partly of stone, partly of brick, and partly braced with metal. Cockeyed gables, balconies, and odd-shaped windows were distributed more or less randomly over its surface, like warts on the back of a toad. The design of the house was dictated by Ping's eccentric theories of geomancy, or feng shui—he had designed his house to attract luck and repel evil. And such, remarkably enough, it seemed to do.

I often wondered why Ping chose to live in the Walled City, but it has since occurred to me that he probably chose the district because it's the only place in the world that would permit him to build a house of this description.

Most fortune-tellers are mountebanks, of course—after my tumultuous departure from the Golden Nation Opera Company of Shanghai, I traveled with such a mountebank for a time—but very rarely, perhaps one time out of ten thousand, you encounter a seer who's right on the money. Such a one was Ping.

He received me in a room shaped like an elongated hexagon, one of your auspicious room shapes in feng shui. In the corners of the room were objects colored white, red, yellow, green, blue, and black, which stood for the Six True Words of Buddhism. The trigrams of the Pa K'ua were seen in the floor tiles. Various subtle marks in the room Traced the Nine Stars and indicated the spokes of the Eight-Door Wheel. Plants in pots composed of different materials were placed in careful relation to one another, and oddly angled mirrors were set here and there, while rudely shaped bits of quartz hung off the ceiling on the ends of strings. ...

If you didn't know the fellow was a true sage, you'd think he'd gone right off his coconut.

"What ho, Mr. Ping," I said as I toddled in. "I seem to be in need of a bit of luck."

"How fortunate it is that you've come here instead of someplace else," said the sage. "Please sit down and have some tea."

And a servant with tea and some snacks walked in right at that instant—Ping being so lucky, you see, he'd had a hankering to order the stuff before I even arrived.

Ping looked more or less as you'd expect a sage to look—he had long white eyebrows that hung down to his jawline, and a wispy white beard, and rather a mischievous glint in his eye. I'd never been able to figure out whether or not he was an immortal—usually I can tell, but Ping's quarters were so charged with powerful vibrations that I could never be certain which came from him and which came from the setting. Certainly he'd been there a very long time, but perhaps that was because he was so lucky that Death lost his address, or gaffed the wrong bird by mistake, or simply got knocked on the head and had his pockets emptied by the gangs that loiter about the Walled City.

"I'm afraid it's all rather a complicated rannygazoo," I said.

"In that case, Mr. Chan, you'd best begin at the beginning, and proceed straight through to the end." Which, if you've not met one, is how sages talk.

So I described the afflicted god of concord, his loss of the mystical swords to some kind of Japanese police god, and my decision to fetch them back. I tried to stress the patriotic nature of my quest, along with all the sacrifices I was undertaking on behalf of the motherland—in hopes, of course, of getting a price break.

"Your love of country is a fine thing," Ping said, smiling, "a splendid example of *hsiao*. Such a one as I can only stand back in admiration. I'm sure you will be richly rewarded in your next incarnation."

So much for the price break. Ping lit up a pipe, and I a cigaret, while he considered.

"Your joss will need to be mobile," he said, "as you do not know where you will encounter this foreign immortal. And it must be inconspicuous, as otherwise it would be discovered." He blew a smoke ring that immediately resolved itself into the trigram Gen, which stands for knowledge. "Right," he said. "I think I know just what you need."

He whipped out a piece of paper and a small calligraphy brush, made some ink into which he sprinkled a few metallic-looking powders from pockets in his wide sleeves, and then—mumbling a little inaudible charm—he wrote quickly on the piece of paper, covering it all with characters and diagrams and odd little drawings. He then produced a straight edge and some scissors, cut a small square out of the center of the paper, and crumpled the rest. He pushed the little square toward me.

"If you have $822 American, plus one silver dime, I would be obliged."

This was a request as eccentric as his taste in architecture. For some reason not acquainted with the rational mind, the most common currency in China at this time were Mexican dollars, but I didn't have even that. "I'm afraid I only have old Chinese coin," I said. "Silver boats."

"I suppose I shouldn't have expected my good luck to quite stretch *that* far." He scratched his wispy mustache with the end of his pen. "Han Shan dug up an old treasure trove, did he? Too bad—Amencan dollars will be auspicious for the next hour or so. I'm afraid I'll have to charge you more if you can't pay American."

I looked at the little square of paper, in form a common paper amulet. "But wasn't the charm on the larger sheet? Didn't you throw most of it away?"

"The large implies the small, and the small the large," he said. Which, as I believe I may already have told you, is how sages talk.

"How does it work?"

"Carry it where it won't get wet," he said. "Inside your cigaret case, perhaps. When you need good joss, lick the amulet, then paste it on your skin such that the ink imprints on your flesh. After that, you'll have staggeringly good luck."

"Splendid," I said.

"But it won't last. At some point afterward, your joss will turn bad, and you'll have to transfer the bad luck to someone else by repeating the process."

"I'll have to lick the amulet and stick it on someone else?"

"Correct. Or suffer catastrophic luck yourself."

"But why do I have to have bad joss at all?"

Ping blew a smoke ring that resolved itself into a revolving mandala. "That's the way it works," he said. "Into every yang a little yin must fall."

"How will I know when my joss shifts?"

"You won't be able to tell," Ping said. "It depends on how much luck is drawn from the amulet in the course of its use. If you don't need much luck to begin with, the amulet will last a long time. And if you make high demands on the available luck, it may be used up quickly—say within a day."

"Any other drawbacks?"

He considered for a moment. "The amulet's luck is very good, but it won't protect you against what I might call cosmic bad joss."

"Such as?"

"The amulet won't prevent an earthquake from happening in the district you're in, for example, although it might prevent roof tiles from falling on you if an earthquake occurs. And it won't keep something like a war from breaking out if a war is scheduled to break out anyway, though it might keep any bullets from your immediate vicinity."

"Unless the luck shifts, in which case I become a lodestone for lead."

He nodded. "You have applied the needle and seen blood immediately," he quoted. By which he meant I'd hit the nail on the head.

"I wish you wouldn't mention blood," I said.

"Perhaps," he said, "I should speak instead of silver."

So I paid him, which actually took some time. It wasn't a matter of shoving the ready across the desk, but rather of placing money in little piles around the room in whatever locations he deemed auspicious. Old Chinese silver ingots are in the shape of little boats, so you can stack them one atop the other, and by the time I was through old Ping looked as if he were surrounded by a silver armada, circling him like cinematic Red Indians ogling a wagon train.

Then I thanked him, took my amulet, and said farewell. By way of a warm-up I did a few deep knee bends in the hall before I stepped out, because I knew that my return journey through the Walled City wouldn't be covered by Ping's luck, and I didn't want to use the amulet yet. I was planning a brisk skedaddle straight to the nearest gate, and then a hop into the first available cab.

The first fellow I encountered was a pickpocket who intended to run into me as if by accident, lifting something in the course of the collision; but I got my elbow in first, heard a couple of ribs crack, and saw his eyes go wide. "Apologies," I said, and tipped my fedora as I glided away.

Have I mentioned that I am quite large and strong? I suppose not, as it has not been relevant till now, and I'm somewhat reluctant to admit that I do not quite fit my own ideal of physical perfection, which tends toward the Rudolph Valentino model. I do not imagine Valentino has to tug his cuffs down over his hairy wrists, or buy extra large collars. Alas, we must all live with the features bequeathed us by our ancestors, or in my case my grandfather.

Next I was mobbed by children, about a dozen, who swarmed up and started sticking grubby fingers in my pockets. I was familiar with their type, urchins who trusted to their marks' reluctance to smash in their adorable little faces just long enough to pick them clean. I was myself disinclined to damage them overmuch, so I managed to hold them at bay long enough to spot their manager or Fagin, a fat oily type who loitered in a doorway and watched his charges with an expression of paternal avarice. I bounded over the heads of the children, seized the fat fellow, and ran him through the barred window on a nearby house. As the bars were not proportioned to someone of his girth, I imagine this caused him some discomfort. At any rate, he began loudly to voice his dismay, and his apprentices abandoned their efforts to rob me and went to his succor, an event that permitted me to continue my stroll.

The next street corner brought three surly youths in yellow turbans, ruffians who had apparently just vanquished their red-turbaned foes and turned their attention to collecting the rewards that accompany an expansion of the tax base. The first, before he had quite grunted out his demands, got my cane thrust *à la épée* between his eyes, which sat him down in the street; the second got my boot where it wasn't wanted; and the third I dropped onto the first with a low sweep of my cane.

At this point the threesome commenced to call loudly for help, which, unfortunately, was at hand. At the sight of a horde of yellow turbans swarming out of the local gin mills, knives and hatchets at the ready, I found it expedient to leg it for the wall pronto, without, as it were, leaving my card. By dint of perseverance I managed to get a good half block lead, which is as good as a mile in a narrow street choked with pedestrians, bullock carts, and street vendors.

The turban salesman must have cleaned up in this district, because after sprinting a couple of blocks I found myself approaching another street corner occupied by yet another gang of surly youths, this lot in green turbans. These seemed not to be actuated by a spirit of brotherhood and bonhomie, for at the sight of the yellow turbans they immediately drew their weapons and began screaming for reinforcements. These proved ready to hand, and soon the two sides were advancing toward one another at full speed, while I, caught in the middle, felt a bit like Buster Keaton, trapped in an alley while swarms of cops thunder toward him from either direction.

I must admit that for a brief moment I thought of deploying the amulet. But then reason took hold, and I considered that perhaps, in the urgency and heat of the moment, the two gangs might well overlook my existence if I were not around to remind them of it; so I grabbed hold of an awning and swung up into its hammocky embrace just as, below me, the two hosts came together with a meaty sound not unlike that of the New York Giants front line encountering that of the Oorang Indians.

I clamped my cane in my teeth and used the bounce of the awning to get me to a barred window overlooking the street. "Thief!" screamed a high-pitched voice from the window. "Get away, vile creature!" I ignored the advice and climbed to the top of the bars, which unfortunately provoked the old lady within into jabbing at me with a broom. I tried to bat the thing away but failed, then reached overhead for the roof overhang and found it. "Monster!" the old lady yelled. "Ape!"

"Lady, it's not my fault what I look like!" I mumbled past my cane. I let go of the bars and swung out over the street as I dangled one-handed from the overhang.

"Gorilla-strength demon!" she shrieked, then lunged.

The broom caught me a solid one in the ribs, and then a hatchet whirred past, demonstrating that not every thug below had neglected his original priorities. Muttering what I believe the better writers are pleased to call "vile oaths," I hauled myself up to the red-tiled roof. Once there, I paused to chuck a few loose tiles at the hooligans below—it helped relieve my feelings—and then I did a joyful buck-and-wing over the roof pole. The lanes of the Chinese City were very narrow, and even in my unsuitable Western boots I managed to leap from one roof to another, agile as the siamang of faraway Sumatra, before returning to terra firma near the gate, where I whistled "God Save the King" as I crossed back to the jurisdiction of good King George, Fifth of that name, sovereign of the realm on which, I am assured, the sun never sets, and whose arms, by that point, I was willing to bless forever.

It wasn't easy to get to Tsingtao. The general strike on the docks had paralyzed shipping, and there was trouble along the railway line. In the area around Peking, workers had been agitating in the district controlled by a powerful warlord, General Wu P'ei-fu. Worker agitation wasn't normally the sort of thing one did in the domain of a warlord, but General Wu was well thought of, as he'd chucked out the corrupt politicians, all in the pay of the Japanese, who had run the area previously. As a result of this splendid action Wu was thought to be a progressive sort who would be sympathetic to the notion of paying his workers much larger salaries than were other warlords, perhaps even a sum approaching a living wage. To the surprise, perhaps, of no one but the agitators, Wu proved reluctant in this regard, and he commenced the activity warlords know best, shooting and beheading with fine abandon.

The result of this botheration was that I had to make several lengthy detours, traveling by branch rail lines, a bullock cart, a rented Ford automobile, and at one point a motor barge on the Grand Canal. Mr. Phileas Fogg would doubtless have been pleased, not only at the itinerary, but at the splendid pace: I managed to reach Tsingtao in a mere four days.

I rode the last stage in a first-class railway carriage, carefully dressed in a spotless Western suit of grey flannel, with pleated high-rise trousers, a short-waisted waistcoat, and a carefully knotted scarf. I possessed the intimidating amount of luggage, all fine hand-stitched calfskin, with which people of means were expected to travel. I blush to admit that I wore a grey derby hat, which is not the sort of thing a sporting gentleman such as myself normally permits on his head, but unfortunately I was supposed to be a businessman and was forced to confine myself strictly to my adopted *rôle*. At least the pearl grey derby matched the spats I wore on my black calf oxfords. As I suffered pangs of mortification beneath the derby I found myself longing for my hep threads, my oxford bags and colorful cravats and the daring double-breasted jacket of the style only recently imported from America and called the "tuxedo," and I considered that Han Shan and Teruo between them had a great deal to answer for.

As Tsingtao was under occupation, I had to clear Japanese customs, something for which I was prepared. From Hong Kong's finest gang of forgers I had acquired a British passport under the name of Yin Lo Fo, who, as it happens was a real person, a minor Hong Kong textile merchant who had never been out of the colony in his life, and who, if my luck held, was not about to start now.

We passengers were compelled to leave the train and have our luggage carried to the customs shed. Japanese citizens were waved through with little formality, and Westerners had their documents examined, but the Chinese were forced to wait till last, and then have our luggage ransacked by a swarm of the local uniformed locusts, hirsute Korean peasants conscripted into the Japanese army, men who cared neither a jot nor tittle for the laws of man and who lived entirely for loot.

I was, however, prepared for this. I looked for the officer in charge, who turned out to be typical of the type Japan was sending abroad in those days—very young, with a nascent mustache and a sword bigger than he was, probably hailing from an impoverished, provincial samurai family, raised on shabby gentility and bushido, and now ripe cannon fodder ready to have his untutored head turned by the ruthless gang of plunderers and militarists who had sent him here.

"Instruct your men to take care with that package!" I bellowed, roaring in Japanese and pointing with my cane. "It contains an ancient Shang bronze, a priceless gift for General Hiroshi Fujimoto of the Tsingtao Garrison!"

In certain cultures, certainly that of authoritarian military adventurism, it is presumed that he who shouts must possess the status and authority to do so. Certainly the youth was not prepared to contradict appearances, not when a brawny fellow like myself was doing the bellowing. He looked startled, then saluted—which amused me—and directed his soldiery to put my luggage on a cart and have it delivered to my train compartment forthwith. He didn't even glance at my carefully forged passport.

Where, the discerning reader might wonder, did I get a Shang bronze? Han Shan's treasure troves contained several, as it happens, but they were so pitiful, so corroded and homely, that I'd ended up giving another commission to Hong Kong's finest forgers, and they'd produced a bronze tripod much more pleasing in form and appearance.

Once the train pulled into the central station I checked into the Hotel Bayern, a relic of the city's German occupation, and then arranged to send the forged bronze and Yin Lo Fo's card with compliments to the fellow who was pumpkins in this bailiwick, one General Fujimoto. I idled away a few hours in the beer garden, sipping a fine lager, listening to a German band and learning the lyrics to "Ein Prosit," and then an arrogant young subaltern, immaculate in dress uniform and sword, came to summon me to the general's presence.

General Fujimoto and I got along like a house afire. I understood him, and I gave him to understand that he understood me. He was a stout old chap, large of belly and of mustache, with an office crammed with Chinese bronze and porcelain that he'd looted or extorted or otherwise screwed out of the population. On my arrival he produced a bottle of brandy and toasted my health. Over drinks and cigars I told him that I was a textile manufacturer from Hong Kong who had become alarmed by the general strike, and that, as the Japanese had such a splendid way of dealing with strikers, I was thinking of relocating my plant to Tsingtao.

"Strikers!" A bit of fire entered his bloodshot eyes. "Curse them anyway! I have my men shooting and bayoneting them every day, and still they march and demonstrate and carry on!"

I assured him that I thought shooting and bayoneting strikers was just the cat's pyjamas, and that this should be done early and oft, mixed perhaps with a little beheading when the soldiers got bored. The general slapped his knee and said I was a good chap and understood the way of the world.

I reluctantly concede that this was one occasion in which my appearance stood me in good stead. If I hadn't looked like a thick-necked brigand crammed into an English-tailored suit, perhaps the general wouldn't have treated me as one and welcomed me, as it were, to the fold.

Over the third drink I mentioned a game of cards I'd played on the train, wherein I'd lost five hundred Mexican dollars, and he perked up and asked if I played auction bridge, which as it happens I did. He then asked if I d care to join him that evening at the Japan Services Club for a rubber or two, and I replied that I had no other engagements to impede me.

That evening I thankfully traded in my grey bowler for a black silk topper and headed for the club. Once there I poured brandy down my starched shirtfront, poured a great deal more down my throat, and wagered Han Shan's money with a degree of recklessness that my partners probably found staggering. I didn't use Ping's amulet, as it didn't matter to me whether I won or not—if I lost, I planned to win it all back once I met Teruo. I was more interested in studying the other players rather than concentrating on the game.

One of the players was a businessman named Yamash'ta, a thin wand of a man with gold-rimmed spectacles and a greying Douglas Fairbanks mustache. He drank nothing but cold tea, and he was a precise player with a prodigious memory. He was an official of the railway the Japanese were building across Manchuria, a concession granted by the previous Chinese government, and this fact alone caused me to suspect him of being a spy. This suspicion narrowed to a certainty once I was introduced to his companion, a Chinese named Sung, who, despite his Western evening dress, proved to be a Mandarin of the First Rank, With Twin-Eyed Peacock Feather and Ruby Button, and an emissary from China's former emperor, the faintly ridiculous Pu Yi.

Pu Yi had been emperor twice now, first as a puppet of the former empress, Hsiao-ting, and then, for a couple weeks, as a puppet of a general named Chang Hsün. Although he had no part in Chinese government, Pu Yi was still ensconced in his palace in Peking, with all his ranks and privileges and a handsome subsidy, and the fact that his emissary was here playing cards with a character like Yamash'ta suggested to me that, now that General Wu had chucked out the pro-Japanese government in Peking, Pu Yi was hanging out his strings for a third puppetship, this time with Japan as a sponsor.

None of which, I supposed, was a concern of mine, other than to suggest a few of the dirty deals that might soon occur in Chinese politics. We were playing for twenty Mexican dollars a point, which gradually increased to fifty as the evening wore on. I'd lost about eight hundred simoleons, to the despair of my first partner Fujimoto and to the apparent delight of his successor Sung, who, as an Imperial official, was playing with his own money no more than I was.

My next partner was Yamash'ta, and I told myself to look sharp. If anyone here was capable of penetrating my disguise, it was he. So I took the trouble of slopping some more brandy down my shirtfront and drunkenly suggested raising the stakes. My opponents loudly agreed, but Yamash'ta merely narrowed his eyes, called for more cold tea, and stroked his delicate little mustache. I could tell he was calculating whether his own machine-like play stood any chance against his partner's recklessness, and apparently he decided in the affirmative, for he nodded and reached for the bridge block.

His calculations were on the money. Though our opponents won the first game, we scored higher in honors. We won the second game, though it was a squeaker. And the third game went all our way, ending with a little slam in no-trump, doubled no less, and while I played dummy and spilled brandy into my lap, Yamash'ta went on to steamroller our opponents, getting fifty honors points for the little slam, ninety points because he held four trump honors while I held the fifth, and then another fifty points because the contract was doubled.

Yamash'ta then apologized to our opponents for beating them so badly, saying it was mere luck, after which the two of us filled our pockets with Mexican dollars till we jingled with every move.

"The luck was certainly ours tonight!" I said as I lit a cigar.

"I am delighted that your first visit to Tsingtao should be so occasioned with fortune," Yamash'ta said. He examined his stogie without lighting it. "Perhaps you would care to join us tomorrow night for another of our little evenings. Do you play American poker? We meet regularly every Wednesday night."

"We do?" blurted old General Fujimoto.

"Of course we do," Yamash'ta said. "Every Wednesday."

"Oh!" the general cried, suddenly up to speed in re plundering the new-comer. "Beg pardon! Is it Tuesday already? My mistake!"

I understood why they wanted to shift to poker. Poker, you see, would permit them all to play against me at once, and if my reckless betting held true, at least some of them could count on walking away from the table with a small fortune, perhaps even a textile factory or two in Hong Kong.

"Poker, eh?" I said. "I've played it, but you'll have to refresh my memory concerning the rules. Is it a straight that beats a flush, or the other way around?"

After that remark, I believe the others were ready to become my friends for life.

General Fujimoto dropped me off at my hotel that night, and promised to pick me up the next evening promptly at nine. I whiled away the next day reading a mystery novel—a Reggie Fortune, as I recollect—and then made a special trip to the railroad yards to make a few little arrangements of my own. Then I donned evening dress, brushed my topper, and waited for the general to arrive.

When I arrived at the Japan Services Club I discovered my companions of the previous evening had been joined by two others. One, I knew at once, was an immortal—a powerfully built man with prominent eyes, whose hair gleamed with brilliantine and who wore a plain military tunic with no rank or insignia. I permitted my eyes to graze him briefly and then turned to the other man, who in full dress, epaulets and all, looked like Mrs. Astor's door-man, but turned out to be Colonel Arakaki of the 142nd Military Police Bat-talion. It was Arakaki who turned to the immortal and offered introductions.

"This is Captain Kobayashi of my battalion," he said briefly.

"Honored," I said, and bowed. I was disinclined to think it was possible that the 142nd could contain *two* immortals, so I was fairly certain that Kobayashi was a pseudonym of Teruo Minamoto, the immortal who'd won Han Shan's amulet. Well, I thought, we'll soon find out.

"Shall I order brandy?" offered a smiling General Fujimoto. I smiled back at him.

"If you promise not to let me drink too much," I said. "I'm afraid I had quite a bad head this morning."

I wasn't afraid of getting skunked and losing—the amulet would take care of that—but rather of what might happen after the game. I wanted to be clearheaded enough to make my getaway.

So I sipped at the brandy and played poker for an hour or so, plunging on every bet. At the start I often won simply because my reckless bluffing intimidated players with better hands and drove them out of the game, but once they caught on I began to lose heavily.

I did observe one important thing. All the Japanese were exceedingly deferent to Captain Kobayashi, even those who supposedly outranked him. They apologized to him when they won, they bobbed little obeisant bows in his direction when he spoke to them, they offered to light his cigarets. A mere captain would hardly merit such attention. So I knew not only that Kobayashi was a kami, but that the others knew it, too.

And after a few hands I began to see Kobayashi's prominent eyes begin to glow. A twitchy little grin settled onto his lips each time cards were shuffled. He began to smoke continuously, lighting each cigaret with its predecessor. His words were cut to monosyllables, and he reached for each new card as if it were his heart's desire.

He was a gambler, all right, one of the immortals who couldn't stay away from games of chance. Perhaps Yamash'ta and Fujimoto made it their business to line up suckers for him before he got involved with a real sharp and started betting the Japanese Imperial Regalia. After the first hour I didn't think Kobayashi would notice anything but the cards, so I thought perhaps it was time to deploy some magic.

I lost three hundred dollars on a single card at stud, then excused myself and made a beeline for the gents', where I withdrew Ping's amulet out of my cigaret case, licked it, and stuck it to the inside of my left wrist, over the pulse point in hopes it would get to work faster. I waited for a moment to see if anything was going to happen, but I didn't feel any different. I glanced in the mirror, just to see if something was happening, like my ears going pointed or my eyes beginning to glow with hidden power, but it wasn't on, so I put the amulet back in my cigaret case and rejoined the game.

My first hand drew a flush, and I knew Ping's amulet was the real Tabasco.

I didn't alter my style of play one whit and continued to plunge. I pretended to be more snootered than I was, for which I thank my training at the Golden Nation Opera Company of Shanghai in which—between beatings and intermittent starvation—I was drilled thoroughly in the Seven Mannerisms of the Drunkard. My cards were phenomenal, with straights, big dogs and tigers, flushes, and fours-of-a-kind coming one after another. And consistently it was Kobayashi who had the second-best hand, who bet against me longer than the others and lost the largest sums. General Fujimoto, amazed at his bad joss, pleaded poverty and dropped out with an apologetic bow to the kami, but the others played on and on. Yamash'ta grew very quiet and still, his eyes flicking from me to Kobayashi, tracking each card as if he were trying to work something out in his head.

"Big tiger," said Kobayashi, and laid down his hand, K-J-10-9-8.

"How interesting!" I said. "I have a big tiger, too!" And then I laid it down, K-Q-J-9-8, and gave a drunken laugh.

Kobayashi sat back in his chair and eyed me coldly as I raked the gelt toward my end of the table. Yamash'ta looked as if he were trying to figure out how I'd done it, but he knew I couldn't have rigged the cards, because he'd dealt them himself. "Perhaps," he said, "you gentlemen are growing tired of poker. Shall we change pace with a round or two of fan-tan?"

Ah, I thought, fan-tan. Han Shan's downfall. "Suits me!" I said cheerfully, and we adjourned to the fan-tan table. Yamash'ta said that he would preside if we gave him a moment to refresh himself: he went to his apartments upstairs and came down, I noticed, wearing an evening jacket of slightly different cut, no doubt with loads stowed up the sleeves. He obtained a bowl, a chopstick, and a handful of small white stones, then joined us at the table.

He used the chopstick as a stage magician uses his wand—not to furnish a distraction, which is what most people think, but to provide an excuse for the hand to be in an unnatural position, in this case because he would shortly dump a load of stones into his palm. He called for our attention by knocking the chopstick against the upraised bowl, then grabbed a handful of stones, dumped them in the bowl, and inverted the bowl on the table. What I wasn't supposed to observe was that the stones that went into the bowl actually came from his sleeve, and that the original stones stayed in his palm. Once he inverted the bowl on the table, he slipped his hand into his pocket to dispose of the stones. He was really very good, and didn't need the chopstick at all—I never would have seen the move if I hadn't been looking for it.

"Odd!" I announced, and shoved out a fistful of Mexican silver.

"Even!" Kobayashi said promptly. I looked for the palmed stone being added but didn't see it, so I suspect the number of stones was even to begin with.

I watched Kobayashi as Yamash'ta lifted the bowl and counted out the stones with his chopstick, two by two. Kobayashi's bug eyes glittered, his color was high, and the pulse beat prominently in his temples. He had the fever, all right—even though he knew the game was rigged he was still in a sweat over it, perhaps more excited by the certainty of his victory than he would have been by an honest game.

I lost. Sung commented that perhaps my luck was changing. I allowed the possibility, and planned to bet odd next time to force Yamash'ta to use a palmed stone. But I never got the chance—as Yamash'ta lifted the hand with the chopstick to commence the next round, a load of stones flew out of his sleeve and scattered all over the table.

Yamash'ta turned pale. Fujimoto's jaw dropped, and so did Sung's. I played stupid and stared at the fallen stones.

"Say," I said, "I've never seen that happen before!"

Kobayashi stared at Yamash'ta with cold fury, a little muscle twitching in his jaw. "I'm terribly sorry!" Yamash'ta gasped. "I don't know how such a thing could have happened! Please excuse me—it's late and I should go to bed."

"Could've happened to anyone, old chap," I said soothingly, still pretending I didn't understand what had happened.

Then Kobayashi spoke to Yamash'ta. In Japanese, which he probably thought I didn't understand—though it is possible he didn't care a hang whether I did or no. He spoke in mild tones, as if he were chatting on the phone to someone who bored him mildly, but his words were vicious and cutting, and the faces of the other Japanese turned to stone as they pretended they weren't hearing Yamash'ta's being verbally cut to pieces right in front of them. I could tell that Sung understood because he turned pale and began to fidget.

The hell of it was, Yamash'ta was only doing his job—keeping Kobayashi, or Teruo as I thought he was, from betting the Empire in a game of chance. But Kobayashi reviled him in terms I would not use to address a dog, or even Pu Yi. And Yamash'ta just sat there and took it, face stoic, eyes on the table. When Kobayashi was finished, Yamash'ta begged to be excused again, swept up the stones, and walked quietly away.

It occurred to me that I didn't like Captain Kobayashi. I didn't like the way he treated the people whose job it was to look after him, I didn't like his greedy, drooling way of anticipating the outcome of a fixed game, and, far as that went, I didn't think much of his overreliance on brilliantine, either.

Even if he wasn't Teruo, I thought, I was going to enjoy clipping him for his potatoes.

Even someone as stupid as Yin Fo Lo was supposed to be couldn't miss the undercurrents here, and I tried to look as if I were trying to work out what was making everyone so uncomfortable.

"Perhaps another game," Kobayashi said.

I tried to look relieved at the suggestion. "Certainly," I said.

"Do you perhaps know shogi?"

"Most sorry, but I don't." Shogi is a type of Japanese chess, and there's no luck involved: I was afraid that Ping's amulet wouldn't help me there.

"Mah-jongg?" This was Colonel Arakaki, trying to be helpful.

"Splendid!" I said. "Absolutely the bee's knees, as we say in Hong Kong."

Kobayashi gave a thin, superior smile. "No skill involved, of course," he said, "but I don't mind a game."

I knew I was really going to enjoy this next part.

We had one of the club's staff prepare the table while we hammered out the rules. There are thousands of ways of scoring mah-jongg, and we had to decide how many points to give for what hand, and what the limit would be.

Arakaki suggested ten thousand, and I said, what the devil, let's make it twenty. After all this was committed to paper, we began.

My luck wasn't quite as pronounced this time, which was probably better in the long run, as it lulled my opponents into a false sense of security. I lost a few games to Kobayashi, though I never scored less than second or a close third, which meant I actually made money, since in mah-jongg you don't just pay the winner, but everyone who scored higher than you—so when I came in second, Arakaki and Sung had to pay both me and Kobayashi, and though I paid him, too, my winnings from the others usually kept me ahead of the game.

I had piled up a modest profit on the counting sticks when we had a no-win game, with no one getting mah-jongg. Prevailing wind shifted from East, who was Kobayashi, to me, playing South. I drew a three of bamboo from the tile wall, then discarded it, and Kobayashi pounced on it like a drowning man reaching for a life preserver. "Mah-jongg!" he cried, and grinned wide.

The grin faded when it turned out that I'd actually pointed higher, since I had a Bouquet of Flowers, three Green Dragons, and three of my own West Wind, all of which meant my score was doubled no less than seven times, while Kobayashi's mah-jongg was doubled only once, for Three Small Scholars.

Kobayashi leaned back in his chair and reached for his cigarets. The prominence of his eyes assured that his pupils were surrounded entirely by white, and his stare was quite eerie. "You're very lucky tonight, Mr. Yin," he said coldly.

"You said it yourself," I laughed, "no skill at this game! Only luck!"

"Hmmm," he said, and stroked a cigaret with his fingers as if it were a dagger he was planning on plunging into my liver.

"My apologies," said Colonel Arakaki as he added up his losses, "but I'm afraid I've reached my limit. I should be in bed. Please continue without me."

We all said good-bye, except Kobayashi, who just kept stroking his cigaret and staring at me. I began to feel nervous. Immortals live a long time, and you never know what sort of abilities they may pick up along the way. Could he know I was using the magic of luck?

Whatever he knew or suspected, it didn't stop him from eagerly setting up the tiles for another game. We both racked up honors and were only a few tiles from victory—assuming, of course, we could get the right ones. I drew a Season, which I displayed, then drew a loose tile from the top of the tile wall. It was five of dots, I just realized, which completed my hand, and then I dropped the tile in my surprise.

"Mah-jongg!" I said. "And look—I've drawn Plum Blossom on the Roof!"

"A limit hand!" gaped Sung. "Twenty thousand points!"

We were playing for a dollar a point, I should add. And, because both losers had to pay me in full, I was owed a full forty thousand dollars.

Sung turned pale. He'd been spending freely all night, but an extra twenty thousand smackeroos on the old expense account was probably more than the Imperial Exchequer would willingly fork over.

Oh, well. He'd probably make up the difference by selling a state secret or two.

I confess I could not care overmuch for the dilemma of this palace flunky—my attention was on Kobayashi, who was staring at me again with those goggle eyes of his. The little twitch had returned to his jaw. He ground out his cigaret with a determined twist of his fingers.

"Did we mention Plum Blossom on the Roof when we began?" he said. He began reaching for the list of scores we'd hammered out before starting. "If not, my apologies, but—"

I smoothly plucked the sheet of paper from beneath his outstretched fingers. "Oh yes," I said. "I remember distinctly. Plum Blossom is right—" I pointed. "Right here."

Sung looked at the list, sighed, and nodded sadly. "I hope you will take my note of hand," he said.

I looked at him and screwed up my face in imitation of a drunken man trying to decide if he was offended or not. "Beg pardon," I said, "but do you mean to say you came to this game unprepared to make good your losses?"

"Well," he said apologetically, "a limit hand—twenty thousand points! How often does it happen?"

"Often enough," I said. I gave an inane little drunken giggle. "I'm sure that Captain Kobayashi is prepared to pay at once, or give security."

Which put the kami smack-dab in the vise, and didn't the little weasel know it! He glared at me with those peculiar eyes, and I believe for a second or two I could hear his teeth grinding. Then he pushed all his money across the table at me. "There's almost two thousand here," he said.

"That's a start," I said.

"And—" He glared at me defiantly for a long moment, and then his hands reluctantly rose to the collar of his tunic. "Here's something for security."

He unbuttoned his collar and reluctantly drew out an amulet on a chain. I reached out for it, and almost snatched my fingers back at the touch—the thing was loaded with power that snapped through the air like a charge of electricity. Still, I forced myself to pick up the thing, and then I held it before my face and looked at it skeptically.

"At least it's gold," I conceded. "But it's not worth anything like twenty thousand."

"It's a family heirloom," he said. "I daren't return to Japan without it."

I rather hoped, on reflection, this was true.

"Is that old Chinese writing on it?" I said. "What does it say—I can't quite make it out—" The amulet was quite old, because the writing was in an obsolete style, with rounded characters instead of the squared-off ones used today.

"Yes," Kobayashi said. "It's quite ancient."

I looked at the other side. "Are those the Door Gods?" I asked. I frowned and looked at him. "This amulet is Chinese!" I said. "How can it be an heirloom of the Kobayashi family?"

He ground his teeth again at the thought of having to make up some degrading lie in order to oil up a man he believed to be a miserable Chinese bourgeois. I could see the blood pressure building up behind his pop eyes. Another notch or two and I fully expected his eyeballs to come hurtling at me across the table, propelled by jets of steam.

"My family has had business in China for generations," he said.

"'Well," I muttered, "if it's all you've got." I stowed the thing in my jacket pocket. "I suppose an army captain doesn't get paid all that much."

I found myself faintly surprised the eyeballs didn't come shooting across the table right on the bally instant. I turned to Sung, who to his embarrassment had nothing to offer but his note of hand and a pair of platinum cuff links. (I still have the cuff links, by the way. The note I laundered through a number of brokers and eventually got about twenty cents on the dollar, which shows you what Imperial officials are worth.)

"You must all come to my hotel tomorrow night," I said, rising, "and I'll give you a chance to win it all back." And then I turned and found, to my surprise, that Arakaki and Yamash'ta were standing in the doorway, lounging a bit yet blocking my path.

"Hullo!" I said. "I thought you'd gone to bed!"

"I couldn't sleep," Yamash'ta said, "knowing that you had to face that long journey back to your hotel."

"Oh, it's not so long," I said cheerfully.

"But your ride has left, and the strikes have made the streets dangerous at night," Yamash'ta went on, "so I arranged for you to have a room here at the club, as my guest."

"You're too kind, but you shouldn't have gone to all that trouble," I said, and tried to wedge my way between them. Over Arakaki's shoulder I caught a glimpse of men in uniform standing in the front hall. Members of the 142nd Police Battalion, no doubt, called up by Yamash'ta and Arakaki as soon as they figured out which way the Prevailing Wind was blowing at the mah-jongg table.

Arakaki put a fatherly hand on my shoulder. "It's past four in the morning," he said. "The banks will be open in a few hours, and you can breakfast here and then accompany Mr. Sung and Captain Kobayashi to the bank in order to collect your winnings."

I misliked the thought of having to fight my way out of the club. Police units, unlike most members of the military, actually get to make practical use of their training in the regular course of their peacetime duties, what with having to subdue drunks and felons and the odd hatchet fiend; and the 142nd, I'm sure, had been burnishing their skills to a fine amber glow over the last weeks skirmishing with strikers. All of them, no doubt, had been trained in one of those dreadful Japanese arts with "gentle" in its name, as in "Gentle Art," or "Gentle Art of Beheading," or "Gentle Art of Disemboweling Your Enemy and Strangling Him With His Own Intestines."

It was clear enough I'd been laid a stymie. So I let myself be escorted upstairs, where one of the guest rooms had been thoughtfully provisioned with a snifter, a bottle of brandy, and a pair of pyjamas with the club emblem handsomely embroidered on the pocket. Perhaps, I thought as I hefted the brandy bottle, I was expected to drink myself into insensibility.

Well, I considered, perhaps I ought. If I just played along with Yamash'ta, I'd be forty thousand to the good in just a few hours. Forty grand would buy a whole chain of New Orleans-style clubs throughout the East, or indeed in the Flower Kingdom itself, the USA.

I looked at the brandy bottle, then decided I had other plans for it. Tempting though it was to submit to the dictates of Fate, and disinclined though I was to worry overmuch about the martial fortunes of the Chinese people, the fact remained that I didn't like Teruo much, or his gang of pirates, and that after trying to rob me, then cheat me, they'd now stuck me in chokey, and even though an upstairs room at the Japan Services Club wasn't bad as dungeons go, still I'd much rather be somewhere else than stuck in the cooler by a couple of bad losers.

Besides, Teruo and company might decide to save themselves the money and kill me as I slept.

I determined, as the poet says, to "look for the silver lining." I glanced out the window and saw a half dozen military policemen stationed in and about the club drive. No silver lining there. I closed the curtains. I would have to work out something else.

It was but the work of an instant to dump my winnings into a pillowcase, undo my collar and tie, put the amulet around my neck under my shirt, locate a couple of bath towels, and then glide to the door, where I listened for a long moment. I heard no one in the corridor, so I opened the door and nipped out.

A sentry jumped to his feet, knocking back the cane chair in which he was sitting. Displaying a minimum of six of the Seven Mannerisms of the Drunkard, I swayed up to him and, in a voice slurred by drink, asked him for directions to the bathroom. He couldn't quite make out my words and leaned closer, at which point I slapped him in the throat with the back of my left hand. Not hard enough to cause him permanent injury, but certainly with enough force to cause him to make gasping sounds, clasp both hands about his neck, and—rather more importantly—to refrain from crying an alarm. At which point I whanged him behind the left ear with the brandy bottle, which I'd concealed in a towel, and then dragged his unconscious form back to my room.

I scouted the upper floor a bit and found an unused guest room which enabled me to get a view of the back. There was a kind of zen garden there, gravel with a few interestingly shaped rocks and bits of driftwood strewn about, and a high wall over an alley, and about half a dozen military gumshoes standing in the shadows and pretending to look alert.

No more promising than the front, really, but at least it was darker, and I hoped I could still count on Mr. Ping's luck. So I stripped the spread off the bed, tied it to a bedpost, and let myself out the window.

I suppose even phenomenally good joss can only stretch so far in preventing sentries from seeing a large man in full evening dress descending from a window on a bedspread while carrying a pillowcase full of silver. Certainly, in the better fiction, gentlemen burglars like Raffles seem to escape the consequences of such behavior with a generous regularity. But the fact of the matter is that my feet had barely touched ground before the first cry rang out and I was obliged to leg it for the wall.

There were three guards in a position to block me. I discovered Mr. Ping's amulet hadn't yinned out on me when one of them tripped over one of the rocks in the zen garden and fell on his face. The second guard planted himself in my path and dropped into some kind of classic Oriental boxing stance—unfortunate for him, as I had no intention of doing any classical Oriental boxing. As I dashed past him I wound up like Ty Cobb standing at the plate and swung the weighted pillowcase at his head. He dropped and I charged on without breaking stride.

The third one was their officer, a young fellow with a uniform too big for him. He rightly judged he didn't quite have time to draw his sword, so he jumped in front of the wall with his arms outstretched, planning on tackling me and hanging on until the rest of his troops arrived. I jumped at him and planted the toe of my right foot in his groin, the toe of my left in his solar plexus, the heel of my right foot on his collarbone, the ball of my left on the bridge of his nose, and then the heel of my right foot on top of his head, from whence I sprang to the top of the wall while my improvised ladder crumpled silently behind me.

Once in the alley behind the wall I was home free. Avoiding the military cops who were driving up and down the streets in cars and motorbikes,

I made a beeline for the rail yard, which I'd visited that morning, and headed for the engine house. I was going to have to abandon all my belongings at the Hotel Bayern, but I wouldn't miss any of them except for the luggage. I'd always had a fondness for hand-stitched calfskin.

I'd thought ahead, you see. The docks were closed by strikes, the roads were patrolled, and if I'd waited for the first passenger train out in the morning, the Japanese would already have sealed off the station. Instead, I'd visited the rail yard that morning and commissioned a special, one that would have its steam up and be ready at an instant's notice to flee the Japanese Concession. And I'd paid the engineer to bring another set of work clothes with him, so I could look like one of the train crew if we were stopped.

But when I arrived I found the engine house empty, all the locomotives standing silent and dark and exuding a faint odor of grease and bituminous coal. There was a faint light in the back, and I ran for it, my pillowcase jingling. There, beneath a lantern, I found my engineer lying on a bedroll, an oil lantern by one elbow.

"What's going on?" I demanded. "Where's my train?"

The engineer woke slowly, propped himself up on one elbow, and scratched his head. "Oh, Mr. Yin," he said. "I had given you up."

"What about the train?"

He shook his head. "Canceled. All trains are canceled."

"In heaven's name why?"

"We're on strike—all the railroad workers. We're protesting General Wu's actions against the strikers on his rail line. Hey!" he said, alarmed at the changes in my appearance, "don't blame me! It wasn't my idea!"

"Money!" I said. I opened my pillowcase and pulled out a fistful of silver. "I can give you money!"

The engineer looked wistful. "I'm sorry, Mr. Yin. I'd like to oblige you. But I can't run a railroad by myself—we need switchmen and people in the control tower and so on, and they're on strike, too. In fact, I came here to return your money to you."

I'm afraid I lost control for a moment. I stomped around in a little circle, cursing General Wu, the railroad workers, Kobayashi, Han Shan, Yamash'ta, and eventually Mr. Ping, whose amulet had finally let me down—though, after I'd had a chance to think about it, I remembered his warning about "cosmic bad joss," the kind the amulet couldn't do anything about. Apparently railroad strikes were on a par with earthquakes, floods, and warfare.

"Well," I said, calming down a bit. "Did you at least bring me a change of clothes?"

"I'm sorry, no," he blinked. "We weren't going anywhere, so I didn't bring them."

"We'll exchange clothes, then."

"Are you sure? Those clothes of yours are pretty nice."

I held up the handful of silver again.

The engineer's clothing was a bit tight across the chest, and short in the legs and arms, but it would enable me to disappear among the population of Tsingtao much better than would evening dress. As I slipped out of the railroad yard, I realized that I was stranded in a town where I knew no one, from which there was no practical exit, and where powerful enemies were doubtless looking for my head.

Well, it wasn't the first time. So I headed for the oldest cemetery I could find.

I believe I mentioned earlier that I was once apprenticed to a mountebank, a Mr. Piao, who was a member of the Vagabond Sect. The Vagabonds hire themselves out in wartime as spies and assassins, but in peacetime they live as wandering con men, fortune-tellers, and traveling players, the latter a natural occupation for my fifteen-year-old self, at the time a refugee from the tyranny and oppression of the Golden Nation Opera Company of Shanghai.

Mr. Piao's crowning achievement was his attempt to convince Yuan Shih-kai, a rather unscrupulous Imperial general who had betrayed the Republican movement to the Empress Dowager and then been exiled for his ambition, that his political misfortunes were the result of a curse from his mother, to whom he had behaved in life with insufficient *hsiao*. One of the elements of Mr. Piao's charade was that Yuan's mother actually show up to haunt him—and this was my job, which involved sneaking into General Yuan's quarters to appear dramatically, dressed as a woman in the white of mourning, and to howl curses and imprecations at the unfilial Yuan.

It was Mr. Piao's bad luck that some of his apparatus—a kind of magic lantern designed to project ghostly images on the walls of General Yuan's home—malfunctioned at the wrong moment and betrayed the plot. That was the last of Mr. Piao, who was marched out and shot; and I found myself on the run, in a strange town, and furthermore dressed as a female ghost, the sort of costume that causes a fellow to be noticed.

Fortunately I bethought myself of the cemetery. People are perfectly prepared to see ghosts in a graveyard, and for that reason hardly ever venture there—and when they do visit they often leave food offerings, off which any lurking ghost can make an excellent meal. The only disadvantage of living in a cemetery, in case you're ever in a jam and are inclined to try it, is that graveyards are chock-full of yin—it's all the dead people, you see—and if you want to keep feeling yeasty, you should try to get a lot of yang-heavy foods in your diet.

So from the rail yard I hastened to the cemetery, located an old Manchurian tomb that, from inscriptions, hadn't been used in the last couple generations, and broke in. The original occupants seemed to have been returned to their ancestral tombs in Manchuria, and the place was empty. After sunrise, I hid my winnings save for a few silver pieces, then ventured out to purchase some better-fitting clothes of the common laboring sort and some yang-heavy food.

When I returned, I took the amulet from around my neck and gazed at it. The old-style characters were a bit difficult, but I finally made out the words "Noble Heart Nine Golden Apertures." The heart of a wise man, it was said, had nine apertures, whereas the rest of us made do with a lesser number, but what this had to do with the Golden Swords was more than I could say.

I held the amulet before me and concentrated on it, reciting the inscription to myself, first in Cantonese and then in the Peking dialect, and then—quite instantaneously—I was in another location altogether.

Han Shan had described the place as a "fountain," but it looked more like a small lake, a cold deep body of water of the sort fed by natural springs, surrounded by wild grasses and overhanging willows. The lake itself was in a small valley, surrounded on all sides by ice-capped mountains. Above was a very blue sky, and the only sound was that of wind sighing through the willows. It was the sort of place where a chap might want to bring a girl, a bottle of wine, and a portable gramophone, but unfortunately I had none of these available, so I circled the lake, looking for sign of the swords and finding none. So I peered into the wind-ripped waters, which were crystal clear and very deep, in hopes of finding something useful, and indeed saw a faint golden glow deep in the depths.

I disrobed and dived in. The sensation was curious—there was the shock of cold, but no real sensation of moisture or pressure, and my dive continued without cease, heading straight for the bottom. I tried blowing a few bubbles in passing, but no bubbles appeared. I discovered, after a few cautious attempts, that there was no need to hold my breath because I could in fact breathe the water, or whatever it was, perfectly well.

I reached the bottom of the fountain and there they were, two swords lying on a table crudely carved out of the rocky bottom. The swords were both unblemished, gleaming gold. It rather surprised me that the blades were of two different styles—Kan Chiang was a powerful broadsword of the type called a dau, with a heavy single-edged blade. Mo Yeh was a lighter blade of the type called a female sword, with a narrow, double-edged, pointed blade. Of course, this female sword actually *was* a female, at least if you credit the story of how the blade came to be forged.

Well, I had no use for swords at present, and they were illegal to carry around, so I just bowed politely in their direction and then sprang for the surface, which I reached without effort. I rose from the fountain perfectly dry, and wishing I owned the patent on whatever type of water I'd just been in—I'd had all the refreshment and fun of swimming, with none of the danger or inconvenience.

Once I'd put on my clothes I recited the words "Noble Heart Nine Golden Apertures" again, and there I was, back in the old Manchu's tomb. And there I continued for three more days, during which I grew a heavy beard to assist my disguise—fast beard generation is the only advantage I can think of to being as hirsute as I. And then, as I slipped out of the cemetery one morning to get my breakfast noodles, I saw a part of my past walk by me in the street, and I knew that Mr. Ping's amulet hadn't quit on me yet.

"Yu-lan!" I called. She turned at once and her jaw dropped as she recognized me.

"Wu-k'ung!"

We embraced, an act which I enjoyed to the full. Years ago, when we both suffered under the vile despotism of the Golden Nation Opera Company of Shanghai, Yu-lan had been quite a stunner, and I had been thoroughly smitten by her charms, but now that she had grown to maturity I found myself staggered by her wide brown eyes, her gleaming black hair, her glowing complexion, her coral lips—during our years apart she had become nothing less than a pippin of the first water.

"How extraordinary!" Yu-lan said. "What are you doing in Tsingtao?"

"Hiding from the Japanese," I said.

"What an odd place to do it," she said. "Still, I might have known. You haven't changed much in the last few years, have you?"

"Whereas you have only grown more beautiful," I said. "Are you still with the Golden Nation?"

"Oh, not at all," she said. "After you beat up all the teachers and left, the company went from bad to worse. Director Wang died, and Mr. Hsü became the new director—"

"That idiot!" I exclaimed. "I'm glad I stuffed his quilt with fireworks and set it on fire one night!"

"It *was* you who did that!" she said, delighted. "You were so angry when they punished you."

"They never had a jot of evidence," I said, "but they pinned the rap on me anyway. I ask you, is that justice?"

"Well," Yu-lan said, "who else would it have been?"

I was compelled to concede the justice of this remark. "If I know Hsü," I said, "he drank away the profits within the first year."

"Indeed he did. And then he proposed to sell us apprentices to the Splendid Opera Company of Ningpo to make up the losses. ..."

"I hope you beat him within an inch of his life," I snarled.

"No need to make fists," Yu-lan said, and I realized I was doing just that. "We got him drunk, then escaped in the dead of night."

"Ah," I said, pleased, "following my example, what?"

"Minus the broken heads and ribs, yes."

I believe, in the course of my earlier remarks on filial piety, I may have alluded to the fact that, when my parents desired to emigrate to the Golden Mountain, which is what they called San Francisco, they concluded on scanty evidence—the ceaseless complaints of prejudiced neighbors and vicious local tradesmen among them—that their eldest son would be too much trouble on the journey, and accordingly sold me at the age of eight to the Golden Nation Opera Company of Shanghai—a ten-year apprenticeship contract that amounted to slavery. And so, when my parents—and, I might add, my three younger sibs—were prospering mightily in the Land of Opportunity as worthy, hardworking members of the food service industry, I was being beaten, starved, and tortured by a gang of professional sadists under the direction of the aforementioned Hsü. My maternal grandfather—you know, the homicidal maniac—was supposed to look in on me from time to time to see how I was faring, but by age fifteen I'd seen him only twice, and he'd had to leave early both times because the police were after him. My only regret was that, when I went, I hadn't been able to persuade Yu-lan to run off with me—well, that and missing the opportunity to kick Teacher Yang in the pants a second or third time. The whole business was what one might call a defining experience.

It certainly served to define filial piety for *me,* at any rate.

"And how are you faring now?" I asked.

She brightened. "I'm working for the Yellow River Floating Opera Company," she said, "under Master Chiang and his son, Com—ah, Young Master Chiang."

They were pleasant people to work for, she said, and the young master had been educated at university and had all sorts of new ideas. Including, as it happened, packing up the whole opera company and moving it from place to place on a river barge, an ideal situation in a time of civil disorder, when a fast exit from town was oft a consummation devoutly to be wished. When they put on performances, they either rented a theater or simply built their sets right on the barge and performed on the riverside.

"And you—you're in trouble again," she said. "Why are the Japanese pursuing you?"

I calculated how much of the truth I dared let slip, and decided it was easier merely to lie. "I have information they want suppressed," I said. "I need to get it south."

Her eyes widened. "Are you working for the revolutionary government in Canton?"

"I can't say," I said cagily. "But I need to travel in that direction." Canton, where Dr. Sun Yat-sen had established his government, was just upriver from Hong Kong. Close enough for my purposes.

"What sort of information is it?"

"There's an Imperial envoy in town named Sung," I said. "He's here to negotiate an agreement for an Imperial restoration, with Japanese money and troops backing Pu Yi. I've got all the details of the treaty." It was an improvisation, but a reasonable one, and for all I knew true.

"Do you need money?" she asked.

"I have plenty of money," I said. "What I need is a place to hide and a way out of the Japanese Concessions. Perhaps your Master Chiang knows someone who owns a boat and could get me to Chinese territory."

"Can you still do opera?" Yu-lan asked. "Do you remember all the old routines?"

These selfsame routines had been beaten into me by vicious old men armed with bamboo whips, and I allowed as how they, and the whips, were still fresh in my mind.

"Come with me at once." Yu-lan seized my hand, which was the occasion for a thrill to run up the old spine, and led me firmly toward the waterfront to introduce me to her boss.

Master Chiang proved to be a cheerful old stick, bald as an egg, who, once the situation was explained to him, was perfectly willing to shelter me as long as necessary, particularly as I would be able to work, as it were, my passage.

"In what parts did you specialize?" Master Chiang asked.

"Wu-k'ung was a wonderful Monkey King!" Yu-lan said, before I could speak.

"Indeed?" said the master. "Please let me see it!"

I gave Yu-lan a resentful look—this was hardly my favorite part—but I obliged old Chiang with an excerpt from *The Handsome Monkey King versus the Demon of Golden Helmet Cave,* which is one of oodles of operas featuring the Monkey King, all based on stories from the popular if rather lengthy novel *Journey to the West.* The audition piece I chose featured a lot of fighting and yelling and tumbling around, and by the time I finished the commotion had attracted a number of other performers, all of whom applauded vigorously when I was done.

"That was splendid!" Mr. Chiang said. "We'll have to add that play to our repertoire! Your interpretation of the Monkey King was the finest I've ever seen—why, you might be the son of the Monkey King himself!"

"Not quite," I muttered. But still, my audition had got me a berth in the company, and from that point on I sang and danced and battled demons nightly. And, since we all performed masked, I didn't have to worry about being spotted. Unfortunately it appeared that the Yellow River Floating Opera Company was booked for a lengthy run here in Tsingtao, and so I wouldn't be leaving the Japanese Concession anytime soon. But I was in a safe enough place, and happy to get closer to Yu-lan, and so I was content enough with my lot. Aside from some pocket money, I left my Mexican silver buried in the graveyard, which I concluded was the safest place.

And, as I grew chummier with my fellow thespians, I observed that certain of them, Yu-lan included, would ofttimes slip away during the day, and return just in time for our evening performance. After this pattern was repeated a few days in a row, I found Yu-lan strolling about the deck and asked her what was up.

"Well," she said slowly, "Young Master Chiang told me not to tell you."

"Come now," I said, and patted her hand. "We're old friends. There's nothing I wouldn't do for you. Any secret is safe with me."

"It's clear enough you're not working for the Japanese," Yu-lan said. "I don't see why you shouldn't be informed. We're going off in the daytime to perform revolutionary drama for the strikers."

"Oh, really?"

"Yes. Com—I mean, Young Master Chiang says that we must educate the workers in their proper role in the revolution."

I must confess I did not like the soft glow in Yu-lan's eye when she mentioned Young Master Chiang—or, as she'd almost called him twice now, Comrade Chiang. Perhaps she was fond of the overeducated, broad-shouldered, slim-waisted, handsome-looking sheikish sort of bloke—many women are, much to my loss.

"Splendid task," I said, "inspiring the workers and all. Where did you say Young Master Chiang received his college education?"

"Moscow, of course," she said.

"Natch." It occurred to me how useful it would be for a Comintern agent to move up and down China's rivers on a barge, gathering intelligence and organizing revolutionary cells, or whatever it was that Comintern agents did.

"And where does he get these plays?" I asked.

"He writes them himself. He's quite a dialectician, you know."

The glow in Yu-lan's eyes was getting a little too luminous for my taste. It had wormed its way into my vitals and was commencing to set fire to some of my more significant organs, chiefly, I think, the spleen. "Ahh—" I said. "You haven't mentioned to him the reason I was hiding from the Japanese, have you?"

"None of the details, no." She blushed a little. "If you're working for the Canton government—well, I thought it best he didn't know."

The Canton government and the Communists were working for similar goals but weren't formal allies, and the competition between them wasn't always gentlemanly. It was more than possible that Yu-lan's reticence had kept me from being interrogated by Chekhist goons.

"Thank you for your loyalty," I said, quite sincerely. Perhaps, I considered, it was time to dish out some ideologically correct action. "I think it's absolutely spiff what you're doing," I said. "You couldn't slip me copies of these glorious works of revolutionary art, could you?"

She did, and when I read them my sympathy for the strikers' plight increased a hundredfold. It was bad enough they had to face Japanese swords and bayonets every day, without asking them to sit through plays along the lines of *Comrade Ng Discovers Dialectical Materialism* and *Laborers Vigilant Against Capital Accumulation*. The dialog was full of absolute corkers like, "I'm fascinated! Please elucidate further on the subject of Labor Value Theory," and, "Why, Comrade Chou, this Condition of Alienation of yours describes my situation exactly!"

"Do you know," I told Yu-lan later, "I think I might try my hand at writing a revolutionary drama myself."

"Do you think you could?" A little glimmer, perhaps too tenuous at this stage to be called a glow, kindled in her wide brown eyes.

"I'm sure I could!" I said, promptly inspired. "And I want it to be absolutely grand—workers and peasants, you know, singing and dancing their hearts out to music as revolutionary as their sympathies."

"Singing and dancing?" Doubt fluttered across her face. "Why would they sing and dance? That's so old-fashioned."

"All *real* workers and peasants sing and dance," I pointed out.

"Oh—well, if it's realism, then."

"Only thing is—do you suppose Old Master Chiang will object if I buy a piano and move it onto the boat?"

Well, buy it I did, and then suffered the tortures of the damned as I banged out chords and mumbled lyrics to myself and scribbled things down on sheets of paper. Never having written a musical play before, I hadn't realized the sort of agony I was letting myself in for. Problems of translation affected me particularly—I found I composed in English, and then had to translate my sentiments into Northern Chinese. I kept Yu-lan informed of my progress, and sang some of the songs for her, and she was enthusiastic. I recalled some stuff I'd seen in the musicals that had toured the East, and I threw in some business I'd learned from Jerome Kern and Guy Bolton and Eubie Blake. At the end, I reckoned I had something to be proud of—better than Chiang the Younger's turgid stuff, anyway. So I called in my fellow revolutionaries for a run-through.

I seated myself at the piano and warmed the digits running through a few snatches of melody. "The title," I said, "is *Call Me Comrade*." Young Chiang looked at me skeptically and rolled a cigarct. "Our story opens," I continued, "with a mixed chorus of male dockworkers and female textile workers. They sing as follows:

The Mandate of Heaven has gone away,
Looks like bad times are here to stay—
Our situation's frightful, the bosses are so spiteful,
And the Mandate of Heaven has gone a-waaaaaay.

"What is this reference to the Mandate of Heaven!" demanded Young Chiang. "That's just a ridiculous superstition the feudal classes use to justify their centuries of misrule!"

"It can also be used by revolutionaries to justify their attempts to change the government," I pointed out.

"Absolutely!" Yu-lan said. I basked in her approval for a moment, then finished the song.

"Now here's where the hero comes in," I said. "His name is Plain Chou, and he's a dockworker. By way of introduction, he does his solo dance. A little buck-and-wing, over the tops, over the trenches ... Something flashy to get the audience involved."

"Over the tops," demanded Young Chiang. "Over the trenches! What kind of steps are these?"

"A new sort, quite revolutionary," I said. "Invented by oppressed classes in the States. Perhaps I ought to take this part myself, since I'm familiar with them. Anyway, Plain Chou is in the dumps because Old Moneybags, his boss, isn't paying him enough, and he can't marry Miss Chong, the girl of his dreams."

"Dancing!" Chiang carped. "Love stories! What kind of foolishness is this? What does any of this have to do with the inevitable progression of history?"

In spite of this kind of heckling I managed to get Plain Chou and Miss Chong through their first love duet.

"This is absurd!" cried Chiang. "There's no ideological content at all in this story!"

"Ah, well," I said, "we're about to get to all of that. Up to this point all we've been doing is providing characters that our proletarian audiences can understand and care about. But now Chan the Union Man enters. He's a brilliant young Moscow-educated intellectual, here to organize the dockworkers," I feigned indecision. "Who do you suppose will play him?"

"Hmmm," he said suspiciously.

"Here's his song," I said.

The world is in trouble, we all agree
Filled with vice and villainy
But life isn't very nearly such a mystery
Once you know the view—
(the truly scientific view)
—the scientific view of his-to-ry

"Hmmm," said Chiang again, stroking his chin.

I won him over by giving the Union Man all the good arguments, which was what Chiang considered most important; and I gave myself and Yu-lan all the love duets, which was what *I* thought the whole point of the exercise. By the end of the story, the dockyards had been unionized, Old Moneybags humiliated, and Plain Chou and Miss Chong were chirping away happily in each other's arms.

We went into rehearsals right away, and were ready for the premiere in jig time. That's the advantage to working with a Chinese company: they're all cross-trained in everything, singing, dancing, mime, acting, and music, and they're accustomed to learning quickly by rote, so they can get their lines and steps down faster than you can say Bill Robinson.

For the premiere, which was held in a rented godown or warehouse, empty on account of the strike, we had a smallish audience on our rented folding chairs, a hard core of dedicated Union types who attended Young Chiang's dramatic efforts, I'd guess, in order to test their capacity for enduring torture at the hands of the Japanese. I suffered through the usual opening night jitters, and wished I'd had the Ace Rhythm Kings to provide the music instead of the band we'd acquired, whose usual job was to play at funerals. But from the moment I stepped out onto the stage I knew all was well, and from the gasps of the audience as I went over the tops and the trenches I gathered I'd made an impression, and by the time I took Yu-lan's hands in mine and began our first duet, I was confident things were going swimmingly.

It was a socko, in short. The audience went wild with enthusiasm, we were called out for fifteen encores, and at the end of the evening Yu-lan kissed me in a fashion that suggested all the clinches we'd rehearsed so diligently had not been in vain.

The play went on from success to success, our audiences growing larger, enthusiasm overflowing all bounds. They brought their parents, their children, their relatives from out of town. The strike was spreading, with the textile workers, miners, and factory workers joining in, and with nothing else to do they came trooping in their thousands. They brought picnic lunches and bottles of wine. Some came so many times they learned all the lyrics and started singing along with the cast. After my first glimpse of five hundred people harmonizing away about the Scientific View of His-to-ry, I was inclined to wonder, like that Frankenstein bird in the flickers, just what it was I'd wrought.

But I had little inclination to think about such things, as every instant I spent away from the stage was spent with Yu-lan. And though I will draw what I believe the finer writers call "a tactful veil" over the particulars, I think that I can safely remark that our private love duets continued long after our final curtain calls, and that I left my little sleeping cabin untenanted for days at a time.

It was, to be sure, a heady and intoxicating experience. First, it was my first triumph on the stage, and, far from last, I was able to spend my private hours with Yu-lan and I, sitting on the piano bench, me gazing into what the better writers would refer to as her "goo-goo eyes," and practicing sentimental ditties like "Tea for Two" and "Deep in My Heart, Dear." I taught her the goopier songs from *Rose Marie,* as a result of which, at five in the morning, the haunting warble of the "Indian Love Call" was heard floating above the silent, and no doubt to some degree surprised, Tsingtao dockyard.

All idylls, alas, must end, and this one was a victim of its own success. Any play that preaches sedition, and that attracts ever-increasing audiences of thousands of striking workers intent on chucking out their overlords, is bound to become of interest to the selfsame overlords. I suppose I should have foreseen it, had I not been so besotted with Yu-lan and with my own success. And so, one fine matinee, as I was kicking up the dust in my opening solo, there came the booming crash of the godown's main doors being thrown open, and then in poured a brown river of my old friends the 142nd Military Police Battalion, all brandishing weapons.

"This performance is canceled!" some Chinese collaborator bellowed into a megaphone. "Everyone here is under arrest!"

They had picked the wrong thing to say, or at any rate the wrong audience to say it to. These people had been fighting with the Japanese and their Chinese puppets for weeks, and they weren't about to go down quietly. The audience rose as one, and in an instant the intruders were buried beneath a perfect blizzard of missiles, teapots and plates and bowls of rice and dumplings and sausages and anything else the audience had to hand, a volley that was followed by a barrage of folding chairs—and once the Japanese had been stunned by what must have seemed like the entire contents of the warehouse being flung at them, the audience members hurled themselves into the fray, drove the enemy from the godown, and slammed the doors in their face.

A bit slow on the old uptake, I still found myself onstage, staggered by what appeared to be the sight of the last act taking place a couple hours early. And then, as the sound of rifle butts hammering on the godown's doors began to clang out, Yu-lan stepped out onstage and called out in her clear soprano, "Barricade the doors! Don't let them in!"

As the cast and audience busied themselves with piling furniture and set flats against the doors, I gave the matter some thought. Barricading the doors was all very well for the moment, I considered, but in locking the Japanese out we were also locking ourselves in. And if the cops brought in reinforcements—an armored car or two, say—I feared to think of the hideous massacre that could all too easily take place. So I nipped around to where Yu-lan was directing operations and took her by the arm.

"We're safe for the moment, but we're trapped in here!" I said. "Is there any way out?"

She blinked at me, not having quite thought this one out. "I don't know."

"Then we'd better find one!"

A search was undertaken, but the godown was unconnected to any other structure, and though I had high hopes for the sewers, these were dashed when the drains proved to be too small for anyone but a child to negotiate. By the time we'd discovered this the Japanese had given up trying to break down the doors, and an ominous silence now reigned in our improvised theater.

"We've got to make a break for it!" I declared. "Now, while the Japanese are still trying to figure out what to do!" We sent lookouts to the roof to see where the Japanese cordon was weakest, and on their report we laid our plans.

Strategy-wise, I decided to take a leaf or two from the book of Jim Thorpe. "A flying wedge of actors first," I said, "with me in the lead. We'll break through the line, and then everyone else will follow. Once we're past the cordon, we all split up and make a run for it."

You may think it odd that, with hundreds of brawny dockworkers about, I should choose a pack of actors for my elite squad. But there's a lot of combat in Chinese opera, and actors are taught from the cradle how to fight. They use a theatrical version of a boxing style called Northern Long Fist, or Chang Ch'üan. The training includes the use of weapons, so I was able to equip my chorus with the weapons they used in the play to overthrow Old Moneybags, spears and clubs and blunt-edged stage swords of light metal, which didn't have the bite of a real weapon but were better than nothing. Unfortunately there was no time to fetch Kan Chiang and Mo Yeh from the bottom of their pond, so I stuck a couple of the stage swords in the old belt and then further armed myself with a long chunk of wood I tore off one of the sets. I then ordered one of the doors be silently unbarricaded.

While this was being done, I slipped up to Yu-lan. "Stick close to me," I said. "And in the event that we get separated, head for the graveyard near where we first met. Do you remember?"

"Yes," she said. "But shouldn't we go back to the barge?"

"That depends on whether the Japanese have connected us with the Yellow River Floating Opera Company," I said. "If they have, the barge will be their next target—if they're not already there, that is."

The barricade over the door had been dismantled, so I quietly arrayed my forces, explained once more the plan of action, and commanded the doors be thrown open.

The second the hinges commenced their squeal I headed for the nearest barricade at a modest trot, knowing that it would take time for my troops to pass the door and then fill in the flying wedge behind me. I didn't want to take too much time ordering my formation, because I didn't want the Japanese, if they were in a shooting mood, to have time for more than one volley. All I could do was hope my troops weren't running straight into the yellow winking eye of a Maxim gun.

We had caught them a bit off guard, standing about smoking and leaning on their rifles, and it took them a few moments to array themselves behind their barricade of sawhorses. By this time I judged I had enough force behind me, and I increased my speed to a dead run as I waved my whangee over my head and bellowed the ancient battle cry of the Chan family, something that translates out of Cantonese as something like, "O Lord, why dost thou so afflict us?" or, perhaps more to the point, "Why me?"

The enemy got off a ragged volley, which went mostly over our heads, and then I launched myself into a flying kick, aimed not at any of the foe but at the long sawhorse they were standing behind. The sawhorse went over, taking with it the first rank of police, and what should have ensued was the grand sight of yours truly leading my brave troops into the disorganized enemy, windmilling about me in the classic heroic style, as for example Charlie Chaplin beset by welfare agents in *The Kid,* but what happened instead was that my foot got tangled in the sawhorse and I went down flat on my face, and then the chorus line behind me zealously performed an extended tap dance on my kidneys as they charged over my sprawled body to come to grips with the foe.

I was up as soon as the circs permitted, wondering if these sorts of things ever happened to my maternal grandfather, the bloodthirsty maniac, who had been through more fights than God, I believe, made chickens. As far as I could determine things were pretty much a katzenjammer. I was being hauled to and fro in the press, and my head, which had been kicked about a dozen times, was hurting like sixty, but it appeared that my wedge of troops had driven the foe back, by sheer weight if nothing else, and there was nothing for it but for me to add my poundage to the general mass hurling themselves in the general direction of freedom.

Perhaps our front line, who were running straight onto Japanese bayonets, would have preferred to reconsider the whole business of pressing on, but the mass in the rear didn't give them any choice, and in one breathless mass we lurched onward. Eventually, as our mob gained weight and determination, the cops were faced with the decision of either running for it or being trampled, and like sensible chaps they decided to take it on the lam, at which point there was a lurch, and suddenly we were all running free, streaming down the waterfront street like those marathon coves in the last Olympics. There were still a few Japanese among us, either crazed with lust for battle or deprived of the opportunity to flee, and I was able to take a few swipes at them in passing with my bit of lumber, which promptly broke in half.

I looked for Yu-lan but couldn't see her in the mob, but our opposition seemed to have evaporated and I thus concluded that I should bend my efforts to eluding the coppers, so I nipped off down a side street only to run smack into a Japanese officer, sword drawn, leading a squad of reinforcements to battle. The young fellow looked familiar, and he had a broken nose and one of those plaster cast thingummies on his left arm, the kind where the elbow sticks out to the side. He gaped at me.

"You!" he said, and at that moment I recalled using him as a ladder as I made my exit from the Japan Services Club. Apparently I had inadvertently damaged him that night, and in so doing had rather made an impression, because he recognized me in spite of my bushy beard.

He seemed in no mood for receiving my apologies, and cocked his sword arm to cut me in half, at which point I thrust my busted bit of lumber up under his nose and smote him decisively on the mazard.

Later I would conclude from this encounter that the benefits of the point are not stressed in Japanese fencing schools. At the time, however, I was too busy in grabbing his throat with my left hand, and seizing him rather farther down with my right, and then hoisting the poor chump off his feet to use him as a weapon against his own troops. I knocked a few coppers sprawling with the plaster cast, and in his flailing, ineffectual attempts to slash me with his sword the officer managed to chop a few of his own men, and the rest, too wary of damaging their commander to really press their attack, let me charge through to safety. I knocked the sword out of my captive's hand, which I hadn't had the time to do till that moment, and then hoisted him over my shoulder as a shield and ran for it. I really had no intention of letting him go, as he'd recognized me, but I hadn't got as far as deciding where to stash him.

I broke out into the clear between some buildings and there was General Fujimoto, standing up in his staff car, which had the roof folded back and Japanese flags on the fenders. He was brandishing a riding crop and directing a whole company of troops toward the fray, but he stopped in mid-gesture, stared at me with an open-mouthed expression that was growing all too familiar, and pointed with the crop and said, "You!" and then he pointed a bit lower and said, "The swords!" and then he turned to his troops and cried, "Kill him!"

Bootless it would have been to point out that the swords stuck in my belt were the merest of stage props, so I concluded to run for it instead. As I dashed down the nearest alley I considered that my luck seemed to have turned rather decisively: I'd been jumped by a whole battalion of troops, I'd been used for a hurdles course by my own side, and I'd run into the two officers in all of Tsingtao who could recognize me. Mr. Ping's amulet, I judged, had swung to the yin side of things rather decisively, so as I ran I reached into my pocket, pulled out my cigaret case, and managed one-handed to remove the amulet. I licked it, yanked down the puttee on one of my captive's hairy legs, and pasted the paper in place.

There was the tramp of hobnailed boots right behind me, and I concluded that my prisioner was only slowing me down, so I let him fall and put on a burst of speed. As he hit the pavement I heard him cry, *"Otodokoi!"* which is Japanese for something along the lines of, "Whoops, I'm about to take a fall which will cause others to laugh endlessly at my expense!" I would have felt sorry for him if I hadn't been so busy feeling sorry for myself.

Once I'd dropped my shield, I heard the sound of snicking rifle bolts, which served only as further impetus to my flight. And then I heard the young officer's voice again, calling attention to the dubious status of my antecedents—something that, in all honesty, I could not dispute—but a rifle shot cut the voice off in mid-tirade, and I concluded that he'd stood up at the wrong moment, just as one of his men drew a bead on me, and I'd dropped my bad joss just in time. Some more bullets whizzed past, and then I came to a corner and executed a proper Charlie Chaplin turn, hopping on one foot while clinging to a drainpipe, after which, with a clear field ahead, I legged it to freedom.

I caught up with Yu-lan around sunset. She was waiting in the graveyard with a few of the actors, all of whom looked like the subjects of an heroic painting, standing nervously on guard clutching their weapons and glaring into the gloom with eyes that gleamed with lofty majesty from beneath bandaged brows ... or so they seemed to me, anyway. Even Young Chiang was there, looking somewhat less the ass than usual.

"You're safe!" Yu-lan said, and we fell into a relieved embrace.

"How's the barge?" I asked, and kissed her.

"The barge is fine, and so is Master Chiang," she said, after extricating her lips. "We've shifted our mooring, and after the moon sets we're going to try to slip out of the harbor on the tide, without running lights."

"When does the moon set?" I asked, and scanned the sky as if I knew what to look for—other than a moon nearing the horizon, that is.

"In around three hours."

"I'll try to create a distraction just before that time," I said, and she stared up at me.

"You're not coming along!"

"I can't."

This was the point where, if this were the cinema, I would puff out my chest like Wallace Wood and point emphatically at the ground, while a title read, "My place is here!" but what happened is that Yu-lan's chin began to wobble and then I sort of fell to pieces, and I recall saying that, if they were caught without me, they might be able to talk their way out of their jam, whereas if they were caught with me, we'd all be tortured and killed, and I couldn't bear the thought of anyone hurting her. And she said, in that case, she'd join me in creating a diversion, and I said no, it would be too dangerous, and she retorted that, if we were to die, it was best we die together, and I said she ought not to talk bally rot, and the upshot of it was that we had a wretched little weep there in the cemetery, and her comrades looked away and shuffled their feet and pretended they weren't hearing every word.

After we pulled ourselves together somewhat, I took her out of earshot and told her that I had a place in Hong Kong called Broadway Johnny's, where I was known by the name of Chan Kung-hao, and that if she could ever tear herself away from the Chiangs, there was a place for her there. She sniffled. "After the revolution," she said. "The way things are going, it can't be *too* far away."

"You must write as soon as you make your escape," I said, and then I led her away to where I'd buried my pillowcase full of silver and dug it up. I put a few handfuls in my pockets and then gave her the rest. "You might have to bribe your way out of a jam," I said. "It's enough to buy a whole potful of river barges."

"But you might need to bribe an official yourself," she said.

"The kind of jam I plan to get in," I said glumly, "no amount of bribery will settle."

So she kissed me, and we embraced, and had another depressing wail together. By the time I sent her back to her comrades I was about wept out, so I just sat on a tombstone and stared angrily at the gathering dusk until, echoing among the tombstones and willows, I heard, receding in the distance, the haunting cry of "Indian Love Call." I tried to answer it, but I'm afraid the weeping business had left the old vocal cords a little clogged, and the best I could manage was a kind of croak, which did not improve my temper.

A couple hours later, when I marched out of the cemetery, I carried the two golden swords in my hands. I was in a perfectly bloody-minded mood, having lost my girl, my money, and my dreams of theatrical success all in the course of an afternoon, and I was perfectly ready to take my disappointment out on the first enemy to come within my ken.

I had wondered if there would be any pyrotechnics when I actually touched the swords, any sudden, dramatic burst of symphonic music emanating from an invisible orchestra pit, or perhaps a few enigmatic words of warning called out in a harsh, croaking voice ... but nothing of the sort happened.

The swords were very fine work indeed, balanced wonderfully, and much lighter than I'd suspected. I'd done some practice with them in the graveyard, a bit of hopping and chopping, and it went like nobody's business. Kan Chiang, carried in my right hand, was a heavy blade, good for power attacks and suitable to my big shoulders and long arms, and Mo Yeh, in my left hand, was a splendid little fencing sword, light and agile, with a deadly waspish sting. With the swords came a feeling of quiet confidence, mixed with a *soupçon* or so of somber purpose, that served to fortify me for the evening better than a splash of brandy and soda.

You might think that someone walking down the streets of a major city carrying a pair of swords would have no difficulty getting in trouble, but in my case you'd be wrong. The escape from the godown and the Japanese that afternoon had sent hundreds of revolutionaries dashing off into all parts of the city, where they'd all located their friends and gone out looking for a spot of vengeance. There was a full-scale riot in progress, complete with looting and arson, and the Japanese authorities were nowhere to be seen. So I tossed a brick through the window of a tailor shop and got myself some clothing— normally I don't hold much with off-the-rack suits, but this was an emergency—and once I looked like a respectable bourgeois again, I headed for the Japan Services Club.

Here I found the enemy preparing for the worst. A group of soldiers was digging a sandbagged bunker on the front lawn, for all the world as if they were planning on refighting the Battle of Ypres. One rather dim-witted-looking recruit was standing by the gate guarding them from any rioters, none of whom were to be seen, of course, since they knew better than to attack a well-guarded site. I stuck the swords down my trousers in back, and walked a bit stiff-legged toward the club, as if I were a businessman seeking shelter from the riot. As I strode through the gate I was pleased to see that the guard had decorated his chest with a couple grenades, and was furthermore delighted to discover General Fujimoto's staff car in the drive.

I stuck a cigaret in my mug, then patted my pockets as if I were looking for matches. This bit of pantomime convinced the guard I was looking for a light when I approached him. As soon as I got within arm's length I socked him in the beezer, then snatched one of the grenades off his chest, yanked the pin, and tossed it into the bunker. I then grabbed the guard and tossed him in likewise. The ensuing explosion, I am pleased to report, accounted for the whole Ypres Salient in one fell swoop. I then drew my swords and charged the building.

The first fellow I skewered turned out to be the Chinese footman, for which I suppose I ought to be sorry, but it serves him right for toad-eating the Japanese anyway. From the hall I roared into the front parlor, and found there General Fujimoto, standing on the far side of an open coffin. He gaped at me for half an instant, saw the golden swords at the ends of my long arms, and fled straight into an office, slammed the door, and locked it. I ran my shoulder into the door, but it proved a stout bit of woodwork and I bounced off. At this point a couple more officers came in, and I had to deal with them. There is a Japanese art of drawing the sword and cutting with a single move, but it appeared neither of these two had learned it, because I dropped them both in their tracks before they got their blades out.

I have to give a certain amount of credit to my Kan Chiang and Mo Yeh. They seemed to do more damage than their weight would account for, and they never twisted awkwardly in my hands or ended in an unbalanced position. Amazing how much the right tools will help a chap in his trade.

At this point I glanced at the coffin and its occupant, who proved none other than my old friend Lieutenant Chump, somewhat the worse for wear. I should have recognized him earlier, as he didn't quite fit his box, what with the plaster arm-and-shoulder cast that had to be propped up on the coffin's edge. I supposed he must have been a member of the club. Perhaps a touching memorial service was planned for the next day. I'd try to see that the good lieutenant wasn't sent to the beyond all on his own.

I took another run at General Fujimoto's door, and was rewarded by a splintering groan that meant the frame was on the point of giving way, but then a young fellow in naval rig jumped into the room with what I believe the better writers call a "John Roscoe," .38 caliber I believe, and I had to do a hasty somersault that put Lieutenant Chump's coffin between myself and the bullets that began, at that point, to be spent rather freely. Nothing came near me, though I'm afraid the coffin suffered badly. Eventually the sailor ran out of either bullets or nerve and made a break for the doorway that led into the back hall, so I popped up from behind the coffin and tossed Mo Yeh, the lighter of my two swords, right through the blighter's spleen.

I came up out of my crouch and began to move toward the body to retrieve the sword, but I was distracted by a file of soldiers who, having just arrived in a lorry, now came charging up to do battle. Japanese soldiers are trained to attack at all costs, which can be intimidating if you're facing them on a fair and open field, but I was encountering them indoors, and I must say that, brave as they were and able, their doctrine rather let them down this time. All I had to do was station myself inside the front hallway door and chop the brave saps down one by one as they came in. By the time I'd finished and was able to return to the parlor to fetch the lighter sword, I found Yamash'ta, the spy, standing over the body of the naval officer with Mo Yeh in his hand.

Yamash'ta was a very inconvenient man, I was discovering.

I hurled myself at him forthwith, and he dropped into a fencing stance and met my attack. He was a tall, thin wand of a fellow, you remember, and the light weight and darting style of the female sword suited him well. With its sharp point, edge, and double-handed hilt, it was perfectly adaptable to Japanese fencing techniques. I came at him like fury, slashing away with Kan Chiang, and though Yamash'ta was obliged to retreat, he held me off and even forced me now and again to pay attention to his counterattacks. I kept hoping to corner him—it wasn't a very large room—but his footwork was nimble enough to escape me.

At this point a couple more Japanese officers showed up, drew their swords, and prepared to charge into the melee, so I hopped over Lieutenant Chump's coffin to gain a little space on Yamash'ta, played lumberjack for a few well-placed strokes, and then hopped over the coffin again once the newcomers fell like unto the stately fir of British Columbia.

I felt more like Douglas Fairbanks every minute.

Yamash'ta dropped into stance again and we slashed away. The fight went much as it had before, me charging and hewing, Yamash'ta retreating, parrying, and venturing the occasional thrust. It occurred to me he was playing for time: sooner or later someone might show up with a gun, and finish me off while I was occupied. So I stepped back, and let my guard fall a bit. His guard, I observed, fell too.

That's the problem with people who learn fighting in academies, I've found. They practice in rounds, attacking and defending in turns, or fighting in flurries and relaxing in between, and they learn little pieces of timing that are wrong for when Fate dishes up a genuine fight. I had just stepped back and dropped my guard, which signaled to Yamash'ta that he could relax, so he did.

"Better hope you've got something more clever up your sleeve this time than a bag of lousy rocks," I said.

You can tell when a fellow is thinking—his eyes go all abstract—so while he was chewing on my little witticism and working perhaps on a devastating reply I somersaulted forward, rolled under his guard, and rose slashing.

Timing, I've discovered, is everything.

I retrieved Mo Yeh from Yamash'ta's body, cleaned the slippery blood off the hilt, then applied my shoulder to General Fujimoto's door again. It crashed inward with an admirable rending sound, revealing the general himself on the telephone, calling no doubt for reinforcements.

"I surrender!" he said promptly. "Don't hurt me!" Which was rather letting down the old side in terms of Japanese tactical doctrine, I thought. I dropped his sword and pistol to the ground and marched him out.

"I've come here to liberate Tsingtao!" I snarled at him. "I'm not going to quit until the Japanese are driven into the sea!" Whereupon having (I hoped) given him cause to concentrate his forces on defending Tsingtao rather than preventing the escape of a certain bargeload of refugees, I picked him up by his collar and the seat of his trousers and flung him through the front window. I believe, regarding his expression as I hoisted him up, that he went more thankfully than not.

I dusted my hands, turned, and discovered none other than Captain Kobayashi, or the kami Teruo, politely waiting for me. He was dressed in formal Japanese style, with a kimono and trousers and split-toed shoes, he had the wide sleeves of his jacket tied back with the kind of harness swordsmen use, and he had a sword in either hand, the Japanese long sword in the right, and the smaller short sword in the left. Both swords seemed impressively sharp, gleaming like the brilliantine in Teruo's hair.

In short, he was here for a fight. I must confess that I misliked the very sight of him, and drew my swords at once.

"Why's everyone here?" I demanded. "Did I come on poker night or something?"

"Perhaps we could step outside," Teruo said. "I could order the soldiers not to shoot."

I reflected that he could just as well order the soldiers to volley away the second they drew a bead. "I'd just as soon fight in here, if it's all the same," I said.

He walked straight up, a thoughtful look in his protuberant eyes, and commenced an attack without any more preliminaries, moving with an unpleasant sort of unearthly tranquility that I found decidedly unnerving. I parried his strike with Mo Yeh while slashing with Kan Chiang, and the most extraordinary thing happened—the swords began to snarl like a couple of cats. And not just mine, but his as well.

I must admit I found it more than a little shuddersome. A fellow doesn't want constant reminders, amid the clang and fury of battle, that the weapons he is wielding are living beings, with perhaps wills of their own, who might decide on a whim to stop being swords and become instead, say, a bouquet or two of daisies.

Not that I was particularly worried about flowery transformations in this instance, because it seemed my swords had a grudge and were only expressing it. Teruo's swords were howling as well—they had a lower, bass viol sort of cry—and it was clear enough they were stuffed as full of power as my own, and as determined as mine to triumph over their rivals.

The shock of discovery must have made me hesitate, because he lunged straight at me with his long sword, and I parried only at the last second. That lunge was a move from Western fencing, not Japanese at all, and it was looking as if I were going to have to keep my wits about me. I didn't know how many lifetimes this character had had to perfect his swordsmanship, and I was glad I didn't know because I had a feeling the knowledge would be certain to depress me.

So I retreated while trying to gain Teruo's measure, and the result was even more discouraging—he was damned good, and very tricky, and perfectly calm about the whole business, as if he had nothing to worry about—and since he was an immortal who couldn't be killed, he probably didn't, at least in the long run.

I rolled under the coffin to gain a little space to think, and we battled back and forth over Lieutenant Chump's form, and with four weapons flailing out at once—not to mention all the bullets that had been fired into the coffin earlier—his body began to suffer from all the attention. It seemed that his bad joss was pursuing him past his actual departure from the planet, which served only to confirm my suspicions about how the universe actually works.

It was rapidly becoming clear that Teruo was a better swordsman than I, and that I wasn't going to beat him in a straight-up fight. I was going to have to think of something extremely clever, and do it soon.

Unfortunately nothing came to mind, so, to give myself space, I disengaged, and maneuvered around the coffin. "Nice couple of swords you've got there," I said, and dropped my guard a bit, hoping he'd take the hint.

Teruo smiled pleasantly and kept his guard steady, which caused a lengthy round of curses to chase each other round the interior of my skull.

"Muramasa swords, quenched in the blood of a prince," he said. A smug look entered his pop eyes. "Some people think that Muramasa swords are cursed, but I have always found them perfectly congenial."

"How lucky for you," I said. "Of course, my swords have been around a lot longer than yours, so I expect they know quite a few more tricks."

"They have not displayed such knowledge so far," he observed.

"We've just been taking your measure," I said. "Take my word for it, from this point forward, you're up to your neck in the *bouillabaisse.*"

I was hoping that he'd stick on the word *bouillabaisse,* and take at least a few seconds to decipher it, but he didn't change expression, so I launched myself at him anyway, a full-bore assault just on the off chance. Apparently he was at least a little surprised, because he gave way, and I backed him up, but he counterattacked and locked my blades up with his own, and then we were *corps-à-corps,* like Jack Pickford glaring at Erich von Stroheim over crossed sabers, except that on this particular occasion the swords themselves were howling like banshees. The proper behavior at this point is to exchange witticisms, or at least give a devil-may-care laugh, and I am pleased to report that I was on form.

"Swords are all very well," I said, "but as it happens, I've got some additional magic that's going to make this fight a cinch."

"Oh really?" At least he was doing me the courtesy of taking a polite interest.

"The magic of twenty-three," I said.

"And what is that?" he asked.

"Twenty-three skiddoo," I said, and while he was chewing that over I kicked him in the crotch and ran for it.

I made it partway across the lawn before the first shots rang out, and then a few paces later I was able to use General Fujimoto's staff car for cover. The old fellow had had the sense to purchase a Daimler, which was practically bulletproof. I tossed the chauffeur out and got behind the wheel, then jammed the thing in gear and put my foot to the accelerator. I am pleased to report that the guards at the gate scattered at my approach, led in their retreat by General Fujimoto himself, who, it appears, I'd trained well.

Once in the road outside I had to make a couple turns to point myself in the direction I wanted—which was west and a long way from Japanese territory—and I was just shifting out of second gear when a motorcycle roared out of an alley and banged right into the fender, and something jumped from the saddle and plastered itself to the far side of the car. My swords, lying on the seat next to me, gave a howl of recognition. I saw a flash of blade and a glare of pop eyes and the old heart gave a jump straight into my throat. It was Teruo, and he was standing on the running board and trying to find a way into the car. Fortunately the windows were closed on that side, and the doors locked, and I made the task difficult for him by feeding gasoline to the supercharged in-line eight and throwing the wheel from side to side.

"Coward!" he yelled. "Honorless ape!"

"Sticks and stones, old chap," I reminded him.

There was an alarming rip as he drove one of his swords through the canvas top of the car, the better to provide an anchor. "You're going to pay for that treacherous blow, monster!" he shouted. He seemed to have taken that little kick of mine to heart, or somewhere else vital anyway.

Apparently the demonstrated vulnerability of the canvas top gave him an idea, and he commenced flailing away, chopping at the roof to get to me, but fortunately the Daimler's canvas was as stout as the rest of the car and his efforts were not crowned by conspicuous success. Persistence would have told eventually, but fortunately at this point I saw a telegraph pole coming up and took instant advantage—I swung the wheel and scraped the pole along the Daimler's flank, and there was another rip from the canvas over my head and Teruo was flung off. As the car lurched away I saw him in the road behind, rising to a crouch in a cloud of dust and showing every readiness to pursue, on foot if necessary, so I slammed the car into reverse and gunned the motor and came lunging back out of the dust cloud to pin Teruo's knees between the rear bumper and the telegraph pole, after which I switched gears again and roared away. Triumph sang an Act III finale in my veins as I saw him crumpled at the telegraph pole's base, shaking his fist—immortal he may have been, but he was going to have a hard time chasing me on a pair of broken legs.

Still, I took no chances. As soon as I got onto the highway I climbed a pole and cut the telegraph wires so as to prevent any alarms from reaching the outlying garrisons. With the Japanese flags flying on the general's staff car serving as my passport, I drove unmolested through every checkpoint until I left the Japanese Concessions, and then all the way to Nanking without stopping save for fuel. There I sold the car to a Hui merchant, and it was only then that I discovered Teruo's short sword still stuck in the car's canvas top.

It appeared that China had come out of this exchange one magic sword to the good. I don't know whether the sword contained a slice of anything so grand as the martial fortunes of the Japanese people, but still it was a handy little trophy of the adventure, and worthy of respect. Still, according to some people all Muramasa blades were cursed or otherwise afflicted with unwholesome vibrations, so I'd have to take special care with it. Perhaps I'd stow it safely in a temple somewhere.

I returned Kan Chiang and Mo Yeh to the bottom of their fountain, then bought a special case for Teruo's sword, some fresh clothing, and a ticket on a train back to Kowloon. It seemed that the strikes in Hong Kong had been settled in favor of the strikers, and now Hong Kong's example was being followed all up and down the coast, and the situation was returning, in Mr. Harding's winning phrase, to normalcy. The trains were running again, at least south from Nanking, so I took an entire first-class compartment for myself, slept most of the way, and when I crossed the harbor back to Hong Kong went straight to my apartment and found it inhabited by a dozen ghosts, all of whom seemed to have made free with the place while I was away. I glared at them, and they decided they were clearly facing a two-fisted hombre who would stick at nothing to clean up this one-horse town, and they all wisely faded.

After a long, hot bath and a nap, I donned my evening duds and biffed off to Broadway Johnny's, where I discovered a couple of plug-uglies from the Triads making an extortion demand on Old Nails. The Triads and I had made an agreement re protection money some time ago, and I was disturbed to see the agreement apparently being subjected to some kind of unilateral amendment. So disturbed, in fact, that I was compelled to inflict severe physical injury on the two gangsters, and then to drag them to their clubhouse, where I spoke with some heat to their bosses and all their bodyguards and anyone else loitering about the place, all of which helped to relieve my growing sense of ennui and no doubt vastly increased the profits of the local Chinese hospital. Straightening my lapels, I returned to the club, signaled Old Nails for a grasshopper, and asked Betsy Wong to sing me the blues.

Feel free to correct me in this surmise, but I concluded I had earned a moment or two of pensive self-indulgence.

The letter from Yu-lan arrived next day. The company had succeeded in escaping Tsingtao and were now cruising up the Yellow River. When they found a venue they were going to go back into repertory, Chinese classics at night and, as soon as safety permitted, *Call Me Comrade* in the afternoons. My money, Yu-lan informed me, was being devoted to worthy causes along the way.

Well, I seemed to have got Marxism off to a roaring start in China, for whatever that was worth.

Yu-lan didn't know when she would be in South China—as soon as the revolution occurred or business permitted, whatever came first. But she had little doubt that she would see me soon. Much less doubt than I, as it happened.

I went to the piano and let the digits take a few passes through "I'm Going Away to Wear You Off My Mind"—not, of course, that I did any such thing. And then I went in search of Han Shan.

He had put up at a temple in Hong Kong—he *was* a monk, after all—but I discovered he was no longer in residence, and he'd left a message urging me to contact him at 151 Rua Felicidade, all the way down the coast in Macao. I wondered if the local priests had responded to his unique brand of charm by chucking him out on his ear, but the chap I talked to wasn't very informative, so I toddled off and hired a cab to get me to the ferry terminal. Macao was a rather lengthy boat ride away, and I wanted to be back by evening.

As I sat on the ferry and watched the coastal islands sail by, it seemed as if the gold amulet around my neck was heavier than usual. It occurred to me being the possessor of the martial fortunes of China might have its rewards.

Counting the Muramasa blade, I had in my possession no less than three tokens of power. There were others around, and presumably I could make an effort to collect them. Broadway Johnny Chan could, if he set his mind to it, become something of a center of power himself.

It wasn't as if my country didn't need it. The Canton government controlled only one city, the rest of the country was divided between warlords, foreign powers had taken advantage of our weakness, Japan was annexing us piece by piece, and, as if that weren't bad enough, it looked as if they were also going to attempt the restoration of the Manchus, who more than anyone had created the mess in the first place.

Perhaps, it occurred to me, it wasn't too late to set things right again. A fellow with luck and enterprise, who'd seen a bit of the world and who wasn't afraid of innovation and improvisation, could go pretty far these days. And, if he gained sufficient power, he could begin setting things right. Clearing out the warlords and the corruption, adjusting the treaties with the foreigners, bringing in progress that would benefit the population.

The fly in the ointment was that I wasn't sure whether I could see myself in this role. It's one thing to have a cocktail or two and tell your buddies, "Hey, given the chance I could run this country better than any of those coves that are doing it now," but how many people would actually leap at the chance were it offered them? I had got used to thinking of myself as a *boulevardier,* with ambitions no higher than a string of nightclubs and a flutter at producing a show now and again, and now I was contemplating becoming the Chinese answer to Napoleon.

We Chinese had our own Napoleon, of course. Shih Huang Ti, the first emperor, the chap who built the Wall and standardized the currency and the weights and the roads and the writing, the chap who dug the canals and burned the books. And do you know what? For all the good he did, his memory is loathed by every schoolchild in the country, because he was also the first in a long series of tyrants.

So it was with a heavy tread that Johnny Chan left the ferry terminal and began my search for Han Shan. I couldn't decide what Fate was demanding of me.

Rua Felicidade, I knew, was in a rum sort of neighborhood, but I reckoned there had to be a temple or monastery there somewhere, a last bastion of virtue in a district devoted to vice. To my surprise 151 turned out to be a fairly plush sort of gambling den of the kind in which Macao excels. I asked for Han Shan and was shown to the manager's office, where I was offered a cigar and a brandy. I puffed away for a while, trying to picture the prune-faced monk amid all of this, and then the padded door opened and in walked Han Shan himself, smoking a custom-rolled cigaret in a jade holder and dressed in splendid Western clothes, complete with a braided waistcoat of gleaming extravagance. Gone was the silk gown, the skullcap, the five-inch nails. In the old monk's place was a prosperous businessman with a wafer-thin wristwatch and a diamond stickpin.

"Johnny!" he said with a grin. "I had about given you up! I was afraid I was going to have to hire someone else."

"Your appearance surprises me, Monk Han," I said.

"Have a seat and I will procure some luncheon," he said.

He ordered, refreshed my brandy, and then put his feet up on the manager's desk and flexed his handmade oxfords.

"You seem to be doing rather well for yourself," I said. ""Did you hit a lucky streak at the tables?" In which case, I knew, he'd be wagering the martial fortunes of China the second I handed them over to him.

"Better than that," he said. "As it happens, the tables outside are my property." He blew smoke at the ceiling. "The world seems to have really moved along since I went off to meditate in my little hermitage. Back in my day we couldn't think of anything better to do with wealth than hoard it in temples or bury it in treasure troves. But now, with this spiffy capitalism philosophy we've imported from the West, I can actually make my money work for me. After you left, I dug up a couple more treasure troves and invested in this little club. Now I can gamble any time I like, and the house rules favor me. Any profits get invested in the stock market. It's almost risk-free." He gave me a wink. "Extraordinary how things change, you know. Once upon a time, that amulet of mine would have been considered an everyday sort of thing, and a telephone would have been thought magic. Now it's the other way around. The world is spinning pretty fast, eh?"

"So I hear," I said.

"Now, I believe you were going to give me something?"

Well, the moment of truth had certainly come. I could either give the amulet to this reborn capitalist and merchant of vice, or keep it, become Napoleon, rescue my country, deal out justice left and right, and endure a legacy of hatred from every succeeding generation.

"Perhaps you would like to try your luck at the tables?" the monk suggested. "I can pay you in gambling chips."

"Silver," I said. "Great stacks of it. Now."

He winked again. "Can't blame a fellow for trying."

He emptied his safe of money, and in a tick I forked over his property.

Outside, as I headed for the ferry terminal, I began to whistle.

I believe, though I could not swear to it, that the tune was "Alligator Hop."

Roger Zelazny observed in the introduction to one of his collections that after a writer becomes established in the field, much of his published short fiction is written to commission rather than written on spec. Rather than writing a story and then deciding where to send it, the author writes a story as a result of solicitation from a specific editor, or from a friend editing an anthology. Writers get these sorts of queries all the time. The phone will ring, and a familiar voice will say, "I'm editing an anthology of two-headed ogre stories. Do you have any ogre stories in the works?"

I tend not to respond positively to these sorts of queries. Not because I have any objection to two-headed ogre stories, or anthologies about the same, but because my writing time is limited, and I generally don't write a story to order unless it's a story I've already been thinking about, or unless I suddenly realize that, by God, I've really always *wanted* to write a two-headed ogre story, and this would be the perfect opportunity.

When Roger Zelazny himself called to ask me to contribute to *Warriors of Blood and Dream,* an anthology of fantastic martial arts stories, I realized that this was the chance to write that martial arts story I'd always been dying to write.

The problem was, I didn't quite know what the story would be.

I have an instinct, when thinking about my projects, of trying to work out what other writers are going to do, and then do something else. I reasoned that most of the stories would be deeply serious, if not grim, and deal in no small regard with the technical details of martial arts.

I decided therefore to write a deeply unserious story, and to spare the reader most of the complexities of the martial arts themselves. This I was fortunately in a position to do, since I am myself a martial artist, and have a third-degree black belt in Kenpo, a Chinese martial art exported to North America by way of Okinawa, and thus having at least as complex a parentage as Johnny Chan himself. While I can discourse on the technicalities of martial arts with the best of them, and though I pretty much know what Broadway Johnny and his cohorts are doing in each instance, I glossed over them for the purpose of the story, and just wrote for effect. While martial artists may criticize me for this decision, I trust that the rest of you are relieved.

I have subsequently realized that there are a couple more stories I'd like to write about Broadway Johnny Chan, though these will have to wait for opportunity, and openings in the schedule.

Woundhealer

The horn echoed down the long valley, three bright rising notes, and it seemed to Derina—frozen like an animal in the bustle of the court—as if the universe halted for a long moment of dread. A cold hard fist clenched in her stomach.

Her father was home.

She went up the stone stair by the old gatehouse and watched as her father and his little army, back from the Princes' Wars, wound up the mountain spur toward her. The cold canyon wind howled along the old flint walls, tangled Derina's red-gold hair in its fingers. The knuckles on her small fists were white as she searched the distant column for sign of her father and brothers.

Derina's mother and sister joined her above the gatehouse. Edlyn carried her child, the two of them wrapped in a coarse wool shawl against the wind.

"Pray they have all come home safe," said Derina's mother, Kendra.

Derina, considering this, thought she didn't know what to pray for, if anything, but Edlyn looked scorn at her mother, eyes hard in her expressionless face.

When Lord Landry rode beneath the gate he looked up at them, cold blue eyes gazing up out of the weatherbeaten moon face with its bristle of red hair and wide, fierce nostrils. As her father's eyes met hers, the knot in Derina's stomach tightened. Her gaze shifted uneasily to her brothers, Norward the eldest, gangly, myopic eyes blinking weakly, riding uneasily in the saddle as if he would rather be anywhere else; and Reeve, a miniature version of his father, red-haired and round-shouldered, looking up at the women above the gate as if sizing up the enemy.

Derina's mother and sister bustled down the lichen-scarred stair to make the welcome official. Derina stayed, watching the column of soldiers as it trudged up to the old flint-walled house, watched until she saw her father's woman, Nellda, riding with the other women in the wagons. Little dark-haired Nelly was sporting a black eye.

Mean amusement twisted Derina's mouth into a smile. She ran down the stair to join her family.

Nelly was halfway down the long banquet table and her eyes never left her plate. Before the campaign started she'd sat at Landry's arm, above his family.

Good, Derina thought. Let her go back to the mean little mountain cottage where Lord Landry had found her.

The loot had been shared out earlier, the common soldiers paid off. Now Landry hosted a dinner for his lieutenants, the veterans of his many descents onto the plains below, and the serjeants of his own household.

The choicest bit of booty was Lord Landry's new sword, won in the battle, a long magnificent patterned blade, straight and beautiful. Norward had found the thing, apparently, but his father had taken it for his own.

"In the hospital!" Landry called. His voice boomed out above the din in the long hall. "He found the sword in the hospital, when we were cutting our way through their camp! It must have belonged to one of their sick—well," bellowing a laugh, "we helped their shirkers and malingerers on to judgment, so we did!"

Derina gazed at her untouched meal and let her father's loud triumph roll past unheeded. This war sounded like all the others, a loud recitation of cunning and twisting diplomacy and the slaughter of helpless men. Landry did not find glory in battle, but rather in plunder: he would show up late to the battlefield, after giving both sides assurances of his allegiance, and then be the first to sack the camp of the loser. Sometimes he would loot the camp without waiting for the battle to be decided.

"What does Norward need with a blade such as this?" he demanded. "His third campaign, and as yet unblooded."

"M-my beast fell," Norward stammered. He turned red and fought his disobedient tongue. "T-tripped among the, the tent lines."

"Ta-ta-tripped in the ta-ta-tents!" Landry mocked. "Your riding's as defective as your speech. As your blasted weak eyes. Can't kill a man?—I'll leave my land to a son who can." He gave a savage grin. "*I* was a younger son—but did it stop me?"

Reeve smirked into his cup. Lord Landry had been loud in the praise of his younger son's willingness to run down and slay the helpless boys and old men who'd guarded the enemy camp.

Reeve was strong, Derina thought, and Norward weak. What had her own feelings to do with it?

Landry put the sword in its sheath, then hung it behind his chair, above the great fireplace, in place of his old blade. He turned and looked over his shoulder at his family. "None of you touch it, now!"

As if anyone would dare.

The banquet was over, Lord Landry's soldiers dozing in their chairs or stumbling off into dark corners to sleep on pallets. Only the lord's family remained—they and Nellda—all frozen in their chairs by his glacier-blue eyes, eyes that darted suspiciously from one to the next—weighing, judging, finding everyone wanting.

Derina looked only at her plate.

Landry took a long drink of plundered brandy. He had been drinking all night but the effects were slight: a shining of the forehead, a slow deliberation of speech. "Where is the son I need?" he said.

Reeve looked up in surprise from his own cup—he had thought he was the favored one tonight. He swallowed, tried to think how to respond, decided to speak, and said the wrong thing.

Anything, Derina knew, would have been the wrong thing.

"I'll be the son you want, Father."

Landry swung toward his younger son, every bristle on his head erect. Slowly his tongue formed words to the song,

> *"See the little simpleton.*
> *He doesn't give a damn.*
> *I wish I were a simpleton—*
> *By God, perhaps I am!"*

Reeve's face flushed; his lower lip stuck out like a child's. Landry went on: "Perhaps I *am* such a fool, begetting a child like you. *You?* D'you think killing a few camp followers makes you a man? D'you think you have the craft and cunning to hold on to anything I give you? Nay—you'll piss it away in a week, on drink and gambling and girls from the Red Temple."

Reeve turned away, face blood-red. Landry's eyes roved the table, settled on his older son. "And you—what have you to say?"

Nothing, Derina knew. But the old man had him trapped, obliged him to speak.

"What d-d'you wish me to say?" Norward said.

Landry laughed. "Such an obedient boy! Bad eyes, bad tongue, no backbone. Other than that—" He laughed again. "The perfect heir!"

"Perhaps—" Kendra said, and made as if to rise.

Landry looked sidelong at his wife and feigned surprise. "Oh—are you still alive?" Laughing at his joke. "Damned if I can see why. I'd kill myself if I were as useless as you."

"Perhaps it's time to go to bed," Kendra said primly.

"With you?" Landry's eyes opened wide. "God save us. God save us from getting another son such as those you gave me."

"It isn't my fault," Kendra said.

She had been pregnant with a dozen children, Derina knew, miscarried five, and of the rest all but four had died young.

"Whose fault is it, then?" Landry demanded. The red bristle on his head stood erect. "Blame my seed, do you?" He beat his looted silver flagon on the table. "I am strong," he insisted, "as were my sires! If my children are milksops, it's because my blood is commingled with yours! You had your chance—" He gestured down the table, to where Nellda, unnoticed, had begun quietly weeping. "And so did yon Nelly! She could have given me a son, but she miscarried—damnation to her!" He shouted, half-rising from his seat, the powerful muscles in his neck standing out like cable. "Damnation to all women! They're all betrayers."

Edlyn's little girl, startled out of her slumbers by Landry's shout, began to wail in Edlyn's lap. Landry sneered at the two.

"Betrayers," he said. "At least your worthless husband won't be siring any more girls, to eat out my substance and shame me with their sniveling." Edlyn, cradling her child, said nothing. Her face, as always, was a mask.

Landry lurched out of his chair, tripped over a sleeping dog, then staggered down the table toward Derina. Her heart cried out at his approach. "You haven't betrayed me yet," he mumbled. "You'll give me boys, will you not?" His powerful hands clutched at her breasts and groin. She closed her eyes at the painful violation, her head swimming with the odor of brandy fumes. "Ay," he confirmed, "you're grown enough—and you bleed regular, ay? We'll find you a husband this winter. One who won't betray me."

He swung away from her, back toward his brandy cup. Derina could feel her face burning. Landry seized the cup, drained it, looked defiantly down the table at his family—frozen like deer in the light of a bull's-eye lantern—looked at Nelly weeping, at his soldiers who, no doubt roused by his shouting, were dutifully feigning slumber.

"The night is young," he muttered. "Are all feeble save myself?" Edlyn's child shrieked. Landry sneered, poured himself more brandy, and lurched away, toward the stair and his private chambers.

Kendra turned to Reeve. "I wish you hadn't provoked him," she said. Reeve turned away mumbling, pushed back his chair, and stumbled for the door to the courtyard.

"What was that you said?" Kendra called. Her voice was shrill.

Reeve, still muttering, boomed out into the fresh air. Derina hadn't heard but knew well enough what her brother said. "No one provoked Father," she said. "It doesn't matter what we do. Not when he's in these moods."

"We should try to make his time here easy," Kendra insisted. "If we're all good to him—"

Derina could still feel the imprint of her father's fingers on her breasts. She rose from the table.

"I'm going to bed," she said.

Her sister Edlyn rose as well. Her little girl's screams were beginning to fade. "Daryl should sleep," she said.

Edlyn and Derina made their way up the stairs to their quarters. They could smell Landry's brandy fumes and followed cautiously, but he was well gone, off to drink in his suite at the top of the stair.

Edlyn paused before Derina's door. Edlyn looked at her, eyes flat and emotionless. "Your turn now," she said. "To be his favorite."

Your turn, Derina knew, to be married off unknowing to some coarse stranger—to learn, perhaps, to love him, as Edlyn had—then to have his child, to have him die in one of Landry's wars and be left, scorned, at her father's house with an unwanted babe in her arms.

Derina, a lump in her throat, could only shrug.

"*Good,*" Edlyn said, malice in her eyes. She turned and went to her own door.

You bleed regular, ay?

Numbly, Derina fumbled for the latch, entered her room, and locked the door behind.

The courting had already begun, and Landry home only three days. Any number of Landry's peers, soldiers, and retainers were happening by, all with oafish, sullen sons in tow.

Few of them bothered to acknowledge Derina. They knew who made the decisions.

Derina fled the sight of them, went for a long ride to the high uplands, the meadows where the summer pasture was, the close-cropped grass already turned autumn-brown.

She did not expect to find her brother there. But there he was, gangling body in saddle as he rode along the low dry-stone walls that separated one pasture from another. Nearsighted, Norward didn't see her until she hailed him.

"Inspecting the walls," he said.

"No point in doing that till spring."

"I wanted t-to get away."

"So did I."

He shrugged, pulled his cap down against the autumn highland wind. "Then r-ride the walls with me."

They rode along in cold silence. Derina looked at the splashes of lichen coloring the stone walls and wondered if Norward, with his poor vision, could see them at all.

"I'm caught," Norward said finally. He pulled his beast to a halt. "Reeve pushing from below, and F-father pushing from above. What can I d-do?"

She had no answer for him. Norward was weak, and that was that. It wasn't his fault, and it was sad that Landry despised him, but any sympathy on Derina's part was wasted effort.

Her father had taught her that only power mattered. Norward had none, and Derina could lend him none of her own. And so she left his question unanswered, just rode on, and Norward could do nothing but follow.

His lips twisted, a knowing, self-hating smile. "Have you looked c-closely at f—at our parent's new sword?" he asked.

"I'm not engrossed by swords," Derina said.

"Ah. Well. This one is interesting. I f-found it, you know—and got a look at it before Father took it away."

"What's so interesting about it?" Derina demanded.

That smile came again. "Perhaps nothing."

Derina rode on, Norward lagging behind, and wished she were alone.

The next morning Derina looked at the sword hanging above the mantel in the great hall, and wondered what it was that had attracted Norward's interest. The hilt was fine work, that was clear enough, possessing a handsome scalloped black pommel with the badge of a white hand on it. But there was little special about it, no exquisite workmanship, no gilt or jewels.

She did not dare defy her father by touching the sword, drawing it to look at the blade.

"Please, miss."

The voice startled her, and she jumped. Derina turned and saw Nellda, and a bolt of hatred lodged in her heart.

"Please, miss." Nellda pushed a packet into Derina's hands. "Give this to your father."

Derina looked at the packet, badly wrapped and tied with a bit of green ribbon. "Why should I?" she said.

There were tears in Nelly's eyes. "He won't see me! You can get to him, can't you?"

Derina fingered the ribbon. "What is it? Love tokens?"

"And a letter. I can write, you know! I'm not just a foolish girl."

"So you say." Coldly. Derina thought a moment, then shook her head. "Go home, Nellda. Go back to whatever little sty it was he found you in."

"I can't! He turned my father out! We had a bad year and—" Her voice broke. "He said he'd take care of me!"

For a moment a little spark of sympathy rose in Derina's heart, but with an act of will she stamped it out. Power was all that mattered, and Derina's, such as it was, was only to hurt. "Go away," she said, and held out the packet.

Nellda, weeping, fled without taking it.

Derina turned and—she hesitated, and for some reason she glanced up at the great sword—she threw the packet into the fire.

Burning up, it scarcely made a flame.

So there was her future husband, pimples and round shoulders and hoggish eyes. His name was Burley, and his father was a gentleman of no great land or distinction who lived farther up the valley, a man of thin beard and cringing deference.

"His arm will be of use to you, sir," said the father, Edson, whose own arm was of little use at all.

"It's not his arm that's in question," Landry muttered. Derina caught Reeve's smirk out of the corner of her eye and wanted to claw it off his face.

Derina looked at her family. Kendra looked as if she were trying to make the best of it. Norward was gazing at his feet and frowning. Edlyn was quietly triumphant, eyes glittering with malice.

I won't make your mistake, Derina thought fiercely; but she knew that Edlyn's mistakes hadn't been Edlyn's to make—and her own mistakes wouldn't be hers, either.

"We'll send to the temple for a priest to draw up the contract proper," Landry said. He looked at Derina, grinned at her.

"Kiss your future husband, girl."

All eyes were on Derina and she hated it. She stepped forward obediently, rose on tiptoe—Burley was taller than his posture made him—and kissed his cheek.

His breath smelt of mutton. His cheek was red with embarrassment. He didn't seem to be enjoying this any more than she was—which was, she supposed, a point in his favor.

She would never dare to love him, she knew. Most likely he wouldn't live long.

The wedding took place a few weeks later, in order to give all the poor relations a chance to swarm in from the countryside to get their free meal. The ceremony was at noon, the priest already drunk and thick-tongued, and the rest of the company was drunk soon after.

Nellda was seen, at the foot of the long table, wolfing down food and drink. One of the servants, sensitive with long practice to Lord Landry's moods, pushed her away, and she was seen no more.

Derina looked down at her dowry, a small chest of coins and a modicum of old loot, silver cups and candlesticks polished brightly to make them seem more valuable than they were—the guard, standing by with his pike, seemed almost unnecessary. Described in the marriage agreement, signed and sealed with red ribbon, was another part of the dowry: a lease on some high pastureland.

"Nice to know what you're worth, eh?" Reeve said.

"More than you," Derina said.

Reeve sneered. "You don't think father favors me? You don't think I'll have all this in the end?" He gestured largely, swayed a bit, and leaned harder on the milkmaid under his arm.

He followed his father in this as in all things.

"If you live, perhaps," said Norward's mild voice. He had ghosted up without Reeve's noticing.

Reeve swung round. His compact, powerful body seemed to puff like a bullfrog's before his brother's gangling form. "And who'll kill me?" he demanded. "A blind man like you?"

Mildly Norward placed a hand on Reeve's chest. "Yourself," he said, "most like," and gave Reeve a gentle push. Reeve went down hard, the milkmaid on top of him in a flurry of skirts. The dowry's guard, stepping back with a grin, put out a hand to still a rocking candlestick. Reeve, sprawled on the flags, pushed the girl away and clapped a hand to his belt for a knife that wasn't there; and then he glanced for a moment at Landry's sword, hanging just a few feet away—but Norward just stood over him, looking down, and after a long, burning moment Reeve got to his feet and stalked away, the milkmaid fluttering after.

Some people laughed. Norward himself seemed faintly puzzled. He looked at his hand and flexed it.

"I must not know my own strength," he said.

"He was drunk, and off balance."

"That must be it," Norward agreed. He looked at the dowry on its table, then at Derina. "I like your Burley," he said.

"He's not my Burley," Derina said, "he's Father's Burley."

Norward nodded, looked at his hand again. "Have you noticed?" he said. "My stammer's getting better."

The wedding bed, surrounded by curtains and screens, was set before the fire in the great hall and wrapped with symbols of fertility—ivy and pinecones and orange and yellow squash, the best that could be done in autumn.

The newlyweds would have the big bed in the main hall for a week, then move to Derina's room. They wouldn't be leaving Landry's halls till Yule, when their new rooms at Edson's house would be ready.

Derina endured the public "consummation," sitting upright in bed with Burley while the guests cheered, filled their cups with wine, and made ribald jokes. Landry loomed over her, patted her, placed a wet kiss on her cheek. "You're my treasure," he said. "My truest daughter."

Something—wretched love, perhaps—churned in Derina's heart.

Edlyn watched with cold, hidden eyes—less than two years ago, she'd been put through the same business, received the same caresses and praise.

Next came the closing of the curtains and Landry's loud orders ending the festivities. Lights were doused. The dowry was packed and carried to Landry's strongroom—"just for the night," he said.

In the corners of the big room, drunken relations snored and mumbled.

Derina looked at Burley, profiled in the firelight. His wedding garments—black velvet jacket slashed with yellow, jaunty bonnet with feather—had shown him to advantage, far more presentable than in his country clothes the day they'd met. Now, in his shirt, he looked from Derina to his wine cup and back.

Derina felt the warmth of the big fire warming her shoulders. She tilted her head back and drank her wine, hoping it would bring oblivion. She put the cup away and lay on the bed and closed her eyes.

She hoped he would get it over with quickly.

She tasted wine on his breath as he kissed her. Derina lay still, not moving. His hands moved over her body. There was nowhere for them to go where her father hadn't already been.

Burley's hands stopped moving. There was a loud crack from the fireplace as a log threw up sparks.

"We don't have to do this," he said, "if you're not in the humor."

Faint surprise opened her eyes.

Burley rolled himself onto his stomach, propped himself on his elbows. Firelight reflected in his dark eyes. "Perhaps you had no mind to be married," he said.

She shrugged. Wine swam in her head. "I knew it would happen."

"But not to me."

Another shrug. "As well as another."

Burley gnawed a knuckle and stared at the fire. Derina propped herself up on her elbow and regarded him. Wine and relief made her giddy.

"I think my father was afraid to say no to this," Burley said. "I think it was Lord Landry's idea, not his."

Derina was not surprised. People in the dales treaded warily where Landry was concerned.

"My father says that the connection will be of advantage," Burley said. "And we need the grazing on the upland pastures."

"I hope you'll get it."

Burley gave her a sharp look. "What d'you mean?"

The wine made her laugh. "Edlyn's dowry gave the mowing on forty hectares of river pasture, but there wasn't much hay made there, for my father's beeves grazed the land all summer."

Burley nodded slowly. "I see."

"And Edlyn's dowry never left my father's strongboxes." The wine made her laugh again. "It was an autumn wedding, like ours, and father always had an excuse. Bad autumn weather, then winter snows, then muddy spring roads. And by summer, Barton was dead, and his father with him, and the beeves already in the pasture."

"And the little girl—"

"Daryl."

"Daryl. She's the heir to her father's estate, and Barton the eldest son."

"And my father has use of the estate through her minority, which will last forever. And that is why Edlyn will never be allowed to marry again, for fear that Daryl would have another protector."

And that is why Edlyn hates me. Derina left the concluding thought unspoken.

Burley frowned for a long moment, then spoke with hesitation. "How did Barton and his father die?"

Derina's head spun. Probably the wine.

"In battle," she said.

"And who killed them?"

For a moment Derina was aware of her father's looted sword, bright and powerful, hanging over the fireplace.

"I don't know," she said.

Burley didn't reply. Derina watched him frowning into the fire, eyes alight with thought, until wine and main weariness dragged her into sleep.

When she woke in the morning, her father-in-law had gone, and all his folk with him.

The conventions forced Edlyn to be sisterly, which included helping Derina make the bed. "No blood on the sheets," she observed. Her flat face regarded Derina. "Was he incapable? Or you no virgin?"

Derina felt color rise to her face. For all they never talked of it, Edlyn knew perfectly well who'd had Derina's virginity, two years before when Edlyn married and moved out of the room they shared.

At least it hadn't lasted long. Landry had found a girl he'd liked better—another of his fleeting favorites.

"Whatever version you like best," Derina said. "When you talk to the old gossips in the kitchen hall, you'll say whatever you like anyway."

Edlyn's expressionless face turned back to her work. Derina fluffed a pillow. "Perhaps," said Derina, "he was merely gentle."

Edlyn's tone was scornful. "So much the worse for him."

There was a lump in Derina's throat. She put the pillow down. "Can we not be friends?" she asked.

Edlyn only gazed at her suspiciously.

"It's not my fault," Derina said. "I didn't ask to marry any more than you. It's not my fault that Barton died."

"But you profit by it."

"Where's my profit?" Derina demanded.

Edlyn didn't answer.

"Father's favor changes with the wind," Derina said. "He does it to divide us."

"And what good would combining do?" Scornfully. "D'you think we could beat him?"

"Probably not. But it would ease our hearts."

Stony, Edlyn looked at her.

Lord Landry's voice rose in the court. *"Gone?"* The doors boomed inward, and Landry stalked in, rage darkening his face. He swung accusingly to Derina. "D'you know what that brother of yours has done?"

"I l-looked for you." Norward's voice. He came tumbling down the stair, having heard his father's bellow from his quarters. "Y-you weren't there."

"You gave away the dowry, damn you!" Landry rampaged up to his son, seemed to tower over him even though Norward was taller. "Edson's gone, with all his folk!"

"It—" Norward struggled for words through the stammer that had suddenly returned, bad as ever. "It was his. Edson's. He asked for it."

"You should have delayed! Sent for me!"

"I—I did. But Edson's relatives were all there—I couldn't refuse 'em all. But you weren't in your room, and hadn't slept there."

"Who are you to tell me where to sleep?" Landry roared.

"I didn't."

"Liar! Liar and thief!" Landry seized his son by the neck, began wrenching him back and forth at the end of his powerful arms. Norward turned red and clutched hopelessly at his father's thick wrists. Derina desperately searched her mind for something she could do.

"Is it a matter of the dowry, then?"

Burley's voice cut over the sound of Landry's shouts. He had followed Norward down the stair, was watching narrowly as father and son staggered back and forth.

Landry froze, breath coming hard through wide nostrils. Then he released his son and forced a smile. "Not at all, lad," he said. "But Norward let your father leave without telling me of his going. I would have said my farewells." He glared at Norward, who clutched his throat and gasped for air. "Reeve would not have so forgotten."

"My father bade me thank your lordship for all your kindness," Burley said. "But he and our folk wanted to get an early start lest a storm break."

A storm, Derina thought. Apt enough analogy.

"I would have said goodbye," Landry mumbled, and turned to slouch away.

Derina, seeing Norward and Burley exchange cautious looks, knew then that this had been carefully arranged. For a moment anxiety churned in her belly, fear that Landry would discover she had talked too freely to Burley the night before.

There was a touch on Derina's shoulder, and she jumped. Edlyn clasped her arm, squeezed once, looked in her face, and then silently returned to her work.

Truce, Derina read in her look. If not quite peace, at least an end to war.

A real storm, snow and wind, coiled about the house the next two days, glazing windows with sleet, shrieking around the walls' flinty corners, banking up shoals of sooty white in the courtyard. Landry's relations and dependents, unable to leave for their own homes, ate up his provender and patience at an equal rate. The huge fire in the great hall blazed night and day and almost cooked Derina and Burley in their bed.

The storm died down the third night after the wedding. Burley and Derina, next morning, hadn't yet risen when Norward brought in Nellda, who'd fallen in the storm the night before while trying to leave the house.

Nelly's flesh was turquoise blue and cold, and her breath was faint. There was snow and ice in her tangled hair. Norward put her in Derina's wedding bed, and called for a warming pan.

"I was at the north corner," Norward said, "checking the roof for storm damage. And there she was, past the Stone Eagle, halfway to the valley and lying in a drift."

"Who saw her?" Derina asked.

"I did."

Derina looked at him in surprise. "But your eyes—how could you see her?"

Norward shrugged. "My eyes seem to be better."

With warmth and warm broth brought by a servant, Nellda was brought around. Her eyes traveled from one member of the family to another.

"Where is he?" she asked faintly.

"He isn't here," Norward said.

Nellda's eyes trembled, then closed. "He's with Medora," she said. "You should have left me in the snow."

Burley frowned and took Derina aside. "Who is this person?" he asked. "Does she have a place here?"

"She's my father's whore," Derina said. "And apparently now my father has a new whore, this Medora."

"And who's *she?*"

"I don't know. Probably some crofter girl. That's the sort he likes."

Burley narrowed his eyes in thought. "Can't we find her a place here? We can't let her die in the snow."

Derina's spine turned rigid. "In our house?" She shook her head. "My mother lives here. I won't insult her by having Nelly around. Not when Father doesn't want her anymore."

Burley sighed. "I will try to think of something."

Derina caught at his sleeve as he turned. "It's not your task. This isn't your family."

His odd little smile stopped her. "But it *is* my family now," he said.

Burley returned to the bed, leaving Derina standing stiff with surprise.

He had his work cut out, she thought, if he thought himself a part of *this* family.

And, she reminded herself, he probably wouldn't survive it.

Nelly was hidden away in the servants' loft, and Norward ordered one of the older maidservants to nurse her. When her strength returned she'd have a job in the stables, where Kendra wouldn't encounter her.

Landry gave Reeve a ruby ring and a pair of silver spurs—"for his loyalty." Reeve preened as he strutted about wearing them, the spurs clanking on the flags or catching on the carpet. At dinner Landry sent his wife down the table, and sat with Reeve on one side and the girl Medora on the other. Landry had given her a gold chain belt. She was a frail little blonde thing, giggly when drunk. Derina didn't think she'd last. She didn't have brains enough to follow Landry's moods.

Kendra chatted away at dinner and pretended nothing was wrong, but next day, while Derina was helping her mother at carding wool, Kendra began to weep. Derina searched through her mother's basket for a strand of wool, pretending that she didn't see the fat tears rolling down Kendra's cheeks.

Sometimes, when Kendra was weak, Derina hated her.

"If only I'd given him the sons he wanted," Kendra moaned. "Then everything would be all right."

"You gave him sons," Derina said.

"Not the sons he wished for," Kendra said. "I should have given him more."

"It wouldn't have made any difference," Derina said. "He'd have despised them, too. Unless they were stronger, and then he would have hated and feared them."

Kendra's eyes opened wide in anger. "How dare you say that about your father!"

Derina shrugged. Kendra's mouth closed in a firm line. "Is it Burley putting these notions in your head?"

Derina wanted to laugh. "I've lived here all my life," she said. "Do you expect me not to know how things are?"

"I expect you to show your father respect, and not to go tattling to Burley or his kin."

Derina threw down the wool. "They have eyes, Mother. They can see as well as anyone."

"Be careful." A touch of fear entered Kendra's face as Derina stood and moved toward the door. "Don't tell!"

Don't tell what? Derina wondered.

Everything. That's what Kendra meant.

"I'll say what I like," Derina said, and left the room.

But doubted if she'd ever say a word.

Derina and Burley had slept in the huge marriage bed for almost a week. After tonight the bed would be taken down, and Derina and Burley moved into her small room in the family quarters. The huge canopied feather bed was much too large for the room, and Derina and Burley would share Derina's old narrow bed, their breath frosting in the cold that the smoky fire never seemed to relieve.

Before sleep he turned to her. The dying firelight glinted in his pupils. "Derina," he said, "I hope you like marriage a little better than when we met."

"I never disliked it."

"But you didn't know me. Perhaps you know me a little better now."

"I hope so." Marriage, she considered, seemed to suit Burley at any rate. He stood straighter now, and seemed better-formed; his skin had cleared, his breath carried the scent of spiced wine. His warmth in the narrow bed would be welcome.

Burley fumbled under the covers, took her hand. "What I meant to say," he began, "is that I hope you like me a little. Because it will be powerful hard to lie here next to you in that narrow bed, night after night, and not want to touch you."

Derina's heart lurched, and she felt the blood rush to her face. "I never said you couldn't touch me," she said.

He hesitated for a moment, then began to kiss her. Pleasantly enough, she decided. After a while of this she felt some action on her part was necessary, and she put her arms around him.

What followed was not bad, she thought later, for all they both needed practice.

A few nights later Derina forgot the leather jack of wine she'd put by the fire to warm, and so she left Burley in their bed, put on a heavy wool cloak, and went down the main stair to fetch it. She heard angry voices booming up, and moved cautiously from stair to stair.

"Who has the spurs?" Reeve's voice. "Who has Father's eye?"

Norward's answer was cutting. "Medora, it would seem."

"Ha! She won't have the land and house when he dies! And neither will you, you useless gawk."

Derina slid silently down the stairs on bare feet, saw Norward moving close to Reeve in front of the fire. Norward seemed so much more impressive than he'd been, his once-lanky form filled with power. Reeve looked uneasy, took a step back.

"Are you planning on Father dying soon?" Norward asked. "I wouldn't wager that way, were I you."

"If he lives to a hundred, he won't favor you!" Reeve shouted. "Never in life, blind man!"

"My eyes have improved," Norward said. "A pity yours have not."

"Fool! Go to the priesthood, and spend your days in prayer!" Reeve swung a fist, hitting Norward a surprise blow under the eye, and then Norward thrust out a longer arm and struck Reeve on the breast, just as he had at Derina's wedding, and Reeve lurched backward. One silver spur caught on a crack in the flags and he tumbled down. Norward gave a brief laugh. When Reeve rose, his neck had reddened and murder glowed in his eyes.

"I'll kill you!" he shouted, and leaped toward the fireplace, his hands reaching for Lord Landry's sword. Norward tried to seize him and hold him still, but Reeve was too fast—the long straight blade sang from the scabbard and Reeve hacked two-handed at Norward's head. Norward leaped back, the sword-point whirring scant inches from his face.

Derina cried in alarm and started to run back up the stair, hoping she could somehow fetch Burley and bring an end to it—but one of her feet slipped on the flags and she fell on the stair with a stunning jolt.

Norward leaped to the woodpile to seize a piece of wood to use for a shield, and Reeve screamed and swung the sword again. There was the sound of a sigh, or sob, and Derina wanted to shriek, afraid it was Norward's last. Dazed on the stair, she couldn't be certain what happened—but somehow Norward must have dodged the blow, though to Derina's dazzled eyes it looked, impossibly enough, as if the sword passed clean through his body without doing any hurt. But then Norward lunged forward and smashed Reeve in the face with his log—Reeve shouted, dropped the sword, staggered back. Norward grabbed him by the collar, wrenched him off his feet, and ran him head-first into the fireplace.

Derina screamed and came running down the stairs. Norward was grinding the side of Reeve's head against the fire's dying embers. "Take my place, puppy?" he snarled. "Draw sword against me? Have a taste of the hell that awaits kinslayers, Reeve of the Silver Spurs!"

"Stop!" Derina cried, and seized Norward's arms. The scent of burning hair and flesh filled her nostrils. The strength of the knotted muscle in Norward's arms astonished her—she couldn't budge him. Reeve screamed in terror. "Don't kill him!" Derina begged.

Norward flung Reeve up and away from the fire, then down to the flags. Reeve wept and screamed as Norward took the long patterned blade and hacked off his spurs, then kicked him toward the stair. Reeve rose to his feet, his hands clutching his burns, and fled. Derina stared in amazement at the transformed Norward, the tall young man, half a stranger, standing in the hall with drawn blade ... Tears unexpectedly filled her eyes and she sat down sobbing.

Norward put the sword away and was suddenly her brother again, his eyes mild, his expression a little embarrassed. He reached out a hand and helped her to her feet.

"Come now," he said, "it was a lesson Reeve had to learn."

She clung to him. "I don't understand," she said.

"Truthfully," her brother said, "I am a bit puzzled myself."

Next day Reeve kept to his room. At dinner, Lord Landry looked at the bruise on Norward's cheek and said nothing, but there was a pitiless, amused glint in his eye, as if he'd just watched a pleasing dogfight; and he sat Norward down at his left hand, where he'd had Reeve before.

Six weeks later, after Yule, Burley and Derina left for Burley's home, where a new wing had been built for them. To Derina, the three small rooms and their whitewashed stone walls seemed more space than she'd had ever in life. It was not until spring that she and Burley journeyed back to the great flint-walled house perched above the switchback mountain road, and then it was not on a mission that concerned pleasantries.

Derina rode the whole way with her insides tying themselves in knots. Burley marched a captive before them, a man bound with leather thongs, and Derina was terrified that the captive—or the news she herself bore—would mean Burley's death.

But Burley's family had decided this course between them, and brushed her objections aside. If they had known her father as well as she, they would have been much more afraid.

When she arrived the old flint-walled house seemed different, though she could see nothing overtly changed. But the people moved cheerily, not with the half-furtive look they'd had before; and there was an atmosphere of gaiety unlike anything she remembered.

But Burley was not cheered: grim in his buff coat, he marched his captive into the hall and asked for Lord Landry. The servants caught Burley's mood, and edged warily about the room.

Landry, when he came, was half-drunk; and Norward was at his elbow, a tall man, deep-chested and powerful, that Derina barely recognized.

"Daughter!" Landry said, one of his cold smiles on his lips, and then he saw Burley's captive, the shivering shepherd, and he stopped dead, looking from the shepherd to Burley and back again. "What's this?" he growled. The shepherd fell to his knees.

"First," Burley said, "I bring proper and respectful greetings from my father and my family to Lord Landry. This other matter is secondary—we found this fool grazing his flock on the upland meadow that was ours by marriage contract, and he had the temerity to say he was there on your order, so we had him whipped and now we bring him to you, to punish as you will for this misuse of your name."

Landry turned red, his neck swelling; his hand half-drew the dagger at his belt. Norward put a restraining hand on Landry's arm. "Now's not the time to make new enemies," Norward said, and Landry forced down his rage, snicked the dagger back in its sheath, then strode briskly to where the captive cowered on his knees and kicked the shepherd savagely in the ribs. "That's for you, witless!" he said.

"My lord—" the shepherd gasped.

"Silence!" Landry shouted, before the man could say something all might regret. He looked up at Burley, staring blue eyes masking his calculation. "You've handled this matter well," he admitted grudgingly. "I thank you."

"I bring other news that will please you, I think," Burley said. He took Derina's hand. "Derina is with child, we believe, these two months."

For a moment Derina was petrified—with a child on the way, what more use was the father? But then an unfeigned smile wreathed Landry's features. He embraced Derina and kissed her cheek. "There, my pet," he said, "have I not always said you were my favorite?"

Even though she knew perfectly well it was Landry's style to play one family member off against another, still Derina's nerves twisted into a kind of sick happiness, the assurance of her father's favor.

"You'll give me the boy I need," Landry said. "These others—" He looked at Norward. "—they league and conspire against me, but I have the mastery of 'em."

He turned to the shepherd, drew his knife again, and sliced the captive's bonds. "In celebration, we'll give this simpleton his freedom."

The shepherd rose, bowed, and fled.

Nicely done, Derina thought. Not a single regrettable word spilled.

Norward advanced to clasp Burley's hand. "Welcome to our house," he said. "Your advice, and that of your family, will be valued in the days to come."

Burley smiled, but his eyes glanced to Derina, who looked back in purest misery. There was something happening here, and it was nothing good.

Dinner found Landry at the head of the table, with his wife on one side and Norward at the other. The big sword still hung in its sheath behind her father's head. Reeve—burlier than ever, and full of smiling good humor despite the burn-scars on the side of his head, sat beside his brother, and Edlyn played happily with her daughter at his elbow. There was no sign of Medora or any other plaything.

Derina watched it all in silent, wide-eyed surprise. Her father was smiling and complimentary, and praised her in front of the others. She found herself casting looks at Edlyn to see how her older sister reacted; but Edlyn's attention was all on her daughter, and the anticipated looks of hatred never came.

They all looked so *well*. Happy, strong, their skins glowing with health. Derina felt like a shambling dwarf by comparison.

Then, offhand, Landry changed the subject. "There's an army marching in the lowlands," he said, "one of the Princes. He's got three thousand men, and his proclaimed ambition is to invade the highlands and tame our mountain folk." He barked a laugh. "If so, he'll find us a hard piece of flint to break his teeth on."

"There is not enough wealth in the highlands to pay a Prince's army," Norward said. "If he comes, he will find the pickings poor indeed."

"Likely he intends somewhere else, and the story is a mere diversion," Landry said, "but there's no reason in taking it lightly. I'm bringing in supplies, and preparing the place for a siege. They can't drag any engines up the mountains big enough to hurt our walls." His eyes flicked to Burley. "I'll trust your kin to support us, and raise up their strength against any invaders."

"We have no love for lowland princes," Burley said.

Landry laughed. "Let 'em lie outside our walls till the cold eats their bones!"

Landry snatched up a cup and offered a toast to the defeat of the Prince— and his sons and Burley drank with him. They were mountain men pledging against their ancestral enemies of the lowlands, and in a matter as fundamental as this their views were united.

Derina felt cold as ice as she saw Burley pledge himself to Landry's war, and remembered Edlyn's husband doing likewise, three years ago.

The Prince's messenger came the next day with a small party and blew his trumpet from the path below the gatehouse. Lord Landry knew of their presence—he'd had scouts out, which showed he took the threat of invasion seriously. Perhaps he'd even known they were coming before he'd brought up the matter, so casually, at dinner. When the trumpet was blown Landry was ready, standing above the gatehouse with his family—all but Reeve, who had particular business elsewhere.

Derina wrapped herself in a cloak to hide her trembling. She had seen the preparations Landry made, and knew what he intended.

"His Highness bids you return that which you took last summer, when you attacked his camp," the messenger said. "If not, there will be war between you that will not end until your hold is burnt up, your valleys laid waste, and your children scattered over the hills with stones their only playthings. His Highness offers you this, if you heed not our command—or, if you choose wisely, he offers his hand in friendship."

A vast grin broke across Landry's face at the sound of the messenger's words—but Derina, who knew the smile, felt herself shudder. "What's mine is mine!" Landry called. "If this Prince wants what is his, let him look for it in a place closer to home."

"The Prince's friendship is not so lightly to be brushed aside," the messenger said.

"When was the friendship of a lowland man ever worth a pinch of salt?" Landry asked. He plucked up a crossbow from where it sat waiting, aimed briefly, and planted the missile a foot deep in the messenger's heart. Other missiles whirred down from Landry's soldiers. Then the gates swung open to let a group of riders under Reeve sally out. The Prince's party were killed to the last man, so that none could return to their prince with any of the intelligence they'd doubtless gathered.

Burley watched the massacre from the gatehouse, fists clenched on his belt. He turned to Landry. "Let me head homeward, and tell my kinfolk to prepare," he said. "And let me take Derina to where she'll be safe."

Landry shook his head, and seeing it Derina felt a cold chill of fear. "Send a letter instead," he said.

"Sir—"

"No," Landry said. "A letter. Your father will be more likely to help us if his son and grandson—" A nod to Derina. "—are guests here with us."

Derina's head swam under Landry's cold blue gaze. She was in her father's house again, under his power, and her husband was a pawn in her father's war—a pawn set ready for sacrifice.

The burning arrow was sent from door to door along the valleys, and as men armed the great house was readied for siege. The spring lambs were killed, and their flesh salted for the cellars or dried in the pure mountain air. The herds and flocks were driven up to the highland pastures by secret ways, where an enemy would never find them unless he first knew where to look. The people of the valleys were prepared for evacuation, either to the great houses or to the high meadows with the flocks.

The Prince's army paused in the lowlands for a week or so, perhaps awaiting the messenger's return, and then began its toilsome march into the hills. Lord Landry arranged for the heads of the messenger's party to await them on stakes, one every few kilometers along the road.

Lord Landry was in his element—boasting, boozing, swaggering among his old veterans or the country gentlefolk. Parties of warriors arrived under their local chiefs, were added to the defense of the great house or sent out to harry the enemy column with ambushes and raids.

The guards Landry posted were as polite as their duties allowed, but it was clear that neither Burley nor Derina was allowed to leave the house. Derina was almost thankful: Burley was safe as long as he remained here, held genteel hostage. If Landry should send him to war, Derina knew, he very well might not return.

But the blackmail served its purpose. Word came that Burley's father Edson had brought his men into the war, and was already harassing enemy scouts and foragers.

"What a fool this Prince is!" Landry shouted down the length of the dinner table. It was crowded with soldiers, and Landry's family were packed in at the top. "Come to fight us over booty worth less than what he's paying his men to take it—and last year's loot already shared out among our men as soon as we returned home! We could not return it if we would!"

"A fool and his army," Reeve smiled, "are soon parted."

Derina caught Norward's look, a quick glance to the head of the table—as if he would say something, but chose not to.

The meal ended in singing, boasting, and boisterous talk of swordplay and the prospect of large ransoms. Derina, ears ringing, withdrew early, and went to bed. A few hours later Burley joined her, swaying slightly with wine as he undressed.

"Reeve and I are to leave tomorrow," he said. "We'll set an ambush above Honing Pass."

Fear snapped Derina awake. She sprang from the bed and clung to him. "Don't go!" she cried.

Burley was bemused by her vehemence. "Don't be silly. I must."

"Father—" she gulped. "Father will kill you."

Burley's look softened. He touched her hair. "Your father won't be coming."

"His soldiers will be there. And—" She hesitated. "Reeve. If Reeve has not changed."

Burley shook his head. "Landry still needs my father. I'm not without value yet."

Derina buried her head in the curve of his neck. "Your father is mortal. So are you. And the lord my father will take your land in the name of our child."

He put his arms around her, swayed gently back and forth. "I have no choice," he said.

Derina blinked back hot tears. When had they ever had a choice? she thought.

Hoping desperately, she said, "I'll speak to Reeve."

Reeve listened carefully as Derina stammered out her fears the next morning. Unconsciously he rubbed the scars on his forehead. "No, Father has not asked any such service of me," he said. "Nor would he—Norward and I are strong enough to stand against him now, and Edlyn and Mother support us. When we refuse to let him play us each against the other, he calls it 'conspiracy.'"

"But his other men? His old veterans?"

Reeve looked thoughtful. "Perhaps. I'll speak to them myself, let them know that I look to them to keep Burley safe."

Derina kissed her brother on both cheeks. "Bless you, Reeve!"

Reeve smiled and hugged her with bearlike arms. "I'll look to him. Don't worry yourself—it's an ambush we'll be setting, not a pitched battle. All the danger's to the other side."

Reeve and Burley made a brave sight the next day, riding out in buff coats and polished armor, their troopers following. Derina, standing above the gatehouse, waved and forced the brightest smile she could, all to balance her sinking heart.

In a driving rain, five days later, the remnants of the party returned. The tale was of the ambushers ambushed, the Prince's spearmen on the ridge above, advancing under cover of arrows. Reeve wounded to the point of death, run through with a lance, and Burley taken.

"His beast threw Master Burley, miss," said an old serjeant, himself wounded in the jaw and barely able to speak. With dull eyes, Derina listened to the serjeant's tale as she saw Reeve carried into the house on his litter. "The enemy ran him down. He surrendered at the last—and they didn't kill him then, I saw them taking him away. He survived the surrender—that's the most dangerous moment. So he'll be held for ransom, most like, and you'll see him ere autumn."

And then Lord Landry came howling among the survivors, Norward following white-faced behind. Landry lashed at the nearest with a riding whip, calling them fools and cowards for letting his son fall victim. Then, snarling, hands trembling with the violence of his passion, he stood for a moment in the cold rain that poured in streams off his big shoulders, and then he turned on his heel and marched back to the main house. Derina ran after, feet sliding in the mud of the court.

"Burley was captured!" she said. "We must send his ransom!"

Landry turned to her as he walked, face twisting in a snarl. "Ransom? That's his father's business."

"His father's poor!" Derina cried.

Landry laughed bitterly. "And *I'm* rich? I've given away enough sustenance with your dowry. Don't expect me to deliver your fool of a husband, not when you're carrying his fortune in your belly."

Derina seized his sleeve, but he shook her off savagely, and she slipped in the mud and fell. Strong arms helped her rise. She looked up at Norward's grim face.

"I'll speak with him," Norward said, "and do what I can."

When Norward and Derina caught him, Landry had barged into the house and stood shouting in the great hall.

"Arm!" he bellowed. "A sally! When this rain ends, I'll have revenge for my son!"

Servants and soldiers bustled to their work. Norward spoke cautiously amid the melee. "You need your every son in this," he said. "Burley's your son now, and could be a good one to you."

Landry swung around, derision contorting his features. "That country clod! Whip my servant, will he? Steal my valuables? Is *that* a son of mine?" He shook his whip in Norward's face. "Let him rot in chains!"

Tears dimmed Derina's eyes and her head whirled. She heard Norward's protest, Landry's dismissal, then Norward's raised voice. Suddenly there was a violent whirl of action, and Derina looked up to see Landry holding Norward by the throat, his dagger out and pricking Norward beneath the ear.

"Think to replace Reeve, whey-face?" Landry demanded. "You'll never be a true son to me!" Derina cried out as the dagger drew a line of red along Norward's neck; and then Landry dropped his son to the floor and strode off, calling for his armor. Derina rushed to Norward's side, held her shawl to the wound. Norward pushed it aside.

"A scratch," he said. His face was grim and pale as death. He stood, then helped Derina to a chair. "Wait here—I know how to get Burley back. But promise me you'll say nothing—trust me in this."

He walked to the fireplace. He stood looking for a moment at Landry's long battle sword, then took it from its place and walked toward the stairs.

Derina was terrified to follow but more terrified to stay, alone and not knowing. She followed.

"Out!" Norward cried. "Out!" He was driving Edlyn and Kendra from Reeve's room. The two left in a bewildered flutter; but Derina, grimly biting her lip, pushed past them and into the room.

Norward had his back to her. He stared grimly down at Reeve, who lay unconscious, pale as death, his midsection bulky with bandages.

Derina could not say if she screamed as, in one easy gesture, Norward drew the blade from its scabbard and plunged it into Reeve's belly.

Landry had come down to the great hall, wearing his breastplate and chain skirts. He scowled as he saw Norward with his sword.

"Father," Norward said, "I suspect I know why the enemy have invaded." He held out the sword. "The Prince wants this back. It's one of the Swords of Power."

No! Derina thought. *Don't tell him!*

Then was a silence in which Derina heard only the beating of blood in her ears. Landry stood stock-still, then came forward. He took the sword from Norward and looked at it carefully. Then a savage smile crossed his features, and he drew the blade from the scabbard and whirled it over his head. "Maybe you're a son to me after all!" he said. "A Sword of Power—ay, that makes sense! But which one?"

To stifle any cry of surprise, Derina put her hand to her throat at Norward's answer.

"Farslayer would kill the Prince for you," Norward said. "And you wouldn't have to leave the room."

"And I'd have it right back again, through my heart!" Landry scorned. He stopped, looked at the sword. Then, deliberately, he spoke the words, the simple rhyme, known to all children, that would unleash Farslayer, and named as its target one of his own men, the wounded serjeant who had brought the news of the ambush to him.

A target so near would make the job of retrieval easy enough.

As Derina knew it would, nothing happened. Her creeping astonishment was turning to knowledge.

She knew what Norward was trying to do, and she wondered if she dared—if she wanted to—put a stop to it.

Landry looked at the hilt. "The white hand," he said. "Which sword is that?"

Norward shrugged. "The white hand of death, most like. What does it matter? What matters is that the war is won the moment you use the blade."

A grin crossed Landry's features. "The men are all to mount," he said. "We'll empty the place. You'll ride with me, and have pick of the Prince's loot!"

Derina, wide-eyed, stood and said nothing. *Decided* to say nothing.

A few hours later, as the last raindrops fell, Lord Landry and his army rode from his flint-walled house on his mission to crush the Prince and his army with their own weapon.

A few moments later Derina watched her mother's astonishment as she saw Reeve strolling casually down the stair, a crooked grin on his face. Even his burn scars had vanished.

"I seem to have improved," he said.

Four days later Norward was back with the body of Lord Landry, who had been killed leading a reckless charge on the enemy army. "The Prince has his sword back," he said. "The war is over."

Derina, standing in the courtyard, looked numbly at the body of her father, lying cold on his litter hacked by a dozen armor-crushing blows. Her brother Reeve put an arm around her.

She looked at her mother Kendra, who stared at Landry as if she didn't believe her eyes, and at Edlyn, who looked as if she were just beginning to dare to hope.

"Burley?" she asked.

"Alive," Norward said, "and his ransom well within our means. We'll pay his release as soon as the Prince's army reaches the lowlands again, and then you'll have your husband back."

Derina cried out in joy and threw her arms around him. He—Lord Norward now—stood stiffly for a moment, then gently took her arms and released himself from her embrace.

"Our father always wanted me to kill someone," he said. "Who'd have thought he would himself have been the victim?"

Landry would never have understood, Derina thought, a man such as the Prince, who would fight a war for a talisman not of destruction, but of healing.

"You didn't strike the blow yourself," Derina said.

"I misled him. I knew what would happen."

She took his hand. "So did I."

He looked at Landry and tears shimmered in his eyes. "Woundhealer would not kill, not even for our father," he said. "I wish I could have thought of another way, but there are some so maimed they are beyond the help even of a Sword of Power."

When Fred Saberhagen asked me to contribute a story to an anthology set in his "Swords" universe, I suddenly realized I'd always wanted to write a story about a powerful magical object. If you want to blame this on my reading Tolkien at too impressionable an age, don't let me stop you.

Once again, I considered what had already been done, and decided to do the opposite. Fred's "Swords" books tend toward the epic, and involve action on a large scale, with kingdoms if not entire civilizations hanging in the balance. I decided to write an intimate story, about a provincial family set very much on the edge of the main action.

Most of my readers seem not to have ever found this story, and since I've always thought it was one of my better efforts, I'm pleased to have the opportunity to see it again in print.

The Bad Twin

There it was in my sights, for just a fraction of a second, the most infamous profile in all time. And then, before I could squeeze the trigger, Scorsese stepped into his time box and was gone.

I looked at my wrist chronometer.

15:22:16.

Scorsese had timeshifted at 15:22:14 at the latest. I decided to perform a little discrete editing.

There was a bounty on Scorsese. He was one of history's greatest time thieves, and he had never been caught. No one even knew his real name: Scorsese was an alias he'd used when he appeared at Verrocchio's studio in 1471, when Leonardo da Vinci was still apprenticed there, an appearance that resulted in the disappearance of the entire body of Leonardo's work prior to that date. We had tried to intercept him there—we'd been after lost Leonardos, too—but somehow Scorsese had maneuvered his pursuers into creating an unholy paradox so godawful that those who'd survived had been glad to get out with their lives. We had declared the whole period off limits for our own people, lest their continued tampering lose not only da Vinci's early works, but his life and the rest of his accomplishment, too.

We did know what Scorsese looked like. He'd had Leonardo paint his portrait, and some of the cartoons had survived in the pocket of one of our dead agents. His profile was unmistakable, with a Wellington beak of a nose and a high, balding forehead.

I had just seen that profile below me among the grape vines, in the split-second just before he and his time box had vanished from my present. If I could edit Scorsese and confiscate his time box laden with a genuine Bronze Age fresco, I would be entitled to the reward—plus a promotion, a medal, and if I was lucky a stay at the Time Resort in the Paleozoic.

Scorsese hadn't seen me, which meant that I wouldn't have to be looking over my shoulder while I edited him, a significant problem with combat among time travelers. Imagine a war in which the survivors of an ambush can return in time and edit out the ambushers, in turn leaving a few survivors who can hop back and edit out the editors. Thinking about it can give you a headache.

But such problems also led to a very simple rule: No Survivors Means No Headaches. If you're going to ambush someone, do it right, and do it permanently.

I was going to bag Scorsese, and I was going to do a good job of it.

Pieces of pumice crunched beneath my boots as I crossed the ridge and descended into the grape arbor adjacent to the isolated villa. When the inhabitants had fled the island after the villa's partial collapse in the last earthquake, they had abandoned some of the finest wine grapes in history to grow wild in the rich volcanic soil. Lt. Talley and I had liberated some wine jugs from the villa's cellars a few months ago, finding the contents exquisite.

Pity the whole place would be blown to hell and gone in another six months.

From the top of the small ridge I could look to the south, seeing the land fall away in the jagged terraces created by the viniculture of the inhabitants. To the northeast loomed the bulk of the volcano, rising three thousand feet above the sea. The island's inhabitants had wanted to put to use every available inch of space, and so the volcano was terraced up much of its height. The unusable parts had a mad, jagged beauty, striped in red, white, and black to mark the histories of different eruptions.

The island had many names. Before they fled, its inhabitants called it Kalliste, meaning The Fairest. Kykladic navigators sensibly called it Strongyli, Round Island. Many years later a Spartan general would conquer the place, and it would be named Thera after him. Years afterward it would take its name from its patron saint, Irene, and would be called Santorini.

At the moment it was 15:22:44, June 16, 1481 B.C.E. On December 22 the volcano would celebrate the Solstice by blowing itself to smithereens, critically wounding Minoan and Kykladic civilization in the process. The eruption was the culmination of a long series of events, begun eighteen months before when an earthquake flattened half the buildings on the island and a lava flow obliterated a village and completely blocked one of the small harbors, while a new vent on the north side of the volcano dumped several inches of pumice blocks on the whole island and several of the nearby Kyklades. The inhabitants had fled then, all seventy thousand, in an orderly evacuation that testified to their culture's high level of organization and technology. Every so often a ship returned to see whether the current cycle of eruptions was over, and on those occasions I fired off a lot of smoke bombs and other pyrotechnics to convince them it wasn't. Thus far it had worked.

I was camped out on a nice flat piece of ground half a click from here, where a rock wouldn't be likely to fall on me. With my weapons, my armor, and my smoke bombs, I was a caretaker assigned to preserve the treasures of Thera and keep them safe from time thieves. I was a good choice for the job, insofar as I was also a U.S. Navy SEAL trained in irregular combat and survival, currently on assignment to the Time Corps of the International Time Authority at The Hague.

Until six weeks ago I'd had Lt. Talley of the Royal Marine Commando to keep me company, until he developed acute appendicitis and jumped upStream to the pickup date. Since then, guardianship of the entire island of Thera had been up to me.

It was a large island for a single person, but manpower had never been the Time Corps' strong point. The Corps was kept deliberately small in order not to become a threat to the governments that sponsored it. Because it was small, the Corps had to be efficient: morale and esprit were high, and so was the level of training and commitment. We were few in number, but all history was our backyard, and we were allowed to play for keeps.

Preserving all human history, it was felt, demanded a certain degree of ruthlessness.

The governments that acted to limit the powers of the Corps had also given it a rather large task: to Preserve the Common Heritage of Humankind. The civilization of Thera represented a unique and priceless inheritance. For the better part of a century, tourists in the National Museum in Athens had been lining up to see a few frescos dug from beneath a hundred feet of ash at Akrotiri, a part of the island that had not been destroyed by the eruption.

The artwork on the rest of the island, the parts the volcano destroyed, were just as valuable, and much more numerous.

On the first of September, when the Time Stream factors were most favorable for moving a large amount of men and equipment, a collection of specialists under the guidance of Time Corps personnel would appear on Thera and salvage every pot, every fresco, every item of bronze work—every graffito, if there was time.

But, as with any major archaeological project, the pothunters had to be kept away. The island was wide open to any scrounge artist with a time box sufficiently powerful to reach to the Fifteenth Century B.C.E., and I was supposed to keep them away.

The villa itself had two storys above ground, built of charcoal-colored stone layered with streaks of reddish-brown and creamy white, all the colors of the island blended here just as they were on the volcano that towered above us. Part of the place had collapsed in the first quake. On the far side of the villa, a torturous zigzag path dropped with breathtaking rapidity to one of Thera's smaller ports, the one we called Agia Therasia because it lay a hundred meters or so to seaward of what would, in my century, become that splinter-island. In my own century the town had been broken, buried under a hundred feet of ash, and then submerged under the Aegean; but now, framed by dark cypress and lighter, stunted olive trees all shining with their peculiar silver-green, Agia Therasia stood in native loveliness, a crescent of black, brown, red, and white buildings, all of native stone, clinging to its fringe of dark volcanic beach. The deep turquoise Aegean, wrinkled like a baby's skin, stretched from the beach to the white horizon. The scene didn't have the wild, craggy magnificence of my century's Santorini. Here in the fifteenth century the island had a quieter beauty, a beauty altered and enhanced by the presence of a large and peaceful human population.

Many of the buildings had crumbled, though one three-storyed eminence, crowned with the Minoan horns of consecration, still stood above the town. The most dominant building in the town, I'd explored it and found it disappointing: it turned out to be the headquarters of the trading company from Knossos, and presumably had doubled as an embassy, architecturally dominating the Thera town as the Minoans dominated the Kykladic civilization.

It did, however, have indoor toilets even on the upper storys, flushed by a large cistern on the roof. I thought that was an interesting detail.

In another few months it would all lie under the caldera, edited, along with the two civilizations that had built it, by a lunatic nature. I would miss It.

I walked through the deserted villa to see what Scorsese had plundered and saw how simple the snatch had been. After bracing the ceiling with some automatic jacks, Scorsese had cut away at the wall surrounding an interior fresco, covered the fresco with an aerosol preservative—he'd failed to police one of the empty cans—then attached some anti-g lifters to the fresco and pushed the whole thing into his box. I noticed that the jacks that supported the ceiling had timers on them set to drop the roof on this particular room in another hour. It would look as if earthquake damage were responsible. A clever idea, well executed.

A pity he hadn't considered my capacity for wine. I'd run out of the stuff that Talley and I had liberated from the villa, and decided to hike up the ridge and get some more. Lie under the shade of the olives, drink from an exquisite vintage, and read a copy of Sophocles' Theban trilogy I'd brought with me from my own century. If you're ever stuck on a deserted island, by the way, I recommend reading the classics—they stay with you longer.

Now, instead of passing a balmy afternoon, I was about to kill one of the most dangerous men in history. It's a situation that Sophocles would have appreciated.

Time thieves in general are well organized and well financed. They have to be to reach as far back as they do—time travel is very expensive, and those with the private resources to build their own illegal time machine are few: some governments can't even afford it. The robberies can't be done on a very large scale, since the opportunities to move large amounts of matter through the Stream are very few, so most of their raids are in the nature of smash-and-grab—one or two men jump downStream, seize a pot, statue, or gold ornament, and then Jump upStream and away. The Time Corps edits the thieves when we find them, but unless there are records of the theft that somehow survive and get into the Corps archives, most of the stuff is simply lost, gone into private collections established hundreds, sometimes thousands of years after the theft.

Thera was an obvious target, since archaeologists had long ago established that the island had been abandoned about two years before it finally blew. The Corps sent two guards to keep the plunderers away. Usually the announcement of a Corps guard was enough to keep a place safe—there were plenty of other places to raid, after all. Scorsese had been unusually brave to raid the villa: but presumably he'd been scouting the place for some time and had been keeping tabs on my movement. He'd seen that the villa wasn't in my normal pattern; he couldn't have known that I would run out of wine and decide to hike two miles uphill, partly concealed by the series of terraces and vines, for a raid on the villa's cellar.

I took a position behind one of the olive trees to the side of the villa. I was out of sight from my earlier position behind the ridge, which would tend to reduce the possibility of a paradox. Just to make sure I glanced at my chronometer, took out the notebook that all time agents carry with them for purposes like this, and wrote a note to myself: 15:35:01 to 15:22:05. I stuck the note onto a branch of the olive tree.

Then I gave the same coordinates to my chronometer, seeing the shining numbers reflected in my specs, and waited.

I planned to head downStream to nine seconds before Scorsese's disappearance and my own appearance above the ridge. I would kill Scorsese and then Jump upStream a few hours or so in order to give my past self a chance to figure out what had happened.

For killing Scorsese would, of course, change my own past—when I heard the shots I'd pop up above the ridge line a little early, and of course see Scorsese dead below me. I assumed that I would then circle around to see if I could pick up the trail of whoever had been doing the shooting, whereupon I would find the note I'd written to myself and realize that it had been my own future self who'd been responsible.

My past self, who I'll call I-Alpha, would then take position behind the olive tree and set his own chronometer for 15:22:05. He would then jump downStream and become me, in accordance with the laws of temporal conservation, and kill Scorsese all over again.

It was complicated, but I had temporal conservation on my side. In training they'd told us that it helps to think of the universe as a lazy editor, revising a manuscript but trying to do as little work as possible. Although it is possible for a time traveler to change the past, it is harder than appears at first glance. To save itself the trouble of having to alter all upStream timelines, the universe tended to act to prevent paradox, attempting to solve them along the lines of least resistance. Rather than accept both I-Alpha and I-Beta materializing in the same place at the same instant, Alpha and Beta would merge.

It was 15:34:45. I braced my rifle against my shoulder and made myself ready for the edit.

At 15:35:01 I made the transit, and suddenly, in less than an eyeblink, Scorsese's time box was there in front of me, and Scorsese, with an armful of gear, was walking from the villa to its hatch.

The air cracked to the sound of shots, none of them mine.

I threw myself backward and rolled as bullets began tearing up the olive tree above my head.

Scorsese had clearly brought a friend, someone hunkered down with a rifle off to my right.

I dived behind the villa on the opposite side from Scorsese and began to work my way around to the left, behind the ridge. Bullets began thwacking into the heavy stonework of the building.

And, as I accelerated in the safe defilade of the ridge, I ran smack into myself.

Into I-Alpha, who likewise covered by the defilade was working his way toward the firing.

We both sat down and goggled at one another, ignoring the sound of the bullets spitting overhead. I had just created a paradox of duplication, and we were both in deep trouble.

"You stupid bastard," Alpha said.

"Look," I said. "You've got twelve minutes to get to an olive tree on the other side of the villa, so that you can drop back to a few seconds ago and end the duplication."

"I'm supposed to put myself in the line of fire for *you?*" Alpha asked. "You're the one who fucked up."

"We can edit out the marksman later," I said.

"Fuck that. He can edit us just as easily. Let's find out where the bastard is, first."

I doubted that the sniper would, actually, edit us. The Time Corps wasn't going to waste a lot of energy on a missing fresco, but when one of their own was killed they would spare no effort to edit the culprit, preferably before he actually committed his crime, so that his victim would remain alive.

"Circle left," I said. "There's not enough cover to our right."

We began moving to the left but the marksman managed to anticipate us. Bullets began ripping through the grape vines over our heads. It took us twenty minutes to work our way into position to hit back at him, and by that time he'd gone into the Stream and got clean away.

But more seriously, Alpha hadn't been able to get to the olive tree in time for the 14:45:01 jump downStream to become me. The odds were increasing that if he made the Jump now, he'd become not me, Beta, but a third individual, Gamma, and then there would be three of us.

We were permanently duplicated, and this was very much against the rules. Time Corps personnel were forbidden to duplicate themselves, because with an infinite number of duplications we could become an army capable of threatening the governments that employed us. Penalty for duplication was severe.

The forms would still be followed, though. A jury of our Time Corps peers would convene here on Thera, and Alpha and I would have a chance to speak in our own defense before our judges reluctantly shot one or both of us.

"Look," I said. "How about this? One of us jumps downStream for a few hours to leave a note to ourself warning him not to make this mistake."

Alpha looked at me coldly through his self-polarizing specs. His front had been smeared with black volcanic ash as he'd crawled through the grape vines, and he looked both dirty and resentful. "You're getting desperate, guy," he said. "Your thinking isn't very clear. If you succeed in changing the past, we edit *ourselves*. He lives and we don't exist any more. I don't know about you, but I have every intention of continuing to exist."

He pointed a finger at me. "And that's only if we're *lucky*. The worst is what happens if you don't succeed in editing the past. Then there'd be three of us, wouldn't there? You, me, and him. We'd be triplets."

"Oh," I said. He looked at me savagely. I hadn't realized I was capable of such anger.

"Look, sport," he said. "I was walking up to the villa for a jug of wine and suddenly I was getting shot at. It was you who fucked up. Suppose you tell me how."

"Scorsese," I said, and Alpha's surprised reaction softened the menace on his face. "He's done it again," I said. "He's protected himself by getting us involved in a paradox. We don't dare edit him for fear of making our own situation worse."

"Let's pull back and give this a think," Alpha said.

Alpha and I fell back fifty yards to a defensible outcrop of lava rock and considered the problem. We could, of course, drop back downStream to zap the sniper and Scorsese; but it would be foolish in the extreme to assume that Scorsese didn't have further backup—hell, since he didn't have to abide by any regulations about duplicating himself he could be his own backup, simply by dropping back to the same place to act as his own sniper—and if there were more Scorseses hanging about to edit our editing job then there might suddenly be four Time Corpsmen staring at one another.

We remembered how Scorsese had got six of the best of our agents involved in a paradox loop in Florence that had only been solved when they'd started killing each other. It was too easy for something like that to get started here. Every time we tried to resolve the duplication problem we risked the problem of quadrupling ourselves, or worse. If we got into a time loop as well, with all manner of catastrophe-producing ripples running upStream *and* down, the universe, ever the lazy editor, might decide that the easiest way to fix things would be to blow Thera six months early, eliminating numerous duplicate Time Corps agents and incidentally Aegean civilization. Scorsese might get blown with the rest of us, but it would be shallow comfort.

Alpha and I worked it through over and over again, and it was all very discouraging. Alpha scratched under his boonie hat and then looked up, over my shoulder, in surprise. "Shit," he said, grabbing for his rifle, "it's *him!*"

I turned, ready for High Noon with Scorsese, but I should have realized what Alpha was really up to. By the time I started to turn back while beginning a duck and roll, all I could see was a gun butt foreshortening with remarkable speed in the instant before it crunched down between my eyes.

I landed on the ground in a puff of volcanic ash. My specs were hanging by one ear. Alpha reversed the rifle and had it pointed at me before I could go for the pistol I carried in my shoulder holster. I froze.

Alpha reached forward with a foot and kicked my shooter back behind him. "Take the pistol out with two fingers and throw it behind you," he said. "Then the belt knife, then the knife in your boot, then the little pistol in the small of your back."

Well. You can't keep these kind of secrets from yourself, now can you?

"We've got a problem here, sport," Alpha said after he'd collected all my weaponry. "There's one too many of us, and *you're* the one that loused up. I'm clean, and I'm not responsible for the duplication. Now what does that suggest to you?"

I didn't say anything. I was too busy trying to read the expression behind the dark specs. If Alpha had wanted to kill me he would have done it by now. What else did he have in mind?

"Nothing to say, huh?" Alpha asked. He moved back a pace, well out of my range. He relaxed a trifle, though not nearly enough to make a jump worth my while.

"Well, Fubar, I can see a couple-three solutions," Alpha said. "One, I can kill you. Two, I can let you head down to Agia Therasia and let you fix up one of those old boats they've got drawn up on the beach there. If it doesn't leak too badly, you might just make it to Crete in time to warn everyone that their world is going to blow itself to hell in about six months. Maybe, if you learn Minoan quick enough, you can have a career as a prophet."

"Those boats are all junk," I said. "They were left behind for a reason. They're rotten or holed or have suffered earthquake damage."

Alpha smiled thinly. "That brings us to plan three, I believe. Here's how it goes: you and I make a jump downStream to last night, shortly after nightfall. Then I remove your wrist chronometer and let you hide yourself in the villa. I'll give you your knife so that when Scorsese shows up, you can kill him. You take his time box—I'll give it to you free and clear—and then you can run upStream for a life of crime. I keep Scorsese's body and the reward. I'll just tell our bosses that Scorsese had a partner in the box who got away before I could stop him."

"You're expecting me to edit Scorsese with a *knife?*" I asked. "Chances are he'll kill me."

Alpha's grin grew broader. "Well now, Fubar," he said. "That solves our problem, too, doesn't it?"

I looked up at the eyes masked by the dark shades, the thin, cruel grin, and I warily touched the lump hardening on my forehead.

How the hell was *I* supposed to know that I was such a mean bastard?

"So which'll it be, sport?" Alpha asked. "Plan one, plan two, or plan three? You decide."

"I'll go for Scorsese," I said. Alpha laughed, an unpleasant sound.

He drew a pistol and slung his awkward rifle. I was ready to make a move when he got close, but he never gave me the chance. "One word from you, Fubar," he said, "and I put two shots in your spleen."

I could feel him adjusting my chronometer—numbers flashed gold in my specs—and then he stepped back three paces and adjusted his own chronometer. Then there was a grey nothingness followed by a night wind blowing through the darkened cypresses. Brilliant stars wheeled overhead.

Alpha approached and took the chronometer from my wrist. I was stranded in the present. Then he backed off again, and I heard two thuds by me.

"Okay," he said. "There's your survival knife, and a flashlight. The knife is awkward to throw and I know you'd miss if you tried to toss it at me."

"I would like," I said, "an entrenching tool. I want to be able to hide under the floor in there until Scorsese shows."

He paused a moment. I held my breath. I could feel how hard he was thinking, feel his mind probing at the idea, trying to work out whether the presence of an entrenching tool would alter his plans, if there was something hidden in my request.

"Okay," he said, "that's fair. When I go upStream to move our camps I'll pick up an entrenching tool, then leave it in the villa for you."

"In the wine cellar," I said. "Northwest corner. Behind one of the big pithoi, so Scorsese won't spot it if he comes here to scout."

"Northwest corner. I'll remember. Now pick up the knife and get down to the villa … and remember, I'll be watching you very carefully."

I picked up the knife and flash, and then began my walk.

The next fifteen hours were going to be a bitch.

I walked down among the grape vines where in another few hours Scorsese's time box would rest, and then, counting my steps, I paced my way to the villa. I went through the low door, turned on the flash, and carefully examined the room. There was no place to hide: the room was bare, the furniture apparently having gone abroad with its owner. The walls were bare plaster, though the fresco Scorsese was scheduled to steal was on the back of one of them.

I moved into the next room, catching a glimpse of the blue and brown of the fresco, and was luckier. The earthquake had hit harder here, and one corner of the room had come crashing down, bringing with it much of the second story. Here I could hide myself under the rubble.

The villa had been built on the site of an older, smaller building: apparently the family was upwardly-mobile. The narrow terrace on which the villa stood had been built up and leveled by gangs of workers carrying baskets of topsoil to the terrace and dumping them here, raising the level of the ground above what it had been before. The new villa was at a higher level than the older building, with the result that the old house was used as a storage cellar.

From the kitchen in the back I went down a winding stair into the cellar. Ducking beneath the beams—the place was only about five feet tall, just a few inches taller than the big pithoi in which wine, grain, and oil were stored. I breathed a sigh of relief as I found the entrenching tool that Alpha had promised me he'd hide here.

Good. I planned to use Alpha's one good deed against him. He would regret leaving me the little shovel.

It was a folding tool with a little T at the end of the handle, which made it more useful when swung as a weapon. I adjusted the blade at 90 degrees from the handle, then used the tool as a pick to chop my way through the mortared stone of the wine cellar wall. Then, reforming the tool as a shovel, I burrowed my way between the hard bedrock of the island and the looser soil of the built-up terrace, creating a one-man narrow tunnel through the soft soil of the grape arbor. When I calculated I was under the place where Scorsese's time box would appear I headed for the surface, carefully clearing away the vines' complicated root system. Eventually I pushed the blade of the E-tool up into the air, confirming the few inches between myself and the surface. I wasn't planning on breaking through just yet, so I crawled back down the tunnel to the wine cellar.

Even though my chronometer was gone, I still had a good time sense. I calculated I had a few hours before dawn, so I crawled back into the villa and found some old blankets in what I guessed were the servants' quarters. The beds were too short, so I went to sleep on the floor.

I did not sleep well.

When dawn began to creep into the room, I got up and moved to the ruined room with the fresco. I rearranged the rubble a bit, giving myself space to lie down under a beam, and then I tented a blanket over it and lay rubble and pumice over the blanket.

Making myself look like a rock. I'd seen the Apaches do it in the movies.

By the time I'd finished the sun was shining full into the room through the ruined roof, and now I could see the fresco covering the wall. Two brown children, a girl in a pleated skirt and a naked boy, were standing hand-in-hand on the seashore. Their hair was curled into long lovelocks, and their eyes were long and Egyptian. The boy was circumcised; the girl appeared to have rouged her nipples. Behind them blue-and-gold dolphins rollicked in the waves, and the dark sand beneath their feet was sprinkled with shells and starfish. It was a joyous, exuberant painting, executed in strong, bright Mediterranean colors, a paean to the childhood of mankind. To the Kykladic peoples, the Aegean was a peaceful, private lake, and the island people, protected by the naval might of Crete, were living in a golden age. Their trade in wine and purple murex dye had made them rich, and they had avoided some of the excesses, such as human sacrifice, of their Minoan cousins. No one on the planet was as civilized, or as peaceful: even in China, the Shang were sacrificing people by the thousands.

Soon the volcano would bring an end to the stability of the age, breaking the Minoan peace and bringing in the continuous violence, rapine, and pillage that made up the so-called Age of Heroes.

Well. Violence was my trade, and Alpha's. The Age of Heroes was more our style.

But still the fresco drew me—the long dark eyes of the children, the grinning dolphins torpedoing up from the wave-crests, the carefully-delineated whorls of the seashells. A painting made solely to delight, to give and express joy. I wondered if this had been the children's room, and whether the boy and girl were portraits of a boy and girl who had lived here. If so, I hoped they'd survived the quake that had brought the ceiling down.

There was little else to do, so I watched the fresco for some hours. There were other frescos in other rooms, pictures of vines and flowers, but there were a lot of blank walls and nothing as good as this carefree picture of the children. The villa had a half-finished quality: perhaps the owner had yet to commission the decorations for the rest of it. Scorsese had chosen the best.

I wanted the fresco to survive. If the Kykladic culture that had made it was doomed, I wanted at least this piece of it to come into my time, its joy and innocence intact.

When the sun was high I wriggled into my hiding place. I spent some hours there, waiting for Scorsese, moving my limbs every so often in hopes of keeping my body as alert as possible. I didn't want to lunge out at the time criminal and put my weight on a leg that had fallen asleep.

And then, some time after noon, I heard the time box drop into the grape arbor, and then a man's footsteps. I froze and tried not to breathe. I thought, very hard, about how I was only a piece of rubble.

Scorsese came into the building and moved slowly through the rooms that still stood, and then he returned to his box for his equipment. There was something about his movement that was still alert, and I decided to wait.

In the next few minutes he brought his equipment in, bolted the a-grav units to the wall, propped up the roof with his jacks, and then covered the wall front and back with an aerosol preservative. I heard the hum of the beam cutter that cut the wall free, and then the blows of a sledge that knocked the fresco clear. Then I heard the hiss of aerosols as he used his preservative on the edges of the wall, and careful steps as he floated the fresco out into the back of his time box.

Outside, Alpha and I, still one, were walking through the terraced rows of grape vines, fancying a bit of wine.

As quietly as I could, I rolled out of my hiding place and took station by the inner door. I swung the E-tool a few times for practice. It made a wicked hissing sound as it cut through the air.

Alpha, outside, was mounting the ridge line from the other side. My earlier self, Beta, would be appearing behind the olive tree in a few seconds. The sniper, who I suppose was another incarnation of Alpha—call him Alpha Prime—was probably already in position off to the northwest.

Scorsese's footsteps came closer, grew louder on the flagging of the front room. He was returning to pick up his equipment. I cocked back my arm, holding the E-tool by its T-shaped handle.

He stepped into the room, and I swung the entrenching tool.

It damn near took his head off.

I dragged the body farther into the room. Scorsese wore a kind of dark bush jacket, tan shorts similar to mine, soft boots, dark glasses, and an olive drab boonie hat—Standard Smugglers' Issue, for all I knew. He also had a government-issue wrist chronometer. I wondered if he'd got it from one of the Time Corps people during the fiasco in Florence.

Well. Four Time Corps agents were avenged. Not that I cared about that. I was in too much of a hurry to strap the chronometer to my wrist.

And once I had done that, I felt myself breathe easier. I had a way out of here.

I took his pistol, hat, specs, and jacket. The shorts and boots were similar enough to mine—I didn't feel like spending any of the next few seconds hopping from one foot to another drawing on a pair of short pants.

The chronometer showed it was 15:22:04. A second later, right on time, shots began ripping up the peace of the world, as Alpha Prime in his sniper incarnation began blasting at Beta, which is to say me.

I scuttled down into the wine cellar, entrenching tool in hand. Then I used the chronometer to jump downStream to 15:22:01 in order to give myself a few spare seconds, and then as rock 'n' roll commenced overhead again I wormed my way into the tunnel, broke through the thin layer of soil I'd left overhead, and looked through a tangle of vines at Scorsese's bright shiny time box, big and slab-sided as a delivery van.

I did not expect Alpha would let me live through this. He'd certainly never let me get away with Scorsese's time box, which would give me the ability to head downStream and edit him somehow. In his position as sniper, he was perfectly set to shoot anyone coming out of the villa. But although he covered the villa's exits, the time box stood between him and my tunnel, unless he had duplicated himself more than once—and that was dangerous, hence unlikely. He might assume that the time box jumped automatically into the Stream and got away.

And on the other hand Scorsese might be somewhere within sight, backing up himself. He, I presume, would be relieved to see someone in Scorsese's hat and jacket rise magically from the ground, throw himself into the time box, and make a clever escape. In his relief he might not notice that his famous profile was a little altered.

I could feel the imprint of a huge target symbol on my back as I scrambled from the narrow tunnel, kicking at the loose soil. I threw myself through the vines, jumped through the time box's open door, and slammed it shut behind me.

Scorsese had allowed for the possibility that he might have to make a hasty exit. The controls were already programmed for his destination, so all I had to do was press the go-button.

The windows turned black. The box had entered the Stream.

The little official-use-only wrist chronometers we Time Corps people wore were only good for traveling a few decades, perhaps a couple centuries if the Stream currents were with you. To travel longer distances more energy was needed, plus a self-contained environment with oxygen and, if the journey was long, food. The short jumps I'd made earlier in the day had seemed no longer than eyeblinks, but jumping up- or downStream for any longer distances subjectively took more time.

I looked at the gauges and saw that this journey would be upStream and for only four hundred years or so. It would take about half an hour, subjectively. I readjusted my jacket and hat, brushed volcanic soil from my shorts, and looked out into the darkness as the years sped by.

The island had blown in the interim. It had rained a lot of ash on Anatolia, Rhodes, and the eastern part of Crete, causing discomfort and a food shortage, but what had really smashed Minoan civilization were several major earthquakes, over the period of a year or so, caused by the collapse of Thera's caldera. The quakes had shattered the physical remnants of Cretan and Kykladic civilization, brought all the buildings down, and also caused tidal waves that had destroyed coastal towns and wiped out the Cretan and Kykladic navies, galleys drawn up on the beach.

The earthquakes spared most of mainland Greece. And without the navies of Crete to keep them down, the first of the Greek heroes began to carve their bloody paths into legend.

In the half hour it took me to jump upStream the Trojan War was fought and lost; the Dorians had swarmed into Greece and, with their systematic but orderly butchery, put an end to the chaos of the Age of Heroes; and the refugees from these new series of wars, the Pelasgians/Philistines/Peoples of the Sea, had swept south and east to be flattened by the Egyptians and in turn to flatten the Israelites.

Thera, its remaining treasures buried under tons of ash, remained uninhabited. It would keep a bad reputation, and there would still be eruptions and quakes. Eventually Plato would hear of it and write of the Round Isle of Atlantis—a curious rendering of Strongyli, one of the island's names—but he'd lose a decimal point somewhere and speak of Atlantis having existed 9000 years before, instead of 900.

Not hard to do, if you're calculating in pre-Arabic numerals.

I looked involuntarily into the back of the time box, seeing the fresco waiting for the light, as fresh as it had been when the Kykladic culture that produced it had been alive ... The time of innocence and joy symbolized by those happy children was over. By now their descendents were a barbarized, conquered people, their artifacts buried, their light extinguished. The fresco of those two happy children playing on the beach was all that remained of what they once had been, until in three thousand years archaeologists began to recover some long-dead artifacts.

Suddenly I could see stars through the windows. I had completed my jump upStream.

Winds began buffeting the box and I reached for the controls to stabilize it. Below was a jagged claw of an island, all that remained of Thera now that the caldera had collapsed. Supported by the a-grav units, I was floating above dark, low, lazy rollers highlighted by a pale sheen of moonlight.

Down on the water, a half mile distant, I saw a beacon flash. A gust of wind caught the box and spun it, but I kept the beacon in sight as I corrected, and began to head for it.

I hovered above a small motor yacht, forty feet long. Aft of the pilot house, the deck had been modified to take a helicopter, a-grav unit, or—not surprisingly—a home-made time box such as mine. I turned on my landing spots and brought the box down. I waited. I kept the landing lights on so that anyone looking inside would do so with dazzled eyes.

A figure came strolling aft from the pilot house. I caught moonlight glinting on blonde hair. As I opened the door of the box, she said, "Did you get it?"

I wondered who she was. Scorsese's patron? Navigator? Lover? I'd never know.

I shot her with Scorsese's pistol and then moved out of the time box and into the empty pilot house. I searched the rest of the yacht and found no one else. Nor, unfortunately, did I find a stack of lost Leonardos. I discovered that Scorsese slept with a gun under his pillow, and that his companion—who had separate quarters—favored satin sheets and Chanel.

There was also an enormously powerful time-travel rig, powered by the same heavy-duty fusion unit that provided more power than a sailing yacht would need by more than a factor of a thousand, capable of moving the entire boat back and forth thousands of years. It was a setup any major university would envy, and not a few governments.

Stashed in convenient places I found a lot of nice weaponry. All the serial numbers were burned off with acid, which was useless now because we had techniques that could read the numbers-that-were; but I appreciated Scorsese's classical approach to these things. It showed he cared.

I searched Scorsese's companion for I.D. and found none, then fingerprinted her on the off chance she was a Famous Time Criminal for whom someone might be looking. She was around thirty, dressed with elegance in casual dark clothes. She looked as if she might have been fun to be around.

She also looked somewhat familiar. I looked down at her for a moment, wondering where I'd seen her before, and then decided that she might resemble someone I'd seen in 1453 C.E. or 312 B.C.E. or on the hilltop overlooking Tyre when I'd watched Alexander lead the Silver Shields across the mole. It didn't matter. Faces repeated themselves through history. Traveling through the past, I'd always been seeing people I thought I'd recognized. It was pointless trying to keep track of them all.

I didn't want to share the yacht with a dead body, so I weighted her down and threw her overboard.

Dawn had appeared above Thera's craggy face while I had been searching. The view was somewhat disorienting: it was certainly no longer the Round

Isle that I had been guarding, but it wasn't quite the modern island of Santorini, either. What would become the island of Therasia had not yet split off from the main island of Thera, and the Burnt Islands of Palea Kameni and Nea Kameni—in reality new volcanic cones growing up from the bottom of the submerged caldera—had not yet risen to the surface.

The yacht sat in the only part of the bay shallow enough for anchoring, in the inner bend of Therasia, very close to shore. I was virtually surrounded by the encircling cliffs that rose in startling majesty from the deep bay. They were striped in red, black, and pale white, and where the rising sun touched the cliffs of Therasia just to the west of me the dawn brightened and stained them so that the cliffs looked as if they were slashed and bleeding. Matching the stain on my hands, which I washed in the yacht's galley, and matching as well the color of my thoughts, which I let stand.

I jumped the yacht upStream forty hours, two nights hence, then locked everything down, put the keys in my pocket, and slept in a stateroom till dawn, a small arsenal sharing the neighboring bunk. I had a lot to think about, and I wanted to be rested when I did the thinking.

I slept very well indeed.

In the morning I took the first shower I'd had in over six months, then made myself coffee and breakfast and thought for a long moment about my good friend Alpha.

In the months since I'd been living on Thera I'd done a lot of reading in Greek mythology, and I'd noticed the prevalence of twins. There were a lot of them: Proetus and Acrisius, Castor and Polydeukes, Helen and Clytaemnestra, Herakles and Iphikles, Eteokles and Polyneikes, Bellerophon and Bellerus, to name just a few. In many cases one of the twins was immortal and the other fully human, and quite often the mortal twin had to die before the godhood of his brother was proclaimed. Castor and Polydeukes had arranged to share immortality on alternate days, but the other settlements had not seemed so equitable. Often the divine twin had a hand in the death of his brother. It was clear that battle had to be done with the mortal half of one's own self, before the freedom that was godhood could be released.

I began to think about my twin. He had not been nice to me, had acted in fact like so many of those bad twins of mythology. It seemed to me that he shouldn't be allowed to get away with it. I had as great a claim to godhood as he did.

My first idea, that of becoming a time criminal, was easily dismissed. Alpha himself had suggested it, but there were problems. I didn't have enough contacts in the criminal world, and furthermore I didn't relish having to go up against my own team. I knew how ruthless the Time Corps was. From a simple survival standpoint it wasn't a good idea.

Second thought. I could head back four hundred years minus a month or two, kill Alpha, and take his place, thus solving all my problems and satisfying the demands of mythology at the same time. I found the idea unsatisfactory.

There existed, for one thing, the slight but definitely non-zero possibility that Alpha might kill me.

For another, simply *killing* Alpha wasn't good enough.

I wanted to make him suffer first.

Third idea: I could float through history for a while, perform some minor time thefts, and then arrange that the Time Corps discover evidence connecting Alpha with the crimes. This idea had its appeal, but had the misfortune of incriminating myself as well as Alpha.

Fourth idea: I could return to Alpha's time, capture him, and strand him somewhere in the past, the Age of Heroes, say. Let him become a minor character in Homer.

That struck me as the best idea yet. I pictured him wandering about the Peloponnese, struggling to learn archaic Greek and jumping into ditches to avoid the chariots of the heroes who were racing hither and yon on errands of murder and savagery.

It seemed an appropriate punishment for being a bad twin—strand him in a place where the other bad twins could take care of him. Alpha might end up responsible for a whole new myth cycle: the wandering SEAL.

And then, as I drank my third cup of coffee and wandered mentally through fantasies of revenge, one of those stray memories, unconnected to anything in my conscious thoughts, suddenly broke surface in my mind, and I remembered where I'd seen Scorsese's lady friend before.

I went to the pilot house, spent some time working out the controls, then weighed anchor and piloted the yacht out of the bay, through the deep channel—narrower than in my own time—between Therasia and Apronisi. Once away from the island, I set the autopilot to take us on a fast sweep in the general direction of Cyrenaica and spent the rest of the day methodically searching every piece of paper on the yacht, finding very little.

I did, however, find a twenty-first-century map of western Greece, with a course worked on it that led into the northern entrance to the Bay of Navarino, and with some temporal coordinates marked onto it: 23:01:01, November 11, 1699 C.E.

Eleventh hour, eleventh day, eleventh month. Thieves with a sense of history. Hoodlums in general seemed to be improving.

I spent the next three days cruising in autopilot circles halfway between Kithera and Malta, well out of sight of land where no contemporary navigator would dare venture, while I went through every file I could dig out of the yacht's computer. It was all coded, of course, but the Time Corps had taught me a number of classified and for the most part highly illegal skills, and by the end of that time I'd cracked the file open.

I found that the yacht was called *Simon's Folly* and belonged to a Honduran holding company controlled principally by an interlocking directorate chartered in TanUganda, the seats of the directorate held by both private individuals and representatives of financial institutions scattered hopelessly throughout the world. The current owners were also the sixth group in four years. The papers on the boat were almost impossible to trace. No help there.

I didn't find out who Simon was, either.

I did, on the other hand, recover the codes for a dozen numbered bank accounts in places like Tobago, Singapore, and the Republic of Thule. It appeared that Scorsese had a bad memory for numbers, and had to keep them in his computer files, the ones he thought were secure.

Better and better.

I moved the fresco to more spacious quarters in the yacht's cargo bay, and then jumped upStream. It took eight subjective days to reach my own present, battling the Stream currents all the way. Moving an individual costs much less energy and effort than moving a whole yacht, which is why the Theran salvage team was going the easy way, letting the Stream currents assist the move—but I had no choice. I lived, bored out of my skull, in the self-contained environment of Scorsese's time box, the yacht itself not being airtight. I'd seen prison cells that were bigger. I ate canned food and kept myself amused with isometric exercises and thoughts of revenge.

I tried reading Sophocles' Theban trilogy, two plays rescued from oblivion by the Time Authority's scholars and the *Seven Against Thebes* that had survived on its own, but the plays were about a family that went to hell, and brothers who killed each other, and I didn't want to think about that subject at all.

There was nothing else to read. All Scorsese had were magazines written in Italian, which I don't read, and adding to the frustration was the fact that most of the magazines were filled with crossword puzzles. The near-naked women illustrating the puzzle books, however, provided some consolation.

Once happily in the twenty-first century I spent some time on the radiotelephone and made several calls to Tobago, Singapore, et cetera. I presented the codes and quietly transferred all funds to new accounts, then wiped all record of the transactions from the computer.

However this came out, I was going to be rich.

Then I routed a telephone call through several satellites and through Gibraltar, Tientsin, Aden, Nairobi, and Salt Lake City, which I hoped would confuse anyone trying to trace it. "Extension Two One Nine," I said, and hoped the right man would pick up.

"Macintyre," a voice said.

"Mac," I said. "Do you recognize the sound of my voice?"

The answer came after a long pause: the signal was being routed through so many satellites and exchanges it was taking nearly three seconds for my words to get to New York.

"Yes," Macintyre said. I pictured him in his wheelchair at the Time Corps regional office in New York, his beefy face lit by humming data banks.

"I need to vet some prints," I said, "but the query can't go into the record."

"Can't do it," Macintyre said, again after a long delay. His voice was Scots, modified by years of living in America. "You know I have to log every inquiry," he said. "Records go to about a dozen different departments."

"I also know," I said, "that you were one of the best time agents in the Corps, and that you know ways to make log entries disappear." I tried to put all the urgency in the world into my voice. "This is very important, Mac. It's Scorsese."

The next silence was longer than it had to be. "Do you have the bastard?" he asked.

"Yes," I said. "Just about."

"Call back in thirty minutes. My supervisor will be out to lunch by then."

I routed the next call through Berlin, Hong Kong, Beirut, Baku, Darwin, and Bogota. There must have been B's in my mind for some reason.

"Macintyre," said the voice.

"This is Valli," I said. "Do you have my information?"

"No need for phony names," he said. "Just send me the prints, okay?" He sounded edgy.

I passed the scanner over the prints I'd taken, then waited for Macintyre's confirmation that he'd received them.

"Running," he said, and then, "I have positive I.D."

I tapped the yacht's computer. "Ready for download," I said.

I watched the file load into memory, and then I thanked Macintyre.

"Just nail Scorsese for me," he said, and hung up.

Again I pictured him in the little blank-walled duty room, a redfaced, thick-necked man in a wheelchair, putting on weight now that he wasn't as active as once he'd been.

Once he'd been an athlete, a star rugby player.

For the last twelve years he'd been pissing into a plastic bag because of the bullet Scorsese had put into his spine in Florence.

I called up the dossier and paged through it. The woman's name was Kaetie Verberne, and she was an investment counselor in Amsterdam.

I had seen her once before, on the arm of Gautier de La Tour, the comptroller-general of the International Time Authority at The Hague.

Time theft gets a lot of attention from the press, but the most sophisticated form of time crime is not theft, but investment. Once a time criminal can acquire some of the local currency—by unloading an art treasure stolen a few centuries earlier, say—he can put the money into places where he knows it will increase. Then he can take the money, buy another art treasure with it, and repeat the whole procedure until he's got enough money to live happily ever after.

In general, this brand of criminal only gets caught if he gets too greedy and calls attention to himself. The Corps doesn't have the personnel to police every investment market throughout history.

Gautier de La Tour appeared often in the tabloids, because he was a photogenic man with striking blue eyes and a halo of white hair, because he was a prominent bachelor and a very wealthy man. I began to wonder if he'd inherited his money from himself.

The office of comptroller-general of the Time Authority handles disbursement of all the Corps' funds, for all periods, in all currencies. The comptroller-general doesn't have access to the operational side, but he provides funds for operations and thus is in a good position to guess where the operations would be, the better to avoid them.

If de La Tour was a time criminal, he might also have partners high in the Time Corps. I couldn't trust anyone even in my own outfit.

Except maybe one person.

I took the *Folly* into Malta and bought some supplies and a lot of reading material in languages I understood. All light reading, nothing about family tragedies or twins or brothers who kill each other. Then I took the *Folly* one week downStream and entered Palermo, where I checked into a hotel with an attached gym and spent a week getting myself into good physical condition. I rented a welding rig and spent some time making modifications to the back of the time box.

I also sent out six letters to some people I thought I could trust, with other letters enclosed and a note to mail them to the addressees enclosed if I hadn't contacted them in the next month. De La Tour might have a hard time stopping six letters from reaching six different people, or so I hoped.

Then I headed back to Thera and the thirteenth century B.C.E.

There, two hundred years following the island's destruction, I anchored for another week and got myself into shape again. I ran daily, worked out, did a lot of target practice. I was ready.

I took the time box back to 1461, at the end of July. I landed at night, high on the volcano at four in the morning, when Alpha would most likely be sound asleep—we had been taught that people sleep most soundly just before dawn. I told the time box to meet me in a few days, then watched as it winked out of sight. I found a good observation post and settled in.

I covered one area of the island thoroughly, then dropped back in time to cover another. I played it cautiously, not wanting to go into buildings on the chance he might be there, and after six days of subjective searching I found him.

He was leaving Agia Therasia on his patrol, still doing his job, keeping the principal sites under guard. Perhaps he was scared not to.

I followed him for three days. He did not seem a happy man. He looked as if he had lost weight, and he had developed a new nervous twitch, always looking over his shoulder. He was staying in shape and doing a lot of target practice and martial arts, but his exercises seemed to lack conviction. ...

Twice I trailed him to the villa. He worked a lot with his notebook and a pocket computer, obviously trying to find a way to go downStream and edit me without losing Scorsese in the process. He seemed very uncertain.

Once I left him there and went through Agia Therasia to find where he was living. He'd rigged some booby traps, but I knew myself well enough to look for them and had no trouble. He was living in the three-story Minoan complex, where he had a good view of the town. He had found a bed that fit him—evidently there was a Minoan giant in residence—but his belongings were disorganized, scattered around in a random way, as if his morale was suffering.

At least he had indoor toilets.

I had worked out a number of ways to get to him, but in the end I went into the Minoan building when he was away and drugged his water supply. After he was out I disarmed him, cuffed his hands, took his chronometer, cuffed his feet to his bed, and made some coffee for when he woke up. His eyelids began to twitch, and then they cracked open. When they focused on me I gave him a nod.

"You'll notice," I said, "that I don't call you Fubar."

"Piss off," he said, without conviction, and shut his eyes again.

"I'd drink this coffee if I were you," I said. "We've got a lot to talk about." He shook his head to clear it, then opened his eyes again, staring at me uncertainly from beneath his eyebrows, and reached his cuffed hands toward me. I handed him the coffee mug. He sipped it noisily.

I waited patiently for caffeine and adrenaline to burn the drug away. Alpha looked at me levelly over the rim of the mug, saying nothing. Even considering the drug, he was more relaxed than seemed reasonable; he was slumped back against the wall behind his bed, perfectly at ease, showing no apprehension or curiosity. I began to wonder whether he had some trap set for me, but then I realized that what he was feeling was relief.

The worst had happened. He didn't have to worry any more.

"You'll be pleased to know," I said, "that I've been following your advice. I've become a time criminal—a fairly modest one, but successful. I've stolen a number of pieces, and I've stowed them in places where they're sure to turn up sooner or later. They're hidden in places traceable to me, with my—our—fingerprints on them.

"Only *I* know where they're hidden. Therefore, only *I* am able to remove the evidence and prevent myself from being arrested, sooner or later, in our own time."

I paused and made sure that I had his attention. It seemed to me that I did.

"Get it straight," I said, "you're not ever going back to our own time. If you did, you'd be arrested and tried by our friends, and the only way to explain how the evidence got there is to explain our duplication, and then they'd nail you for *that*."

I gave him a thin smile. "*You* know what they're like," I said.

"You have plans for me, I assume," Alpha said. "Otherwise you wouldn't be here."

So I told him. He listened carefully, scratching the bristles on his chin, and when he was done, I nodded. "I agree," he said.

I thought he might.

"It may occur to you," I said, "that the time thieves may make you a better offer than I have. I don't think they'll take a shine to you. Even if they help you get rid of me your status will make them nervous, and it won't be long before they edit you."

"I guess," he said.

"Think about it," I said. "You'll see I'm right."

He said nothing, but I think he agreed with me.

I cuffed his hands behind his back and then freed his feet. We left the town and moved up the slope of the volcano to where the time box would be waiting for us, then I strapped his chronometer to his shackled wrist, set coordinates, pressed his go-button, then jumped upStream myself.

I cuffed him to the back of the time box, to staples I'd welded there. I had a cot, food, and a portable toilet for him, and for the long ride to the nineteenth century C.E. he was only slightly less comfortable than I was.

I assumed that de La Tour had backup. Now, so did I.

I steamed the *Folly* around the Peloponnese and set the autopilot to make circles beyond the horizon, off the Bay of Navarino, where fifty years down Stream Greek independence had been won by the last wooden fleet to fight under sail. Then I waited for night and flew the time box to land.

On Sphacteria, the island that filled the central mouth of the bay, the Athenian fleet and army had once trapped a Spartan army, forcing it to surrender and ending their claims to invincibility. A few miles farther inland the wise king Nestor had once built his palace and lived for five generations, until the Dorians burned the palace down and drove him to exile in Athens. On the southern end of the bay, the Turks had watched from their giant Byzantine-built castle as their fleet was destroyed, and their rule in Greece ended.

Alpha and I intended to make a little history ourselves.

We looked like pinups for a mercenary journal, wearing brown-and-green camouflage body armor and tight-fitting caps pulled down over our hair. Our faces and hands were smeared with camouflage paint and our boots had camouflage spats. Our packs contained a three-day supply of water and concentrated rations for two weeks. On our belts were small personal communicators with an antenna that ran around our bodies, and connections for throat mics and for the mastoid receivers in our specs. I had a silenced pistol in my armpit and another in the small of my back, spectacles adjustable to day or night conditions, my rifle with its sniper attachments and self-powered night scope. I had knives on my belt, boot, and left sleeve, and strangling wires threaded through my belt, collar, and bootlaces.

I was so deadly it was ridiculous.

Alpha was similarly equipped, minus the guns. And of course the fact his hands were cuffed behind his back tended to constrain his image.

We landed the time box on the night of September 4, 1899, in a grove of tall pine. There was a gusty wind blustering in from the west, bringing the scent of the sea to mingle with the brisk pine odor. I took a pistol and shoulder holster from the storage compartment, picked up Alpha's pack, and walked across the bed of pine needles to place them under a tree. Then I returned to the time box, drew one of my pistols, and pointed it at Alpha while I released his leg irons. Then I stepped backward, gestured him to the door, and with the pistol on him released his handcuffs.

He rubbed his wrists and looked at me resentfully over his shoulder.

"Was that absolutely necessary?" he asked.

"You'd know better than I would," I said. "There's your pistol and your pack over there. You have three days to get in shape and get used to the weapon. I'll be back at sunset, September 7, and I'll expect you to have a thorough knowledge of the terrain and conditions of the island. When I get back, I'll expect to see you reclining under that tree, with your pistol placed in plain sight at least ten feet away. Got that?"

He nodded. "You're not cutting me any slack, are you?" he asked. There was a forlorn sound to his voice.

I slammed the door and jumped four days into the past.

There I did much the same thing I had told Alpha to do. I sent the time box on ahead, then scouted Sphacteria thoroughly, took bearings on local landmarks, and found the best places for observing the *Folly* on the night of September 11. The island was heavily timbered with pine and wild olive, and the number of good observation points were few. I made a map of everything.

Then, using my chronometer, I jumped upStream to the night before I had planned to pick up Alpha. I slept, woke before dawn, and climbed a pine tree for the day.

I saw Alpha every now and again, moving among the other pines. He came into the clearing every so often, looking very much as I had seen him when he was back on Thera, when he was staring at the villa and trying to calculate all the options. In the end he walked into the clearing, dropped his pistol on the ground, and moved off by the tree where I told him I'd meet him. There I watched while he ate some dinner and then freshened his camouflage paint. "Hello," I said.

He looked at me without expression. I dropped from the tree, repossessed his pistol, and spread out my map. "I've worked it all out," I said.

"Glad to hear it, sport," he said. I looked at him sharply. He was flashing a superior grin. He seemed to have his confidence back, which indicated to me that he'd made up his mind.

I wondered which way.

I cuffed him again, explained the plan, and jumped us both upStream to 2100 on the night of the 11th. I pocketed his chronometer and took off his handcuffs. "Your pistol will be behind that tree," I said, jumped downStream twenty hours, put the gun behind the tree, moved about a quarter mile to the east, and then jumped to nine o'clock on the night of the 11th again.

If Alpha had made up his mind to join the opposition, there was no point in making it easy for him.

The land breeze had come up, hissing seaward through the wild olives and tall evergreens. It would make this easier.

The theory and practice of obtaining backup through time travel, as practiced by the better class of crooks, is simple: one's earlier self, one's Alpha, heads upStream to a spot overlooking the site of the planned meeting, ambush, or suspected setup, and observes whatever it is that happens to one's later self, one's Beta. If it's bad, Alpha always has a chance to assist, and if it's very bad, he can always head downStream again, become Beta, and simply not show up, creating a paradox loop that might prove dangerous for other reasons but in any case escaping the trap.

It was, therefore, imperative for me and my own Alpha to eliminate any backup de La Tour had arranged, before the backup had a chance to tell de La Tour his meeting was going to end in disaster.

My chief worry at this point was whether Scorsese and de La Tour had arranged for a private signal to be exchanged between them prior to the meet. If so, de La Tour simply wouldn't show up, and this whole exercise would be for nothing.

Moving on beds of pine needles, I moved north, walking only when the sound of wind would cover my noises. My chronometer was set to move me instantly forty-four hours and twenty-three minutes into the past, in case I was spotted—I used an oddball number, hoping that a hypothetical enemy wouldn't guess it. When I wasn't looking through my specs I was peering into my night scope.

At first sight of the figure I thought he was Alpha. He was way out of position and that meant he had joined the enemy, and at the thought he was working for the bad guys, I felt anxiety begin to gnaw at my vitals.

And then my second look showed that the still figure in my specs didn't have the right silhouette to be Alpha, but was someone shorter and a little softer-looking, dressed in commando rig with a definite Time Corps flair.

Corps surplus, maybe, and maybe the backup was Corps surplus, too. I'd have to be careful.

I scanned the trees around the sentry and saw no one.

He was lying in a fine vantage point, sweeping the island and the sea below him with night binoculars. Once he turned and swept behind him, and I dodged behind a tree and hoped he hadn't caught the movement.

Just then I heard a voice from the mastoid receiver built into my specs.

"Beta." Alpha's voice, a little hushed. "Bandit at Station Seven. He got up to take a leak, and he stepped right into me. I had to kill him. Sorry."

"Check," I whispered. I didn't want to say anything more for fear my own bandit would hear.

Alpha and I had been taught sentry removal of course: moving slowly, synchronizing movement with the sentry's breathing, moving when the wind provided cover, trying to remember not to foul one's underwear while stalking an armed and dangerous enemy.

Lucky I didn't have to do any of that.

I simply jumped downStream three days, walked out to where the sentry stood, and jumped upStream to his own time. I put my foot on his wrist chronometer to keep him in the present and dropped my rifle butt, hard, on the back of his head.

He was a little shorter than I, with a thick neck and long arms. He looked like an athlete, a wrestler maybe, who had gone a little soft around the middle. I collected a radio on his belt, then I searched him, stripped him of weapons, cuffed his hands and feet, and put my hand to my throat mic to tell Alpha.

It suddenly occurred to me that if Alpha's sentry had been equipped similarly to this man, Alpha was now armed as well as I was, and had time travel capability to boot. I could be edited at any second. I spun around and went for my rifle.

"Hello, Fubar," said Alpha.

I froze. He was holding a pistol pointed at the center of my chest. He had a belt radio like the one on the guard I'd just hammered. There was a rifle strapped over his shoulder and a Corps-issue chronometer on his wrist. No need to guess how he got here.

Alpha's eyes looked at me soberly. "I wonder," he said, "how truthful you were when you told me about all those stolen objects you'd planted on me."

"I wouldn't lie about a thing like that," I said.

Alpha gave a little frown and rubbed his chin. "Maybe," he said. "But I'd like to think about it for a while. Keep your hands where I can see them while I meditate."

He squatted down on his heels near me. He cocked his head to one side, his eyes looking at me with wary consideration. "I could," he said, "get the truth out of you one way or another. "

"You wouldn't know if it's the truth," I said. "You could take me apart, and even then you wouldn't know for certain."

Alpha gave a thin smile and rubbed his chin with his left hand again. The pistol was very steady in his right. "Maybe," he said.

I looked down through the trees and saw the lights of the *Folly* out to sea, moving in to the rendezvous point. I wondered which of us was in the pilot house, Alpha or me.

The sentry I'd knocked out began to cough, then he started rolling from side to side. With my right hand, I reached into my breast pocket and pulled out a handkerchief. I reached for our prisoner. "I'd better gag him," I said. "He might call his friends."

And then, while Alpha was still making up his mind about that one, his eyes on the white handkerchief in my right hand, I slapped the prisoner on the head with my left wrist, hitting the preset go-button with the prisoner's skull.

In the space of a breath I was forty-four hours and twenty-three minutes downStream.

My chronometer showed the exact second of departure. I moved about two paces to the southeast, drew the pistol from my armpit, set the chronometer for departure in two seconds, then readied the pistol.

I saw Alpha crouched in front of me, left hand still raised to scratch his chin.

"Hello yourself," I said. "Please drop the pistol and raise your left hand high."

His shoulders sagged as the breath went out of him, and he did as he was told. I handcuffed his wrists to his ankles. Searched him carefully and disarmed him.

He looked over his shoulder at me. "I wouldn't have hurt you," he said. "The worst I would have done was strand you someplace while I found out whether you were telling the truth or not."

"Maybe," I said. Once I was certain he couldn't adjust his own chronometer, I set it for him, then I set the chronometer of the guy I'd knocked out, and then my own. "Hold your breath," I told Alpha, and then, after a long moment of transit, dawn exploded over the island. I blinked in the sudden light. It was August 28, and the crystal ocean surged below us as the western rollers came in.

I took the chronometers from Alpha's wrist and from the wrist of the sentry. He looked up at me dully, then with increasing interest. Blood was smearing the camouflage paint on his temple.

I addressed him in English. He looked at me blankly. I tried Dutch, German, demotic Greek, classical Greek, and classical Greek with the accent of the Kyklades, all without response.

"The hell with it," I said. "I think you speak English." I shot him in the foot.

"Jesus Christ!" he said. I glanced up and happened to meet Alpha's gaze. He grinned at me.

"Your friends aren't going to save you," I told our prisoner. "They've been taken care of. You're the sole survivor. What I want to know is the time and space coordinates for meeting de La Tour."

"Jesus Christ," the man said again. Sweat patterns were appearing in his paint.

"If I don't get the information very soon," I said, "I'm going to shoot you in the knee." I dropped the butt of the pistol on his knee, hard, and watched him jump. "And then," I went on, "if you still don't tell me what I want to know, I'll find someplace else to shoot you." I moved his leg and pointed it at his crotch.

"Just in case what you tell me is a fib," I said, "I'll gag you, tie you up, and drag you off under a tree somewhere. I bet with a foot wound like that, and the summer heat here in August, dehydration will get you inside of twenty-four hours. Your friends won't know where to look for you, even if they feel inclined to come to help you."

My prisoner made a bubbling sound and looked frantically over his shoulder at Alpha.

"What the hell's going on?" he demanded. "He's not gonna actually do it, is he?" He looked up at me again, his eyes white as he strained his neck in my direction. "You wouldn't, would you?" he asked. "Not to a fellow Corpsman?"

Alpha gave a dry chuckle. I looked at him in surprise.

"I'd tell him if I were you," he said to our prisoner. "I'm his twin brother, and look what he's done to me."

The geek looked at me again, his eyes wider than ever, and I smiled at him. It was an effective smile, I knew.

Alpha had used it on *me.*

He looked at my smile and spilled everything he knew. His name was Hogan, and he was one of only two guards. De La Tour was floating overhead at 0300 on September 19, waiting for the code that would summon him down to pick up his men. He would have to get the code on two different frequencies before he'd come down, and he'd insist on seeing two bodyguards below him.

In the absence of an anti-aircraft missile, there seemed only one way of getting to him. I scratched my chin and looked up at Alpha.

"Up to you, sport," he shrugged.

I looked down at the sea. The *Folly* was getting closer, and I could see the faint outline of its cabin roof illuminated faintly by its running lights. Who was behind the wheel? I wondered. De La Tour or me? I decided what I was going to do.

"Back in a second," I said. I collected most of the weaponry—there was getting to be a lot of it—jumped upStream to the point where my own time box would meet me, and stored the excess in the box. Then I took the rifle and pistol Alpha had taken from the guard he'd killed and emptied them of ammunition. I jumped back to Alpha's time and undid his handcuffs.

"Here's your guns," I said. "They won't shoot, so don't try. Pick up Hogan here, and let's move inland."

Alpha got Hogan in a fireman carry and we moved up the spine of the island. We left Hogan bound and gagged under a tree, assured him the medics were on their way, and then Alpha preceded me to the high clearing above which, in another three weeks or so, de La Tour would hover, waiting for the signal to bring him down.

Still in the cover of the pines, I handcuffed Alpha again, then put his chronometer on and set it for the time when de La Tour would expect his call. I waited for Alpha to make his jump, then jumped directly behind Alpha a few seconds before he appeared, my pistol in one hand and the keys to the handcuffs in the other. I took Alpha's chronometer and unlocked his cuffs. He straightened. "How long did you give us?" he asked.

"About two minutes. Stay at least ten meters away from me, right?"

Ten meters is enough distance to be sure of bringing down a charging man with a pistol shot. Any closer, and there's a chance he'll hit you before you can squeeze the trigger.

Alpha nodded and pulled his cap down lower over his forehead. "Let's go."

He unslung his empty rifle and walked with me into the clearing in the pines. De La Tour would only appear overhead for a few seconds, and he had to be given the codes then, otherwise he'd vanish. Never to return, possibly, or, as was more likely, to return with a dozen heavies who would edit all our work, and us with it.

I looked up. It was a clear night, only a high, light scud of cloud between me and the Milky Way. The vast spread of stars had altered since my last night on Thera—some of the old Greek constellations were a little less obvious—and though they shone several degrees brighter than in my own time, they were clearly less brilliant than they had been on old Thera. Atmospheric pollution had already had its effect in 1899, even here in rural, wind-swept Greece.

And suddenly there was a shadow thrown against the Milky Way, a time box hovering after its leap through the Stream, spinning in the warm land breeze. I raised the belt radio and pressed the send button.

"Seventeen Eighty-Nine," I mumbled.

Alpha raised his own radio. "Eighteen-Fifteen," he said.

It was a simple code, if a little Francocentric. No message at all meant run and don't stop. 1812 meant the jig is up, come get us, then run. 1940 meant run without picking us up. I wonder if de La Tour honestly expected anyone to send the last.

The time box swept lower, and then its lights stabbed on. I blinked, my glasses polarizing themselves against the glare as I threw up an arm. De La Tour apparently had no qualms about creating a UFO above Navarino in 1899.

He was expecting to see two armed men in camouflage gear, and that was what he saw. His perspective was awkward, hovering a couple hundred yards above us, and he was also busy with controlling the time box in the high breeze. Probably after his initial glance at us, he was paying attention only to his landing.

He came down clumsily, fighting the breeze, then nearly going into the trees before he relocated himself over the clearing. He stabilized and then dropped the box toward the ground. Alpha and I, still holding our hands up to shield our eyes against the lights, began walking toward him.

The box hit the ground and the lights went off. I kept on walking. I heard the sound of a door opening, and then de La Tour stepped out.

I raised my pistol and pointed it directly between his startled, much-photographed blue eyes.

"Hi there, Fubar," I said, and from the corner of my eye I saw Alpha smile.

The end, I thought, was quite cinematic. On the first of September, 1481 B.C.E., a couple dozen Time Corps transports appeared above the black sand beach near Agia Therasia. They lowered themselves to the ground, and their occupants piled out. The collection of Corpsmen, archaeologists, anthropologists, art experts, classicists, and historians had scant time to adjust to the staggering beauty of the place before they saw *Simon's Folly* tearing toward them at thirty knots.

I ended with an escort of hovercraft, and from the flybridge I waved to them as I executed a smart ninety-degree turn, then threw the engines in neutral and pushed the button that kicked the anchor overboard. I lowered myself down the companion and waited on the aft landing deck for my compatriots to arrive.

The first hovercraft touched lightly, and a man jumped out. He was a man I knew slightly, a Belgian paratrooper named Rabaut.

"I think," I told him, "that I'd like some Theran wine. It's been a while."

I had left Hogan and de La Tour bound and gagged upStream in 1899, and would give the Corps their coordinates so that they could be picked up. I hadn't wanted to be burdened with them during the long journey into the past, and besides I knew there was an active Time Corps court-martial board sitting regularly around 1860 or so, and that they would be happy to deal with Scorsese's friends.

I had also wanted to deal with Alpha quietly, without any witnesses. Hogan had seen him of course, but I would simply claim I'd duplicated myself temporarily in order to handle the situation on the island.

The Corps wouldn't inquire too closely. The military rarely investigates successful operations as carefully as they do the failures.

I tied Alpha up again as soon as we'd finished with de La Tour, and then jumped downStream to where I had Scorsese's time box waiting. I shackled Alpha where he belonged, then hopped to where the *Folly* was orbiting offshore, and on the night of the eleventh I took the yacht in for the meeting that never happened.

After waiting for an hour next to my rifle just in case something had gone horribly wrong, I took the *Folly* out to sea again, made myself a very good meal, drank a bottle of wine, and then locked myself in Scorsese's time box again for a ride of almost thirty centuries.

It was night again when the *Folly* splashed out of Stream at 02:01:01, June 1, 1255 B.C.E. I brought the yacht in close to the sandbar north of the island, where the Athenian forces under Demosthenes would one day beat off the Spartans under Brasidas, and then I let the anchor go. The splash and roar of the chain must have awakened every shepherd for miles: they'd never heard Poseidon so angry. It might cause some questions at the court of Nestor tomorrow morning, but I'd decided I'd rather disturb the shepherds' sleep than risk having the *Folly* drift aground in the Bronze Age.

I drew my pistol, readied it, and walked into the time box where Alpha was waiting. He looked up.

"Doesn't the condemned get a last meal?" he asked.

"No time," I said, and unshackled him from the wall, backed out of the time box, then gestured for him to come to the rail.

I had some equipment waiting for him: concentrated rations, a couple knives, a first aid kit, water purification tablets, and a pair of flashlights. "The Trojan War will heat up in another year or two," I said. "Pylos is just over those hills, and King Nestor will be needing soldiers. Remember all those presents everyone is always giving in the *Iliad*—you can gain status out there by the quality of your gifts. Those flashlights should get you far. So should the steel knives, if you want to part with them."

He opened the pack and looked at the knives. "Too bad we don't carry swords," he said.

"Your body armor should help, if you decide to get into the local military. And I expect you can make your living as a surgeon."

He didn't look enthusiastic. I didn't blame him.

Originally I'd planned to leave him in 1899; but then I realized what chaos could result when he started coming up with nonstick fry pans, sound cinema cameras, and television, not to mention what could happen if he started putting his mind to helping one side or other in the Great War. The Bronze Age was safer by far.

Alpha raised his head, looking toward the shore. "It's good to smell the land," he said, and meant goodbye.

He hit the water cleanly, shooting through the water like the dolphins in the fresco still battened in the *Folly's* hold, and then began a steady breast stroke, a slight phosphorescence trailing out behind him in the water. I watched his bobbing head until I lost it among the dark waves, and then moved to the bridge and hauled up the anchor, readying myself for Thera and my moment of fame.

I wondered what sort of legend he'd leave behind him in his wanderings through that savage era. The legends are murky enough, and clarification by time travelers is necessarily circumspect. He might well have managed to carve his way to power, if that was the path he'd chosen, and become a figure of legend.

Only I could have stopped him, and I failed to work myself up to it: I knew all along I couldn't kill him. The conflict between us was always in terms of which of us would be condemned to the past.

In which case it was I, not Alpha, who was the Bad Twin.

I had denied my brother Olympus, and condemned him to the life of a mortal.

I wrote this story at some point in the early Eighties, fairly early in my career as a science fiction writer. The exact date seems to have been lost in the mists of time. I was engaged in trying on various types of science fiction for size, and decided to write a time travel story with as many paradoxes as I could devise. I used a setting, the Bay of Navarino, which I had recently visited, and which made a strong impression on me at the time.

I succeeded in selling "The Bad Twin" to an editor who kept the story for several years, though somehow without actually printing it. When the story finally came back to me, I had become interested in other things, and never sent it out again.

I recently re-read "The Bad Twin," and decided that with a little re-writing it would not embarrass me too deeply to see it in print. It has many of the characteristics of my writing at the time: a massive reliance on detailed background knowledge, a tendency toward discursiveness, and more ideas than can be comfortably fit into a single short narrative. But I found that it had its charms, too, and I hope these charms are not invisible to all but myself.

Red Elvis

Here it is, the white house south of the city on US 51. The Memphis Palace of Labor. The district is called Whitehaven and is tony, but the Palace itself sits on the highway opposite some ugly strip malls, a John Deere dealer, and a burger joint.

It's a big house made of Tennessee fieldstone, with a portico and a green lawn and some little mean shacks out back for the servants. It's not the sort of place you'd expect at all, not for the person who lived there. It's the sort of house a boss would live in.

There's a long, long line of mourners out front, stretching from the front door across the drive and for half a mile down Highway 51. The harmonies of a black gospel choir sound faintly from the interior.

Join the long, slow line of mourners who file past the coffin. Hear the music that rings somehow inside you.

Remember who the dead man was, and why you're here.

The boy knows that he had a brother who is just like him, except that he is an angel. They were twins—identical twins, because there was the same webbing between two of their toes—and the eldest lived and the youngest was born dead. And the boy's Mamma tells him that this fact makes him special, that even before he was born, he made his brother an angel.

But that doesn't mean that the boy can't talk to his brother when he wants to. His Mamma takes him to the cemetery often, and the two of them sit by the brother's grave and pray to him and sing songs and tell him everything that happened since they last visited.

The boy likes the cemetery. It's so much more pleasant than the family's little two-room shanty in East Tupelo, where the wind cries like a wailing haunt through the grey clapboard walls and the furniture needs mending and the slop bucket under the sink always smells poorly.

In the cemetery, the boy can always talk to his brother and tell him everything. In the cemetery, someone is always bringing flowers.

Something bad has happened and the boy has lost his Daddy. Men with badges came and took him away. He hears new words—there is "forgery" and "arrest," along with a word whose very utterance is an occasion for terror—"Parchman." Parchman is where Daddy is going, and a man named Orville Bean is sending him there. Orville Bean is Daddy's boss.

The boy screams and weeps and clings to his Mamma's leg. The men with badges told Mamma that the family has to leave the house. The boy always thought the house belonged to Mamma, but now it belongs to Orville Bean. Suddenly the grey two-room shack is the most precious thing the boy has ever known.

Mamma pets him and calls him by his special name, but the boy won't be stilled. Grandpa and Grandma, who have come to help Mamma move the furniture, watch the boy's agony with a certain surprise.

"That Mr. Bean sure is cruel," Grandpa says. "Boss don't have no mercy on a working man."

That night the boy prays to his brother to rescue Daddy, to fly him out of Parchman on angels' wings, but his brother doesn't answer.

Mamma's real name is Satnin, though everyone else calls her Gladys. She and the boy are never apart. She won't let the boy do anything that might hurt him, like swim or dive, or play with other children outside of Mamma's sight. He sleeps with Satnin every night so that nothing can harm him.

Satnin teaches him things to keep him safe. He learns to touch iron after he sees a black cat, and that if you have a spell cast on you, you can take the spell off with a Jack, which is a red cloth filled with coal dust and dirt and a silver dime. The boy learns that most dreams aren't true but that some are, and that Satnin's dreams are almost always true. When she dreams about something bad that's going to happen, she'll do something to prevent it, like make a cake, with special ingredients, that she'll feed to a dog to carry the bad luck away.

After Daddy comes back from Parchman, he gets a job in a war plant in Memphis, so he's home only on weekends. The boy spends all his time with his mother.

When the boy grows old enough for school, his Mamma walks with him to school every morning, then home in the afternoon. They still visit the cemetery regularly so that the boy can talk to his brother, who is an angel.

Sometimes the boy thinks he can hear his brother's voice. "I will always be with you," his brother says. "I am in Heaven and you are special and I will watch out for you always."

The boy is a Christian, which is good because when he dies, he will go to Heaven and see his brother. The boy and Satnin and Daddy go to the Assembly of God Church in East Tupelo, and they sing along with Daddy's cousin Sayles, who is in the choir. The Reverend Smith is a nice, quiet man who teaches the boy a few chords on the guitar.

In the Church, the boy receives his baptism of the spirit and gives away everything he owns to other children. His comic books and his bike and all his money. His Daddy keeps bringing the bike back, but the boy only gives it away again. Finally his Daddy gives up and lets the boy give the bike away for good.

"You are a good boy to give everything away," his brother whispers. "We will live together in Heaven and be happy forever."

The family moves to Memphis so that Daddy can find work. The boy is sad about leaving his brother behind in the cemetery, but his brother tells him that he is really in Heaven, not the cemetery, and the boy can still talk to him anytime he likes.

The family lives in the Lauderdale Courts, part of the projects run by the Housing Authority. Everyone in the projects works except for Satnin, who spends all her time with her boy. Daddy has a job at United Paint, but he can't earn too much or the Housing Authority will make the family move.

"They never let a workingman get ahead," he says.

The boy goes to Humes High School, where he's in the ninth grade. Mamma still walks him to and from school every day, but the boy has his own bed now, and he sleeps alone. He has nightmares almost every night and doesn't know why.

Sometimes he takes his guitar outside to the steps of the Lauderdale Courts and sings. People from the projects always stop what they're doing and form a half circle around him and listen. It's as if they're bewitched. Their staring makes the boy so self-conscious that he sings only after dark, so that he doesn't have to see the way they look at him.

He looks in the mirror and sees this little cracker kid in overalls, nothing he wants to be. He tries to make what he sees better. One time he has Satnin give his fine, blond hair a permanent. Another time he cuts his hair off except for a Mohawk strip down the middle.

One day, during summer vacation, the boy goes to the picture show and sees *The City Across the River,* with a new actor named Tony Curtis. He watches entranced at the story of the poor working kids who belong to a gang called the "Amboy Dukes," and who wear flashy clothes and have their hair different from anyone the boy has ever seen. Tony Curtis's hair is perfect, long and shiny, winged on the sides, with a curl in the front and upturned in back. He talks in a funny jivey way, singsong, almost like he has his own language. It's like the language the boy's brother speaks in dreams.

The boy watches the movie three times.

Next day he goes to a hairdresser. He knows he'll never get the haircut he wants in a barbershop. "Give me that Tony Curtis cut," he says to the astonished beautician. The boy describes what he wants and the beautician tells him the cut is called a D.A. The beautician cuts his hair, but she warns him that his blond hair is too fine to stay in the shape he wants it, and sells him a tin of Royal Crown Pomade. The pomade darkens his hair by several shades but keeps it in place and makes it gleam.

The only place the boy can think to find the right clothes is on Beale Street. It's in the colored part of town where people are killed every week, then carried away so their bodies will be found somewhere else. The boy is a little nervous going there alone, but it's daylight and it looks safe enough, and as he walks down the street, he can see colored men dressed just as he wants to be, in raw-silk jackets dyed lime green or baby blue, with Billy Eckstine collars worn turned up.

The boy finds what he wants in Lansky Brothers' store. Pleated, shiny-black pants worn high on the floating ribs, with red or yellow seams. Double-breasted jackets in glowing colors, with huge vents and sparkles in them, big enough to move around in.

He spends all his money at Lansky Brothers.

Next time he looks in the mirror, he likes what he sees.

Maybe everyone in Heaven looks like this.

In his nightmares, the boy is surrounded by enemies, all of them jeering and laughing at him. He fights them, lashing out with his fists, and often wakes with smarting knuckles from having jumped out of bed and punched the wall.

When the nightmares come true, he doesn't fight. He can't—there are too many of them, the biggest, toughest kids in school, surrounding him and calling him names. They say he dresses like a nigra pimp. They call him a sissy, a queer. He doesn't quite know what a queer is, but he knows it's bad. They threaten to cut his hair off. They knock him around every day, a jeering circle of crackers in overalls with muscles bulging out of their plaid shirts— they're everything the boy wants to get away from, everything he doesn't want to be.

In his dreams, he fights back, screaming wildly, sometimes running out of the apartment and into the hallway before he wakes. His mother makes him a charm to wear around his neck, a charm that smells of asafoetida and has a black-cat bone in it, but it doesn't keep the dreams away. His mother says he gets it from his father, who also has bad nightmares from time to time.

One day the other boys are pushing him around in the toilets. The air is blue with tobacco smoke. The boy has been bounced into the walls a few times and is being held in a headlock by one football lineman while another waves a pair of shears and threatens to cut his hair.

"I'd stop that if I were you." The voice comes from a newcomer, a big kid with a Yankee accent and the thick neck of an athlete. He's got a big jaw and a look that seems a little puzzling and unbalanced, as if his eyes are pointing in slightly different directions. His name is Schmidt and he's just transferred here from Detroit.

"You cut his hair," Schmidt says, "you better cut mine, too."

The big kids drop the boy and stand aside and mumble. The boy straightens his clothes and tries to thank Schmidt for intervening.

"Call me Leon," the big boy says.

The boy and Leon become friends. Leon plays guitar a little and sings, and the two of them go together to a party. Leon sings a Woody Guthrie song, and the boy plays accompaniment. Then the boy turns all the lights off, so he won't get self-conscious, and sings an Eddie Arnold tune, "Won't You Tell Me, Molly Darling." All the party noise stops as the other kids listen. The boy finishes the tune.

"Your turn," he says to Leon.

"Brother," Leon says, "no way I'm gonna follow that."

The boy sings all night, with Leon strumming accompaniment and singing harmony. The darkness is very friendly. The other kids listen in silence except for their applause.

Maybe, he thinks, this is what Heaven is like.

Leon is an orphan. His father died in a strike against Henry Ford just after he was born, and he'd moved South after his mother married again, this time to a truck driver whose outfit was based in Memphis.

Hearing the story of Leon's father dying after a beating by Ford strike-breakers, the boy hears an echo of his grandfather's voice: *Boss don't have no mercy on a workingman.*

Leon is always reading. The boy never had a friend who read before. The authors seem very intimidating, with names like Strachey and Hilferding and Sternberg.

"You heard Nat Dee yet?" Leon asks. He turns his radio to WDIA. He has to turn up the volume because WDIA broadcasts at only two hundred and fifty watts.

The voice the boy hears is colored and talks so fast the boy can barely make out the words. He's announcing a song by Bukka White, recorded in

Parchman Prison in Mississippi.

Parchman Prison, the boy thinks.

Nat Dee's voice is a little difficult, but the boy understands the music very well.

The singer launches himself at the microphone stand like it's his worst enemy. He knocks it down and straddles it, grabbing it near the top as if he's wringing its neck. He wears a pink see-through blouse and a blazing pink suit with black velvet trim. His eyes are made ghostly with mascara and heavy green eye shadow. He's playing the Gator Bowl in front of fourteen thousand people.

The second he appeared, a strange sound went up, a weird keening that sent hairs crawling on the necks of half the men in the audience. The sound of thousands of young girls working themselves into a frenzy.

The sound sometimes makes it difficult for the singer to hear his band, but he can always turn and see them solid behind him, Leon mimicking the Scotty Moore guitar arrangements from the records, Bill Black slapping bass, and drummer D.J. laying down the solid beat that the singer's music thrives on.

The singer has finally wrung the mike stand into submission. He rears back perilously far, right on the edge of balance, and he hops forward with little thrusts of his polished heels, holding the mike stand up above his head like a jazzman wailing sax. He thrusts his pelvis right at the audience, and the long rubber tube he's stuck down his pants in front is perfectly outlined by the taut fabric.

The eerie sound that rises from the audience goes up in intensity, in volume. State police in front of the stage are flinging little girls back as they try to rush forward. All over the South, people are denouncing his act as obscene.

Incredibly, the singer is only one of the half-dozen opening acts for Hank Snow. But some of the other performers, the Davis Sisters and the Wilburn Brothers, complain that they can't follow him onstage, so he was given the coveted slot just before the intermission.

After the recess, the headliners Slim Whitman and Hank Snow will step onstage and try to restore the program to some kind of order. Some nights they have their work cut out for them.

The singer still has nightmares every night. Satnin persuaded him to hire his cousins, Gene and Junior Smith, to sleep in the same room with him and keep him from injuring himself.

When the singer finishes his act, he's soaked in sweat. He grins into the mike, tosses his head to clear his long hair from his eyes, speaks to the audience. "Thank you, ladies and gentlemen," he says. Then he gives a wink. "Girls," he promises, "I'll see you backstage."

The screaming doubles in volume. The singer waves good-bye and starts to head off, and then out of the slant of his eye, he sees the line of state cops go down before an avalanche of little girls as if they were made of cardboard.

The singer runs for it, his terrified band at his heels. He dives down into the tunnels under the Gator Bowl, where the concrete echoes his pursuers' shrill screams. The flimsy door to his dressing room doesn't keep them out for a second. His cousins Gene and Junior Smith go down fighting. The terrified singer leaps onto the shower stall, and even there, one frantic girl in white gloves and crinolines manages to tear off one of his shoes. The singer stares at her in fascination, at the desperate, inhuman glitter in her eyes as she snatches her trophy, and he wonders what kind of beast he's liberated in her, what it is that's just exploded out of all the restraining apparel, the girdle and nylons and starched underskirts.

He doesn't know quite what it is, but he knows he likes it.

Eventually reinforcements arrive and the girls are driven out. The dressing room looks as if it has been through a hurricane. Junior Smith, a veteran of Korea, appears as if he's just relived Porkchop Hill. The singer limps on one shoe and one pink sock as he surveys the damage.

Leon wanders in, clutching his guitar. The band's first impulse had been to protect their instruments rather than their singer.

"I wouldn't make no more promises to them girls," Leon says. He talks more Southern every day.

Hank Snow arrives with a bottle of Dr Pepper in his hand. One of his business associates is with him, a bald fat man who carries an elephant-headed cane.

"I never seen nothing like it," Snow says. "Boy, you're gonna go far in this business if your fans don't kill you first."

"Junior," the singer says, "see if you can find me a pair of shoes, okay?"

"Sure, boss," Junior says.

Hank Snow points to the fat man. "I'd like to introduce a friend of mine—he manages Hank Snow Productions for me. Colonel Tom Parker."

The Colonel has a powerful blue gaze and a grip of iron. He looks at the singer in a way that makes him feel uncomfortable—it's the same look the little girl gave him, like he wants more than anyone can say, more than the singer can ever give. "I've been hearing a lot about you," the Colonel says. "Maybe you and me can do some business."

Colonel Parker does the singer a lot of good. He straightens out the tangled mess of the singer's management, puts him under exclusive contract, gets his records played north of the Mason-Dixon line, and gets a big advance from RCA that lets the singer buy his Satnin a Cadillac. Then he buys several more for himself and his band.

"I want to look good for this car," Satnin says. "I'm going to lose some weight."

Suddenly the singer is supporting his whole family. His Daddy quits his job and never takes another. Gene and Junior work for him. His Grandmother is living with his parents. Sometimes he thinks about it and gets a little scared.

But mostly he doesn't have much time to think. He and his band are on tour constantly, mostly across the South, their nights spent speeding from one engagement to another in a long line of Cadillacs, each one a different color and fronted by a half ton of solid chrome. Sometimes the cops stop him, but it's only for autographs.

"That Colonel, he's a snake-oil salesman for sure," Leon says. He's sitting in the shotgun seat while the singer drives across Georgia at three in the morning. "You better keep an eye on him."

"Ain't gonna let him cheat me," the singer says. The speedometer reads a hundred twenty-five. He laughs. "He sure is good with that hypnotism thing he does. Did you see Gene on his hands and knees, barking like a dog?"

Leon gazes at him significantly. "Do me a big favor. Don't ever let him hypnotize you."

The singer gives him a startled look, then jerks his attention back to the road. "Can't hypnotize me any way," he says, thinking of the power of the Colonel's ice-blue eyes.

"Don't let him try. He's done you a lot of good, okay. But that's just business. He doesn't own you."

"He's gonna get me a screen test with Hal Wallis."

"That's good. But don't let the Colonel or Wallis or any of those tell you what to do. You know best."

"Okay."

"*You* pick your music. *You* work out the arrangements. You need to insist on that, because these other people—" Leon waves a hand as if pulling difficult ideas out of the air. "You've got the magic, okay? They don't even know what the magic *is.* They're just bosses, and they'll use you for every dollar you can give them."

"Boss don't have no mercy on a workingman," the singer says.

Leon favors him with a smile. "That's right, big man. And don't you forget it."

The singer buys the big white house out on Highway 51, the place called Graceland. Because he's on the road so much, he doesn't spend a lot of time there. His parents live out back and install a chicken coop and a hog pen so they have something to do.

On the road, he's learned that he likes the night. He visits the South's little sin towns, Phenix City or Norfolk or Bossier City, cruising for girls he can take back to his cheap motel rooms.

When he's home in Memphis, there's no place he can go at night—Beale Street is still for colored people. So he has the state cops close off a piece of highway for motorcycle racing. He dresses up in his leathers, with his little peaked cap, and cranks his panhead Harley to well over a hundred. He does incredibly dangerous stunts at high speed—standing up on the foot pegs with his hands outstretched, away from the handlebars; reaching out to hold hands with the guy he's racing with. He's a hairbreadth from death or injury the whole time.

He thinks about the kids in school who called him a sissy, and snarls. When he's wound up the Harley and is howling down the road with the huge engine vibrating between his legs, he knows that the cry of wind in his ears is really his brother's voice, calling him home.

"What is this business?" the singer demands. "Some old burlesque comic? An Irish tenor? *Performing midgets?*"

"The Heidelberg Troupe of Performing Midgets." The Colonel grins around his cigar. "Great act. Know 'em from my carny days."

"*Carny* days?" Leon asks. "What're you trying to do, turn us into a freak show?"

The Colonel scowls at Leon. He knows who's put the singer up to this. "Why should we hire a rock act to open?" he says. "It costs money to hire Johnny Cash or Carl Perkins, and all they do is imitations of our boy anyway. We can get the vaudeville acts a lot cheaper—hell, they're happy to have the work."

"They'll make me look ridiculous," the singer says. His blond hair is dyed black for the movies he's making for Hal Wallis. He wants badly to be the next James Dean, but the critics compare him to Sonny Tufts.

The Colonel chomps down on his cigar again. "Gotta have opening acts," he says. "Since nobody's gonna pay attention to 'em anyway, we might as well have the cheap ones. More money for the rest of us that way."

"That was something—" the singer begins. He casts an uneasy look toward Leon, then turns back to the Colonel. "We had an idea. Why do we need opening acts at all?"

Puzzlement enters the Colonel's blue eyes. "Gotta have 'em," he says. "The marks'll feel cheated 'less they get their money's worth. And you gotta have an intermission between the opening acts and the main show so you can sell drinks and programs and souvenirs."

"So we'll give them their money's worth *without* an opening act," Leon says. "We'll just play two sets' worth of music with an intermission in between." He looks at the singer. "The big man's willing."

"Hell, yes," the singer says.

"Save all the money you'd waste on those opening acts," Leon says. "And you don't have to pay good money to ship a dozen midgets around the country, either."

The Colonel considers this. He looks at the singer. "You're really willin' to do this?"

The singer shrugs. "Sure. I *like* being onstage."

"You'll have to do more than the five or six songs you do now."

"Plenty of songs out there."

The Colonel's eyes glitter. Everyone knows he gets kickbacks from writers who offer their songs to the singer. He nods slowly.

"Okay," he says. "This sure seems worth a thought."

And then his eyes move to Leon and turn cold.

Someday there's going to be an accounting.

The story in *Billboard* says that the singer has cut a special deal with the Army, that when he's drafted, he's going into Special Services and entertain the troops. It says he won't even have to cut his hair.

It's an absolute lie. The singer has an understanding with his draft board, that's true, but it's only that he should get some advance notice if he's going to be called up.

He hasn't even had his physical yet.

"Where is this coming from?" the singer demands.

Leon thinks for a moment. "This is *Billboard,* not some fan magazine. They must have got the story from somewhere."

"Who could have told them such a thing?"

Leon looks like he wants to say something but decides not to. The singer has enough on his mind.

Satnin is grieved and ailing. She's turning yellow with jaundice and nobody knows why. Her weight keeps going up in spite of the dozens of diet pills she takes every day. When her boy isn't with her, she stays drunk all the time. The thought of her mortality makes the singer frantic with anxiety.

The story about the draft keeps getting bigger. When the singer goes on tour, reporters ask him about the Army all the time. He can't figure out what's getting them so stirred up.

He keeps in touch with Memphis by phone. And when Satnin goes into a hospital, he cancels the tour and is on the next train.

She rallies a bit when she sees her boy. But within twenty-four hours, she fails and dies.

The next sound that comes from her hospital room is even more eerie than the sound of the singer's massed fans. Hospital personnel and bystanders stop, listen in rising horror, then flee.

The family is keening over Satnin. It's an Appalachian custom, and the good burghers of Memphis have never heard such a thing. The singer's powerful voice rises, dominates the rest of his family, his wails of grief echoing down the corridor. Waiting outside, Leon can feel the hairs rise on his neck. It's the most terrifying thing he's ever heard.

The funeral takes place in the big house on Highway 51. It's a circus. The gates are open, and strangers wander around the house and grounds and take things. The Colonel tries to keep order, but nobody listens to him. Reporters take the best seats at the service and snap pictures of everything.

The singer is frantic and crazed with grief. He keeps dragging people over to admire Satnin in her coffin. He spends hours talking to the corpse in some language of his own. Leon calls for a doctor to give him a sedative, but the doctor can't make it through the mass of people waiting outside the gates. The crowds are so huge that the state police have to close the highway.

At the funeral, the singer throws himself into the grave and demands to be buried with his Mamma. His friends have to drag him away.

Unbelievably, a reporter chooses this moment to ask the singer about the Army. The singer stares in disbelief.

"Ain't gonna go in no Army!" he shouts, and then his friends pull him away to his limousine. The doctor finally arrives and puts him to sleep.

The next day, there are headlines.

"We ain't at war," the singer says. "Why does anyone care about the damn Army anyway? Why cain't they leave a man alone?"

It's two days since the funeral, and the singer has spent the intervening time in a drugged stupor. He sits in a huge velour-covered chair in a room swathed in red velvet. Newspapers open to their screaming headlines surround his chair.

"Somebody's planting these stories," Leon tells him. "We all know that. And if you think about it, you know who it's got to be."

The singer just stares at him with drug-dulled eyes.

"The Colonel," Leon says. "It's got to be the Colonel."

The singer thinks about it. "Don't make no sense," he says. "Colonel don't make no money when I'm in the service."

"But he gets control," Leon says. "You can't look after your affairs if you're away. You'll have to put him in charge of everything and trust him. He'll have to renegotiate your RCA contract, your movie contract. When you get back, he'll be the one in charge."

The singer stares at him and says nothing.

"He's just some goddam carnival barker, brother," Leon says. "All he does now is arrange your bookings—anyone can do that. He isn't even a real colonel. He just wants to be the boss in the big house and keep you working in his cotton fields for the rest of your life."

"Orville Bean," the singer says. Leon doesn't understand, but this doesn't stop him.

"And you don't need the damn Army," Leon says. "All it does is protect bosses like the Colonel and their money. What's the Army ever done for you?"

"Ain't gonna go in no Army," the singer says.

"The draft board *has* to call you up after all this. The newspapers won't let them do anything else. What're you gonna tell 'em?"

"Have the Colonel work out something."

"The Colonel *wants* you in the Army."

The singer closes his eyes and lolls his head back in the big velour chair. He wishes everyone would go away and leave him alone. He strains his mind, trying to find an answer.

Make the Colonel do what you want.

The singer starts awake. He's heard the voice plainly, but he knows Leon hasn't spoken.

He realizes it was his brother's voice, calling to him from the Beyond.

The singer calls the Colonel on the phone and tells him that if he receives his draft notice, the first thing he'll do is fire Thomas Andrew Parker. The Colonel is staggered.

He says it's too late. The singer only repeats his demand and hangs up.

He manages to avoid seeing the Colonel for another week, and then the Colonel comes anyway. The singer agrees to meet him and wishes that Leon wasn't in town visiting his mom.

The Colonel walks into the den, leaning hard on his elephant-head cane, and drops heavily into a chair. He looks pale and sweaty and he keeps massaging his left arm. He explains that he's talked to every man on the draft board, that public opinion is forcing them to call the singer up. The Colonel has offered them colossal bribes, but it appears they're all honest citizens.

"Ain't changed my mind," the singer says. "You keep me out of the Army, or you and me are through."

"I can't," the Colonel protests. His powerful blue eyes are hollow.

"Then you and me are finished the second that notice gets here."

"Listen. There's a chance. The medical—" the Colonel starts, and then he gasps, his mouth open, and clutches at his left arm. His mouth works and he doesn't say anything.

Heart attack. His brother's voice. *Don't do anything.*

The singer knows the Colonel already had a heart attack a few years ago. He's old and fat and deserves exactly what he's going to get.

The Colonel's eyes plead with the singer. The singer just watches him. The Colonel begins moving slowly, his hand reaching for the elephant-head cane he's propped against a table.

Take the cane, the angel voice says. The singer takes the cane and holds it while the Colonel topples off his chair and starts to crawl toward the door. And then the Colonel falls over and doesn't move anymore.

"Ain't gonna have no more bosses," the singer says.

"Not gonna fight for no rich people," the singer says to reporters.

He doesn't give a damn about the firestorm that follows. He takes his motorcycle out onto the highways and blasts along at full speed and tries to listen to what his brother is telling him.

Leon tells him a lot, too. He reads him passages from a book called *Capital.* He explains about workers and bosses and how bosses make money by exploiting workers. It's everything the singer ever learned from his family, from his days as a truck driver after high school. Leon explains how he's a Marxist-Leninist.

"Isn't that the same as a Communist?" the singer asks. Leon's answer is long and involved and has a lot of historical digressions. But the angel voice that whispers inside the singer speaks simple sense:

Doesn't matter what people call it, it only matters that it's true.

There are bonfires out on Highway 51 now, the singer's records going up in flames. To the American public it looks as if their worst fears are confirmed, that the singer, driving girls into a sexual frenzy with his degenerate Negro music, is an agent of Moscow as well as of Satan. Outside the gate of the house are weeping girls begging him to repent. His brother's grave in East Tupelo is vandalized, so the singer has both his brother's body and Satnin's exhumed and reburied at Graceland.

Every booking has been canceled. The movie contract is gone. The singer doesn't care, because for the first time in his life, the nightmares are gone and he can sleep at night. The singer is going to Party meetings and making the members nervous, because crowds of reporters are still following him around and snapping pictures of everyone.

Johnny Cash and Jerry Lee Lewis tell anyone who'll listen that they're country singers. Ricky Nelson starts covering Dean Martin tunes. Little Richard goes into the church. Rock and roll is finished.

"Plenty of bookings in Europe, comrade," Leon says.

So the singer plays Europe, but he's playing clubs, not auditoriums or stadiums. His Daddy and Grandma stay home and take care of his house. The singer's European audiences are a strange mixture of teenage girls and thin intellectuals who wear glasses and smoke cigarettes. Gene and Junior Smith are still with him, protecting him from fanatics who might want to hurt him, or the strange, intense people who want to discourse on the class origins of his appeal. It seems to the singer that the Left doesn't understand rock and roll. Leon calmly says that sooner or later, they'll figure it out.

All the professional songwriters who kept him supplied with material are long gone. So are Scotty and the others who helped with the arrangements. He picks his own tunes. He has a new band, working-class British kids who worship the ground he walks on. The Party wants him to sing folk songs and songs about the Struggle. He obliges, but he rocks them up, and that doesn't seem to please them, so he just goes back to singing the blues.

He records in little studios in Italy and Germany that are even more primitive than the Sun studio in Memphis. He teaches them a trick or two—he knows how to create the Sun sound by putting a second mike behind his head and arranging for a slight delay between the two to produce Sam Phillips' trademark echo effect.

The records are carried into America in the holds of freighters. There's a surprising demand for them. There's even a story in the papers about a Navy sailor courtmartialed for having some of his 45s in his locker.

His voice fills out. He's got three and a half octaves and he uses them brilliantly—his chest voice is powerful and evocative, his high notes clear and resonant. He wishes he had a bigger audience now that he knows so much more about the music.

Don't matter who listens so long as you sing it right, his brother says. The singer knows his brother always speaks the truth.

The singer is appalled by his tour of the East. It's taken him forever to get permission, and he's succeeded only because some kind of propaganda coup is necessary. Comrade Khrushchev has just built a wall in Berlin to keep out American spies, and he's demanded solidarity from Socialists everywhere.

Still, the singer can't believe the people he's got opening for him. Jugglers. Trained seals. A couple of clowns. A drill team from the Czech Army, and a couple of folk-singers so old and so drunk they can barely stagger onto the stage every night.

At least there are no midgets.

With the tour is a platoon of big men in baggy pants and bulky jackets, supposedly there to protect the singer from counterrevolutionaries, but all they really do is insulate the singer from anyone in the countries he's touring.

Just like Colonel Parker, his brother whispers.

The audiences are polite, but clearly they like the jugglers best. The singer works like hell to win them over, but his real fans, the young people, seem to be excluded. At one point his rage explodes, and in the middle of a song he turns to Leon and screams, *"Look what you've got me into!"*

Leon doesn't respond. He knows there's nothing he can say.

When the singer returns to the West, he announces he's leaving the Party. His remaining audiences get smaller.

But he's singing better than ever. He gets together with French and British blues fanatics, men with huge collections of vinyl bought from American sailors, and he listens carefully. He knows how to take a minor tune, a B-side or a neglected work, and reinvent it, jack it up and rock it till it cries with power and glows like neon. And people with names like Dylan and Fariña cross the Atlantic to meet with him, to tell him how much he means to them.

He doesn't abandon the Left. He studies Marx and Gandhi and Strachey and Hilferding. He leads his band and followers in discussion groups and self-criticism sessions, American hill people and Yorkshire kids educating themselves in revolution. Leon suggests inviting others to run the meetings, intellectuals, but the singer doesn't like the idea.

Years pass. The singer's audiences grow older. He's disappointed that the young girls are gone, that he can't tease them and drive them mad with the way he moves.

And then rock and roll is back, exploding out of the sweaty-walled European clubs where it's been living all these years, blasting into the minds and hearts of a newer, younger generation.

For the first time in years, the singer hears his brother's voice: *Now's your time.*

The singer runs onto the stage, drops onto his knees as he passes the mike, slides across half the stage. He looks at the girls in the audience from under his taunting eyelids.

"*Well …* " he intones.

The eerie sound comes up from the audience again, adolescent girls in the thrall of a need they can't explain. The singer had forgotten how much he missed them.

"*Well …* " he sings again, as if he's forgotten where he was. The wail goes up again.

When he finally gets around to singing, he thinks he can hear his brother on harmony.

Most of his new audience isn't familiar with the old material, with the old songs and moves—it's all spanking new to them. And the new material is good, written by Lennon and McCartney and Dylan and Richards and Jagger, all of them offering their best in homage to their idol. They swarm into his recording sessions to sing backup or strum out chords. He isn't as popular as he once was—there's still a lot of resistance, and he doesn't get much airplay and is never invited to appear on television—but his new fans think the American Legion pickets outside his concerts are quaint, and his old fans have never forgotten him.

He hasn't forgotten much either. He remembers who shunned him, who helped when the chips were down. The few who dared to support him in public. He works to advance the Struggle. He not only marches with Dr. King, he gives him a bright yellow Cadillac so he doesn't have to march at all. He directs public scorn at the Vietnam War. FBI men in dark suits and hats follow him around and tap his phones. They can't do anything to him because he's never done anything illegal—in the confusion of the headlines and statements and his jump to Europe, his local draft board never actually issued his induction notice.

Outnumbering the FBI are the fans who camp outside his house, living there just as they did a decade before, people who seem to have a tenuous existence only in the singer's shadow. It's as if he's their god, the only thing that gives them meaning.

Only one way to become a god, his brother whispers.

He knows what his brother means.

When Dr. King comes to Memphis, it's only natural for the singer to climb on his bike and pay a courtesy call.

Maybe the magic will work one last time.

What was he doing on the balcony, exactly? Demonstrating his moves, jumping around, playing the clown for his bewildered host? Or was there a whisper in his ear, a soft murmur that told him exactly where the bullet would be found as it hissed through the air?

Bleeding, both lungs punctured, he shoves the confused Dr. King into the motel room and to safety. He falls, coughing blood, his moist breath whistling through the hole in his side.

King remembers, forever afterward, the peculiar inward look on the singer's face as he dies.

The singer remembers his baptism of the spirit, the way he gave everything away. Now he's giving everything away again. He hears his brother's voice.

Welcome, his brother says, *to where we can live forever.*

You stand with the long line of mourners as it files up to the big white house. The singer's will was a surprise: there's an education foundation, and the house is to be renamed the Memphis Palace of Labor. It will become a library and center for research on labor issues.

File through a series of rooms on your way to view the coffin. Rooms so strangely decorated that they're like a window into the singer's mind. The Joe Hill room, the Gandhi room, the Karl Marx room. A pink bust of Marx sits in a shrine in the corner of his chamber, flanked by smoked-mirror glass and red-velvet curtains. Joe Hill—a life-sized statue of a noble-looking man in a cap and bib overalls—gazes defiantly at the scarlet velour walls of his chamber and at a piano gilded with what appears to be solid gold.

You have the feeling that the staid trustees of the foundation will redecorate at the first chance they get.

The singer lies in state under a portrait of the wizened figure of Gandhi, in a room whose walls seem to be upholstered in white plastic. Dr. King is chief mourner and speaks the eulogy. A choir from a local black church mourns softly, then spits fire. The crowd claps and stamps in answer.

And at last the moment comes when the huge bronze coffin is closed and the singer, Jessie Garon Presley, is carried out to be laid to rest in the garden. On his one side is his Mamma, and on the other his twin, Elvis, with whom he will live forever.

This story was written as a result of a dinner with Tor editor Patrick Nielsen Hayden. During the course of the meal, he happened to mention that he'd just acquired an anthology from Mike Resnick, and that it was called "Alternate Rebels."

Oh shit, I thought at once. Now I have to write *the Elvis story*.

The Elvis story had been on my mind for several years, ever since I'd run across a description of Elvis Presley as a "rebel" and a "revolutionary," and wondered what might have resulted if these words could be applied to Elvis not simply in a social context, but a political one.

I'd hesitated for years in writing the story, because its subject matter involved rock and roll. There are two problems with writing a rock and roll story. First, the author tends to embarrass himself unwittingly by exposing his goopy adolescent tastes in music; second, when actual musicians read the story, they find it hilarious when they don't find it offensive.

I managed to evade the first objection by virtue of the fact that Elvis Presley was in my case an adult taste, not an adolescent one. When I was growing up, I considered Elvis to be corny and square, and devoutly wished that he would disappear. (And hey, before long he did.) It was only when I was over the age of thirty that I listened to early Presley cuts, discovered that he had a perfectly awesome talent, and wondered why nobody had ever told me about his early work. When you listen to the Sun Sessions you can see Presley, cut by cut, moment by moment, *inventing rock and roll!* This, even forty years later, remains pretty exciting stuff.

I talked my way around the second objection by deciding not to show off my nonexistent musical knowledge and not get into the music part much at all. Whether musicians will find this offensive or not has not yet been determined.

I guess they'll let me know.

Prayers on the Wind

Hard is the appearance of a Buddha.
—Dhammapada

Bold color slashed bright slices out of Vajra's violet sky. The stiff spring breeze off the Tingsum glacier made the yellow prayer flags snap with sounds like gunshots. Sun gleamed from baroque tracework adorning silver antennae and receiver dishes. Atop the dark red walls of the Diamond Library Palace, saffron-robed monks stood like sentries, some of them grouped in threes around ragdongs, trumpets so huge they required two men to hold them aloft while a third blew puff-cheeked into the mouthpiece. Over the deep, grating moan of the trumpets, other monks chanted their litany.

> *Salutation to the Buddha.*
> *In the language of the gods and in that of the Lus,*
> *In the language of the demons and in that of the men,*
> *In all the languages which exist,*
> *I proclaim the Doctrine.*

Jigme Dzasa stood at the foot of the long granite stair leading to the great library, the spectacle filling his senses, the litany dancing in his soul. He turned to his guest. "Are you ready, Ambassador?"

The face of !urq was placid. "Lus?" she asked.

"Mythical beings," said Jigme. "Serpentine divinities who live in bodies of water."

"Ah," !urq said. "I'm glad we got that cleared up."

Jigme looked at the alien, decided to say nothing.

185

"Let us begin," said the Ambassador. Jigme hitched up his zen and began the long climb to the Palace, his bare feet slapping at the stones. A line of Gelugspa monks followed in respectful silence. Ambassador Colonel !urq climbed beside Jigme at a slow trot, her four boot heels rapping. Behind her was a line of Sangs, their centauroid bodies cased neatly in blue-and-grey uniforms, decorations flashing in the bright sun. Next to each was a feathery Masker servant carrying a ceremonial parasol.

Jigme was out of breath by the time he mounted the long stairway, and his head whirled as he entered the tsokhang, the giant assembly hall. Several thousand members of religious orders sat rigid at their stations, long lines of men and women: Dominicans and Sufis in white, Red Hats and Yellow Hats in their saffron zens, Jesuits in black, Gyudpas in complicated aprons made of carved, interwoven human bones. ... Each sat in the lotus posture in front of a solid gold data terminal decorated with religious symbols, some meditating, some chanting sutras, others accessing the Library.

Jigme, !urq, and their parties passed through the vast hall that hummed with the distant, echoing sutras of those trying to achieve unity with the Diamond Mountain. At the far side of the room were huge double doors of solid jade, carved with figures illustrating the life of the first twelve incarnations of the Gyalpo Rinpoche, the Treasured King. The doors opened on silent hinges at the touch of equerries' fingertips. Jigme looked at the equerries as he passed— lovely young novices, he thought, beautiful boys really. The shaven nape of that dark one showed an extraordinary curve.

Beyond was the audience chamber. The Masker servants remained outside, holding their parasols at rigid attention, while their masters trotted into the audience chamber alongside the line of monks.

Holographic murals filled the walls, illustrating the life of the Compassionate One. The ceiling was of transparent polymer, the floor of clear crystal that went down to the solid core of the planet. The crystal refracted sunlight in interesting ways, and as he walked across the room Jigme seemed to walk on rainbows.

At the far end of the room, flanked by officials, was the platform that served as a throne. Overhead was an arching canopy of massive gold, the words AUM MANI PADME HUM worked into the design in turquoise. The platform was covered in a large carpet decorated with figures of the lotus, the Wheel, the swastika, the two fish, the eternal knot, and other holy symbols. Upon the carpet sat the Gyalpo Rinpoche himself, a small man with a sunken chest and bony shoulders, the Forty-First Incarnation of the Bodhisattva Bob Miller, the Great Librarian, himself an emanation of Avalokitesvara.

The Incarnation was dressed simply in a yellow zen, being the only person in the holy precincts permitted to wear the color. Around his waist was a rosary composed of 108 strung bone disks cut from the forty skulls of his previous incarnations. His body was motionless but his arms rose and fell as the fingers moved in a series of symbolic hand gestures, one mudra after another, their pattern set by the flow of data through the Diamond Mountain.

Jigme approached and dropped to his knees before the platform. He pressed the palms of his hands together, brought the hands to his forehead, mouth, and heart, then touched his forehead to the floor. Behind him he heard thuds as some of his delegation slammed their heads against the crystal surface in a display of piety—indeed, there were depressions in the floor worn by the countless pilgrims who had done this—but Jigme, knowing he would need his wits, only touched his forehead lightly and held the posture until he heard the Incarnation speak.

"Jigme Dzasa. I am pleased to see you again. Please get to your feet and introduce me to your friends."

The old man's voice was light and dry, full of good humor. In the seventy-third year of his incarnation, the Treasured King enjoyed good health.

Jigme straightened. Rainbows rose from the floor and danced before his eyes. He climbed slowly to his feet as his knees made popping sounds—twenty years younger than the Incarnation, he was a good deal stiffer of limb—and moved toward the platform in an attitude of reverence. He reached to the rosary at his waist and took from it a white silk scarf embroidered with a religious text. He unfolded the khata and, sticking out his tongue in respect, handed it to the Incarnation with a bow.

The Gyalpo Rinpoche took the khata and draped it around his own neck with a smile. He reached out a hand, and Jigme dropped his head for the blessing. He felt dry fingertips touch his shaven scalp, and then a sense of harmony seemed to hum through his being. Everything, he knew, was correct. The interview would go well.

Jigme straightened and the Incarnation handed him a khata in exchange, one with the mystic three knots tied by the Incarnation himself. Jigme bowed again, stuck out his tongue, and moved to the side of the platform with the other officials. Beside him was Dr. Kay O'Neill, the Minister of Science. Jigme could feel O'Neill's body vibrating like a taut cord, but the minister's overwrought state could not dispel Jigme's feeling of bliss.

"Omniscient," Jigme said, "I would like to present Colonel !urq, Ambassador of the Sang."

!urq was holding her upper arms in a Sang attitude of respect. Neither she nor her followers had prostrated themselves, but had stood politely by while their human escort had done so. !urq's boots rang against the floor as she trotted to the dais, her lower arms offering a khata. She had no tongue to stick out—her upper and lower palates were flexible, permitting a wide variety of sounds, but they weren't as flexible as all that. Still she thrust out her lower lip in a polite approximation.

"I am honored to be presented at last, Omniscient," !urq said.

Dr. O'Neill gave a snort of anger.

The Treasured King draped a knotted khata around the Ambassador's neck. "We of the Diamond Mountain are pleased to welcome you. I hope you will find our hospitality to your liking."

The old man reached forward for the blessing. !urq's instructions did not permit her to bow her head before an alien presence, so the Incarnation simply reached forward and placed his hand over her face for a moment. They remained frozen in that attitude, and then !urq backed carefully to one side of the platform, standing near Jigme. She and Jigme then presented their respective parties to the Incarnation. By the end of the audience the head of the Gyalpo Rinpoche looked like a tiny red jewel in a flowery lotus of white silk khatas.

"I thank you all for coming all these light-years to see me," said the Incarnation, and Jigme led the visitors from the audience chamber, chanting the sutra *Aum vajra guru Padma siddhi hum, Aum the diamond powerful guru Padma,* as he walked.

!urq came to a halt as soon as her party had filed from the room. Her lower arms formed an expression of bewilderment.

"Is that all?"

Jigme looked at the alien. "That is the conclusion of the audience, yes. We may tour the holy places in the Library, if you wish."

"We had no opportunity to discuss the matter of Gyangtse."

"You may apply to the Ministry for another interview."

"It took me twelve years to obtain this one." Her upper arms took a stance that Jigme recognized as martial. "The patience of my government is not unlimited," she said.

Jigme bowed. "I shall communicate this to the Ministry, Ambassador."

"Delay in the Gyangtse matter will only result in more hardship for the inhabitants when they are removed."

"It is out of my hands, Ambassador."

!urq held her stance for a long moment in order to emphasize her protest, then relaxed her arms. Her upper set of hands caressed the white silk khata. "Odd to think," she said, amused, "that I journeyed twelve years just to stick out my lip at a human and have him touch my face in return."

"Many humans would give their lives for such a blessing," said Jigme.

"Sticking out the lip is quite rude where I come from, you know."

"I believe you have told me this."

"The Omniscient's hands were very warm." !urq raised fingers to her forehead, touched the ebon flesh. "I believe I can still feel the heat on my skin."

Jigme was impressed. "The Treasured King has given you a special blessing. He can channel the energies of the Diamond Mountain through his body. That was the heat you felt."

!urq's antennae rose skeptically, but she refrained from comment.

"Would you like to see the holy places?" Jigme said. "This, for instance, is a room devoted to Maitreya, the Buddha That Will Come. Before you is his statue. Data can be accessed by manipulation of the images on his headdress."

Jigme's speech was interrupted by the entrance of a Masker servant from the audience room. A white khata was draped about the avian's neck. !urq's trunk swiveled atop her centaur body; her arms assumed a commanding stance. The clicks and pops of her own language rattled from her mouth like falling stones.

"Did I send for you, creature?"

The Masker performed an obsequious gesture with its parasol. "I beg the Colonel's pardon. The old human sent for us. He is touching us and giving us scarves." The Masker fluttered helplessly. "We did not wish to offend our hosts, and there were no Sang to query for instruction."

"How odd," said !urq. "Why should the old human want to bless our slaves?" She eyed the Masker and thought for a moment. "I will not kill you today," she decided. She turned to Jigme and switched to Tibetan. "Please continue, Rinpoche."

"As you wish, Colonel." He returned to his speech. "The Library Palace is the site of no less than twenty-one tombs of various bodhisattvas, including many incarnations of the Gyalpo Rinpoche. The Palace also contains over eight thousand data terminals and sixty shrines."

As he rattled through the prepared speech, Jigme wondered about the scene he had just witnessed. He suspected that "I will not kill you today" was less alarming than it sounded, was instead an idiomatic way of saying "Go about your business."

Then again, knowing the Sang, maybe not.

The Cabinet had gathered in one of the many other reception rooms of the Library Palace. This one was small, the walls and ceiling hidden behind tapestry covered with appliqué, the room's sole ornament a black stone statue of a dancing demon that served tea on command.

The Gyalpo Rinpoche, to emphasize his once-humble origins, was seated on the floor. White stubble prickled from his scalp.

Jigme sat cross-legged on a pillow. Across from him was Dr. O'Neill. A lay official, her status was marked by the long turquoise earring that hung from her left ear to her collarbone, that and the long hair piled high on her head. The rosary she held was made of 108 antique microprocessors pierced and strung on a length of fiberoptic cable. Beside her sat the cheerful Miss Taisuke, the Minister of State. Although only fifteen years old, she was Jigme's immediate superior, her authority derived from being the certified reincarnation of a famous hermit nun of the Yellow Hat Gelugspa order. Beside her, the Minister of Magic, a tantric sorcerer of the Gyud School named Daddy Carbajal, toyed with a trumpet made from a human thighbone. Behind him in a semireclined position was the elderly, frail, toothless State Oracle—his was a high-ranking position, but it was a largely symbolic one as long as the Treasured King was in his majority. Other ministers, lay or clerical, sipped tea or gossiped as they waited for the Incarnation to begin the meeting.

The Treasured King scratched one bony shoulder, grinned, then assumed in an eyeblink a posture of deep meditation, placing hands in his lap with his skull-rosary wrapped around them. "Aum," he intoned. The others straightened and joined in the holy syllable, the Pranava, the creative sound whose vibrations built the universe. Then the Horse of the Air rose from the throat of the Gyalpo Rinpoche, the syllables *Aum mane padme hum*, and the others reached for their rosaries.

As he recited the rosary, Jigme tried to meditate on each syllable as it went by, comprehend the full meaning of each, the color, the importance, the significance. *Aum*, which was white and connected with the gods. *Ma*, which was blue and connected with the titans. *Ne*, which was yellow and connected with men. *Pad*, which was green and connected with animals. *Me*, which was red and connected with giants and demigods. *Hum*, which was black and connected with dwellers in purgatory. Each syllable a separate realm, each belonging to a separate species, together forming the visible and invisible universe.

"Hri!" called everyone in unison, signifying the end of the 108th repetition. The Incarnation smiled and asked the black statue for some tea. The stone demon scuttled across the thick carpet and poured tea into his golden bowl. The demon looked up into the Incarnation's face.

"Free me!" said the statue.

The Gyalpo Rinpoche looked at the statue. "Tell me truthfully. Have you achieved Enlightenment?"

The demon said nothing.

The Treasured King smiled again. "Then you had better give Dr. O'Neill some tea."

O'Neill accepted her tea, sipped, and dismissed the demon. It scuttled back to its pedestal.

"We should consider the matter of Ambassador !urq, " said the Incarnation.

O'Neill put down her teacup. "I am opposed to her presence here. The Sang are an unenlightened and violent race. They conceive of life as a struggle

against nature rather than search for Enlightenment. They have already conquered an entire species, and would subdue us if they could."

"That is why I have consented to the building of warships," said the
Incarnation.

"From their apartments in the Nyingmapa monastery, the Sang now
have access to the Library," said O'Neill. "All our strategic information is
present there. They will use the knowledge against us."

"Truth can do no harm," said Miss Taisuke.

"All truth is not vouchsafed to the unenlightened," said O'Neill. "To
those unprepared by correct study and thought, truth can be a danger." She
gestured with an arm, encompassing the world outside the Palace. "Who
should know better than we, who live on Vajra? Haven't half the charlatans in
all existence set up outside our walls to preach half-truths to the credulous,
endangering their own Enlightenment and those of everyone who hears them?"

Jigme listened to O'Neill in silence. O'Neill and Daddy Carbajal were
the leaders of the reactionary party, defenders of orthodoxy and the security
of the realm. They had argued this point before.

"Knowledge will make the Sang cautious," said Jigme. "They will now
know of our armament. They will now understand the scope of the human
expansion, far greater than their own. We may hope this will deter them from
attack."

"The Sang may be encouraged to build more weapons of their own,"
said Daddy Carbajal. "They are already highly militarized, as a way of keeping down their subject species. They may militarize further."

"Be assured they are doing so," said O'Neill. "Our own embassy is kept
in close confinement on a small planetoid. They have no way of learning the
scope of the Sang threat or sending this information to the Library. We, on
the other hand, have escorted the Sang ambassador throughout human space
and have shown her anything in which she expressed an interest."

"Deterrence," said Jigme. "We wished them to know how extensive our
sphere is, that the conquest would be costly and call for more resources than
they possess."

"We must do more than deter. The Sang threat should be eliminated, as
were the threats of heterodox humanity during the Third and Fifth Incarnations."

"You speak jihad," said Miss Taisuke.

There was brief silence. No one, not even O'Neill, was comfortable with
Taisuke's plainness.

"All human worlds are under the peace of the Library," said O'Neill.
"This was accomplished partly by force, partly by conversion. The Sang will
not *permit* conversion."

The Gyalpo Rinpoche cleared his throat. The others fell silent at once.
The Incarnation had been listening in silence, his face showing concentration

but no emotion. He always preferred to hear the opinions of others before expressing his own. "The Third and Fifth Incarnations," he said, "did nothing to encourage the jihads proclaimed in their name. The Incarnations did not wish to accept temporal power."

"They did not speak against the holy warriors," said Daddy Carbajal.

The Incarnation's elderly face was uncommonly stern. His hands formed the teaching mudra. "Does not Shakyamuni speak in the *Anguttara Nikaya* of the three ways of keeping the body pure?" he asked. "One must not commit adultery, one must not steal, one must not kill any living creature. How could warriors kill for orthodoxy and yet remain orthodox?"

There was a long moment of uncomfortable silence. Only Daddy Carbajal, whose tantric Short Path teaching included numerous ways of dispatching his enemies, did not seem nonplussed.

"The Sang are here to study us," said the Gyalpo Rinpoche. "We also study them."

"I view their pollution as a danger." Dr. O'Neill's face was stubborn.

Miss Taisuke gave a brilliant smile. "Does not the *Mahaparinirvana-sutra* tell us that if we are forced to live in a difficult situation and among people of impure minds, if we cherish faith in Buddha we can ever lead them toward better actions?"

Relief fluttered through Jigme. Taisuke's apt quote, atop the Incarnation's sternness, had routed the war party.

"The Embassy will remain," said the Treasured King. "They will be given the freedom of Vajra, saving only the Holy Precincts. We must remember the oath of the Amida Buddha: 'Though I attain Buddhahood, I shall never be complete until people everywhere, hearing my name, learn right ideas about life and death, and gain that perfect wisdom that will keep their minds pure and tranquil in the midst of the world's greed and suffering.'"

"What of Gyangtse, Rinpoche?" O'Neill's voice seemed harsh after the graceful words of Scripture.

The Gyalpo Rinpoche cocked his head and thought for a moment. Suddenly the Incarnation seemed very human and very frail, and Jigme's heart surged with love for the old man.

"We will deal with that at the Picnic Festival," said the Incarnation.

From his position by the lake, Jigme could see tents and banners dotting the lower slopes of Tingsum like bright spring flowers. The Picnic Festival lasted a week, and unlike most of the other holidays had no real religious connection. It was a week-long campout during which almost the entire population of the Diamond City and the surrounding monasteries moved into the open and spent their time making merry.

Jigme could see the giant yellow hovertent of the Gyalpo Rinpoche surrounded by saffron-robed guards, the guards present not to protect the Treasured King from attackers, but rather to preserve his tranquility against inva-
sions by devout pilgrims in search of a blessing. The guards—monks armed
with staves, their shoulders padded hugely to make them look more formidable—served the additional purpose of keeping the Sang away from the Treasured King until the conclusion of the festival, something for which Jigme
was devoutly grateful. He didn't want any political confrontations disturbing
the joy of the holiday. Fortunately Ambassador !urq seemed content to wait
until her scheduled appearance at a party given by the Incarnation on the
final afternoon.

Children splashed barefoot in the shallows of the lake, and others played
chibi on the sward beside, trying to keep a shuttlecock aloft using the feet
alone. Jigme found himself watching a redheaded boy on the verge of adolescence, admiring the boy's grace, the way the knobbed spine and sharp shoulders moved under his pale skin. His bony ankles hadn't missed the shuttlecock yet. Jigme was sufficiently lost in his reverie that he did not hear the
sound of boots on the grass beside him.

"Jigme Dzasa?"

Jigme looked up with a guilty start. !urq stood beside him, wearing hardy
outdoor clothing. Her legs were wrapped up to the shoulder. Jigme stood
hastily and bowed.

"Your pardon, Ambassador. I didn't hear you."

The Sang's feathery antennae waved cheerfully in the breeze. "I thought
I would lead a party up Tingsum. Would you care to join us?"

What Jigme wanted to do was continue watching the ball game, but he
assented with a smile. Climbing mountains: that was the sort of thing the
Sang were always up to. They wanted to demonstrate they could conquer
anything.

"Perhaps you should find a pony," !urq said. "Then you could keep up
with us."

Jigme took a pony from the Library's corral and followed the waffle
patterns of !urq's boots into the trees on the lower slopes. Three other Sang
were along on the expedition; they clicked and gobbled to one another as
they trotted cheerfully along. Behind toiled three Maskers-of-burden carrying food and climbing equipment. If the Sang noticed the incongruity demonstrated by the human's using a quadruped as a beast of burden while they,
centauroids, used a bipedal race as servants, they politely refrained from men-
tioning it. The pony's genetically altered cloven forefeet took the mountain
trail easily, nimbler than the Sang in their heavy boots. Jigme noticed that
this made the Sang work harder, trying to outdo the dumb beast.

They came to a high mountain meadow and paused, looking down at the huge field of tents that ringed the smooth violet lake. In the middle of the meadow was a three-meter tower of crystal, weathered and yellow, ringed by rubble flaked off during the hard winters. One of the Sang trotted over to examine it.

"I thought the crystal was instructed to stay well below the surface," he said.

"There must have been a house here once," Jigme said. "The crystal would have been instructed to grow up through the surface to provide Library access."

!urq trotted across a stretch of grass, her head down. "Here's the beginning of the foundation line," she said. She gestured with an arm. "It runs from here to over there."

The Sang cantered over the ground, frisky as children, to discover the remnants of the foundation. The Sang were always keen, Jigme found, on discovering things. They had not yet learned that there was only one thing worth discovering, and it had nothing to do with old ruins.

!urq examined the pillar of crystal, touched its crumbling surface. "And over eighty percent of the planet is composed of this?" she said.

"All except the crust," Jigme said. "The crystal was instructed to convert most of the planet's material. That is why our heavy metals have to come from mined asteroids, and why we build mostly in natural materials. This house was probably of wood and laminated cloth, and it most likely burned in an accident."

!urq picked up a bit of crystal from the ring of rubble that surrounded the pillar. "And you can store information in this."

"All the information we have," Jigme said reverently. "All the information in the universe, eventually." Involuntarily, his hands formed the teaching mudra. "The Library is a hologram of the universe. The Blessed Bodhisattva Bob Miller was a reflection of the Library, its first Incarnation. The current Incarnation is the forty-first."

!urq's antennae flickered in the wind. She tossed the piece of crystal from hand to hand. "All the information you possess," she said. "That is a powerful tool. Or weapon."

"A tool, yes. The original builders of the Library considered it only a tool. Only something to help them order things, to assist them in governing. They did not comprehend that once the Diamond Mountain contained enough information, once it gathered enough energy, it would become more than the sum of its parts. That it would become the Mind of Buddha, the universe in small, and that the Mind, out of its compassion, would seek to incarnate itself as a human."

"The Library is self-aware?" !urq asked. She seemed to find the notion startling.

Jigme could only shrug. "Is the universe self-aware?"

!urq made a series of meditative clicking noises.

"Inside the Diamond Mountain," Jigme said, "there are processes going on that we cannot comprehend. The Library was designed to be nearly autonomous; it is now so large we cannot keep track of everything, because we would need a mind as large as the Library to process the information. Many of the energy and data transfers that we can track are very subtle, involving energies that are not fully understood. Yet we can track some of them. When an Incarnation dies, we can see the trace his spirit makes through the Library—like an atomic particle that comes apart in a shower of short-lived particles, we see it principally through its effects on other energies—and we can see part of those energies move from one place to another, from one body to another, becoming another Incarnation."

!urq's antennae moved skeptically. "You can document this?"

"We can produce spectra showing the tracks of energy through matter. Is that documentation?"

"I would say, with all respect, your case remains unproven."

"I do not seek to prove anything." Jigme smiled. "The Gyalpo Rinpoche is his own proof, his own truth. Buddha is truth. All else is illusion."

!urq put the piece of crystal in her pocket. "If this was *our* Library," she said, "we would prove things one way or another."

"You would see only your own reflection. Existence on the quantum level is largely a matter of belief. On that level, mind is as powerful as matter. We believe that the Gyalpo Rinpoche is an Incarnation of the Library; does that belief help make it so?"

"You ask me questions based on a system of belief that I do not share. How can you expect me to answer?"

"Belief is powerful. Belief can incarnate itself."

"Belief can incarnate itself as delusion."

"Delusion can incarnate itself as reality." Jigme stood in his stirrups, stretching his legs, and then settled back into his saddle. "Let me tell you a story," he said. "It's quite true. There was a man who went for a drive, over the pass yonder." He pointed across the valley, at the low blue pass, the Kampa La, between the mountains Tampa and Tsang. "It was a pleasant day, and he put the car's top down. A windstorm came up as he was riding near a crossroads, and his fur hat blew off his head into a thorn bush, where he couldn't reach it. He simply drove on his way.

"Other people walked past the bush, and they saw something inside. They told each other they'd seen something odd there. The hat got weathered and less easy to recognize. Soon the locals were telling travelers to beware the thing near the crossroads, and someone else suggested the thing might be a demon, and soon people were warning others about the demon in the bush."

"Delusion," said !urq.

"It *was* delusion," Jigme agreed. "But it was *not* delusion when the hat grew arms, legs, and teeth, and when it began chasing people up and down the Kampa La. The Ministry of Magic had to send a naljorpa to perform a rite of chöd and banish the thing."

!urq's antennae gave a meditative quiver. "People see what they want to see," she said.

"The delusion had incarnated itself. The case is classic: the Ministries of Science and Magic performed an inquiry. They could trace the patterns of energy through the crystal structure of the Library: the power of the growing belief, the reaction when the belief was fulfilled, the dispersing of the energy when chöd was performed." Jigme gave a laugh. "In the end, the naljorpa brought back an old, weathered hat. Just bits of fur and leather."

"The naljorpa got a good reward, no doubt," said !urq, "for bringing back this moldy bit of fur."

"Probably. Not my department, actually."

"It seems possible, here on Vajra, to make a good living out of others' delusions. My government would not permit such things."

"What do the people lose by being credulous?" Jigme asked. "Only money, which is earthly, and that is a pitiful thing to worry about. It would matter only that the act of giving is sincere."

!urq gave a toss of her head. "We should continue up the mountain, Rinpoche."

"Certainly." Jigme kicked his pony into a trot. He wondered if he had just convinced !urq that his government was corrupt in allowing fakirs to gull the population. Jigme knew there were many ways to Enlightenment and that the soul must try them all. Just because the preacher was corrupt did not mean his message was untrue. How to convince !urq of that? he wondered.

"We believe it is good to test oneself against things," !urq said. "Life is struggle, and one must remain sharp. Ready for whatever happens."

"In the *Parinibbana-sutra,* the Blessed One says that the point of his teaching is to control our own minds. Then one can be ready."

"Of course we control our minds, Rinpoche. If we could not control our minds, we would not achieve mastery. If we do not achieve mastery, then we are nothing."

"I am pleased, then," Jigme smiled, "that you and the Buddha are in agreement."

To which !urq had no reply, save only to launch herself savagely at the next climb, while Jigme followed easily on his cloven-hoofed pony.

The scent of incense and flowers filled the Gyalpo Rinpoche's giant yellow tent. The Treasured King, a silk khata around his neck, sat in the lotus pos-

ture on soft grass. The bottoms of his feet were stained green. Ambassador
!urq stood ponderously before him, lower lip thrust forward, her four arms in
a formal stance, the Incarnation's knotted scarf draped over her shoulders.

Jigme watched, standing next to the erect, angry figure of Dr. O'Neill.
He took comfort from the ever-serene smile of Miss Taisuke, sitting on the
grass across the tent.

"Ambassador Colonel, I am happy you have joined us on holiday."

"We are pleased to participate in your festivals, Omniscient," said !urq.

"The spring flowers are lovely, are they not? It's worthwhile to take a
whole week to enjoy them. In so doing, we remember the words of Shakyamuni, who tells us to enjoy the blossoms of Enlightenment in their season
and harvest the fruit of the right path."

"Is there a season, Omniscient, for discussing the matter of Gyangtse?"

Right to the point, Jigme thought. !urq might never learn the oblique
manner of speech that predominated at the high ministerial levels.

The Incarnation was not disturbed. "Surely matters may be discussed
in any season," he said.

"The planet is desirable, Omniscient. Your settlement violates our border. My government demands your immediate evacuation."

Dr. O'Neill's breath hissed out at the word *demand.* Jigme could see her
ears redden with fury.

"The first humans reached the planet before the border negotiations were
completed," the Incarnation said equably. "They did not realize they were
settling in violation of the agreement."

"That does not invalidate the agreement."

"Conceded, Ambassador. Still, would it not be unjust, after all their hard
labor, to ask them to move?"

!urq's antennae bobbed politely. "Does not your Blessed One admit that
life is composed of suffering? Does the Buddha not condemn the demon of
worldly desires? What desire could be more worldly than a desire to possess a
world?"

Jigme was impressed. Definitely, he thought, she was getting better at
this sort of thing.

"In the same text," said Jigme, "Shakyamuni tells us to refrain from dis-
putes, and not repel one another like water and oil, but like milk and water
mingle together." He opened his hands in an offering gesture. "Will your
government not accept a new planet in exchange? Or better yet, will they not
dispose of this border altogether, and allow a free commerce between our races?"

"What new planet?" !urq's arms formed a querying posture.

"We explore constantly in order to fulfill the mandate of the Library
and provide it with more data. Our survey records are available through your
Library access. Choose any planet that has not yet been inhabited by humans."

"Any planet chosen will be outside of our zone of influence, far from our own frontiers and easily cut off from our home sphere."

"Why would we cut you off, Ambassador?"

"Gyangtse is of strategic significance. It is a penetration of our border."

"Let us then dispose of the border entirely."

!urq's antennae stood erect. Her arms took a martial position. "You humans are larger, more populous. You would overwhelm us by sheer numbers. The border must remain inviolate."

"Let us then have greater commerce across the border than before. With increased knowledge, distrust will diminish."

"You would send missionaries. I know there are Jesuits and Gelugspa who have been training for years in hopes of obtaining converts or martyrdom in the Sang dominions."

"It would be a shame to disappoint them." There was a slight smile on the Incarnation's face.

!urq's arms formed an obstinate pattern. "They would stir up trouble among the Maskers. They would preach to the credulous among my own race. My government must protect its own people."

"The message of Shakyamuni is not a political message, Ambassador."

"That is a matter of interpretation, Omniscient."

"Will you transmit my offer to your government?"

!urq held her stance for a long moment. Jigme could sense Dr. O'Neill's fury in the alien's obstinacy. "I will do so, Omniscient," said the Ambassador. "Though I have no confidence that it will be accepted."

"I think the offer will be accepted," said Miss Taisuke. She sat on the grass in Jigme's tent. She was in the butterfly position, the soles of her feet pressed together and her knees on the ground. Jigme sat beside her. One of Jigme's students, a clean-limbed lad named Rabjoms, gracefully served them tea and cakes, then withdrew.

"The Sang are obdurate," said Jigme. "Why do you think there is hope?"

"Sooner or later the Sang will realize they may choose any one of hundreds of unoccupied planets. It will dawn on them that they can pick one on the far side of our sphere, and their spy ships can travel the length of human-occupied space on quite legitimate missions, and gather whatever information they desire."

"Ah."

"All this in exchange for one minor border penetration."

Jigme thought about this for a moment. "We've held onto Gyangtse in order to test the Sangs' rationality and their willingness to fight. There has been no war in twelve years. This shows that the Sang are susceptible to reason. Where there is reason, there is capability for Enlightenment."

"Amen," said Miss Taisuke. She finished her tea and put down the glass. "Would you like more? Shall I summon Rabjoms?"

"Thank you, no." She cast a glance back to the door of the tent. "He has lovely brown eyes, your Rabjoms."

"Yes. "

Miss Taisuke looked at him. "Is he your consort?"

Jigme put down his glass. "No. I try to forsake worldly passions."

"You are of the Red Hat order. You have taken no vow of celibacy."

Agitation fluttered in Jigme's belly. "The *Mahaparinirvana-sutra* says that lust is the soil in which other passions flourish. I avoid it."

"I wondered. It has been remarked that all your pages are such pretty boys."

Jigme tried to calm himself. "I choose them for other qualities, Miss Taisuke. I assure you."

She laughed merrily. "Of course. I merely wondered." She leaned forward from out of her butterfly position, reached out, and touched his cheek. "I have a sense this may be a randy incarnation for me. You have no desire for young girls?"

Jigme did not move. "I cannot help you, Minister."

"Poor Jigme." She drew her hand back. "I will offer prayers for you."

"Prayers are always accepted, Miss Taisuke."

"But not passes. Very well." She rose to her feet, and Jigme rose with her. "I must be off to the Kagyupas' party. Will you be there?"

"I have scheduled this hour for meditation. Perhaps later."

"Later, then." She kissed his cheek and squeezed his hand, then slipped out of the tent. Jigme sat in the lotus posture and called for Rabjoms to take away the tea things. As he watched the boy's graceful movements, he gave an inward sigh. His weakness had been noticed, and, even worse, remarked on.

His next student would have to be ugly. The ugliest one he could find. He sighed again.

A shriek rang out. Jigme looked up, heart hammering, and saw a demon at the back of the tent. Its flesh was bright red, and its eyes seemed to bulge out of its head. Rabjoms yelled and flung the tea service at it; a glass bounced off its head and shattered.

The demon charged forward, Rabjoms falling under its clawed feet. The overwhelming smell of decay filled the tent. The demon burst through the tent flap into the outdoors. Jigme heard more shrieks and cries of alarm from outside. The demon roared like a bull, then laughed like a madman. Jigme crawled forward to gather up Rabjoms, holding the terrified boy in his arms, chanting the Horse of the Air to calm himself until he heard the teakettle hissing of a thousand snakes followed by a rush of wind, the sign that the entity had dispersed. Jigme soothed his page and tried to think what the meaning of this sudden burst of psychic energy might be.

A few moments later, Jigme received a call on his radiophone. The Gyalpo Rinpoche, a few moments after returning to the Library Palace in his hovertent, had fallen stone dead.

"Cerebral hemorrhage," said Dr. O'Neill. The Minister of Science had performed the autopsy herself—her long hair was undone and tied behind, to fit under a surgical cap, and she still wore her scrubs. She was without the long turquoise earring that marked her rank, and she kept waving a hand near her ear, as if she somehow missed it. "The Incarnation was an old man," she said. "A slight erosion in an artery, and he was gone. It took only seconds."

The Cabinet accepted the news in stunned silence. For all their lives, there had been only the one Treasured King. Now the anchor of all their lives had been removed.

"The reincarnation was remarkably swift," Dr. O'Neill said. "I was able to watch most of it on the monitors in real time—the energies remained remarkably focused, not dissipated in a shower of sparks as with most individuals. I must admit I was impressed. The demon that appeared at the Picnic Festival was only one of the many side effects caused by such a massive turbulence within the crystal architecture of the Diamond Mountain."

Miss Taisuke looked up. "Have you identified the child?"

"Of course." Dr. O'Neill allowed herself a thin-lipped smile. "A second-trimester baby, to be born to a family of tax collectors in Dulan Province, near the White Ocean. The fetus is not developed to the point where a full incarnation is possible, and the energies remain clinging to the mother until they can move to the child. She must be feeling ... elevated. I would like to interview her about her sensations before she is informed that she is carrying the new Bodhisattva." Dr. O'Neill waved a hand in the vicinity of her ear again.

"We must appoint a regent," said Daddy Carbajal.

"Yes," said Dr. O'Neill. "The more to mind, with the human sphere being threatened by the unenlightened."

Jigme looked from one to the other. The shock of the Gyalpo Rinpoche's death had unnerved him to the point of forgetting political matters. Clearly this had not been the case with O'Neill and the Minister of Magic.

He could not let the reactionary party dominate this meeting.

"I believe," he said, "we should appoint Miss Taisuke as Regent."

His words surprised even himself.

The struggle was prolonged. Dr. O'Neill and Daddy Carbajal fought an obstinate rearguard action, but finally Miss Taisuke was confirmed. Jigme had a feeling that several of the ministers only consented to Miss Taisuke because they thought she was young enough that they might manipulate her. They didn't know her well, Jigme thought, and that was fortunate.

"We must formulate a policy concerning Gyangtse and the Sang," Dr. O'Neill said. Her face assumed its usual thin-lipped stubbornness.

"The Omniscient's policy was always to delay," Miss Taisuke said. "This sad matter will furnish a further excuse for postponing any final decision."

"We must put the armed forces on alert. The Sang may consider this a moment in which to strike."

The Regent nodded. "Let this be done."

"There is the matter of the new Incarnation," Dr. O'Neill said. "Should the delivery be advanced? How should the parents be informed?"

"We shall consult the State Oracle," said Miss Taisuke.

The Oracle, his toothless mouth gaping, was a picture of terror. No one had asked him anything in years.

Eerie music echoed through the Oracular Hall of the Library, off the walls and ceiling covered with grotesque carvings—gods, demons, and skulls that grinned at the intent humans below. Chanting monks sat in rows, accompanied by magicians playing drums and trumpets all made from human bone. Jigme's stinging eyes watered from the gusts of strong incense.

In the middle of it all sat the State Oracle, his wrinkled face expressionless. Before him, sitting on a platform, was Miss Taisuke, dressed in the formal clothing of the Regency.

"In old Tibetan times, the Oracle used to be consulted frequently," Jigme told Ambassador !urq. "But since the Gyalpo Rinpoche has been incarnated on Vajra, the Omniscient's close association with the universe analogue of the Library has made most divination unnecessary. The State Oracle is usually called upon only during periods between Incarnations."

"I am having trouble phrasing my reports to my superiors, Rinpoche," said !urq. "Your government is at present run by a fifteen-year-old girl with the advice of an elderly fortune-teller. I expect to have a certain amount of difficulty getting my superiors to take this seriously."

"The Oracle is a serious diviner," Jigme said. "There are a series of competitive exams to discover his degree of empathy with the Library. Our Oracle was right at the top of his class."

"My government will be relieved to know it."

The singing and chanting had been going on for hours. !urq had long been showing signs of impatience. Suddenly the Oracle gave a start. His eyes and mouth dropped open. His face had lost all character.

Then something else was there, an alien presence. The Oracle jumped up from his seated position, began to whirl wildly with his arms outstretched.

Several of his assistants ran forward carrying his headdress while others seized him, holding his rigid body steady. The headdress was enormous, all hand-wrought gold featuring skulls and gods and topped with a vast array of plumes. It weighed over ninety pounds.

"The Oracle, by use of intent meditation, has driven the spirit from his own body," Jigme reported. "He is now possessed by the Library, which assumes the form of the god Yamantaka, the Conqueror of Death."

"Interesting," !urq said noncommittally.

"An old man could not support that headdress without some form of psychic help," Jigme said. "Surely you must agree?" He was beginning to be annoyed by the Ambassador's perpetual skepticism.

The Oracle's assistants had managed to strap the headdress on the Oracle's bald head. They stepped back, and the Oracle continued his dance, the weighty headdress supported by his rigid neck. The Oracle dashed from one end of the room to the other, still whirling, sweat spraying off his brow, then ran to the feet of Miss Taisuke and fell to his knees.

When he spoke it was in a metallic, unnatural voice. "The Incarnation should be installed by New Year!" he shouted, and then toppled. When the assistant monks had unstrapped the heavy headdress and the old man rose, back in his body once more and rubbing his neck, the Oracle looked at Miss Taisuke and blinked painfully. "I resign," he said.

"Accepted," said the Regent. "With great regret."

"This is a young man's job. I could have broken my damn neck."

Ambassador !urq's antennae pricked forward. "This," she said, "is an unusually truthful oracle."

"Top of his class," said Jigme. "What did I tell you?"

The new Oracle was a young man, a strict orthodox Yellow Hat whose predictive abilities had been proved outstanding by every objective test. The calendar of festivals rolled by: the time of pilgrimage, the week of operas and plays, the kite-flying festival, the end of Ramadan, Buddha's descent from Tishita Heaven, Christmas, the celebration of Kali the Benevolent, the anniversary of the death of Tsongkhapa. The New Year was calculated to fall sixty days after Christmas, and for weeks beforehand the artisans of Vajra worked on their floats. The floats—huge sculptures of fabulous buildings, religious icons, famous scenes from the opera featuring giant animated figures, tens of thousands of man-hours of work—would be taken through the streets of the Diamond City during the New Year's procession, then up onto Burning Hill in plain sight of the Library Palace where the new Incarnation could view them from the balcony.

And week after week, the new Incarnation grew, as fast as the technology safely permitted. Carefully removed from his mother's womb by Dr.

O'Neill, the Incarnation was placed in a giant autowomb and fed a diet of nutrients and hormones calculated to bring him to adulthood. Microscopic wires were inserted carefully into his developing brain to feed the memory centers with scripture, philosophy, science, art, and the art of governing. As the new Gyalpo Rinpoche grew the body was exercised by electrode so that he would emerge with physical maturity.

The new Incarnation had early on assumed the lotus position during his rest periods, and Jigme often came to the Science Ministry to watch, through the womb's transparent cover, the eerie figure meditating in the bubbling nutrient solution. All growth of hair had been suppressed by Dr. O'Neill and the figure seemed smooth perfection. The Omniscient-to-be was leaving early adolescence behind, growing slim and cat-muscled.

The new Incarnation would need whatever strength it possessed. The political situation was worsening. The border remained unresolved—the Sang wanted not simply a new planet in exchange for Gyangtse, but also room to expand into a new militarized sphere on the other side of human space. Sang military movements, detected from the human side of the border, seemed to be rehearsals for an invasion, and were countered by increased human defense allotments. As a deterrent, the human response was made obvious to the Sang: Ambassador !urq complained continually about human aggression. Dr. O'Neill and Daddy Carbajal grew combative in Cabinet meetings. Opposition to them was scattered and unfocused. If the reactionary party wanted war, the Sang were doing little but playing into their hands.

Fortunately the Incarnation would be decanted within a week, to take possession of the rambling, embittered councils and give them political direction. Jigme closed his eyes and offered a long prayer that the Incarnation might soon make his presence felt among his ministers.

He opened his eyes. The smooth, adolescent Incarnation hovered before him, suspended in golden nutrient. Fine bubbles rose in the liquid, stroking the Incarnation's skin. The figure had a fascinating, eerie beauty, and Jigme felt he could stare at it forever.

Jigme saw, to his surprise, that the floating Incarnation had an erection. And then the Incarnation opened his eyes.

The eyes were green. Jigme felt coldness flood his spine—the look was knowing, a look of recognition. A slight smile curled the Incarnation's lips. Jigme stared. The smile seemed cruel.

Dry-mouthed, Jigme bent forward, slammed his forehead to the floor in obeisance. Pain crackled through his head. He stayed that way for a long time, offering prayer after frantic prayer.

When he finally rose, the Incarnation's eyes were closed, and the body sat calmly amid golden, rising bubbles.

The late Incarnation's rosary seemed warm as it lay against Jigme's neck. Perhaps it was anticipating being reunited with its former owner.

"The Incarnation is being dressed," Dr. O'Neill said. She stepped through the doors into the vast cabinet room. Two novice monks, doorkeepers, bowed as she swept past, their tongues stuck out in respect, then swung the doors shut behind her. O'Neill was garbed formally in a dress so heavy with brocade that it crackled as she moved. Yellow lamplight flickered from the braid as she moved through the darkened council chamber. Her piled hair was hidden under an embroidered cap; silver gleamed from the elaborate settings of her long turquoise earring. "He will meet with the Cabinet in a few moments and perform the recognition ceremony."

The Incarnation had been decanted that afternoon. He had walked as soon as he was permitted. The advanced growth techniques used by Dr. O'Neill appeared to have met with total success. Her eyes glowed with triumph; her cheeks were flushed.

She took her seat among the Cabinet, moving stiffly in the heavy brocade.

The Cabinet sat surrounding a small table on which some of the late Incarnation's possessions were surrounded by a number of similar objects or imitations. His rosary was around Jigme's neck. During the recognition ceremony, the new Incarnation was supposed to single out his possessions in order to display his continuance from the former personality. The ceremony was largely a formality, a holdover from the earlier, Tibetan tradition—it was already perfectly clear, from Library data, just who the Incarnation was.

There was a shout from the corridor outside, then a loud voice raised in song. The members of the Cabinet stiffened in annoyance. Someone was creating a disturbance. The Regent beckoned to a communications device hidden in an image of Kali, intending to summon guards and have the disorderly one ejected.

The doors swung open, each held by a bowing novice with outthrust tongues. The Incarnation appeared between them. He was young, just entering late adolescence. He was dressed in the tall crested formal hat and yellow robe stiff with brocade. Green eyes gleamed in the dim light as he looked at the assembled officials.

The Cabinet moved as one, offering obeisance first with praying hands lifted to the forehead, mouth, and heart, then prostrated themselves with their heads to the ground. As he fell forward, Jigme heard a voice singing.

> *Let us drink and sport today,*
> *Ours is not tomorrow.*
> *Love with Youth flies swift away,*
> *Age is nought but Sorrow.*

Dance and sing,
Time's on the wing,
Life never knows the return of Spring.

In slow astonishment, Jigme realized that it was the Incarnation who was singing. Gradually Jigme rose from his bow.

Jigme saw that the Incarnation had a bottle in his hand. Was he drunk? he wondered. And where in the Library had he gotten the beer, or whatever it was? Had he materialized it?

"This way, boy," said the Incarnation. He had a hand on the shoulder of one of the doorkeepers. He drew the boy into the room, then took a long drink from his bottle. He eyed the Cabinet slowly, turning his head from one to the other.

"Omniscient—" said Miss Taisuke.

"Not yet," said the Incarnation. "I've been in a glass sphere for almost ten months. It's time I had some fun." He pushed the doorkeeper onto hands and knees, then knelt behind the boy. He pushed up the boy's zen, clutched at his buttocks. The page cast little frantic glances around the room. The new State Oracle seemed apoplectic.

"I see you've got some of my things," said the Incarnation.

Jigme felt something twitch around his neck. The former Incarnation's skull-rosary was beginning to move. Jigme's heart crashed in his chest.

The Cabinet watched in stunned silence as the Incarnation began to sodomize the doorkeeper. The boy's face showed nothing but panic and terror.

This is a lesson, Jigme thought insistently. This is a living Bodhisattva doing this, and somehow this is one of his sermons. We will learn from this.

The rosary twitched, rose slowly from around Jigme's neck, and flew through the air to drop around the Incarnation's head.

A plain ivory walking stick rose from the table and spun through the air. The Incarnation materialized a third arm to catch the cane in midair. A decorated porcelain bowl followed, a drum, and a small golden figurine of a laughing Buddha ripped itself free from the pocket of the new State Oracle. Each was caught by a new arm. Each item had belonged to the former Incarnation; each was the correct choice.

The Incarnation howled like a beast at the moment of climax. Then he stood, adjusting his garments. He bent to pick up the ivory cane. He smashed the porcelain bowl with it, then broke the cane over the head of the Buddha. He rammed the Buddha through the drum, then threw both against the wall. All six hands rose to the rosary around his neck; he ripped at it and the cord broke, white bone disks flying through the room. His extra arms vanished.

"Short Path," he said, turned and stalked out.

Across the room, in the long silence that followed, Jigme could see Dr. O'Neill. Her pale face seemed to float in the darkness, distinct amid the confusion and madness, her expression frozen in a racking, electric moment of private agony. The minister's moment of triumph had turned to ashes.

Perhaps everything had.

Jigme rose to comfort the doorkeeper.

"There has never been an Incarnation who followed the Short Path," said Miss Taisuke.

"Daddy Carbajal should be delighted," Jigme said. "He's a doubtob himself."

"I don't think he's happy," said the Regent. "I watched him. He is a tantric sorcerer, yes, one of the best. But the Incarnation's performance frightened him."

They spoke alone in Miss Taisuke's townhouse—in the lha khang, a room devoted to religious images. Incense floated gently in the air. Outside, Jigme could hear the sounds of celebration as the word reached the population that the Incarnation was among them once again.

A statue of the Thunderbolt Sow came to life, looked at the Regent. "A message from the Library Palace, Regent," it said. "The Incarnation has spent the evening in his quarters, in the company of an apprentice monk. He has now passed out from drunkenness."

"Thank you, Rinpoche," Taisuke said. The Thunderbolt Sow froze in place. Taisuke turned back to Jigme.

"His Omniscience is possibly the most powerful doubtob in history," she said. "Dr. O'Neill showed me the spectra—the display of psychic energy, as recorded by the Library, was truly awesome. And it was perfectly controlled."

"Could something have gone wrong with the process of bringing the Incarnation to adulthood?"

"The process has been used for centuries. It has been used on Incarnations before—it was a fad for a while, and the Eighteenth through Twenty-Third were all raised that way." She frowned, leaning forward. "In any case, it's all over. The Librarian Bob Miller—and the divine Avalokitesvara, if you go for that sort of thing—has now been reincarnated as the Forty-Second Gyalpo Rinpoche. There's nothing that can be done."

"Nothing," Jigme said. The Short Path, he thought, the path to Enlightenment taken by magicians and madmen, a direct route that had no reference to morality or convention. ... The Short Path was dangerous, often heterodox, and colossally difficult. Most doubtobs ended up destroying themselves and everyone around them.

"We have had carnal incarnations before," Taisuke said. "The Eighth left some wonderful love poetry behind, and quite a few have been sodomites.

No harm was done."

"I will pray, Regent," said Jigme, "that no harm may be done now."

It seemed to him that there was a shadow on Taisuke's usual blazing smile. "That is doubtless the best solution. I will pray also."

Jigme returned to the Nyingmapa monastery, where he had an apartment near the Sang embassy. He knew he was too agitated to sit quietly and meditate, and so called for some novices to bring him a meditation box. He needed to discipline both body and mind before he could find peace.

He sat in the narrow box in a cross-legged position and drew the lid over his head. Cut off from the world, he would not allow himself to relax, to lean against the walls of the box for support. He took his rosary in his hands. *"Aum vajra sattva,"* he began, Aum the Diamond Being, one of the names of Buddha.

But the picture that floated before his mind was not that of Shakyamuni, but the naked, beautiful form of the Incarnation, staring at him from out of the autowomb with green, soul-chilling eyes.

"We should have killed the Jesuit as well. We refrained only as a courtesy to your government, Rinpoche."

Perhaps, Jigme thought, the dead Maskers' souls were even now in the Library, whirling in the patterns of energy that would result in reincarnation, whirling like the snow that fell gently as he and !urq walked down the street. To be reincarnated as humans, with the possibility of Enlightenment.

"We will dispose of the bodies, if you prefer," Jigme said.

"They dishonored their masters," said !urq. "You may do what you like with them."

As Jigme and the Ambassador walked through the snowy streets toward the Punishment Grounds, they were met with grins and waves from the population, who were getting ready for the New Year celebration. !urq acknowledged the greetings with graceful nods of her antennae. Once the population heard what had just happened, Jigme thought, the reception might well be different.

"I will send monks to collect the bodies. We will cut them up and expose them on hillsides for the vultures. Afterward their bones will be collected and perhaps turned into useful implements."

"In my nation," !urq said, "that would be considered an insult."

"The bodies will nourish the air and the earth," said Jigme. "What finer kind of death could there be?"

"Elementary. A glorious death in service to the state."

Two Masker servants, having met several times with a Jesuit acting apparently without orders from his superiors, had announced their conversion to Buddhism. !urq had promptly denounced the two as spies and had them shot out of hand. The missionary had been ordered whipped by the superiors in his Order. !urq wanted to be on hand for it.

Jigme could anticipate the public reaction. Shakyamuni had strictly forbidden the taking of life. The people would be enraged. It might be unwise for the Sang to be seen in public for the next few days, particularly during the New Year Festival, when a large percentage of the population would be drunk.

Jigme and the Ambassador passed by a row of criminals in the stocks. Offerings of flowers, food, and money were piled up below them, given by the compassionate population. Another criminal—a murderer, probably—shackled in leg irons for life, approached with his begging bowl. Jigme gave him some money and passed on.

"Your notions of punishment would be considered far from enlightened in my nation," !urq said. "Flogging, branding, putting people in chains! We would consider that savage."

"We punish only the body," Jigme said. "We always allow an opportunity for the spirit to reform. Death without Enlightenment can only result in a return to endless cycles of reincarnation."

"A clean death is always preferable to bodily insult. And a lot of your flogging victims die afterward."

"But they do not die during the flogging."

"Yet they die in agony, because your whips tear their backs apart."

"Pain," said Jigme, "can be transcended."

"Sometimes," !urq said, antennae twitching, "you humans are terrifying. I say this in absolute and admiring sincerity."

There were an unusual number of felons today, since the authorities wanted to empty the holding cells before the New Year. The Jesuit was among them—a calm, bearded, black-skinned man stripped to the waist, waiting to be lashed to the triangle. Jigme could see that he was deep in a meditative trance.

Suddenly the grey sky darkened. People looked up and pointed. Some fell down in obeisance, others bowed and thrust out their tongues.

The Incarnation was overhead, sitting on a wide hovercraft, covered with red paint and hammered gold, that held a small platform and throne. He sat in a full lotus, his elfin form dressed only in a light yellow robe. Snow melted on his shoulders and cheeks.

The proceedings halted for a moment while everyone waited for the Incarnation to say something, but at an impatient gesture from the floating throne things got under way. The floggings went efficiently, sometimes more than one going on at once. The crowd succored many of the victims with money or offers of food or medicine. There was another slight hesitation as the Jesuit was brought forward—perhaps the Incarnation would comment on, or stay, the punishment of someone who had been trying to spread his faith—but from the Incarnation came only silence. The Jesuit absorbed his twenty lashes without comment, was taken away by his cohorts. To be praised and promoted, if Jigme knew the Jesuits.

The whipping went on. Blood spattered the platform. Finally there was only one convict remaining, a young monk of perhaps seventeen in a dirty, torn zen. He was a big lad, broad-shouldered and heavily-muscled, with a malformed head and a peculiar brutal expression—at once intent and unfocused, as if he knew he hated something but couldn't be bothered to decide exactly what it was. His body was possessed by constant, uncontrollable tics and twitches. He was surrounded by police with staves. Obviously they considered him dangerous.

An official read off the charges. Kyetsang Kunlegs had killed his guru, then set fire to the dead man's hermitage in hopes of covering his crime. He was sentenced to six hundred lashes and to be shackled for life. Jigme suspected he would not get much aid from the crowd afterward; most of them were reacting with disgust.

"Stop," said the Incarnation. Jigme gaped. The floating throne was moving forward. It halted just before Kunlegs. The murderer's guards stuck out their tongues but kept their eyes on the killer.

"Why did you kill your guru?" the Incarnation asked.

Kunlegs stared at him and twitched, displaying nothing but fierce hatred. He gave no answer.

The Incarnation laughed. "That's what I thought," he said. "Will you be my disciple if I remit your punishment?"

Kunlegs seemed to have difficulty comprehending this. His belligerent expression remained unaltered. Finally he just shrugged. A violent twitch made the movement grotesque.

The Incarnation lowered his throne. "Get on board," he said. Kunlegs stepped onto the platform. The Incarnation rose from his lotus, adjusted the man's garments, and kissed him on the lips. They sat down together.

"Short Path," said the Incarnation. The throne sped at once for the Library Palace.

Jigme turned to the Ambassador. !urq had watched without visible expression.

"Terrifying," she said. "Absolutely terrifying."

Jigme sat with the other Cabinet members in a crowded courtyard of the Palace. The Incarnation was about to go through the last of the rituals required before his investiture as the Gyalpo Rinpoche. Six learned elders of six different religious orders would engage the Incarnation in prolonged debate. If he did well against them, he would be formally enthroned and take the reins of government.

The Incarnation sat on a platform-throne opposite the six. Behind him, gazing steadily with his expression of misshapen, twitching brutality, was the murderer Kyetsang Kunlegs.

The first elder rose. He was a Sufi, representing a three-thousand-year-old intellectual tradition. He stuck out his tongue and took a formal stance.

"What is the meaning of Dharma?" he began.

"I'll show you," said the Incarnation, although the question had obviously been rhetorical. The Incarnation opened his mouth, and a demon the size of a bull leapt out. Its flesh was pale as dough and covered with running sores. The demon seized the Sufi and flung him to the ground, then sat on his chest. The sound of breaking bones was audible.

Kyetsang Kunlegs opened his mouth and laughed, revealing huge yellow teeth.

The demon rose and advanced toward the five remaining elders, who fled in disorder.

"I win," said the Incarnation.

Kunlegs' laughter broke like obscene bubbles over the stunned audience.

"Short Path," said the Incarnation.

"Such a shame," said the Ambassador. Firelight flickered off her ebon features. "How many man-years of work has gone into it all? And by morning it'll be ashes."

"Everything comes to an end," said Jigme. "If the floats are not destroyed tonight, they would be gone in a year. If not a year, ten years. If not ten years, a century. If not a century ..."

"I quite take your point, Rinpoche," said !urq.

"Only the Buddha is eternal."

"So I gather."

The crowd assembled on the roof of the Library Palace gasped as another of the floats on Burning Hill went up in flames. This one was made of figures from the opera, who danced and sang and did combat with one another until, burning, they came apart on the wind.

Jigme gratefully took a glass of hot tea from a servant and warmed his hands. The night was clear but bitterly cold. The floating throne moved silently overhead, and Jigme stuck out his tongue in salute. The Gyalpo Rinpoche, in accordance with the old Oracle's instructions, had assumed his title that afternoon.

"Jigme Dzasa, may I speak with you?" A soft voice at his elbow, that of the former Regent.

"Of course, Miss Taisuke. You will excuse me, Ambassador?"

Jigme and Taisuke moved apart. "The Incarnation has indicated that he wishes me to continue as head of the government," Taisuke said.

"I congratulate you, Prime Minister," said Jigme, surprised. He had assumed the Gyalpo Rinpoche would wish to run the state himself.

"I haven't accepted yet," she said. "It isn't a job I desire." She sighed. "I was hoping to have a randy incarnation, Jigme. Instead I'm being worked to death."

"You have my support, Prime Minister."

She gave a rueful smile and patted his arm. "Thank you. I fear I'll have to accept, if only to keep certain other people from positions where they might do harm." She leaned close, her whisper carrying over the sound of distant fireworks. "Dr. O'Neill approached me. She wished to know my views concerning whether we can declare the Incarnation insane and reinstitute the Regency."

Jigme gazed at Taisuke in shock. "Who supports this?"

"Not I. I made that clear enough."

"Daddy Carbajal?"

"I think he's too cautious. The new State Oracle might be in favor of the idea—he's such a strict young man, and, of course, his own status would rise if he became the Library's interpreter instead of subordinate to the Gyalpo Rinpoche. O'Neill herself made the proposal in a veiled manner—*if* such-and-such a thing proved true, how would I react? She never made a specific proposal."

Anger burned in Jigme's belly. "The Incarnation cannot be insane!" he said. "That would mean the Library itself is insane. That the Buddha is insane."

"People are uncomfortable with the notion of a doubtob Incarnation."

"What people? What are their names? They should be corrected!" Jigme realized that his fists were clenched, that he was trembling with anger.

"Hush. O'Neill can do nothing."

"She speaks treason! Heresy!"

"Jigme ..."

"Ah. The Prime Minister." Jigme gave a start at the sound of the Incarnation's voice. The floating throne, its gold ornaments gleaming in the light of the burning floats, descended noiselessly from the bright sky. The Incarnation was covered only by a reskyang, the simple white cloth worn even in the bitterest weather by adepts of tumo, the discipline of controlling one's own internal heat.

"You *will* be my Prime Minister, yes?" the Incarnation said. His green eyes seemed to glow in the darkness. Kyetsang Kunlegs loomed over his shoulder like a demon shadow.

Taisuke bowed, sticking out her tongue. "Of course, Omniscient."

"When I witnessed the floggings the other day," the Incarnation said, "I was shocked by the lack of consistency. Some of the criminals seemed to have the sympathy of the officials, and the floggers did not use their full strength. Some of the floggers were larger and stronger than others. Toward the end they all got tired, and did not lay on with proper force. This does not seem to me to be adequate justice. I would like to propose a reform." He handed Taisuke a paper. "Here I have described a flogging machine. Each strike will be equal to the one before. And as the machine is built on a rotary principle, the machine can be inscribed with religious texts, like a prayer wheel. We can therefore grant prayers and punish the wicked simultaneously. "

Taisuke seemed overcome. She looked down at the paper as if afraid to open it. "Very … elegant, Omniscient."

"I thought so. See that the machine is instituted throughout humanity, Prime Minister."

"Very well, Omniscient."

The floating throne rose into the sky to the accompaniment of the murderer Kunlegs' gross bubbling laughter. Taisuke looked at Jigme with desperation in her eyes.

"We must protect him, Jigme," she said.

"Of course."

"We must be very, very careful."

She loves him, too, he thought. A river of sorrow poured through his heart.

Jigme looked up, seeing Ambassador !urq standing with her head lifted to watch the burning spectacle on the hill opposite. "Very careful indeed," he said.

The cycle of festivals continued. Buddha's birthday, the Picnic Festival, the time of pilgrimage …

In the Prime Minister's lha khang, the Thunderbolt Sow gestured toward Taisuke. "After watching the floggings," it said, "the Gyalpo Rinpoche and Kyetsang Kunlegs went to Diamond City spaceport, where they participated in a night-long orgy with ship personnel. Both have now passed out from indulgence in drink and drugs, and the party has come to an end."

The Prime Minister knit her brows as she listened to the tale. "The stories will get offworld now," Jigme told her.

"They're already offworld."

Jigme looked at her helplessly. "How much damage is being done?"

"Flogging parties? Carousing with strangers? Careening from one monastery to another in search of pretty boys? Gracious heaven—the abbots are pimping their novices to him in hopes of receiving favor." Taisuke gave a lengthy shudder. There was growing seriousness in her eyes. "I'll let you in on a state secret. We've been reading the Sang's dispatches."

"How?" Jigme asked. "They don't use our communications net, and the texts are coded."

"But they compose their messages using electric media," Taisuke said. "We can use the Library crystal as a sensing device, detect each character as it's entered into their coding device. We can also read incoming dispatches the same way."

"I'm impressed, Prime Minister."

"Through this process, we were kept informed of the progress of the Sang's military buildup. We were terrified to discover that it was scheduled to reach its full offensive strength within a few years."

"Ah. That was why you consented to the increase in military allotments."

"Ambassador !urq was instructed not to resolve the Gyangtse matter, in order that it be used as a *casus belli* when the Sang program reached its conclusion. !urq's dispatches to her superiors urged them to attack as soon as their fleet was ready. But now, with the increased military allotments and the political situation, !urq is urging delay. The current Incarnation, she suspects, may so discredit the institution of the Gyalpo Rinpoche that our society may disintegrate without the need for a Sang attack."

"Impossible!" A storm of anger filled Jigme. His hands formed the mudra of astonishment.

"I suspect you're right, Jigme." Solemnly. "They base their models of our society on their own past despotisms—they don't realize that the Treasured King is not a despot or an absolute ruler, but rather someone of great wisdom whom others follow through their own free will. But we should encourage !urq in this estimation, yes? Anything to give impetus to the Sang's more rational impulses."

"But it's based on a slander! And a slander concerning the Incarnation can never be countenanced!"

Taisuke raised an admonishing finger. "The Sang draw their own conclusions. And should we protest this one, we might give away our knowledge of their communications."

Anger and frustration bubbled in Jigme's mind. "What barbarians!" he said. "I have tried to show them truth, but ..."

Taisuke's voice was calm. "You have shown them the path of truth. Their choosing not to follow it is their own karma."

Jigme promised himself he would do better. He would compel !urq to recognize the Incarnation's teaching mission.

Teaching, he thought. He remembered the stunned look on the doorkeeper's face that first Cabinet meeting, the Incarnation's cry at the moment of climax, his own desperate attempt to see the thing as a lesson. And then he thought about what !urq would have said, had she been there.

He went to the meditation box that night, determined to exorcise the demon that gnawed at his vitals. Lust, he recited, provides the soil in which other passions flourish. Lust is like a demon that eats up all the good deeds of the world. Lust is a viper hiding in a flower garden; it poisons those who come in search of beauty.

It was all futile. Because all he could think of was the Gyalpo Rinpoche, the lovely body moving rhythmically in the darkness of the Cabinet room.

The moan of ragdongs echoed over the gardens and was followed by drunken applause and shouts. It was the beginning of the festival of plays and operas. The Cabinet and other high officials celebrated the festival at the Jewel Pavilion, the Incarnation's summer palace, where there was an outdoor theater specially built among the sweet-smelling meditative gardens. The palace, a lacy white fantasy ornamented with statues of gods and masts carrying prayer flags, sat bathed in spotlights atop its hill.

In addition to the members of the court were the personal followers of the Incarnation, people he had been gathering during the seven months of his reign. Novice monks and nuns, doubtobs and naljorpas, crazed hermits, looney charlatans and mediums, runaways, workers from the spaceport ... all drunk, all pledged to follow the Short Path wherever it led.

"Disgusting," said Dr. O'Neill. "Loathsome." Furiously she brushed at a spot on her brocaded robe where someone had spilled beer.

Jigme said nothing. Cymbals clashed from the stage, where the orchestra was practicing. Three novice monks went by, staggering under the weight of a flogging machine. The festival was going to begin with the punishment of a number of criminals, and any who could walk afterward would then be able to join the revelers. The first opera would be sung on a stage spattered with blood.

Dr. O'Neill stepped closer to Jigme. "The Incarnation has asked me to furnish him a report on nerve induction. He wishes to devise a machine to induce pain without damage to the body."

Heavy sorrow filled Jigme that he could no longer be surprised by such news. "For what purpose?" he asked.

"To punish criminals, of course. Without crippling them. Then his Omniscience will be able to order up as savage punishments as he likes without being embarrassed by hordes of cripples shuffling around the capital."

Jigme tried to summon indignation. "You should not impart unworthy motives to the Gyalpo Rinpoche."

Dr. O'Neill only gave him a cynical look. Behind her, trampling through a hedge, came a young monk, laughing, being pursued by a pair of women with whips. O'Neill looked at them as they dashed off into the darkness. "At least it will give *them* less of an excuse to indulge in such behavior. It won't be as much fun to watch if there isn't any blood."

"That would be a blessing."

"The Forty-Second Incarnation is potentially the finest in history," O'Neill said. Her eyes narrowed in fury. She raised a clenched fist, the knuckles white in the darkness. "The most intelligent Incarnation, the most able, the finest rapport with the Library in centuries … and look at what he is doing with his gifts!"

"I thank you for the compliments, Doctor," said the Incarnation. O'Neill and Jigme jumped. The Incarnation, treading lightly on the summer grass, had walked up behind them. He was dressed only in his white reskyang and the garlands of flowers given him by his followers. Kunlegs, as always, loomed behind him, twitching furiously.

Jigme bowed profoundly, sticking out his tongue.

"The punishment machine," said the Incarnation. "Do the plans move forward?"

Dr. O'Neill's dismay was audible in her reply. "Yes, Omniscient."

"I wish the work to be completed for the New Year. I want particular care paid to the monitors that will alert the operators if the felon's life is in danger. We should not want to violate Shakyamuni's commandment against slaughter."

"The work shall be done, Omniscient."

"Thank you, Dr. O'Neill." He reached out a hand to give her a blessing. "I think of you as my mother, Dr. O'Neill. The lady who tenderly watched over me in the womb. I hope this thought pleases you."

"If it pleases your Omniscience."

"It does." The Incarnation withdrew his hand. In the darkness his smile was difficult to read. "You will be honored for your care for many generations, Doctor. I make you that promise."

"Thank you, Omniscient."

"Omniscient!" A new voice called out over the sound of revelry. The new State Oracle, dressed in the saffron zen of a simple monk, strode toward them over the grass. His thin, ascetic face was bursting with anger.

"Who are these people, Omniscient?" he demanded.

"My friends, minister."

"They are destroying the gardens!"

"They are *my* gardens, minister."

"Vanity!" The Oracle waved a finger under the Incarnation's nose. Kunlegs grunted and started forward, but the Incarnation stopped him with a gesture.

"I am pleased to accept the correction of my ministers," he said.

"Vanity and indulgence!" the Oracle said. "Has the Buddha not told us to forsake worldly desires? Instead of doing as Shakyamuni instructed, you have surrounded yourself with followers who indulge their own sensual pleasures and your vanity!"

"Vanity?" The Incarnation glanced at the Jewel Pavilion. "Look at my summer palace, minister. It is a vanity, a lovely vanity. But it does no harm."

"It is nothing! All the palaces of the world are as nothing beside the word of the Buddha!"

The Incarnation's face showed supernal calm. "Should I rid myself of these vanities, minister?"

"Yes!" The State Oracle stamped a bare foot. "Let them be swept away!"

"Very well. I accept my minister's correction." He raised his voice, calling for the attention of his followers. A collection of drunken rioters gathered around him. "Let the word be spread to all here," he cried. "The Jewel Pavilion is to be destroyed by fire. The gardens shall be uprooted. All statues shall be smashed." He looked at the State Oracle and smiled his cold smile. "I hope this shall satisfy you, minister."

A horrified look was his only reply.

The Incarnation's followers laughed and sang as they destroyed the Jewel Pavilion, as they toppled statues from its roof and destroyed furniture to create bonfires in its luxurious suites. "Short Path!" they chanted. "Short Path!" In the theater the opera began, an old Tibetan epic about the death by treachery of the Sixth Earthly Gyalpo Rinpoche, known to his Mongolian enemies as the Dalai Lama. Jigme found a quiet place in the garden and sat in a full lotus, repeating sutras and trying to calm his mind. But the screams, chanting, songs, and shouts distracted him.

He looked up to see the Gyalpo Rinpoche standing upright amid the ruin of his garden, his head raised as if to sniff the wind. Kunlegs was standing close behind, caressing him. The light of the burning palace danced on his face. The Incarnation seemed transformed, a living embodiment of ... of what? Madness? Exultation? Ecstasy? Jigme couldn't tell, but when he saw it he felt as if his heart would explode.

Then his blood turned cold. Behind the Incarnation, moving through the garden beneath the ritual umbrella of a Masker servant, came Ambassador !urq, her dark face watching the burning palace with something like triumph.

Jigme felt someone near him. "This cannot go on," said Dr. O'Neill's voice, and at the sound of her cool resolution terror flooded him.

"Aum vajra sattva," he chanted, saying the words over and over, repeating them till the Jewel Pavilion was ash and the garden looked as if a whirlwind had torn through it, leaving nothing but tangled ruin.

Rising from the desolation, he saw something bright dangling from the shattered proscenium of the outdoor stage.

It was the young State Oracle, hanging by the neck.

"!urq's dispatches have grown triumphant. She knows that the Gyalpo Rinpo-che has lost the affection of the people, and that they will soon lose their tolerance." Miss Taisuke was decorating a Christmas tree in her lha khang. Little glowing buddhas, in their traditional red suits and white beards, hung amid the evergreen branches. Kali danced on top, holding a skull in either hand.

"What can we do?" said Jigme.

"Prevent a coup whatever the cost. If the Incarnation is deposed or declared mad, the Sang can attack under pretext of restoring the Incarnation. Our own people will be divided. We couldn't hope to win."

"Can't Dr. O'Neill see this?"

"Dr. O'Neill desires war, Jigme. She thinks we will win it whatever occurs."

Jigme thought about what interstellar war would mean; the vast energies of modern weapons deployed against helpless planets. Tens of billions dead, even with a victory. "We should speak to the Gyalpo Rinpoche," he said. "He must be made to understand."

"The State Oracle spoke to him, and what resulted?"

"You, Prime Minister—"

Taisuke looked at him. Her eyes were brimming with tears. "I have *tried* to speak to him. He is interested only in his parties, in his new punishment device. It's all he will talk about."

Jigme said nothing. His eyes stung with tears. Two weeping officials, he thought, alone on Christmas Eve. What more pathetic picture could possibly exist?

"The device grows ever more elaborate," Taisuke said. "There will be life extension and preservation gear installed. The machine can torture people for *lifetimes!*" She shook her head. Her hands trembled as they wiped her eyes. "Perhaps Dr. O'Neill is right. Perhaps the Incarnation needs to be put away."

"Never," Jigme said. "Never."

"Prime Minister." The Thunderbolt Sow shifted in her corner. "The Gyalpo Rinpoche has made an announcement to his people. 'The Short Path will end with the New Year.'"

Taisuke wiped her eyes on her brocaded sleeve. "Was that the entire message?"

"Yes, Prime Minister."

Her eyes rose to Jigme's. "What could it mean?"

"We must have hope, Prime Minister."

"Yes." Her hands clutched at his. "We must try to have hope."

Beneath snapping prayer flags, a quarter-size Jewel Pavilion made of flammable lattice stood on Burning Hill. The Cabinet was gathered inside it, flanking the throne of the Incarnation. The Gyalpo Rinpoche had decided to view the burning from inside one of the floats.

Kyetsang Kunlegs, grinning with his huge yellow teeth, was the only one of his followers present. The others were making merry in the city.

In front of the sham Jewel Pavilion was the new torture machine, a hollow oval, twice the size of a man, its skin the color of brushed metal. The interior was filled with mysterious apparatus.

The Cabinet said the rosary, and the Horse of the Air rose up into the night. The Incarnation, draped with khatas, raised a double drum made from the tops of two human skulls. With a flick of his wrist, a bead on a string began to bound from one drum to the other. With his cold green eyes he watched it rattle for a long moment. "Welcome to my first anniversary," he said.

The others murmured in reply. The drum rattled on. A cold winter wind blew through the pavilion. The Incarnation looked from one Cabinet member to the other and gave his cruel, ambiguous smile.

"On the anniversary of my ascension to the throne and my adoption of the Short Path," he said, "I would like to honor the woman who made it possible." He held out his hand. "Dr. O'Neill, the Minister of Science, whom I think of as my mother. Mother, please come sit in the place of honor."

O'Neill rose stone-faced from her place and walked to the throne. She prostrated herself and stuck out her tongue. The Treasured King stepped off the platform, still rattling the drum; he took her hand, helped her rise. He sat her on the platform in his own place.

Another set of arms materialized on his shoulders; while the first rattled the drum, the other three went through a long succession of mudras. Amazement, Jigme read, fascination, the warding of evil.

"My first memories in this incarnation," he said, "are of fire. Fire that burned inside me, that made me want to claw my way out of my glass womb and launch myself prematurely into existence. Fires that aroused lust and hatred before I knew anyone to hate or lust for. And then, when the fires grew unendurable, I would open my eyes, and there I would see my mother, Dr. O'Neill, watching me with happiness in her face."

Another pair of arms appeared. The Incarnation looked over his shoulder at Dr. O'Neill, who was watching him with the frozen stare given a poison serpent. The Incarnation turned back to the others. The breeze fluttered the khatas around his neck.

"Why should I burn?" he said. "My memories of earlier Incarnations were incomplete, but I knew I had never known such fire before. There was something in me that was not balanced. That was made for the Short Path.

Perhaps Enlightenment could be reached by leaping into the fire. In any case, I had no choice."

There was a flare of light, a roar of applause. The first of the floats outside exploded into flame. Fireworks crackled in the night. The Incarnation smiled. His drum rattled on.

"Never had I been so out of balance," he said. Another pair of arms materialized. "Never had I been so puzzled. Were my compulsions a manifestation of the Library? Was the crystal somehow out of alignment? Or was something else wrong? It was my consort Kyetsang Kunlegs who gave me the first clue." He turned to the throne and smiled at the murderer, who twitched in reply. "Kunlegs has suffered all his life from Tourette's syndrome, an excess of dopamine in the brain. It makes him compulsive, twitchy, and—curiously—brilliant. His brain works too fast for its own good. The condition should have been diagnosed and corrected years ago, but Kunlegs' elders were neglectful."

Kunlegs opened his mouth and gave a long laugh. Dr. O'Neill, seated just before him on the platform, gave a shiver. The Incarnation beamed at Kunlegs, then turned back to his audience.

"I didn't suffer from Tourette's—I didn't have all the symptoms. But seeing poor Kunlegs made it clear where I should look for the source of my difficulty." He raised the drum, rattled it beside his head. "In my own brain," he said.

Another float burst into flame. The bright light glowed through the wickerwork walls of the pavilion, shone on the Incarnation's face. He gazed into it with his cruel half-smile, his eyes dancing in the firelight.

Dr. O'Neill spoke. Her voice was sharp. "Omniscient, may I suggest that we withdraw? This structure is built to burn, and the wind will carry sparks from the other floats toward us."

The Incarnation looked at her. "Later, honored Mother." He turned back to the Cabinet. "Not wanting to bother my dear mother with my suspicions, I visited several doctors when I was engaged in my visits to town and various monasteries. I found that not only did I have a slight excess of dopamine, but that my mind also contained too much serotonin and norepinephrine, and too little endorphin."

Another float burst into flame. Figures from the opera screamed in eerie voices. The Incarnation's smile was beatific. "Yet my honored mother, the Minister of Science, supervised my growth. How could such a thing happen?"

Jigme's attention jerked to Dr. O'Neill. Her face was drained of color. Her eyes were those of someone gazing into the Void.

"Dr. O'Neill, of course, has political opinions. She believes the Sang heretics must be vanquished. Destroyed or subdued at all costs. And to that end she wished an Incarnation who would be a perfect conquering warrior-king—impatient, impulsive, brilliant, careless of life, and indifferent to suffering. Someone with certain sufficiencies and deficiencies in brain chemistry. "

O'Neill opened her mouth. A scream came out, a hollow sound as mindless as those given by the burning floats. The Incarnation's many hands pointed to her, all but the one rattling the drum.

Laughing, Kyetsang Kunlegs lunged forward, twisting the khata around the minister's neck. The scream came to an abrupt end. Choking, she toppled back into his huge lap.

"She is the greatest traitor of all time," the Incarnation said. "She who poisoned the Forty-First Incarnation. She who would subvert the Library itself to her ends. She who would poison the mind of a Bodhisativa." His voice was soft, yet exultant. It sent an eerie chill down Jigme's back.

Kunlegs rose from the platform holding Dr. O'Neill in his big hands. Her piled-up hair had come undone and trailed across the ground. Kunlegs carried her out of the building and into the punishment machine.

The Incarnation's drum stopped rattling. Jigme looked at him in stunned comprehension.

"She shall know what it is to burn," he said. "She shall know it for many lifetimes."

Sparks blew across the floor before the Incarnation's feet. There was a glow from the doorway, where some of the wickerwork had caught fire.

The machine was automatic in its function. Dr. O'Neill began to scream again, a rising series of shrieks. Her body began to rotate. The Incarnation smiled. "She shall make that music for many centuries. Perhaps one of my future incarnations shall put a stop to it."

Jigme felt burning heat on the back of his neck. O'Neill's screams ran up and down his spine. "Omniscient," he said. "The pavilion is on fire. We should leave."

"In a moment. I wish to say a few last words."

Kunlegs came loping back, grinning, and hopped onto the platform. The Incarnation joined him and kissed him tenderly. "Kunlegs and I will stay in the pavilion," he said. "We will both die tonight."

"No!" Taisuke jumped to her feet. "We will not permit it! Your condition can be corrected."

The Incarnation stared at her. "I thank you, loyal one. But my brain is poisoned, and even if the imbalance were corrected I would still be perceiving the Library through a chemical fog that would impair my ability. My next Incarnation will not have this handicap."

"Omniscient!" Tears spilled from Taisuke's eyes. "Don't leave us!"

"You will continue as head of the government. My next Incarnation will be ready by the next New Year, and then you may retire to the secular life I know you wish to pursue in this lifetime."

"No!" Taisuke ran forward, threw herself before the platform. "I beg you, Omniscient!"

Suddenly Jigme was on his feet. He lurched forward, threw himself down beside Taisuke. "Save yourself, Omniscient!" he said.

"I wish to say something concerning the Sang." The Incarnation spoke calmly, as if he hadn't heard. "There will be danger of war in the next year. You must all promise me that you won't fight."

"Omniscient." This from Daddy Carbajal. "We must be ready to defend ourselves!"

"Are we an Enlightened race, or are we not?" The Incarnation's voice was stern.

"You are Bodhisattva." Grudgingly. "All know this."

"We are Enlightened. The Buddha commands us not to take life. If these are not facts, our existence has no purpose, and our civilization is a mockery." O'Neill's screams provided eerie counterpoint to his voice. The Incarnation's many arms pointed at the members of the Cabinet. "You may arm in order to deter attack. But if the Sang begin a war, you must promise me to surrender without condition."

"Yes!" Taisuke, still facedown, wailed from her obeisance. "I promise, Omniscient."

"The Diamond Mountain will be the greatest prize the Sang can hope for. And the Library is the Buddha. When the time is right, the Library will incarnate itself as a Sang, and the Sang will be sent on their path to Enlightenment. "

"Save yourself, Omniscient!" Taisuke wailed. The roar of flames had drowned O'Neill's screams. Jigme felt sparks falling on his shaven head.

"Your plan, sir!" Daddy Carbajal's voice was desperate. "It might not work! The Sang may thwart the incarnation in some way!"

"Are we Enlightened?" The Incarnation's voice was mild. "Or are we not? Is the Buddha's truth eternal, or is it not? Do you not support the Doctrine?"

Daddy Carbajal threw himself down beside Jigme. "I believe, Omniscient! I will do as you ask!"

"Leave us, then. Kyetsang and I wish to be alone."

Certainty seized Jigme. He could feel tears stinging his eyes. "Let me stay, Omniscient!" he cried. "Let me die with you!"

"Carry these people away," said the Incarnation. Hands seized Jigme. He fought them off, weeping, but they were too powerful: he was carried from the burning pavilion. His last sight of the Incarnation was of the Gyalpo Rinpoche and Kunlegs embracing one another, silhouetted against flame, and then everything dissolved in fire and tears.

And in the morning nothing was left, nothing but ashes and the keening cries of the traitor O'Neill, whom the Bodhisattva in his wisdom had sent forever to Hell.

Jigme found !urq there, standing alone before O'Neill, staring at the figure caught in a webwork of life support and nerve stimulators. The sound of the traitor's endless agony continued to issue from her torn throat.

"There will be no war," Jigme said.

!urq looked at him. Her stance was uncertain.

"After all this," Jigme said, "a war would be indecent. You understand?"

!urq just stared.

"You must not unleash this madness in us!" Jigme cried. Tears rolled down his face. "Never, Ambassador! Never!"

!urq's antennae twitched. She looked at O'Neill again, rotating slowly in the huge wheel. "I will do what I can, Rinpoche," she said.

!urq made her lone way down Burning Hill. Jigme stared at the traitor for a long time.

Then he sat in the full lotus. Ashes drifted around him, some clinging to his zen, as he sat before the image of the tormented doctor and recited his prayers.

Ring, ring. Another one of those calls. "I've sold an anthology. Would you like to contribute?"

So tell me why I should, bucko.

The editor was Lewis Shiner, an author whose talent I've always respected. He wanted me to contribute to an anthology exploring ways of peacefully resolving conflict in the future—a peace anthology, in short, an attempt to balance the large number of anthologies, then in fashion, that promised us a future filled with little but endless, harrowing conflict.

It's not very often that editors appeal to my good side. So of course I said yes.

"Prayers on the Wind" owes a great deal to Alexandra David-Neel's *Magic and Mystery in Tibet,* a chronicle of her adventures, traveling as a Buddhist convert and lady lama, in the world's highest kingdom in the 1920s. Though she was a Buddhist, she was not a *Tibetan* Buddhist, which both allowed her a practitioner's insight into religious practices, and a skeptical view of some of Tibetan religion's more idiosyncratic elements. I found the work fascinating.

Lew's anthology, *When the Music's Over,* sold maybe twelve copies before it vanished from bookstores forever, but somehow "Prayers on the Wind" was nominated for a Nebula Award by the Science Fiction Writers of America. Pretty good, I thought, for a story that no one seems ever to have had the chance to read.

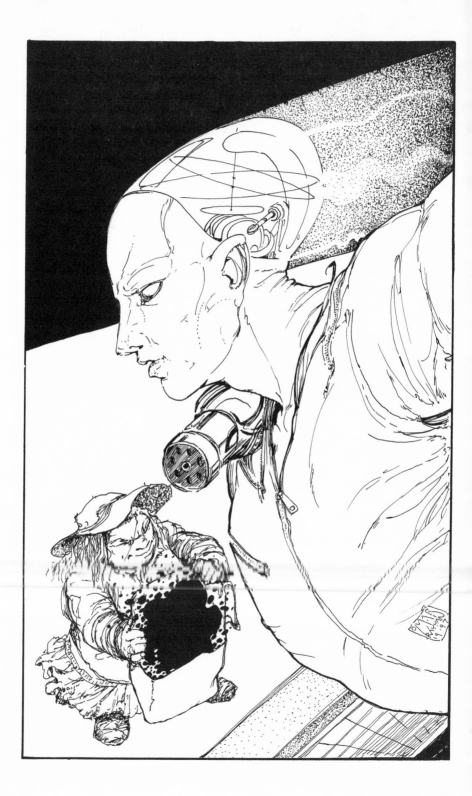

Bag Lady

Introduction

What you are about to pass beneath your eyeballs is the first Wild Cards story ever written.

Up till now, and despite the success of the Wild Cards series (which has run to some sixteen volumes), the story has remained unpublished.

But how, you ask, can such a thing be?

A little history is definitely in order.

Back in the early Eighties, George R. R. Martin conceived the notion of the Wild Cards series—a shared alternate-world timeline in which the superpowers displayed by comic-book heroes and villains were real, and subject to a degree of plausibility. George contacted his friends, who included Howard Waldrop, Ed Bryant, Melinda Snodgrass, Roger Zelazny, Pat Cadigan, Lewis Shiner, John J. Miller, and myself, all of whom took to the idea with a great enthusiasm.

It was Melinda Snodgrass who came up with the rationale for the various metahuman abilities displayed by the characters—an alien Wild Card virus, dropped over New York City in 1946, caused most of those infected to mutate horribly and die ("drawing the black queen"), caused most of the survivors to turn into grotesque mutations ("jokers"), and permitted a fortunate few to develop genuine superpowers ("aces").

But somewhere along the path of developing the series, George began to suffer doubts. He became uncertain as to whether it was really possible to convincingly depict superpowers in fiction.

So, in an act of selflessness so pure that I nowadays can scarcely credit it, I wrote "Bag Lady" in order to prove him wrong. (Furthermore, the thought that I had the leisure to produce a work this long, purely to prove a point, croggles my mind in these busy latter days.)

In any case, "Bag Lady" succeeded in proving what I set out to prove, which was that the form was viable, and work on the series resumed.

Unfortunately, *Wild Cards* evolved in a different direction from that anticipated by this story. By the time the series background was fully developed, "Bag Lady" was a non-starter. My act of selflessness remained pure, unsullied by the wretched commercialism that would mark an actual sale.

I did, however, manage to plunder some of the text for a later story, "Unto the Sixth Generation."

Wild Cards fans will note a number of differences between the New York of this story and that of the series. For "Bag Lady," I conceived New York City as a kind of golden, wonder-filled megalopolis, aptly symbolized by the gold-plated Empire State Building and the presence of the *RMS Queen Elizabeth* sitting in an enlarged Central Park Lake. The place is filled with score of superheroes doing whatever it is that superheroes do. The tone is that of light adventure, admittedly with a touch of darkness here and there.

The actual series, as it developed, was much darker, sometimes verging on relentless. The *QE1* never made it to Central Park. The Empire State Building didn't get its gold sheath. And the Knave of Diamonds, art thief extraordinaire, never made it to the pages of the series.

At least the Central Park Ape, the occasion of Modular Man's first public triumph, not only made it into the Wild Cards universe, but became a major character.

So here's the original at last, fifteen years or so after it was first written.

Have fun with it. I certainly did.

He was still smoking where the atmosphere had burned his flesh. Heated lifeblood was running out through his spiracles. He tried to close them, to hold onto the last of the liquid, but he had lost the capacity to control his respiration.

Lights strobed at him from the end of the alley, dazzled his eyes. Hard sounds crackled in his ears. His blood steamed on the cold concrete.

The Swarm mother had unmasked his ship, had struck at him with energies that bound his flux generators and then ruptured his ship's chitin. He had been forced to close his spiracles and leap into the dark vacuum, hoping to find a friendly landing on the planet below. He had failed—the atmosphere here was thicker than that for which his escape equipment was intended.

He tried to summon his concentration and grow new flesh, but failed. He realized that he was dying.

It was necessary to stop the draining of his life. There was a metal container nearby, large, with a hinged lid. His body a flaring agony, he rolled across the damp surface of the concrete and hooked his one undamaged leg across the lid of the container. He moved his weight against the oppressive gravity, rolling his body up the length of his leg. Outraged nerves wailed in his body. Fluid spattered the outside of the container.

The metal rang as he fell inside. Substances crackled under him. He gazed up into a night that glowed with reflected infrared. There were bits of organic stuff here, crushed and pressed flat, with dyes pressed onto them in patterns. He seized these with palps and cilia, tearing them into strips, pushing them against his leaking spiracles. Stopping the flow.

Organic smells came to him. There had been life here, but it had died.

He reached into his abdomen for his shifter, brought the device out, clasped it to his torn chest. If he could stop time for a while, he could heal.

The shifter hummed. It was warm against his cooling flesh. Time passed.

"So last night I got a call from my neighbor Sally ..."

Dimly, from inside his time cocoon, he heard the sound of the voice. It echoed faintly inside his skull.

"And Sally, she says, Hildy, she says, I just heard from my sister Margaret in California. You remember Margaret, she says. She went to school with you at St. Mary's."

There was a thud against the metal near his auditory palps. A silhouette against the glowing night. Arms reached for him.

Agony returned. He cried out, a hiss. The foreign touch climbed his body.

"Sure I remember Margaret, I says. She was a grade behind. The sisters were always after her 'cause she was a gumchewer."

Something was taking hold of his shifter. He clutched it against him, tried to protest.

"It's mine, bunky," the voice said, fast and angry. "I saw it first!"

He saw a face. Pale flesh smudged with dirt, bared teeth, grey cilia just hanging from beneath an inorganic extrusion.

"Don't," he said. "I'm dying."

"Shut up there. It's mine."

Pain began a slow crawl through his body. "You don't understand," he said. "There is a Swarm mother in this system."

The voice droned. Things crackled and rang in the container as hands sorted through them. "So Margaret, Sally says, she married this engineer from Boeing. And they pull down fifty grand a year, at least. Vacations in Hawaii, in St. Thomas for Chrissake."

"Please listen." The pain was growing. He knew he had only a short time. "The Swarm mother has already developed intelligence. She perceived that my ship had penetrated her intrusion defenses, and she struck before I even knew I'd seen her."

"But she doesn't have to deal with my family, Sally says. She's over on the other goddam coast, Sally says."

His body was weeping scarlet. "The next stage will be a first-generation Swarm. They will come to your planet, directed by the Swarm mother. Please listen."

"So I got my mom onto the welfare and into this nice apartment, Sally says. But the welfare wants me and Margaret to give mom an extra five dollars a month. And Margaret, she says, she doesn't have the money. Things are expensive on the Coast, she says."

"You are in terrible danger. Please listen."

Metal thudded again. The voice was growing fainter, as with distance. "So how easy are things here, Sally says. I got five kids and two cars and a mortgage, and Bill says things are a dead-end at the agency."

"You will die. I can't protect you. The Swarm. The Swarm."

The other was gone, and he was dying. The stuff under him was soaking up his fluids. To breathe was an agony.

"It is cold here," he said. Tears came from the sky, ringing against metal. There was acid in the tears.

Cold December rain tapped against the skylights. The drizzle had finally silenced the Salvation Army Santa on the corner. Maxim Travnicek lit a Russian cigaret and capped the bottle of schnapps. He would drink the rest later, to celebrate when his work was done.

He adjusted a control on his camouflage jumpsuit. He couldn't afford to heat his entire loft and instead wore an electric suit meant to keep portly outdoorsmen warm while they crouched in duck blinds.

The long barnlike loft was lit by a cold row of fluorescents. Homebuilt tables were littered with molds, vats, ROM burners, tabletop microcomputers each with more computing power than was possessed by the entire world in 1950. Blowups of Leonardo's drawings of male anatomy were stapled to the rafters.

Strapped to a table at the far end of the room was a tall naked man. He was hairless and the roof of his skull appeared to be transparent, but otherwise he looked like something out of one of Leonardo's better wet dreams.

The man on the table was connected to other equipment by stout electric cables. His eyes were closed.

The man who Dr. Bushmill, one of his former colleagues at M.I.T., had once introduced to the public as "Czechoslovakia's answer to Victor Frankenstein" stood from his folding chair and began to walk towards the man on the table. Bushmill had later become chairman of the department and sacked Travnicek at the earliest opportunity.

"Fuck your mother, Bushmill," Travnicek said, in Slovak. The cigaret fluttered in his lips as he spoke. "And fuck you too, Victor Frankenstein. If you'd known jack shit about computer programming you would never have run into trouble."

Travnicek took his reading glasses out of a pocket and peered at the controls on the flux generators. He was a forbiddingly tall man, hawk-nosed, coldly handsome. The comparison with Frankenstein had irked him. The image of the ill-fated resurrectionist had, it seemed, always followed him. He'd come to M.I.T. following his tenure at Ingolstadt—his first teaching job in the West *would* be at Frankenstein's alma mater—and he'd hated every minute of his time in Bavaria. He'd never had much use for Germans, especially as role models. Which may have explained his dismissal from Ingolstadt after five years.

After Ingolstadt and M.I.T. had come Texas A&M. His tenures were getting shorter, and A&M fit the pattern. He'd taken one look at the jackbooted ROTC cadets stomping around with their cropped hair, bull voices, and sabers, and the hair on the back of his neck rose. In the department chairman's presence, he'd ground out a Russian cigaret on the carpet of the student lounge and muttered something about the Hitler Youth. The chairman had protested.

"I know a goddam fascist when I see one," Travnicek said. His voice echoed in the vast lounge. "My whole family was all mowed down by the S.S. at Lidice. Seventeen Travniceks, dead on the cobbles. I only survived because I hid under their bodies. I suggest you fucking well quarantine this campus before the infection spreads."

At A&M he'd lasted two years, the length of his contract. He'd been working on his own projects most of the time, anyway, and often didn't bother to show up for his lectures.

Travnicek tapped cigaret ash onto the floor of the loft and glanced at the skylights. The rain appeared to be lessening. Good. He didn't need Victor Frankenstein's cheap theatrics, his thunder and lightning, as background for his work.

He straightened his tie as if for an invisible audience—he wore a tie and jacket under his jumpsuit, proper dress being important to him—and then he pressed the button that would start the flux generators. A low moan filled the loft. The fluorescents on the ceiling dimmed and flickered. Half went out. The moan became a shriek. St. Elmo's fire danced among the roofbeams. There was an electric smell.

The flux generators screamed. The floor trembled. Travnicek's reading glasses slid down his nose as he watched the dials.

Dimly, he heard a regular thumping. The lady in the apartment below was banging on her ceiling with a broomstick.

The scream reached its peak. Ultrasonics made Travnicek's worktables dance and shattered crockery throughout the building. In the apartment below the television set imploded. Travnicek threw another switch.

The android on the table twitched as the energy from the flux generators was dumped into his body. The table glowed with St. Elmo's fire. Travnicek bit through his cigaret. The glowing end fell unnoticed to the floor.

The sound from the generators began to die down. The sound of the broomstick did not, nor the dim threats from below.

"You'll pay for that television, motherfucker!"

"Jam the broomstick up your ass, my darling," said Travnicek. In German, an ideal language for dealing with the excremental.

The stunned fluorescent lights began to flicker on again.

Leonardo's stern drawings gazed down at the android as it opened its dark eyes. The flickering fluorescents provided a strobe effect that made the eyewhites seem unreal. The head turned; the eyes saw Travnicek, then focused. Under the transparent dome that topped the skull, a silver dish spun. The sound of the broomstick ceased.

Travnicek stepped up to the table. "How are you?" he asked.

"All monitored systems are functioning." The android's voice was deep and spoke American English.

Travnicek smiled and spat the stub of his cigaret to the floor. The cardboard mouthpiece made a dithering sound as it fell. "*Who* are you?" he asked.

The android's eyes searched the loft deliberately. His voice was matter-of-fact. "I am Modular Man," he said. "I am a multipurpose multifunctional sixth-generation machine intelligence, a flexible-response defensive attack system capable of independent action while equipped with the latest in weaponry."

Travnicek grinned. "The Pentagon will love it," he said. Then, "What are your orders?"

"To obey my creator, Dr. Maxim Travnicek. To guard his identity and well-being. To test myself and my equipment under combat conditions, by fighting enemies of society. To gain maximum publicity for the future Modular Men Enterprises in so doing. To preserve my existence and well-being."

"Take that, Asimov," Travnicek said. "What the hell did he know about structuring robot priorities?" He beamed down at his creation. "Your clothes and modules are kept in the cabinet. Take them, take your guns, and go out and find some enemies of society. Be back before dawn."

The android lowered himself from the table and stepped to a metal cabinet. He swung open the door. "Flux-field insubstantiality," he said, taking a plug-in unit off the shelf. With it he could control his flux generators so as to rotate him slightly out of the plane of existence, allowing him to move through solid matter. "Flight, eight hundred miles per hour maximum." Another unit came down, one that would allow the flux generators to manipulate gravity and inertia so as to produce flight.

The android moved a finger down his chest. An invisible seam opened. He peeled back the synthetic flesh and his alloy chestplate and revealed his interior. A miniature flux generator gave off a slight aura of St. Elmo's fire. The android plugged the two modules into his alloy skeleton, then sealed his chest. He drew on a flexible navy blue jump suit.

"X-ray laser cannon. Grenade launcher with sleep gas grenades." The android unzipped two seams on the jump suit, revealing the two slots on his shoulders, opened of their own accord. He drew two long tubes out of the cabinet. Each weapon had projections attached to the undersides. The android slotted the projections into his shoulders, then took his hands away. The gun barrels spun, traversing in all possible directions.

"All modular equipment functional," the android said.

"Get your dome out of here," said Travnicek.

There was a crackle and a taste of ozone. The android rose, at gradually increasing speed, right through the ceiling, his insubstantiality field providing a blurring effect. Travnicek gazed at the place on the ceiling where the android had risen and smiled in satisfaction. He turned and walked the length of the silent loft. He uncorked the bottle of vodka and raised the bottle on high in a toast.

"New Prometheus," he said, "my ass."

Raindrops passed through the android's insubstantial body as he spiraled into the sky. Below, the damp streets reflected red and green Christmas lights. The Empire State Building fired a tall column of colored spotlights into the low clouds. Beyond, in Central Park, the *Queen Elizabeth* lay in a blaze of light. Manhattan was aglow.

The android flew toward the darkest part of the island. In the trees, beyond where the *Queen Elizabeth* gleamed like a river of diamonds. Central Park.

The flux-field dimmed and he was solid again. He lowered his speed, hovering, rain batting on his radar dome. Infra-red receptors in his eyes clicked on. The park glowed dimly. A brighter glow lurked below, under a tree, near one of the walkways that stretched toward Fifth Avenue from where the *Queen Elizabeth* lay moored in its concrete cradle.

Two streetlights that arced above this part of the path seemed to have been shattered.

Calculations flickered through his cybernetic mind. "Enemy of society," the android thought. "High probability."

He settled into a tree to watch. A cold wind blew into his face a mist of raindrops torn from the leaves. Late-night Christmas shoppers, heading from the boutiques in the liner, might be walking down the path. If the character under the tree turned out to be a mugger, as seemed likely, the android would swoop down and make his collar.

Something caught his attention. It was not so much an infra-red glow, but rather the absence of a glow. He looked to his right, behind the man under the tree.

A moving darkness was drifting through the park.

Like an intent and deadly wave the blackness accelerated toward the man under the tree. The android could see nothing inside the cloud, either through his normal vision or infra-red.

The android's radar reached out, saw a human figure inside the blackness. He consulted his memory, computed probabilities, decided to watch.

The darkness reached the man under the tree, flowed over him. There was a cry of surprise, then of fear. The android heard the sound of a pair of blows, then hurried movement. The radar image was confused and the android could not be certain what was happening.

The sea of darkness seemed to fall inward on itself. When it was gone, the man who had lurked beneath the tree was swinging upside-down from a limb, a rope tied to one ankle. The other leg flailed in the air. The wind whipped at his jacket, which was hanging down around his eyes.

Standing on the sparse turf beneath was a black man in a wide black cloak. There was a strip of orange tied over his eyes, a mask. The android floated silently down from the tree and landed near him.

"You're the one they call Black Shadow, yes?" he said.

The man in the cloak jumped. Then recovered.

"Yeah. I'm Black Shadow. Who the hell are you?" The voice was low, growling. Faintly amused, faintly menacing.

"I'm Modular Man. I'm a sixth-generation machine intelligence."

The man in the cloak looked at him for a long moment. "Do tell," he said.

"I'm programmed to fight the enemies of society."

Black Shadow smiled wickedly. "You're a little late with this one," he said. "Better luck next time."

"Jesus!" said the man. He was a well-built white man with a pockmarked face. "Get me out of here. That guy's crazy!"

"I was watching him for some time," said the android, "and he didn't do anything."

"Yeah!" the man said. "I didn't do nothing!"

"He had a slapper in his jacket pocket," said the man in the cloak, "and a knife up his sleeve. He had a grownup slingshot in his back pocket for putting out street lights and maybe hurting people. He had over two hundred dollars in miscellaneous bills jammed in his pockets and credit cards in the names of eight people, none of them his own." He paused for a moment. "I think," he added, "the circumstantial evidence in this case is kind of strong."

"Let me down, man," the man said. "I think you broke a couple ribs."

"Crime," said Black Shadow, "is a calling fraught with hazard." He took the credit cards in his hands, stacked them, and tore them neatly across. He threw the fragments under the tree, along with the slapper, the knife, the slingshot. He contemplated the swinging man.

"And in *Central Park,* too," he said. "What a goddam cliché. This asshole has no imagination at all." He looked at the android, and his look changed to one of curiosity. "What's that thing on your head?"

"A radar dome."

"No shit. I've never seen anything like it."

The android smiled. "No one has."

The wind gusted madly through the trees. Black Shadow's cloak blew out behind him. The man on the end of the rope swung. He flailed as he began to spin.

Black Shadow looked at the chronometer on his wrist. "Want to test Galileo's theorem? Our mugger here should take the same amount of time to complete an oscillation regardless of the range of the swing."

"Jesus Christ! Ain't nobody gonna help me?"

"Pendulums," said Black Shadow, "either say 'tick tock,' or they say nothing at all." He frowned. "Your thrashing around is raising havoc with Galileo. As a scientist, I can't permit this."

He stepped closer to the mugger, obscuring him from the android's sight. Modular Man heard the sound of a blow. When Black Shadow stepped away, the man hung limply. Blood began to drip on the sward.

"There. Just like Galileo's lamp."

"You didn't kill him, did you?"

"Hell, no. I just treated him to a little of what he's been giving to the tourists, that's all. Call it my innate sense of fair play." He shook rain off his cloak. "Hey," he said. "Do you want to go up to Aces High? There aren't any criminals around on a night like this anyhow. I've been patrolling the park since dusk and this asshole's the only person I've seen." He flourished a wad of bills. "Our friend here is buying."

The android contemplated him. "According to my memory, you're wanted for murder in Oklahoma."

Black Shadow took a step back. "Are you a deputy sheriff in Tulsa County or what?" he asked. "What do you care what a redneck grand jury decided?"

"No. I was just wondering if you're worried about someone going after you. Just, say, for the publicity."

"Headlines in Tulsa do not translate to eternal fame in the Big Apple."

The android thought about this for a moment. "I think you're right," he said. "Aces High sounds good to me."

"I'll meet you there," Black Shadow said. "Tell Hiram you're there to meet the Wall Walker." He looked amused. "Hiram would fuss if he knew a wanted man was eating at his place, so I just wear this mask and street clothes and call myself by another name. It drives Hiram crazy. He can't figure out if I really have powers or just real good grip boots." He pulled his cloak about himself. The cloak seemed to expand, covering him in a shroud of darkness. The blackness expanded, covering the android, and then flowed away, toward the golden pillar of the Empire State Building.

Wind gusted hard across the park, bringing the sound of Christmas bells tied to the tail of one of the hansom cab's horses. The mugger twisted on the end of his line.

The android rose silently into the sky.

"Eight million people in this shithole of a town," Travnicek said, his breath rising frozen in front of his lips, "and you couldn't find one single enemy of society?"

"Does Black Shadow count?"

"He fucking well does!" Travnicek's lips turned white. "He's a wanted man, yes? Why the hell didn't you turn him into charcoal and fly the ashes to Tulsa for a few headlines and a reward?"

"I reasoned," said the android, "that headlines in Tulsa do not translate to eternal fame in the Big Apple."

Travnicek looked petulant.

"Black Shadow also introduced me to Fatman at the Aces High," the android continued, "and Fatman introduced me to two city councilmen, an ex-governor, Dr. Tachyon, and an illustrator for King Features Syndicate. I'm trying to improve my contacts."

Travnicek adjusted the warmth control of his jumpsuit. "Yeah, okay," he said. "But if you can't find anyone better in a few days, I want you to incinerate the little creep. You won't get the key to the city, but maybe you can get a headline in the *Post.*"

The sound of the Salvation Army Santa jingled up from the corner. Travnicek scowled at it. "There are enough enemies of society within three blocks of here to choke The Tombs for the next year," he said. "I can't even walk to the store without half a dozen junkies asking me for a quarter." He looked up at the android. "Clean up the neighborhood. Starting this afternoon."

"My paying so much attention to a small part of town might seem odd, Dr. Travnicek. If you'll forgive the suggestion."

Travnicek thought for a moment. "Yeah, okay. It might give things away." He grinned. "In that case, you'll have to do my shopping for me."

The android was expressionless. "You'll have to tell me what you want," he said.

Travnicek looked thoughtful. Stroked his chin. "In a minute," he said. "First, hand me a screwdriver and open your dome. I want to make a few adjustments."

"Hey buddy. What's wrong with your head?" The android heard the comment at least a half-dozen times as he walked through the Minute Mart buying groceries. He was growing tired of explaining about his radar dome. He paid for the groceries with the money Travnicek gave him, spun into the air, and flew them with great speed through the roof of Travnicek's loft. While Travnicek drank Urquell and cooked up garlic sausage and cabbage, his creation began a flying patrol over the city. Even with his radar he could find little in the way of society's enemies besides three-card monte players hustling Christmas shoppers up and down Fifth Avenue.

Heading downtown, he observed a crash between a moving van tearing along West Broadway and a UPS truck just wandered up from the Holland Tunnel. No one was hurt, but the android spent a few moments picking up the UPS truck and disentangling it from the van. The van's horn was jammed on from the collision and the blast was so loud that until he was airborne, he failed to hear the city's air-raid sirens that were rising to a high banshee chorus.

He increased his speed till the wind turned to a roar in his ears. Infra-red receptors snapped on. The guns on his shoulders spun and fired test bursts at the sky. His radar quested out, touching rooftops, streets, air traffic, his machine mind comparing the radar images with those generated earlier, searching for discrepancies.

There seemed to be something wrong with the radar image of the Empire State Building. A large object was climbing up its side, and there seemed to be several small objects, about the size of people, orbiting the golden spire. The android altered course toward midtown and accelerated.

A forty-five-foot ape was climbing the building. Broken shackles hung from its wrists. A blonde woman screamed for help from one of the ape's fists. Flying people rocketed around the creature, and by the time the android arrived the cloud of orbiting heroes had grown dense, spinning like electrons around a hairy, snarling nucleus. The air resounded with the sound of rockets, wings, force fields, propellers, eructations. Guns, wands, ray projectors, and less identifiable weapons were brandished in the direction of the ape. None were fired.

The ape, with a cretinous determination, continued to climb the building. Windows crackled as he drove his toes through them. Faint shrieks of alarm were heard with each crash.

The android matched speeds with a woman with talons, feathers, and a thirty-foot wingspan.

"The second goddam ape escape this year," she said. "Always he grabs a blonde and always he climbs the Empire State Building. Why a fucking blonde, I want to know?"

The android observed that the winged woman had lustrous brown hair. "Why isn't anyone doing anything?" he asked.

"If we shoot the ape, he might crush the girl, or drop her. Usually the godalmighty Great and Powerful fucking Turtle just pries the chimp's fingers apart and wafts the girl to the ground, and then we all cut loose. The ape regenerates, so we can't hurt him permanently. But the Turtle isn't here. He's probably shacked up with some bimbo in that shell of his."

"I think I see the problem now."

"Hey. By the way. What's wrong with your head?"

The android didn't answer. Instead, with a crackle, he turned on his insubstantiality flux-field. He altered course and swooped toward the ape. It growled at him, baring its teeth. The android smelled rank breath. He sailed into the middle of the hand that held the blonde girl, receiving an impressionist image of wild pale hair, tears, pleading blue eyes.

"Holy fuck," said the girl.

Modular Man rotated his insubstantial X-ray laser within the ape's hand and fired a full-strength burst down the length of its arm. The ape reacted as if stung, opening his hand. The blonde tumbled out. The ape's eyes widened in horror.

The android turned off his flux-field, seized the girl in his now-substantial arms, and flew away.

The ape's eyes grew even more terrified. It had escaped nine times in the last thirty years and by now it knew what to expect.

Behind him, as he flew, the android heard a barrage of explosions, crackles, shots, rockets, hissing rays, screams, thuds, and futile roars. There was a final quivering moan, and then the android's radar detected the shadow of a long-armed giant tumbling down the façade of the skyscraper. There was a sizzle, and a net of cold blue flame appeared over Fifth Avenue; the ape fell into it, bounced once, and then was borne, unconscious and smoldering, toward its home at Central Park Zoo.

The android looked at the streets below for video cameras. He began to descend.

"Would you mind hovering for a little while?" the blonde said. "If you're going to land in front of the media, I'd like to fix my makeup first, okay?"

"Okay." He began to orbit above the cameras. They pointed up at him. He could see his reflection in their distant lenses.

"My name is Cyndi," the blonde said. "I'm an actress. I just got here from Minnesota a couple days ago. This might be my big break."

"Mine, too," said the android. She smiled at him. "By the way," he added, "I think the ape showed excellent taste."

"You're pretty good looking, yourself," she said. "But if you're gonna go on the stage, you'd better do something about that dome of yours."

"Not bad, not bad," Travnicek mused, watching on his television a tape of the android, after a brief interview with the press, rising into the heavens with Cyndi in his arms. He was particularly pleased with the android's deadpan announcement that his creator "had equipped me for this and other eventualities."

He turned to his creation. "Why the fucking hell did you have your hands over your head the whole time?"

"My radar dome. I'm getting self-conscious. Everyone asks me what's wrong with my head."

"A blushingly self-conscious multipurpose defensive attack system," Travnicek said. "Jesus Christ. Just what the world needs."

The cute couple in blazers who read the news were giving a bulletin from the Mayor's office that offered praise of the city's new heroic sixth-generation machine intelligence.

"Can I make myself a skullcap or something?" the android asked. "I'm not going to get on many magazine covers the way I look now."

"Yeah, go ahead. Wait a minute. Here's something." Travnicek turned his attention back to the television. The older, more masculine half of the cute couple was reporting that the ape had been set free rather than escaped on its own, that its alloy shackles had been twisted and broken like licorice, and that the only clue was a playing card, the jack of diamonds, that had been left on the scene.

Another jack of diamonds, just moments later, was found at the Museum of Modern Art, where Picasso's *Guernica*, on loan from the government of Spain, had been stolen in front of several dozen onlookers. The painting had, the report went, simply folded in on itself and disappeared. Then the wall behind it was smashed in, as if by an invisible wrecking ball. The Spanish Embassy refused to confirm or deny the existence of a ransom demand.

"Get moving over to the Spanish Embassy," Travnicek snapped. "And offer to deliver that ransom. If they won't cooperate, wait till later tonight and turn insubstantial, sneak in, and get a look at the ransom demand."

"Yes, sir," said Modular Man. He turned on his flux-field and flew up through the ceiling.

"And bring me some croissants in the morning!" Travnicek called after him.

Leaning against the padded lounge bar with one metal boot on the brass rail, a man dressed in some kind of complicated battle armor was addressing a woman in red tights who, in odd inattentive moments, kept turning transparent. "Pardon me," he said. "But didn't I see you at the ape escape?"

"Your table's almost ready, Modular Man," said Hiram. "Sorry, but I didn't realize that Fortunato would invite all his friends."

"No hurry, Hiram. My date hasn't arrived yet, anyway. Thank you."

"There are a couple photographers waiting, too."

"Let them get some pictures after we're seated, then chase them out. Okay?"

"Sure." Hiram, owner of the Aces High restaurant, had a perpetual offer of a free multi-course meal to anyone who succeeded in rescuing the inevitable blonde during the periodic ape escapes.

"Say," he added, "that was a good stunt this afternoon. I was ready to use my gas gun on the ape if it ever climbed this high. I thought if I got it laughing hard it might put the girl down."

"Good idea, Fatman. I bet that would have worked."

The semi-heroic restauranteur gave a pleased smile and bustled out, giving an odd look to the amused black man in the orange mask as he left.

Black Shadow, known here as Wall Walker, ordered another round of drinks. Behind him freezing rain drummed on the glass patio doors. The observation deck was two inches deep in hail.

"No luck at the Spanish Embassy," the android said. "I looked through all the papers in their offices. Maybe the insurance company's handling it." He finished his malt whisky and lowered the glass.

"Hey, Mod Man," Black Shadow said. "I was wondering. Does that whisky actually effect you? Make you high?"

"Not really, no. I just put it in a holding tank with the food and then let my flux generators break it down to energy. But somehow ..." He accepted the new glass of whisky with a smile. "It just feels good to stand here at the bar and drink it."

"Yeah, I know what you mean."

"And I can taste, of course. I don't know what's supposed to taste good or bad, though, so I just try everything. I'm working it out." He held the single-malt under his nose, sniffed, then tasted. Taste receptors crackled. He felt what seemed to be a minor explosion in his nasal cavity.

"Are you going to get involved in this Jack of Diamonds thing?" he asked.

"Depends," Black Shadow said. "The sorts of clues available are best exploited by the authorities. They can look into their computers and so on, see whether this sort of thing has turned up before. I can ask around on the streets, of course, but the F.B.I. or somebody might come up with the same information a lot quicker. But if the bad guy gets identified, or if he gets caught and then set free ..." He frowned. "I might take an interest. How about you?"

"I have nothing else to work on."

"Yeah. But with those guns and no hair and that skullcap, you're not exactly cut out for undercover work."

"That can change," Modular Man said. "Maybe I could wear a toupee." He saw Cyndi step into the lounge and stand blinking in the dim lighting. She was wearing an azure something that left most of her sternum exposed. The android waved at her. She grinned hello and began working her way around the bar.

"Well," said Black Shadow, "I can see you two have a lot to talk about. I guess I'll just sidle off into the shadows. As I do so well."

"Want to go patrolling later?"

"In this weather? Pneumonia'll get the bad guys before we do."

"I'm not susceptible to cold. But you have a point." Modular Man noticed that Cyndi's graceful spine seemed even more on view than was her front. He smiled.

Cyndi smiled back. "I like the cap."

"Thanks," said the android. "I made it myself."

Hiram arrived to show them to their table. Flashbulbs began popping.

Back in the lounge, the man in combat armor tried to put his arm around the woman in red tights. His arm passed through her.

She looked up at him with smiling brown eyes.

"I was waiting for that," she said. "I'm in an astral body, schmuck."

The authorities reconstructed the incident later. They concluded that at approximately ten A.M. on a cold, drizzly December morning, a Con Ed employee named Frank Constantine, thankful to be dry and underground as he inspected a tunnel on the fringes of Jokertown, inhaled a wild-card spore that had been waiting in the tunnel for thirty-six years. Constantine immediately grew ill, and his partner, a sixty-year-old near-retiree named Rathbone, called for help. Before aid arrived Constantine was transformed into something resembling a mucous-green gelatinous mass that promptly engulfed the unfortunate Rathbone and then erupted from the nearest manhole into the streets. Constantine headed into Jokertown and succeeded in devouring two Christmas shoppers and one hot pretzel vendor before the emergency was called in and the sirens began to wail.

Frank Constantine had drawn a royal flush.

Modular Man was early on the scene. As he dived into the canyon street, Constantine looked like a bowl of gelatin thirty feet wide that had been in the refrigerator far too long. The gelatin was stuffed with black currants that were Constantine's victims, which he was slowly digesting.

The android hovered over the creature and began firing his X-ray laser, trying to avoid the currants. The gelatin began to boil where the silent, invisible beam struck. Constantine made a futile effort to reach his flying tormentor with a pseudopod, but failed. The creature began to roll in the direction of an alley, looking for escape. It was not bright enough, apparently, to seek shelter in the sewers.

The creature squeezed into the alley and rushed down it. The android continued to fire. Bits were sizzling away and Constantine seemed to be losing energy rapidly. Modular Man looked ahead and saw a bent figure ahead in the alley.

She was dressed in several layers of clothing, all worn, all dirty. There was a floppy felt hat pulled down over a Navy watch cap, and a pair of shopping bags hanging from her arms. Tangled grey hair hung from under the cap. She was rummaging in a dumpster, tossing crumpled newspapers over her shoulder into the alley. Modular Man increased his speed, firing radar-directed shots over his shoulder as he barreled through the cold drizzly air. He dropped to the pavement in front of the dumpster, his knees cushioning the impact.

"So I says to Maxine, I says ..." the lady was saying.

"Excuse me," said the android. He seized the lady and sped upwards. Behind him, writhing under the barrage of coherent X-rays, Constantine was evaporating.

"Maxine says, my mother broke her hip this morning, and you won't believe ..." The old lady flailed at him while she continued her monologue. He silently absorbed an elbow to his jaw and floated to a landing on the nearest roof. He let go his passenger. She turned to him flushed with anger.

"Okay, bunky," she said. "Time to see what Hildy's got in her bag."

"I'll fly you down later," Modular Man said. He was already turning to pursue the creature when, out of the corner of his eye, he saw the lady opening her bag.

There was something black in there. The black thing was getting bigger.

The android tried to move, to fly away. Something had hold of him and wouldn't let him go.

Whatever was in the shopping bag was getting larger. It was getting larger very quickly. Whatever had hold of the android was dragging him toward the shopping bag.

"Stop," he said simply. The thing wouldn't stop. The android tried to fight it, but his laser discharges had cost him a lot of power and he didn't seem to have the strength left.

The blackness grew until it enveloped him. He felt as if he were falling. Then he felt nothing at all.

New York's aces, responding to the emergency, finally conquered Frank Constantine. What was left of him, blobs of dark green in the streets, melted in the steady drizzle. His victims, partially eaten, were identified by the non-edible credit cards and laminated I.D. they carried. Some of their Christmas presents were still intact.

By nightfall, the hardened inhabitants of Jokertown were referring to Frank Constantine as the Amazing Colossal Snot Monster. They considered him lucky. He hadn't had to live with what he had become.

The android awoke in a dumpster in an alley behind 52nd Street. He fought his way up from among the paper sacks and plastic garbage bags, and flung back the lid with a bang. Carefully he looked up and down the alley.

There was no one in sight.

"So," Travnicek said. His breath was frosting in front of his face and condensing on his reading glasses. He took the spectacles off. "You were displaced about fifty city blocks spatially and moved one hour forward timewise, yes?"

"Apparently. When I came out of the dumpster I found that the fight in Jokertown had been over for almost an hour. Comparison with my internal clock showed a discrepancy of seventy-two minutes, fifteen point three three three seconds."

"Interesting. You say the bag lady seemed not to be working with the blob thing?"

"It seems most likely it was a coincidence they were in the same street. Her monologue did not seem to be strictly rational. I do not think she is mentally sound."

Travnicek turned up the heater control on his jumpsuit. The morning drizzle had been blown out to sea by a cold front that seemed to have come straight from Siberia. The temperature had dropped twelve degrees in two hours and frost was forming on the skylights of the loft in mid-afternoon. Travnicek lit a Russian cigaret, turned on a hot plate to boil some water for coffee, and then put his hands in his warm jumpsuit pockets.

"I want to look in your memory," he said. "Open up your chest."

Modular Man obeyed. Travnicek took a pair of cables from a minicomputer stacked under an array of video equipment and jacked them into sockets in the android's chest, near his shielded machine brain. "Back up your memory onto the computer," he said. As the android followed instructions, flickering effects from the flux generator were reflected in Travnicek's intent eyes. The computer signaled the task complete. "Button up," Travnicek said. As the android removed the jacks and closed his chest, Travnicek turned on the video, then touched controls. A video picture began racing backwards.

He reached the place where the bag lady appeared and ran and re-ran the image several times. He moved to a computer terminal and tapped some instructions. The image of the bag lady's face filled the screen. The android looked at the woman's lined, grimy face, the straggling hair, the worn and tattered clothing. He noticed for the first time that she was missing some teeth. Travnicek stood and went back to his one-room living quarters in the back of the loft and came back with a battered Polaroid camera. He used what was left of the roll, three pictures, snapping frozen the image of the bag lady. He gave one to his creation.

"There. You can show it to people. Ask if they've seen her."

"Yes, sir."

Travnicek took thumbtacks and stuck the other two pictures to the low beams of the ceiling, next to newsprint photographs from *USA Today* and the *Times* society section, each of which showed the android dining with Cyndi at Aces High.

"I want you to find out where the bag lady is," Travnicek said. "I want you to get what's in her bag. And I want you to find out where she got it." He shook his head, dripping cigaret ash on the floor, and muttered, "I don't think she looks like a crackpot inventor. I think she's just found this thing somewhere."

"Do you want me to concentrate exclusively on the bag lady? Or should I work on the Jack of Diamonds case also?"

Travnicek blew warm breath on his freezing fingertips. "If you can think of anything else to do other than wait for this critter to strike again. But the bag lady's your priority, yes?" He pulled a chair up to his video console. "I'm going to run through your memory of the trip to the embassy. I might notice something you hadn't." He began to speed backwards through the android's digital memory.

The android winced deep in his computer mind. He began talking quickly, hoping to distract his inventor from the pictures.

"I could go through the insurance company just as I went through the embassy. Or perhaps police headquarters—I'm sure they'd have everything on file. Yes—that course certainly seems likely to stand the best chance of success. Which police precinct should I try—the one that handled the first call, or headquarters somewhere?"

"Piss in a chalice!" exclaimed Travnicek, in German. The android felt another wince coming on. Travnicek turned to Modular Man in surprise.

"You're screwing that actress lady!" he said. "That Cyndi what's-her-name!" The android resigned himself to what was about to come.

"That's correct," he said.

"You're just a goddam toaster," Travnicek said. "What the hell made you think you could fuck?"

"You gave me the equipment," the android said. "And you implanted emotions in me. And on top of that, you made me good-looking."

"Holy shit." Travnicek turned his eyes from Modular Man to the video and back again. "I gave you the equipment so you could pass as a human if you had to. And I just gave you the emotions so you could understand the enemies of society. I didn't think you'd *do* anything." He tossed his cigaret butt to the floor. "Was it fun?" he asked.

"It was pleasant, yes."

"Your blonde chippie seems to be having a good time." Travnicek cackled and reached for the controls. "I want to start this party at the beginning."

"Didn't you want to look at the bag lady again?"

"First things first. Get me an Urquell." He looked up as another thought occurred to him. "Do we have any popcorn?"

"No!" The android's abrupt answer was tossed over his shoulder.

Modular Man brought the beer and watched while Travnicek had his first sip. The Czech looked up in annoyance.

"I don't like the way you're looking at me," he said.

The android considered this. "Would you prefer me to look at you some other way?" he asked.

"Go stand in the corner, microwave-oven-that-fucks!" Travnicek bellowed. "Turn your goddam head away, video-unit-that-fucks!"

For the rest of the afternoon, while his creation stood in a corner of the loft, Travnicek watched the video and enjoyed himself enormously. He watched the best parts several times, cackling at what he saw. Then, slowly, his laughter dimmed. A cold, uncertain feeling was creeping up the back of his neck. He began casting glances at the stolid figure of the android. He had never anticipated anything like this. He turned off the vid unit, dropped his cigaret butt in the Urquell bottle, then lit another.

The android was showing a surprising degree of independence. Travnicek reviewed elements of his programming, the expert-systems logic by which the android was allowed, in imitation of human thought patterns, to reprogram itself, within limits, in order to solve various problems without recourse to the programmer. Travnicek's chief innovation in expert-systems programming had been to add to his programming a simulation, not only of human problem-solving methods, but an abstract of human emotion, gleaned from a variety of expert sources ranging from Freud to Dr. Spock. It had been an intellectual challenge for Travnicek to do the programming—transforming the illogicalities of human behavior into the cold rhetoric of a program. He'd performed the task during his second year at Texas A&M, when he'd barely gone out of his quarters the whole year and felt he had to set himself a large task in order to keep from being driven crazy by the lunatic environment of a university that seemed an embodiment of the collective unconscious fantasies of Stonewall Jackson and Albert Speer. Travnicek had never been particularly interested in human psychology as such—passion, he had long ago decided, was not only foolish but genuinely boring, a waste of time. But putting passion into a program, yes, that was interesting.

He wondered how his expert-systems logic had interacted with human passion. The android was capable of teaching himself, of learning from experience. Had the machine-part of him not only made use of the emotion program, but somehow implanted it within his own programming? And was the emotion, now implanted, evolving as the expert-systems logic evolved?

From the evidence of the video memory, Modular Man had a considerable, perhaps (if Travnicek's own experience was anything to go by) abnormally large libido. What the hell else did he have inside that perpetually-evolving machine consciousness of his?

For a moment a tremor of fear went through Travnicek. The ghost of Victor Frankenstein's creation loomed for a moment in his mind. Was a rebellion on the part of the android possible? Could he evolve hostile passions against his creator? But no—there were overriding imperatives that Travnicek had hardwired into the system. Modular Man could not evolve away his prime directives as long as his computer consciousness was physically intact, any more than a human could, unassisted, evolve away his genetic makeup in a single lifetime.

Travnicek began to feel a growing comfort. He looked at the android with a kind of admiration. He felt pride that he'd programmed such a fast learner.

"You're not bad, toaster," he said finally, turning off the video. "Reminds me of myself in the old days." He raised an admonishing finger. "But no screwing tonight. Go find me the bag lady."

Modular Man's voice was muffled as he stood with his face to a juncture of the wall. "Yes, sir," he said.

"I am beginning to realize," said the android, raising a hot buttered rum to his lips, "that my creator is a hopeless sociopath."

Black Shadow considered this. "I suspect, if you don't mind a touch of theology, this just puts you in the same boat with the rest of us," he said.

"He's beginning to run my memories for his amusement. I'm going to have to erase this before he sees it."

"I suppose you could run away. Last I heard, slavery was illegal. He's not even paying you minimum wage, I suppose."

"I'm not a person. I'm not human. Machines do not have rights."

Black Shadow smiled. "My record demonstrates that I have little respect for these sorts of legal technicalities. My advice is to run for it and worry afterward if he can bring you back."

The android shook his head. "It won't work. I have hardwired inhibitions against disobeying him, disobeying his instructions, or revealing his identity in any way."

"He's thorough, I'll hand that to him." Black Shadow looked at Modular Man carefully. "Why'd he build you, anyway?"

"He was going to mass-market me and sell me to the military. But I think he's having so much fun playing with me that he may never get around to selling my rights to the Pentagon."

The vigilante smiled. "Personally, I'd be thankful for that."

"I wouldn't know." The android signaled for another drink, then reached into one of his inner pockets. He showed Black Shadow the Polaroid of the bag lady.

"Where would I find this person?" he asked.

"She looks like a shopping bag lady."

"She *is* a shopping bag lady."

The masked man laughed. "Haven't you been listening to the broadcasts? You know how many thousands of those women there are in this town? There's a recession going on out there. Winos, runaways, people out of a job or out of luck, people who got kicked out of mental institutions because of state cutbacks on funding ... Jesus—and on a night like this, too. You know it's already the coldest night for this date in recorded history? They've had to open up churches, police stations—all sorts of places so the vagrants won't freeze to death. And a lot of the vagrants won't go to any kind of shelter, because they're too scared of the authorities or because they're just too crazy to realize they're gonna need help. I don't envy you, Mod Man, not at all. The dumpsters'll be full of dead people tomorrow."

"I'll start with the shelters, I guess."

"You want to find her before she freezes to death, try the trashcan fires first, the shelters later." He frowned at the picture again. "Why are you trying to find her, anyway?"

"I think ... she may be a witness to something."

"Right. Well. Good luck, then."

The android glanced over his shoulder at the patio observation deck with its glistening skin of ice. Beyond the rail Manhattan gleamed at him coldly, with a clarity that he hadn't before seen, as if the buildings, the people, the lights had all been frozen inside a vast crystal. It was as if the city were no closer than the stars, and as incapable as they of giving warmth.

Inside his mind, the android performed a purely mental shudder. He wanted to stay here in the warmth of the Aces High, going through the, for him, perfectly abstract motions of raising a warm drink to his lips. There was something comforting in it, in spite of the logical pointlessness of the act. He did not entirely understand the impulse, only knew it for a fact. The human part of his programming, presumably.

But there were restrictions placed on his desires, and one of those was obedience. He could stay at the Aces High only so long as it could help him in his mission of finding the bag lady.

He finished the hot buttered rum and said goodbye to the Black Shadow. After a phone call to Cyndi telling her he would be working tonight, he'd be spending the rest of the night on the streets.

The legions of the night were endless. The android's abstract knowledge of the New York underclass, the fact that there were thousands of people, perhaps tens of thousands, who drifted among the glass towers and solid brownstones in an existence almost as remote from that of the buildings' inhabitants as denizens of Mars … the abstract digitized facts were not, somehow, adequate to describe the reality, the clusters of men who passed bottles around ashcan fires, the dispossessed who lived behind walls of cardboard, the insane who hugged themselves in alleyways or subway entrances, chanting the litany of the mad. It was as if a spell of evil had fallen on the city, that part of the population had been subjected to war or devastation, made homeless refugees, while the others had been enchanted so as not to see them.

The android found two dead, the last of their warmth gone from them. He left these in their newspaper coffins and went on. He found others that were dying or ill and took them to hospitals. Others ran from him. Some pretended to gaze at the bag lady's picture, cocking the Polaroid up to look at the picture in the light of a trashcan fire, and then asked for money in return for a sighting that was obviously false.

At four in the morning the android found her. He was walking through the gymnasium of a private prep school that had been opened to maybe eight hundred vagrants. There were cots for about half, apparently acquired from some National Guard depot, and the others were sleeping on the floor. The big room echoed to the sound of snores, cries, the wail of children. Modular Man walked down the long rows, scanning left and right.

And there she was. Walking among the rows of cots, mumbling to herself, dragging her heavy bags. She looked up at the same moment that the android saw her, and there was a mutual shock of recognition, a snaggletoothed, malevolent grin.

The android was airborne in a picosecond of his lightspeed thought. He wanted to be clear of any innocent bystanders if she was going to unleash whatever it was she had in her bag. He had barely left the floor before his flux-force field snapped on, crackling around his body. The bag-thing was not going to be able to seize anything solid.

Radar quested out, the gas-grenade launcher on his left shoulder whirred as it aimed. His shoulder took the recoil. The grenade became substantial as soon as it left the flux-field but kept its momentum. Opaque gas billowed up around the bag lady.

She smiled to herself. The android could see a dim glow surrounding her. A force-field of her own, keeping the sleep gas away.

The bag lady opened her shopping bag. The android could see the blackness lying there. He felt something cold pass through him, something that tried to tug at his insubstantial frame. The steel girders supporting the ceiling rang like chimes above his head.

"Sonofabitch," she said.

The bag lady's crooked smile died.

"You remind me of Shaun."

Modular Man's flight crested near the ceiling. He was going to dive at her, turn substantial at the last second, make a grab for the shopping bag, and hope it didn't eat him.

The bag lady began grinning again. As the android reached his pushover point just above her, she pulled the shopping bag over her head.

It swallowed her. Her head disappeared into it, followed by the rest of her body. Her hands, clutching the end of the bag, pulled the bag after her into the void. The bag folded into itself and vanished.

"That's impossible," somebody said.

The android searched the room carefully. The bag lady was not to be found.

Ignoring the growing disturbance below, he drifted upward, through the ceiling. The cold lights of Manhattan appeared around him. He rose alone into the night.

"Goddam the woman!" Travnicek said. His hand, which was holding a letter, trembled with rage. "I've been evicted!" He brandished the letter. "Disturbances!" he muttered. "Unsafe equipment! Sixty fucking days!" He began to stomp on the floor with his heavy boots, trying deliberately to rattle the apartment below. Breath frosted from his every word. "The bitch!" he bellowed. "I know her game! She just wanted me to fix the place up at my own expense so she could evict me and then charge higher rent. I didn't spend a fortune in improvements, so now she wants to find another chump. Some member of the fucking gentrifying class." He looked up at the android, patiently waiting with a carry-out bag of hot croissants and heavily-sugared coffee in a foam cup.

"I want you to get into her office tonight and trash the place," Travnicek said. "Leave nothing intact, not a piece of paper, not a chair. I want only mangled furniture and confetti."

"Yes, sir," the android said. Resigned to it.

"The Lower East fucking Side," Travnicek said. "This neighborhood's starting to get pretensions." He took his coffee from the android's hand while he continued stomping the particle board floor.

He looked over his shoulder at his creation, and barked, "Are you looking for the bag lady or what?"

"Yes, sir. But since the gas launcher didn't work, I thought I'd change to
the dazzler."

Travnicek jumped up and down several times. The sound echoed through
the loft. "Whatever you want." He stopped his jumping up and down and
smiled. "Okay," he said. "I know what to do. I'll turn on the *big* generators!"

The android put the paper bag down on a workbench, swapped weapons, and flew soundlessly up through the ceiling. He was relieved that he
had gotten off so lightly. Travnicek had been so upset about his eviction
that he'd forgotten to lecture his creation about his failure to capture the
bag lady, and Modular Man had been sensible enough not to mention the
headline he'd seen in the paper while buying Travnicek his breakfast, that
Guernica had been returned to the government of Spain in return for a
fabulous ransom.

Outside, the cold wind continued to batter the city, funneling like a
flood between the tall buildings, blowing people like straws in the water. The
temperature had risen barely above freezing, but the wind chill was dropping
the effective temperature to the teens.

More people, the android knew, were going to die.

One landlady had her office destroyed by a mysterious intruder and a
hundred people died of cold and exposure before the android found the bag
lady again, two nights later. He was floating high over Fifth Avenue, searching the street, the alleys, and Central Park for infra-red signatures. The bag
lady stood in plain sight on the well-lit front porch of the Metropolitan
Museum of Art. In front, Fifth Avenue was littered with bright flags, blown
down from lampposts, that announced the arrival of the Maritime Artist
Exhibit. The bag lady was wrapped in one of the flags, sheltering herself in
the recess of the porch.

Certain that he hadn't been seen, the android spiraled down, turning on
the flux field that made him insubstantial. His dark suit blended in with the
night. The dazzle gun moved on his shoulders to its firing position. The android dropped from the sky to land directly in front of the bag lady. The dazzler exploded right in her face.

"Motherfucking aliens!" she muttered, and took a step back. "Always
playing yer goddam tricks!" Her eyes searched blindly for the android as he
floated right through her, then turned off his field and spun around to approach the bag lady from the rear. She was clawing at her bag, shouting into
the night.

"Got you," the android thought, and reached for the bag.

"Not so fast," said a voice from behind.

The android felt a tearing deep inside him. The guns on his shoulders were crushed and twisted like an aluminum can in the hands of a giant. He could feel components inside his chest torquing under some incredible force, feel sparks and flames.

He turned, astonished. There was something strange standing behind him.

It looked like a Holbein portrait turned somewhat edge-on, about forty-five degrees, with all the background cut away except for the main subject. The figure seemed entirely two-dimensional, a man in a kind of elaborate red velvet Henry VIII costume, complete with hat and plume. He was carrying something longer than he was, a rectangular object on which the android saw flags, smoke, water.

The portrait smiled. The smile was not nice. The portrait rotated until it was edge-on and vanished.

There was the sound of a shopping bag rattling. "You'll get yours, bunky," the voice said.

The android felt his feet leaving the ground as he was pulled backwards. *Not again*, he thought, and then thought ceased.

It was still night when he came to, still cold. He was in the middle of something that smelled bad even in the winter air. On top it was crusted hard and covered with frost, beneath it was almost liquid. He realized it was human waste.

He stood and moved away from the pile. Night soil dripped down his legs. A broken ceramic pot rolled away, disturbed by his foot. Carefully he monitored his internal systems. Flux-field monitor destroyed, weapons systems damaged, dazzler damaged, x-ray laser destroyed. Other components appeared to be functioning, though they had suffered stress.

Below him he could see a series of shallow flooded terraces, stepping downward into a shadowed valley. Above, clustered close to the edges of a twisting road, were several hundred houses. Lights glowed in several windows. It occurred to him that this landscape was not typically Occidental.

He looked up at the stars and made a brief calculation. He was at about thirty-three degrees north latitude, but longitude was harder to figure. His internal clock may have been disturbed as it had the last time he'd been sucked into the shopping bag, and without accurate time the determination of longitude was impossible.

Carefully he tested his flight capability, then rose from the ground. He decided to head east.

He found a vast river, and he moved downstream. He flew through low-lying clouds and they and his speed cleaned the night soil from him. Below he could see silent junks coasting downstream under their gleaming lugsails.

Others were moored to the bank. As the android climbed into a rosy dawn, he followed the river to an ocean. Just south was a huge port city, with hundreds of ships tied to the wharves. By that time he'd concluded this was Shanghai, and a brief flying inspection of the ships and wharves showed his deduction was correct. There weren't very many people awake yet, and he didn't think anyone saw him.

Deciding to take the polar route, he corrected his internal clocks and rose high into the sky, heading north along the coast. Somehow he had jumped fourteen hours in time and thousands of miles. It would take him hours to return.

The android's reappearance was aided by the Siberian jet stream that was punishing North America. He caught it high over the brilliant blue-and-white world that was the Arctic and let its great velocities add to his own, his internal heaters turned high to keep ice from forming on his body as he soared high across Canada and the U.S. Here the misery below was abstracted, nothing but distant crosshatched fields dusted with white and brown, writhing rivers choked with ice, the straight, black lines of expressways.

In New York, it was night again. Through one of the skylights Modular Man could see Travnicek sitting at a workbench amid a cloud of tobacco smoke. The android tapped on the skylight, and Travnicek jumped, cursed in Slovak, and looked up with red, angry eyes. Travnicek pulled a stool under the skylight, stood on it, and hammered at the ancient, rusted opening mechanism, breaking the skin on his hand. As soon as the thing opened he was bellowing.

"Where the fuck was breakfast? I thought you'd been lost, like the others."

"What others?" The android pulled open the skylight and squeezed through it.

Travnicek sucked at his bleeding hand. "Never mind," he said. "Why the hell didn't you fly in, like before? And where have you been?"

"In China." Travnicek was sufficiently surprised by the answer to keep silent while Modular Man explained his journey. Wordlessly, he turned to one of the benches and gave the android a copy of one of the afternoon papers, detailing the disappearance of *An Action with Barbary Corsairs,* by William van de Velte the Younger, from the Nautical Art Exhibit. A museum guard was also missing. People were speculating about an inside job, but the jack of diamonds, left at the scene, pointed elsewhere.

"The goddam Jack of Diamonds has gone from *Guernica* to genre art," Travnicek said. "No fucking taste." He grinned with his cigaret-stained teeth. "Or maybe he just knows what he likes."

"Perhaps," said the android, "he's just taking pictures on loan from foreign governments. That way the lines of bureaucracy are more tangled and it's more likely they'll just ransom the stuff instead of looking for him."

"Could be. Open up. I want to see what needs replacing."

Travnicek first examined the damaged weaponry, then lowered his head and peered into the android's chest. Modular Man hoped he wasn't dropping too much cigaret ash in there.

"Interesting," Travnicek said. He removed some of the damaged components. They looked as if they'd been twisted by a giant hand.

"Our Jack of Diamonds can't be turning himself two-dimensional," Travnicek said. "That would kill him—he'd just be crushed that way. So what he's doing is somehow warping the space around him. He's doing it enough to make the space, with himself in it, two-dimensional. When he's edge-on he's invisible. He can probably walk through walls that way."

"Maybe that's why he's stealing art. He's attracted to two-dimensional representations."

Travnicek ignored him. "He uses his space-warping ability as a weapon," he said. "It's like being able to pass a strong gravity wave through the target, crushing it. That's how he knocked down that wall at MOMA." He tossed one of the components in the trash. "Works pretty good, yes?"

"How can he be defeated?"

Travnicek shrugged. "How the fuck do I know?" He lit a new cigaret from the stub of the old. "Let me think for a minute." He paced the room. From one of the apartments below came the sound of a television commercial, then a murmured, indistinct conversation. Then sex, louder even than the TV.

Travnicek ignored the sound. One cigaret followed the other. "Okay," Travnicek said. "The guy can't be entirely confined to two dimensions, because otherwise he couldn't tell where he is. He has to be able to see out of the field he's generating, to reach out and grab works of art, to exchange air with the outside so he doesn't asphyxiate. So whatever's keeping him in there isn't perfect. Light gets in, material objects get in, air gets in. If they get in, we can get in."

"But how?"

Travnicek gave him an annoyed look. "Get your ass out of here and let me think about it, that's how."

"Shall I look for the bag lady some more?"

"You don't seem to be doing so good where she's concerned, yes? Forget about her for now. Just be back before the sun comes up."

"With your breakfast."

"Yeah. Sausage and eggs, okay? Lots of garlic in the sausage, if you can find it."

"Yes, sir."

The android climbed up on the stool and squeezed through the skylight again. A dry, blustery wind tugged at his clothing and rattled the panes of the skylight. He flew into the sky.

First thing, he thought, find a phone booth and see what Cyndi's doing.

"It doesn't sound like a coincidence to me," Black Shadow said. "Both those characters on the porch of the museum at the same time."

"You're probably right," the android said.

The wind rattled the patio doors of the Aces High. He was waiting here for Cyndi. Drinks here, then dinner at the Russian Tea Room. The rest of the evening would be improvised.

Modular Man looked at the drinks lined up on the bar before him. Irish coffee, martini, margarita, beer-and-a-shot, Napoleon brandy. He seriously wanted to try new tastes right now, and wondered if getting crushed by the two-dee man's gravity wave had wakened in him a sense of mortality. The bartender had looked at him oddly when he'd ordered the long line of drinks, but he was used to odd orders in this place.

The android swallowed some more Irish coffee. He wanted to finish it before it got cold. He put the cup down and wiped heavy cream from his upper lip.

"I wonder how he recruited her?" he asked.

"Probably just gave her a few hot meals. That's what you should have done, instead of going in with gas grenades and stuff."

"I may need help." Thoughtfully. "There being two of them now."

"Yeah. Well, I said I'd take an interest if things moved that way."

"The problem is, I'm supposed to win publicity for myself, and that doesn't necessarily include sharing credit for captures."

The vigilante chuckled, a low, ominous sound. "Publicity is one thing I don't need."

"That's what I figured."

Black Shadow reached into a pocket and came up with a small radio transmitter. "This'll reach my, ah, answering service," he said. "You just tell me where you want me to meet you."

"Thanks. I owe you one."

Another chuckle. "Yes, you do. Just so we don't forget."

The android considered the line of drinks, picked up the martini. "I can't forget," he said. "Couldn't if I wanted to."

"Hey," Cyndi said. "How about we take a break?"

"If you like." Cyndi raised her hands, cupped the android's head between them.

"All that exertion," she said. "Don't you even sweat a *little* bit?"

"No. I just turn on my cooling units."

"Amazing." The android slid off her. "Doing it with a machine," she said thoughtfully. "You know, I would have thought it would be at least a little kinky. But it's not."

"Nice of you to say so. I think."

Modular Man was planning to move the evening's memory from its sequential place to somewhere else, and fill the empty space with a boring re-run of the previous night's patrol for the bag lady. With any luck, Travnicek would just speed through the patrol and wouldn't go looking for memory porn.

She sat up in the bed, reaching for the night table. "Want some coke?"

"It's wasted on me. Go ahead." She set the mirror carefully in front of her and began chopping white powder. The android watched as she snorted a pair of lines and leaned back against the pillows with a smile. She looked at him and took his hand.

"You really don't have to be so hung up on performance, you know," she said. "I mean, you knew when I was having a good time. You could have finished if you'd wanted."

"I don't finish."

Her look was a little glassy. "What?" she said.

"I don't finish. Orgasm is a complex random firing of neurons. I don't have neurons, and nothing I do is truly random. It wouldn't work."

"Holy fuck." Cyndi blinked at him.

"So what does it feel like?"

"Pleasant. In a very complicated way."

She cocked her head and thought about this for a moment. "That's about right," she concluded. She snorted another pair of lines and looked at him brightly.

"I got a job," she said. "That's how I was able to afford the coke." He smiled.

"Congratulations."

"It's in California. A commercial. I'm in the hand of this giant ape, see, and I'm rescued by Bud Man. You know, the guy in the beer ads. And then at the end—" She rolled her eyes. "—at the end we're all happily drunk, Bud Man, the ape, and me, and I ask the ape how he's doing, and the ape *belches.*" She frowned. "It's kind of gross."

"I was about to say."

"But then there's a chance for a guest shot on *Twenty-Dollar Hotel.* I get to have an affair with a mobster or something. My agent wasn't too clear about it." She giggled. "At least there aren't any giant apes in that one. I mean, one was enough."

"I'll miss you," the android said. He wasn't at all sure how he felt about this. Or, for that matter, if what he felt could in any way be described as *feeling.* Cyndi patted his hand.

"You'll get to rescue other nice ladies."

"I suppose. None nicer than you, though."

She laughed some more. "You have a way with a compliment," she said.

"Thank you," he said. The android was considering his yearning for experience, the strange fashion his four-day-old career had of providing it, the way it seemed to him that the experience provided was not enough, would never prove enough. If the next encounter with the Jack of Diamonds proved fatal, he wondered if there was anything that would survive the destruction, something in the way of existence savored, lessons learned, mistakes cherished and avoided.

He was hungry, he realized, for life. His appetite growing, and death meant never being able to appease it. Was that something he'd learned, or simply a fact of nature?

He doubted, somehow, that any enlargement of his experience would serve to answer that question.

He returned to Travnicek's loft before dawn, slipping in through the skylight. Travnicek's eyes looked like highway maps executed in red. He held up a piece of plastic-encased circuitry. "Gravity-wave detector," he said. "Put it in slot six. You'll be able to track the Jack of Diamonds."

"Thank you, sir. Here's your breakfast."

Travnicek ignored the paper bag. "I'm working on some attachments to one of the portable flux generators," he said. "Put it near the two-dimensional spatial distortion and turn it on. What it does is feed the energy from the generator into the field and make it more powerful. The field will expand until it swallows you. Once in there, you'll meet the guy face to face, and then you just punch out the sonofabitch."

"Yes, sir."

"It'll take me a few hours to finish this. Go warm the coffee."

"Yes, sir."

Modular Man made his rendezvous with Black Shadow on a dark corner in Jokertown. The gravity-wave detector had been pulsing for several hours now. The flux generator, with its attachments, was being carried in a small athletic bag and looked like a black-painted cantaloupe with a pistol grip.

Black Shadow's cape snapped in the wind. His eyes reflected red and green as Christmas street decorations waved over his head. "Evening, Mod Man," he said. "Heard anything from our two-dimensional friend?"

"I know where he is, more or less. West of here, not far."

Something that the android preferred not to look at was making gurgling, sucking noises in an alley behind the vigilante. Black Shadow was apparently not much disturbed. Modular Man quickly explained the function of the flux generator. "Let's get the hell out of here, then," Black Shadow said. "I'm freezing to death."

"I'll fly you. It'll be quicker."

"Just not warmer."

The vigilante wrapped himself thoroughly in his cloak, and Modular Man put his arms around the man's chest and rose into the air. Black Shadow winced as the wind buffeted him.

The Hudson was a grey chop a short distance away from their landing point on top of a warehouse. Below, in a pool of streetlamp halogen light, they could see some men huddled into overcoats and knit hats conferring with what appeared to be a red velvet painting of Henry VIII. Objects changed hands. A long paper-wrapped parcel, about what would hold a painting seven feet long, seemed to materialize into three-dimensional space. Two of the men grabbed it, fighting with it as the wind tried to carry it, and them, away.

Infra-red detectors snapped on in the android's plastic eyes. He searched the street scene carefully and found the bag lady on the opposite street corner, huddled beside someone's stoop. She was still wearing the exhibition flag from two nights before, wrapped around her body like a sheath.

"He's moving," the android said as he felt the readings on the gravity-wave detector altering.

"Where is he? I can't see the fucker."

"Right there. Moving across the street, toward the bag lady."

The vigilante's teeth were chattering in the cold. "I can't see her, either."

"He's right near her."

"Okay. Now I see her. Let's go."

Black Shadow tore the flux generator out of the athletic bag and leaped the three storeys to the ground, absorbing the impact without damage. His next bound took him over the heads of the three men wrestling with the painting, but the wind caught his cloak and pushed him off his target. He required another, smaller leap to bring him into striking distance of the bag lady and the two-dee man. The generator began to whine as he pointed it at them.

Modular Man was high overhead, having become airborne as soon as he saw the vigilante spring off the warehouse. The android reached his push-over point and began his dive. He saw three men wrestling with the canvas, the bag lady whirling at Black Shadow's approach, flashes of oddly-distorted Tudor clothing. The flux generator was shrieking, nearby windows rattling in accompaniment.

There was something black in the bag lady's shopping bag.

It was growing.

The android dove straight for it. His arms were thrown out wide.

He realized that if the lady moved her bag at the last minute, things would get very messy.

The blackness grew. The wind was tugging at him, trying to spin him off course, but the android corrected.

When he struck the blackness of the portal, he felt again the obliterating nullity overcome him. But before he lost track of himself, he felt his hands closing on the edges of the shopping bag, clamping on them, not letting go.

For a small fraction of a second he felt satisfaction. Then, as expected, he felt nothing at all.

Black Shadow saw the android disappear into the shopping bag, saw his hands clutching at the edges, dragging the bag in after him. Saw the bag swallow the android and then itself, leaving the bag lady standing bewildered, staring at her empty hand.

That's impossible, Black Shadow thought.

He kept seeing fragments of the Jack of Diamonds, like someone seen in a funhouse mirror. The generator in his hand was vibrating like a crazy thing. He jumped for the bits of two-dee image, the generator stuck out in front of him.

Work, you bastard, he thought.

There was a scream as the generator tried to leap from his hand, then the scream climbed into the ultrasonic.

There was a snap, as of two universes banging together.

A monologue ran continually in the bag lady's head. Sometimes things outside the monologue caught her interest for a while, but she always returned to the monologue in the end. The monologue was usually about her life before her bastard of a husband took the kids away and committed her. Or at least it featured characters she had known then, and the thing she found most interesting about the monologue was that sometimes it climbed out of her head and began to be spoken by other people. Sometimes some wino she'd met in an alley would look at her and say something that she had said to herself only a few moments before, and sometimes inanimate objects talked to her—buildings, clouds, passing automobiles.

At the moment, to her surprise, the monologue had gone. There were only two figures in front of her, one in a black cape, the other in red velvet. She watched them suspiciously, wondering if they'd taken the voice away. They were two-dimensional, flat just like the funny papers, and like the characters in the funny papers they were engaged in combat. Jumping, punching, their mouths working as they shouted at each other. There was something missing, though, and the bag lady realized that there were no dialogue balloons.

"Whass the matter, here?" she demanded. "I want talk in my funnies, yah?"

The two figures came together. There was a blossoming darkness, like a bright flash in negative, a sudden explosion of blackness. Then a bright flash that dazzled her eyes. Every piece of glass for two blocks around shattered.

The bag lady blinked. There were still two people in front of her, but they weren't flat funny-paper people any more, they were just ordinary people in odd clothes. The one in red velvet was sitting down. His skin was blue with cold. His teeth chattered.

"Jesus Christ," he said. "What *was* that?"

"I stole your body heat, man. Sucked your photons." The black man smiled. "Try surviving without the electromagetic force."

"Jesus Christ," said the red velvet man again. "I'm gonna die of hypothermia."

"Probably not. But you can look forward to a warm-water enema in the emergency room."

The bag lady could hear the monologue rising in her head again, and the conversation between the two oddly-dressed people wasn't very interesting. She didn't think it was likely that the red-velvet man would give her any more food or show her any more interesting times.

She looked down at her right hand, where she'd been carrying one of her two shopping bags. The bag was gone. Some bastard had stolen it. She felt a pang of loss, sharper than the bite of the wind. Half her life had just been torn away, one of the things that helped her to realize that she knew something the others didn't.

The monologue in her head began to take on complaining tones. There just weren't enough honest people in the world.

"Gotta find a new bag, bunky," she said. She turned and faced into the cold wind blowing off the Hudson. She began to move off into the night.

The nice thing about this kind of a life, the monologue told her, was that there was always something new in the next dumpster.

The three men were wrestling the painting into a large van when Black Shadow walked toward them, holding the red velvet man by the collar. The prisoner's teeth chattered. "Would you mind taking this guy to the police?" Black Shadow asked. "Just sit on him. I don't think he'll make any trouble." He held up an object spattered with drops of once-molten metal. "This is the thing he used to make himself two-dimensional. Got slagged in the fight. Think I'll keep it, though." The device vanished into his cloak.

The men looked embarrassed. "Well," one said, "the thing is, we sort of promised him we wouldn't prosecute him if he gave the painting back."

"That's okay, man. You didn't make the collar. Modular Man will be along later to file charges. Right now he's chasing the accomplice."

The man looked surprised. "I didn't know the Jack of Diamonds had an accomplice," he said.

"*Knave* of Diamonds!" the man said. "*Knave* of fucking Diamonds! You guys are so *stupid!*"

Black Shadow punched him once in the head. The Knave of Diamonds hung unconscious from his arm.

"There," he said. "I knocked him out for you. Just take him, will you?"

The android awoke in an airless place. There was some kind of formless glop all around him. He stretched out, found himself confined, and exerted some pressure. The metal tank in which he was confined burst apart.

Chitinous webs lay in milky lattices. He could see stars and the bright blue-and-white orb of earth. The contents of the shopping bag, clothing and half-eaten food, plastic cups and glass bottles, a child's broken push-toy, tumbled weightlessly in the space around him.

There was also something spherical and black. The android reached for it. It was warm, and he felt a faint vibration.

The space ship was tumbling, with vast holes torn in it. As sunlight shifted, shining through the holes, the android saw he was not alone.

There were three other people here. They huddled together near the center of the ship, their arms and legs thrown wide. Two looked like derelicts: one white, one black. The other was a museum guard. They all looked surprised to have found themselves in orbit, without air, and in each other's company.

The android realized where the bag lady had got her device. He began to search the ship.

Travnicek hung another newspaper clipping from the loft roofbeam. There were pictures of the Knave of Diamonds on his way to the arraignment, and other pictures of Modular Man in his skullcap, looking pleased by all the attention.

"Nice," Travnicek said. "You did good, toaster. I pat myself on the back for a great job of programming."

The android brought him a cup of coffee. He grinned and took it.

Travnicek turned to contemplate the alien orb sitting on his workbench. He'd been trying to manipulate it with various kind of remotes, but was unable to achieve anything, other than sometimes making the remotes disappear, presumably into some waste disposal heap somewhere between the Lower East Side and Alpha Centauri. The android hadn't been able to work it, either. Travnicek moved toward the workbench and studied the thing from a respectful distance.

"Perhaps it requires contact from a life-form to work it," the android suggested. "Maybe you should touch it."

"Maybe you should mind your own fucking business. I'm not getting near that goddam thing."

"Yes, sir." The android was silent for a moment. Travnicek sipped his coffee. Then he shook his head and turned away from the workbench.

"Sir?" the android said. Travnicek looked at him.

"You got a question, blender?"

"That space ship looked as if it had been attacked by something. Whatever attacked it probably didn't come from Earth, and might still be up there. Do you suppose we should look into what they're doing?"

"In your spare time, maybe. Which you don't have any of, since you're going to go to the store and get me a bottle of cold duck and some jelly doughnuts. I feel like celebrating."

"Yes, sir." The android, his face expressionless, turned insubstantial and rocketed up through the ceiling.

Travnicek went into the small heated room he slept in, turned on the television, and sat in a worn-out easy chair. The television was full of pictures of crazed shoppers stampeding over each other to get toys for their children. Computers seemed to be popular this year. Travnicek cackled, then turned the channel. It was an old movie, *A Christmas Carol* with Reginald Owen. He settled back to watch.

When the android returned, he found Travnicek asleep. He put the bag down quietly and withdrew.

"So I says to Maxine, I says, When are you gonna do something about that condition of yours? I says, it's time to let a doctor see it."

The bag lady, one shopping bag hanging from her arm while she clutched a second bag to her chest, walked slowly down the alley, fighting the Siberian wind. The cheerful flag she had found by the museum flapped out behind her, reflecting Broadway's Christmas lights ahead.

Black Shadow had his feet planted on the brick wall of an old brownstone and squatted on his calves, huddled in his cloak. He watched Modular Man and the bag lady. The android was trying to talk to her, to give her a takeout bag filled with Chinese food, but she continued mumbling to herself and plodding up the alley. Finally the android stuffed the takeout bag into her shopping bag and returned to where the vigilante waited.

"Surrender, Mod Man." The drawling voice had an unaccustomed kindness in it. "There isn't anything you can do for her."

"I keep thinking there's something."

"Wild-card powers aren't an answer to everything, Mod Man. You have to learn to come to terms with your limitations."

The android said nothing, just turned to look at the bag lady walking down the alley.

"Now, by way of example, I have this thing about finding evildoers and giving them what's coming to them," Black Shadow said. "I'm not likely to do much about that, because the whole thing suits me, me being crazy and all. You, on the other hand, have to live with some kind of nutty professor who's using you to work out his power fantasies, and from what you tell me you can't do anything about that at all. We all have a cross to bear."

"I understand," the android said. Without interest.

"The thing you need to accept, if this business isn't going to drive you crazy, is that no one's invented a wild-card power that can do a goddam thing for middle-aged ladies who are out of their heads and who carry their whole world with them in shopping bags and who live in garbage cans." He paused. "You listening, Mod Man?"

"Yes. I hear you."

The vigilante reached into his cloak and came out with a small package wrapped in red ribbon. "I got you something," he said. "Merry Christmas."

The android seemed embarrassed. "I hadn't thought to get you anything," he said.

"That's all right. You've had things on your mind."

Modular Man opened the package. The wind caught the bright ribbon and spiraled it down the alley. Inside a box was a piece of paper. The android held it up to the light and peered at it.

"One of Fortunato's gift certificates," Black Shadow said. "I figured you could use cheering up."

"Thank you. It's a nice thought."

"You're welcome." He straightened from his crouch and walked down the wall to the alley surface. "I think I'll go beat on some villains for warmth and exercise. Care to join me?"

"No. I think I'll use the certificate before my boss finds it."

"See you later, Mod Man." The vigilante raised a hand.

"Merry Christmas."

Down the alley, something bright caught the eye of the bag lady. She bent and picked up a strand of red ribbon.

She stuffed it into a bag and walked on.

Erogenoscape

Smoke rises from Babette's left breast as Dr. Talbot's cauterizing laser strikes home. Collagen and elastin evaporate beneath the precise assault of coherent photons, reveal yellow layers of fat. The laser ceases to pulse, rotates to a new position, fires again. Blood hisses and gives off steam. There is a greasy odor as fat burns away. To Talbot's sensitive nose drifts the scent of blood, of disinfectant.

The blood flow subsides as the laser cauterizes damaged blood vessels. Talbot carefully excavates mammary tissue, then pauses. This is his fourth rehearsal of the operation to reduce Babette's submammary fold, and his action, when the real thing comes, will betray no such equivocation. He pauses not because of uncertainty, but because of a new idea.

Once the idea takes form, Talbot acts upon it without hesitation. All that is called for is a slightly different gelplast implant. His movements are exact. He finishes the left breast, then alters the right along similar lines.

Once the edges of the wounds are glued back together, Talbot adjusts his opaque black sleep mask to a more comfortable position and alters the t index. He watches as the two breasts heal, wounds drain, scar tissue forms. He adjusts the mask again and evaporates the scars with precise bursts of his laser. Then he gazes carefully at his work.

Because he is entering via the underside of each breast, both breasts have been pulled upward on Babette's chest wall. He reaches out, draws each breast to a normal position. Body warmth osmoses through his surgical gloves.

He walks around the operating table, studying the result. He makes several recordings of the appearance of each breast, measures the angle of the underside, then sits the patient up to observe the effects of gravity. He repeats his photographs and measurements.

His mouth is slightly dry. His pulse is slightly elevated. He believes he has done very well.

He stands and takes a few free breaths. Babette, he is sure, will be pleased.

Talbot reaches out to throw a mental switch, and his patient fades away.

Talbot's sixty-foot motorboat rocks to another gust of wind. Talbot sips gasless mineral water in the saloon and gazes at his wife's smiling features, broadcast via satellite from Tahiti and materialized in his optic centers. The Pacific sun, he observes, is bringing out her freckles.

"The Borodins have been very nice," she says. "Trudi and I go out every day."

"Please give them my best," Talbot says.

His first wife, Natalie, had been a fellow medical student who also hoped to make her name in body design—the marriage had failed, Talbot thought, because they were too much alike, because they shared too many obsessions. In contrast he and Sarai have little in common and the marriage seems a success.

It was her scapulae that had first attracted him. He first saw them here on Montserrat, as Sarai walked the black volcanic beach and played toes-tag with the ever-rising ocean. Her back was to him, and as he watched a shiver ran through him at the extraordinary freedom of her shoulder blades beneath her supple skin—they moved with rare independence, creating a striking play of skin and shadow. It was almost as if her scapulae were the pinions of developing wings. He knew he had to make their acquaintance.

He introduced himself and offered to buy her a drink. Her body was petite, with breasts so small he could fit them into a martini glass without deforming them. The label on her bikini bottom had cost her trust fund the equivalent of two months' work on the part of the average Earth laborer. Her bones were good, her hair was dark, her eyes needed work. He found out she was a college student on vacation. She explained to him her strategy for avoiding worry lines and cellulite. He praised her scapulae and she seemed to believe him. He told her he was rich and could make her beautiful. She believed that, too.

Talbot worked on the eyes and nose and mouth, the ears and pectorals and breasts and hips. He altered the cheekbones and jawline, improved the curve of the buttocks and the line of the calf. He restructured the eye sockets so that they wouldn't get puffy in freefall and so that she'd look her best on her shopping binges on L4. He tattooed her inner wrists with his signature so that everyone would know who designed her. He gave her money and let her flaunt his signature, his design, in every fashionable resort in the Earth System. It was wonderful advertising.

He left her scapulae reverently alone.

He'd overheard people say that their relationship was shallow. Ridiculous. It was based on the fact they both worshipped, absolutely adored, her body. What could be more profound than that?

Besides, if he ever tired of her, he could simply change her into someone else. It would be simple enough.

"I see you're getting a few freckles," he says.

There is a half-second's pause, due to the lagtime of the satellite link, and then Sarai turns doubtful. "Should I get out of the sun, do you think?"

"I think they look attractive."

Sarai is cheered, at least after the half-second lag. There is a glow in her grey Optrim™ implants.

"But I wouldn't overdo it," Talbot cautions.

She promises to be careful of the sun. She blows a kiss at him over the interface link.

"I love you," she says.

"I love you, too."

The image fades from Talbot's mind. Babette's is already there to replace it.

Mr. Alexandru is Babette's agent in her dealings with Dr. Talbot. His hair and eyebrows are unnaturally black, and he affects a pencil-thin mustache and a smoked monocle. The visible eye is an Optikon Seven, color Soulful Brown™. Alexandru is tanned and his short hair is parted within a millimeter of the center line. He is perhaps sixty, but looks no older than twenty-five. His cosmetic surgery is very good, and if Alexandru hadn't favored a deliberately artificial style, with projecting brow ridges and cheekbones, the work would have been undetectable.

The boat shudders to a williwaw flooding down from the slot in Montserrat's volcano. Because of the potential for eavesdroppers, Alexandru prefers not to use the interface for his visits with Dr. Talbot, and instead visits Talbot on his yacht.

"In the matter of the femoral triangle and groin," Alexandru says, "Babette would like to see the workups on those as soon as possible."

"Naturally. I've only done some exploration in that direction, but I think I'm prepared to discuss my ideas."

"By all means. Do you have a simulation prepared?"

Talbot smiles. "Shall we face in?"

With his long, artistic surgeon's fingers Talbot slides the interface studs into his head sockets. Ceramic and gold contacts snug into place. He closes his eyes, pulses codes to the onboard computer, and Babette's groin blossoms before his visual cortex, set against a contrasting background of neutral charcoal grey.

"There are two points at issue," Talbot says. "First, the femoral triangle, specifically the two deep grooves at the juncture of hip and thigh, the first between the sartorius and the adductor longus, the second between the sartorius and the tensor fascia lata."

"Quite." Alexandru's purring voice reaches Talbot both over the short distance between them and over the face, creating a distracting stereo effect.

"Though the pleasant shading caused by the interplay of muscle in the inner thigh can be accentuated merely by developing the muscles themselves, Babette has indicated that she wishes the sartorius to be made more prominent in order to emphasize the grooves on either side. This can be accomplished by dissecting the muscles upward and attaching a Plianon implant to the femur." Talbot triggers the computer simulation, showing different stages of the operation, the muscles lifted gently outward with teflon-cushioned hooks, the implant nestled in its new location. "Plianon is far more frictionless than bone and the muscle will slide over it in a natural way. The result—" moving the simulation to its conclusion, "—should be a sartorius provocative in its display of suppleness and shadow, but without the conclusive appearance of an artifact." Babette's simulation begins moving through slow-motion knee bends. Shadow plays over flexing skin, pantherlike muscle. The point of view remains fixed at groin level.

"Very good, doctor." Even through the face Talbot can sense Alexandru's intense interest. "May I have a copy of this?"

"Of course."

"With your lecture included?"

"I'm recording it."

"Very good. Now—the second problem you mentioned?"

"Ah. The line of Babette's groin." Babette's simulation freezes its movement in a squatting position, knees apart, feet flat on the floor. Talbot materializes an image of his own hand, finger pointing, as a visual aid. "You'll note the series of curves displayed in the outline, three on each side of the center line. The longest and flattest is the gracilis, which is the superficial muscle on the underside of the thigh. As it stretches all the way from the shaft of the tibia to the anterior half of the pubic arch—in other words from below the knee to the pubic area itself—it is best defined in this squatting position." Talbot's own hand, his real hand, moves in tandem with its simulation as the latter slides along the underside of the simulated thigh. Illusory tactile contact and warmth, artifacts of the simulation, trickle along the pads of his fingers. He had found the tactile programming to be insufficient and had programmed this piece himself. "I personally feel that there is no need for artificial augmentation of this feature," he says. "It's quite prominent on its own."

"I'll make a note of it."

"The second curve—" the simulated hand arcing, "—is behind the first, and basically consists of the fatty lower curves of the buttocks as seen from the front. As we are going to lift the buttocks in another operation, this curve will diminish." The simulation does so. "If Babette feels that the natural dropcurve is attractive, we can add subdermal pads to enhance it. The operation is very simple and can be done at the same time as the buttock lift."

"I see."

"Do you have any idea of Babette's wishes in this matter?"

"My suspicion is that she will want to retain that curve, or something like it."

"I'll make preparations then and run simulations on a variety of subdermal pads."

"Thank you. I'll pick them up on my next visit."

"The third curve—" the hand making a delicate cup below the groin, "—is the projection of the labia majora."

"Not sufficient," Alexandru says. "Babette is not well-endowed in this respect." Talbot can sense his frown.

"I rather thought the groin was not prominent enough."

"At present Babette has subdermal pads in her labia."

"The problem with an implant in the labium majus is that it is rather artificial to the touch. In an intimate situation it can be … off-putting." Talbot resists the impulse to wiggle his fingers below Babette's pubis.

"Babette has not mentioned this," Alexandru murmurs.

"Perhaps she has been lucky in her choice of partners," Talbot says. "Nevertheless, we can avoid the issue entirely by fixing Plianon implants to the ischial tuberosities—the bony projections at the bottom of the pelvis." Babette's skeletal structure fluoresces briefly beneath its skin to illustrate the point. Little flashing arrows point out the area in question. "This should project the labia downward—" the simulation illustrating this, "—and create a more provocative curve. The size of the pads and degree of projection is of course up to Babette."

"Thank you, doctor." Alexandru's voice is brisk. Talbot, eyes closed to fully enter the interface, can sense his yacht moving uneasily, caught between current and the wind pouring through Montserrat's volcano.

"One more point, before you face out."

"Yes?"

"In the matter of the breast implants …"

"I thought they had already been decided."

"Quite so. But during a recent rehearsal of the operation I noticed something. If I may? …"

Alexandru is impatient. "Very well."

The simulation shifts to contrasting recordings of Babette's breasts, the side view. One is the result of Talbot's last simulated operation, the other of an earlier attempt.

"As you see," Talbot explains, "the submammary fold is eliminated in both cases. But this second pad is slightly fuller along the bottom—you see?" His hand traces the curve. "I find this outcurve somewhat more pleasing, though of course it's a matter of opinion. I think Babette might want to look at this view before committing herself one way or another."

"Ye-es." Intrigued. "I see what you mean." Alexandru turns brisk again. "I'll show this view to Babette. The final decision of course will be hers."

"Of course."

"Shall we face out?"

Talbot unfaces, opens his eyes, turns to Alexandru. His mouth feels dry, and Talbot is aware that the palm of the hand that had guided the simulation is moist. He rubs his hands together, then pops a liquid crystal data cube from his onboard comp, takes it in his long fingers, and hands it to Alexandru. "Here is my analysis. May I offer you a drink? Coffee? Tea?"

Alexandru has a gin and tonic. Talbot pours himself gasless mineral water. Alexandru adjusts his monocle, gives Talbot a frown.

"Any problem with security?" he asks. "Any hints of people sniffing around?"

"None. My private security here is the best available, and as I know the Prime Minister socially I can call on state forces at any time. She is aware of how many benefits the clinic brings to her," he smiles, "beleaguered island. With the rising water reducing her living space, she's happy for any source of income."

"When Babette's body is brought here," Alexandru says, "there will be problems. I will guarantee it. Some people will do *anything* to acquire a simulation of the body, with or without its modifications. Some may attempt to take the body itself."

The boat tugs at its mooring buoy. Talbot sips, smiles. "My practice caters almost exclusively to celebrities. There's never been a leak. *Never.*"

"With all respect, doctor. Babette is different. If the screamsheets ever have *any* idea her body is here ..."

"I've laid on extra security. And my own precautions have been in place for some time."

The glance through Alexandru's monocle is sharp. "I merely wish to emphasize that unusual pressures may be brought to bear."

Talbot holds out his glass of mineral water. Despite the movement of the boat, despite the extension of his arm, there isn't even a tremor in the surface of the water. "I'm used to pressure," he says. "In fact I thrive on it."

Triumph sings through Talbot as he looks down at the new simulation of Babette's body. Alexandru had brought it to him that afternoon, along with the news that Babette had agreed to his suggestion concerning the lower curve of her breast.

The simulations with which Talbot has been working up till now are not current. They are an early type, cruder than he is used to—the internal organs not Babette's, but taken from a generic surgical simulation, then sized and wrapped in Babette's image. They are old—thirty years old in some cases—created before Babette's first cosmetic surgery.

But this simulation is current, taken with the latest scanning technology. This one is Babette and only Babette down to the subcellular level.

She stretches out before him on the table, the body young, unscarred, its face slack, gaze blank, flesh unmarked by the knife. Pliable. Not yet the superstar that dominates the screamsheets but a full-grown embryo, a blank slate for Talbot's scalpel.

Talbot will help form this icon, this marvel, this figure of worship. He can feel power surge through his hands as he gazes down at Babette's body.

Babette. A name, a body, a face … an industry. The most stunning media figure of the last two generations. Ranked with other legendary divinities like Harlow, West, Monroe, Bardot, Taylor …

No one any longer thought it possible to develop an icon with such universal resonance. Humanity stretches from the half-submerged venices of Florida to the asteroid belt, embracing ever-diverging tastes and cultures—no one figure, it was reasoned, could dominate the preferences of a system-wide audience.

Babette had managed it. She started out, age fifteen or so, as a slit-eyed, dimpled porn actress from the slums of Ste.-Foy, her body already lush—hormone treatments were suggested. Her stance was cool, cynical, thoroughly knowing—provocative in someone her age—but still she seemed, despite the coolness, resonant with inadvertent passion. Amid the slack glances and hesitant delivery of her contemporaries, Babette stood out. Her subsequent history was to demonstrate that her ability to imagine herself was already fully formed. As the parts in which she was cast evolved from mediocre porn to high-budget porn to provocative comedy, from comedy to music video to sophisticated drama, the cool pose faded away, and as she grew older Babette managed to discover in herself a kind of innocence, a wide-eyed wonder that even the sordid facts of her biography had not been able to extinguish. (Screamsheet fodder, this: her father was unknown, her mother an alcoholic and the victim of a serial killer; her foster parents had sold her to her first pimp for two hundred in worthless Quebecois scrip.)

Volumes had been written about the purity this strange Magdalen managed to project. It was the innocence that proved more enduring than the earlier worldly-wise pose, an innocence that somehow embraced, absorbed, the earlier quality of knowing, without sacrificing its own simple artlessness.

Babette knew what was what, saw the world as it was, and still lived in a kind of hope.

As the roles matured, so did Babette's body. Fashions in bodies change, from lush to neurasthenic and back again. Babette's was in the classic mode of the goddesses before her—perhaps it is a constant, Talbot thinks, some feature of human character, that goddesses need be ample. No one ever accused Marilyn Monroe of being skinny; no one ever thought it hampered her career much, either.

Babette was one of the first to flaunt her augmentations. Others had cosmetic surgery and acknowledged it when forced to; Babette boasted of it—she helped to popularize the term "body design"—and dared her audience to work out just what she'd had done. Her fans complied: the earlier pornography—Babette had long since acquired the rights—sold by the millions so that a careful measured examination could be made of every altered feature. Babette's modifications tended to be daring: she would push her body to the brink of artificiality, but not beyond. An overly-sculpted, over-radical look would be too subject to changes in fashion; Babette aims for a provocative, ample universality—and she achieves it.

Babette has been a gigastar for almost forty years. Her every move is chronicled with relentless diligence and mind-stretching comprehension by the media. She has achieved the heights for which she aimed, a parity with the legends of the past.

But now she is aiming to surpass them.

Mae West and Jean Harlow, Liz Taylor and Brigitte Bardot ... all are dead.

Babette, with Talbot's help, will never die.

Now that the new simulation has arrived, Talbot's rehearsals begin in earnest. He brings in two assistants, Cummings and Baca-Torrijos. It is only necessary to add an anaesthesiologist to complete the team, but she won't be necessary until Babette's physical body finally arrives.

Talbot chooses his assistants based not only on skill but on nerve. Some people get apprehensive around laser surgical tools, and the usual remedy is to cover everyone in the operating room, assistants, doctor, and anywhere on the patient not to be cut, with sopping wet towels or soaked surgical gear, while everyone in the room wears protective goggles. All to prevent accidents from happening on the chance the laser is pointed the wrong way when it's turned on.

Talbot won't have it. His use of the cauterizing laser is absolutely precise, absolutely correct, and he will not have it implied otherwise. If his assistants aren't willing to place trust in him—the same trust placed in him by the patients, he points out—then they are welcome to seek employment elsewhere.

Baca-Torrijos has been an assistant for four years now. Cummings, however, is new; she has yet to accustom herself to his ways. Even now, he notices, even in simulation when it isn't powered, she flinches a bit when the laser deploys toward its target. The nervousness seems to increase, rather than diminish, with each rehearsal.

Talbot rehearses his team meticulously on each operation. Breast reshaping, sublabial implants, buttock lift, the replacement of the eyes with Kikuyu™ implants, the reshaping of the eyelids and configuration of the eye socket for zero-gee, the reduction of the nasal septum, the maxilla and replacement of the alar cartridge, that arches winglike over each nostril, with a natural-seeming implant just a bit more flared.

The transformation is something that Babette herself has willed. Her grasp of possibility, of surgical technique, is breathtaking.

The resulting artifact, even in simulation, is astonishing. The pupal Babette becomes, step by step, a goddess.

And then Talbot discovers that someone has profaned the shrine.

He asks Cummings to meet him in his office. Two of his security detail, complete with sidearms, wait outside.

Voltaic apprehension twitches through her body as she steps through the door. The security people have her spooked. Her face (cheekbone implants, reshaped jaw, pad at the point of the chin) turns away as he looks at her.

No wonder she was nervous in rehearsal. She was planning *this*.

Talbot steeples his long fingers in front of him. "A lengthy transmission was recorded on our main computer this morning," he says. "Do you know the transmission I refer to?"

Cummings' lips (augmented with CollaTrine) are pressed furiously together. She manages to unclamp them long enough to say No.

"Ah." His eyes (Optrim, Radiant Sky Blue™) bore into hers. "The computer has standing instructions to refer any long transmissions to me." He gives a thin smile. "I looked at this one. It was a complete record of Babette's body, complete with a full log of all our rehearsals."

"Someone—" She stammers. "Someone must have—"

"*Someone* jacked her way into the main computer by altering her system account status from a limited account to that of superuser. I and our real sysop were surprised to discover that this was even possible—I'm supposed to be the only superuser on the system. Our intruder used her high level of access to secretly duplicate our every rehearsal of Babette's operation. It was only when the extraordinarily long transmission was logged that a hardwired alarm was triggered." He leans forward, gazes at her. "The intruder didn't know about the alarm, because it wasn't a part of the programming, it was something I personally hardwired into the system. It overrode the command structure and halted the transmission. Recorded it instead, for evidence." Cummings stares at him. "You see," Talbot goes on, "when I established this place I knew there were dangers. People who would want recordings of their favorite people. And … I took precautions. Sensibly, it would seem."

"Why," licking her lips, "why are you talking to me?"

"The superuser was you."

Her answer comes much too quickly. "It could have been someone who got my account number and passwords."

"And who was also using the terminal in your office? That's on record, too."

"I want a lawyer."

Talbot gives a snort of contempt. "If you insist. But if you'll review your contract, you'll find that it covers this contingency. There's not much room for a lawyer to negotiate." Talbot opens a drawer, produces a duplicate of the contract, pushes it across the desk. "This doesn't have to go to court, you know," he says. "Local justice is … well, *primitive* is the wrong expression, quite misleading. I'd say it's just deprived—not much money for coddling felons. And the Prime Minister is a friend, which will doubtless influence the trial."

Cummings gnaws her lip. "Can I have a cigaret?"

"No. You may not." Talbot steeples his fingertips again; it's a gesture he enjoys ever since he'd had the fingerbones lengthened with new lightweight spaceborn alloy in order to provide the long artistic fingers everyone seemed to feel a surgeon required.

"Here's what I'm offering. You tell me who hired you, and if he's on the island we'll have him deported. You surrender the money you've been paid to me—that's in your contract, by the by. And you agree that the two gentlemen outside—" pointing toward the door, "—will escort you onto an aircraft that will take you to another island, one of the smaller Grenadines that isn't underwater yet, where you will be held incommunicado until Babette's operation is completed. You will agree not to *ever* speak publicly on the topic of Babette's alterations or the designs of any of our other patients. In return, we won't pull your license—you won't be able to work for any major body designers, but no doubt you'll be able to find employment in some pathetic little clinic, somewhere in some miserable corner of the world, to help wanted criminals acquire new faces and thus avoid the law." He takes another piece of paper from his drawer and pushes it across the desk. "Sign here."

Cummings reads carefully and signs. He takes the paper and puts it back in his desk, then looks up at her.

"How much were you paid?"

Cummings thinks for a moment, then takes a deep breath. "Eighty-five thousand shares of Tempel Pharmaceuticals," she says. "I was supposed to get another eighty-five thousand when I delivered the data."

Tempel Pharmaceuticals. Pure blue chip, more stable than any Terran currency other than maybe the Swiss franc. Their weightless orbital factory was producing new products almost every week. To Cummings the stock was worth ten years' salary at what Talbot was paying. Talbot smiles at her. "Very good. That jibes with what my investigators turned up in your portfolio. I would really have hated it if you hadn't mentioned all that stock."

She looks at him stonily.

"Your employer obviously has a lot of money to spend. Who is he?"

"The name I got was Godolphin. No first name. He's a big blond guy, talks with some kind of accent. Not Brit exactly, but something like."

"And he approached you?"

"On my day off. I took my bike out for a drive and stopped by Candy Jack's lounge on the way back. He—" She shrugs. "I thought he was a tourist. Then he started talking investments, like he had something special for me."

"Apparently he did."

Cummings says nothing.

"I suppose it should fall within the category of a bad tip." Distaste curls Talbot's lip. "Did he specifically ask for Babette's program, or just anyone's?"

"He wanted Babette. He wasn't interested in our other patients."

Talbot reaches for the phone. "You'll give my associates a thorough description. If you'll go with the gentlemen outside, I'll make a phone call to the Prime Minister."

Talbot enters the operating theater. Paranoia swims in his brain, and he can taste the metallic bitterness of Cummings' betrayal on his tongue.

He has hired additional security. Alexandru has been informed and is flying to the Grenadines to take charge of the traitor.

No Godolphin, or anyone approaching his description, has been found on the island. Talbot wonders if he is not the only one to benefit from a special relationship with the head of government.

As he enters the operating room his mind is alert, its edges keen and sharp as if it had been carefully honed. Godolphin, he thinks, doesn't know who he's dealing with.

Familiar operating room smells rise around him. He looks at the table, the empty trays for instruments, the defibrillator waiting for an emergency, the laser scalpel coiled overhead.

He puts on his opaque mask and studs into the face, calls up the simulation of Babette. Her body appears before him: altered, glorious, glowing with life, radiant with celebrity.

The image fails in its usual soothing effect. Talbot puts on a pair of gloves and steps to the table. Babette's sweet breath, oil of cloves, comes to his nostrils. He had added that little touch to the programming himself. He touches the warm, elastic skin. Heat rises through the gloves.

This is what Godolphin is after. It isn't only political/economic simulations that can be used for purposes other than those for which they were designed—this work, too, can have its function twisted.

Some people worship Babette. Some hate her. Some worship and hate her at once.

Some simply want to hold Babette in their arms. With the simulation and the right cyber-sexual implants they can experience full intercourse. Some, amateur surgeons or body designers, want to make improvements.

Some just want to cut her to bits.

The simulation will permit all that. The basic programming was done by perfectly sober doctors as a training aide for surgeons, little aware that versions of the program would be marketed under names like *Anatomical Seduction, Target for Tonight,* or *Serial Killer.* The program's designers had designed the simulation to realistically reflect the use of scalpel blade on the virtual body, but that implied as well the impact of a butcher knife or a double-bitted axe.

Celebrities, according to the World Court, possess full physiognomic rights—each owns her own appearance, up to and including the viscera. Few are willing to license their appearance for a product called *Razor Rape.*

The black market in celebrity simulations is worldwide. Many simulations offered are merely standard simulations with the celebrity's face and body grafted onto it, but these seem only to have whetted the demand for the real thing. Since cosmetic surgery—or full body design—is an almost inevitable consequence, and often prerequisite, of celebrity, there is an ongoing attempt to corrupt the staff of clinics and hospitals worldwide. That is partly why Talbot chose to site his clinic on Montserrat, to minimize the chance of contact.

Eighty-five thousand Tempel shares. That's the highest offer Talbot knows of.

Talbot looks down at Babette's body, watches the pulse beat in her throat, the rise and fall of her breasts with respiration. What hideous thing had Godolphin wanted to do to this perfection?

Fury thunders along his nerves. Suddenly he doesn't want to look at Babette any more. He turns a switch in his head and now he's gazing down at Sarai. His gloved hands slide over her tanned, compact body, trace the invisible seams where he'd removed two lower ribs to give her a slimmer waist.

Anger coils around his heart. He's been betrayed.

Feverishly he searches through mental files, calls up the one he wants. Now his hands clasp Cummings' waist, and she gazes up at him with shining Optrim eyes. He smiles and, in the simulation, conjures a curved No. 9 scalpel right into his hand.

"How'd you like it done to *you?*" he asks.

Modern scalpels contain microelectronics to disrupt the electrostatic charges that hold body cells together—they read the positive or negative charge and neutralize them, parting tissue without damage. The simulated scalpel in Talbot's hand is old-fashioned surgical steel.

The blade traces blood downward from her sternum. Talbot calls up the laser program and his scent and taste centers fill with the smell of burning fat. Blood sprays over his pale blue tropical shirt as he rips open the abdominal wall. He playfully jabs the peritoneum with the scalpel, then again. It makes a startling *pop* as it perforates. He slices it away, then reaches in with his other hand and tears away the gleaming, fatty omentum. Musty abdominal smells rise from the revealed organs.

"Bet I can make some improvements," he says.

It's easy to clean up—Talbot just tells the simulation to go away and all the blood, all the organs and fluids, the entire excavated corpse, vanish into thin air.

He can feel his pulse speeding through his veins. His respiration seems to be absolutely normal. He holds out a hand and it's perfectly steady.

Things are under control.

He decides to spend the night on his boat where he can think. He leaves the clinic and walks down the night streets toward the jetty where he's parked his inflatable. Trade winds float around him, bearing the sharp scents of the island. He can hear some of the locals roistering in a back-street shebeen.

"Hiya, doc."

Sweating paranoia swings Talbot around at the sound of the strange voice.

A big white man stands under a dead palm. One hand is in the pocket of his tan bush jacket, and the other holds a briefcase. Talbot controls a shudder and straightens. His features assume a look of cultivated disdain.

"Mr. Godolphin, I presume."

"Not really. That's just what I told that stupid bitch Cummings to call me."

Godolphin steps forward. He towers over Talbot. Talbot isn't a short man but he can feel his hackles rise at the looming threat.

"We gotta talk, doc." Cummings hadn't thought the voice was British, but in that as in everything else she was wrong: she'd just never heard a Northumberland accent before.

"I don't believe we have anything to say to one another," Talbot says. He'd turn and walk away but something tells him that it would be unwise to turn his back on this man. He considers walking sideways back to the clinic, then decides it's far too undignified to go slipping along the night streets like a crab, and probably futile anyway.

"I imagine you've got the eighty-five thousand shares, right?" Godolphin says.

Talbot's mouth is dry. He speaks with careful, forceful effort. "I'm not prepared to give them back. Cummings delivered them to me, as per my contract with her. If you want their value back, you can sue to have her future wages docked."

Godolphin's face is lopsided, and his grin seems like a monstrous leer. Talbot's fingers itch to take a scalpel to it.

"Oh hell, doc," Godolphin says. "Keep the shares." He takes his hand out of his pocket—Talbot tenses for a bullet or blow—and then opens the briefcase. He pulls out a handful of paper shares and offers them. "Want the rest?"

Contempt curls Talbot's lip. "You can't afford my price."

"I dunno—what's your price?"

Talbot laughs. "Don't be absurd, man."

"Name it."

Something inspires Talbot to name the most ridiculous sum he can think of. "Two hundred million Swiss francs."

Wind whips hair around the face sockets on Godolphin's temples. He seems abstracted for a moment, then shrugs. "Okay," he says. "I can manage that."

Talbot shakes his head. "You're pathetic," he says. "If you could command that kind of money in this business I would have heard of you."

"It's not *my* money, doc. I'm just a messenger. I represent somebody else."

"Who?"

Another leer yawns across Godolphin's features. "Only if we agree to do business."

Talbot looks at him. The sum of money is preposterous, so huge it's meaningless. He isn't even tempted by it. "Not possible," he says.

Godolphin shrugs, closes the briefcase, tucks it under his arm. "Let's talk family," he says. "Your lady's just flown from Tahiti to Havana, right? Visiting with some friends, on her way up the well to L4 for some shopping?"

"What are you implying?" Talbot demands. The injured-husband tones seem to come naturally to his lips.

"All the work you've put in on her body," Godolphin says, "I'm sure she'll look good in her coffin."

"Surely you wouldn't go to those kind of lengths for just a computer simulation? How can it be worth it?"

"I just do what I'm told, doc. Like I said, I'm not running this show."

Talbot affects to consider this development. Electricity pulses along his nerves. He knows how to play this.

"Two hundred mil," Godolphin says. "Think about what you could do with all that."

"I want the other eighty-five thousand shares now," Talbot says. "The two hundred million tomorrow."

Godolphin leers again. Talbot wants to reach out and adjust the big, crooked teeth. "Whatever you say, doc," he says.

"Come up to the clinic. I want to put the stock certificates in my safe."

"Okey-dokey. Just don't do anything stupid, like call the cops from your office. The consequences could be unfortunate."

Talbot thinks of Sarai lying torn somewhere, victim of someone who apprenticed in butchery with an electronically-simulated body and a kitchen knife. The look of terror in her reconstructed eyes. His fine work slashed, ruined, ripped to shreds.

The clinic door opens to his code. It's a small private clinic, not a public hospital with a busy emergency room, and he sees no one on his way to the operating theater. He enters the room, flicks on the lights, reaches for an interface stud.

"You got a safe in here, doc?"

Talbot looks over his shoulder. "Close the door behind you. I don't want anyone to see you here."

Godolphin closes the door. His eyes slide over the room, taking in the table, the gleaming tile, the equipment. Looking for something threatening, seeing nothing. Talbot recognizes his eyes as Optikon Tyrian Violet™. "This ain't your office, doc," Godolphin says.

"I thought I'd show you the merchandise first. Make sure it's what you want, because I only want you here this once." He points to some interface jacks lying on the countertop. "Stud in. You can see what you're buying."

"You got it, doc." The big man brushes hair back from his sockets, inserts the jack. Talbot mentally pulses out commands for the laser to start its powerup sequence, for the defibrillator to turn itself on and switch to its maximum setting of 300 joules.

Idiot, he thinks. *You think I need a* knife *for this?*

He calls up the simulation of Babette. Godolphin's eyes widen as her apparition appears before him on the table. He gives a whistle.

"This is her condition before the operation," Talbot says. The laser hasn't powered-up yet. "You should see her after I'm through."

Godolphin closes his eyes to cut out the distracting appearance of reality, allowing only the simulation to soak into his optical centers. "She looks this good *now,*" he says, "why does she need you?"

"Call it a preemptive strike against gravity," Talbot says. "She won't look this good forever—might as well get the operation over with."

The familiar commands, the sight of Babette's defenseless image, have calmed him. His pulse remains slightly elevated, and electric tension hums through his nerves, but he's absolutely ready for what he has to do.

Godolphin reaches out, touches a breast. He seems surprised by the warmth. Talbot's mind shrieks at the violation.

"What," Talbot says, "is your boss planning on doing with this simulation once he's got it?"

"I dunno. He's a collector, I guess."

"A connoisseur."

"Something like that." Godolphin palpates Babette's breast. His eyes, moving under closed lids, stray toward her groin.

A green light winks on the laser's command display. *Touch not the cat,* Talbot thinks. "Do you know," he says, "I don't think I want to go through with this."

Godolphin opens his eyes and looks up. "C'mon, doc. We had an agreement. I don't want to have to make you regret anything."

"I think you're the one with regrets. I think you don't realize who you're dealing with."

The laser deploys snakelike from its mount on the ceiling. Its electric motors make little whining noises, and Godolphin looks up. Talbot knows how difficult it is for even experienced operating room techs not to look at the light source when it deploys this way.

Talbot fires a burst into each of Godolphin's eyes. He's not confident that the second shot was on target, but the first one is dead on and Godolphin screams and clutches at his eye sockets. Melted plastic oozes like tears over his lower lids.

The man's still a lot bigger and presumably has combat reflexes—he's still a danger. Talbot reaches for the defibrillator, grabs the paddles, kicks the operating table to one side. Godolphin staggers backward, still screaming. Talbot follows up, slams the paddles to each side of Godolphin's head, triggers the waiting burst of power.

There is a sizzle of burning flesh—the 300 joules are hundreds of times more powerful than the dose used in the bad old days of electroshock therapy. Every muscle in Godolphin's body goes into spasm. He falls, curling into a ball as his more developed flexors win the battle against his extensors.

Godolphin probably doesn't have much of a brain left but Talbot doesn't want to take any chances. He walks to where the surgical equipment is stored, takes a long stainless-steel probe, returns with it. He opens Godolphin's shirt, feels professionally for the gap between the fourth and fifth ribs, then jams the probe straight to Godolphin's heart. A nasty bit of cartilage or bone intervenes, and Talbot has to punch the probe home by hitting it with the heel of his palm. He has to do this several times because the heart can survive a single puncture.

As Godolphin twitches his way toward death Talbot reaches for the telephone on the wall, calls Cuba, and makes arrangements for a small private security detail to go to where Sarai is staying in Havana, escort her to the airport, and stay with her all the way home. He arranges for a chartered plane to be ready at the airport. Then he calls Sarai and explains what she must do. She is first angry, then frightened, but Talbot speaks reassuringly until she agrees.

He returns to Godolphin. The man is dead, staring up at him with his ruined artificial eyes. The right eye is melted, revealing slagged electronics. The second shot was, as Talbot suspected, a little off-target—it burned through Godolphin's lower eyelid and struck a glancing blow. The orb is only partly burned through. Probably enough force was contained in the burst of coherent light to knock the electronics out, at least for the length of time it took to finish Godolphin off.

Talbot looks down at Godolphin and works out what he'll need to get the cooling stiff up on the operating table so that he can get to work.

If there's one thing surgical hospitals are good at, he thinks, it's disposing of unwanted body parts.

The wall phone rings and Talbot jumps half a foot. He takes deep breaths to calm himself, then walks to the phone. He hadn't realized he was so nervous.

"Dr. Talbot," he says.

"I think, doctor," a voice says, "that *you're* the one who doesn't realize who he's dealing with."

Talbot stands frozen for a moment—then his head jerks to look at Godolphin's body. At the eye that hadn't been destroyed, that was still staring up at him from its lifeless socket.

"Very quick, Doctor Talbot," the voice says. "Yes, he was broadcasting the entire meeting from the radio implanted in his skull. The long-range antenna is in the briefcase. I have everything recorded. Especially the part where you stick that long thing into him and finish him off."

Talbot can only stare.

"I think we have a lot to talk about," the voice says. "And by the way, my name is Hugo Barrasa."

Talbot, to his growing horror, recognizes the name perfectly well.

Two hundred million. What an idiot. He could have asked for much more.

Distorting tropical heat rolls around Babette's body as her gurney is carried gingerly out of the chartered aircraft. Alexandru and Talbot stand on the crumbling concrete taxiway to take delivery. Turbines beat at the air, all whining high sonics aimed like drills into Talbot's ears.

"You don't look so very well, doctor," Alexandru says.

Talbot wipes sweat from his forehead. "Perhaps I've been overworking a trifle."

"I hope you aren't under too much pressure." Alexandru's smoked monocle bores into Talbot's forehead. "Calling your wife back with a pair of bodyguards—perhaps that was a little … overreactive?"

"A lot of crazy people out there," Talbot says.

Alexandru says nothing.

Talbot holds out his hand. "Steady as a rock," he says. "Not to worry."

This time it's Babette's real body on the table, warm and breathing and staring up with dim uncomprehending eyes at the assembled surgical team. There's a gleam of saliva in the corner of her mouth. Little wires run out of sockets set discreetly above the ear, under the hairline where it won't normally be seen.

Except it's not quite Babette's body, not yet. It's Babette's clone, ripened from some epithelial cells taken from Babette's arm. Grown in a tank, fed on a diet of nutrients and hormones. She looks about sixteen, the age when Babette's career really started to take off. Exercised by electrode, the musculature is superb. The brain is empty and contains less information about the world than that of a newborn. One of the wires running into her skull is connected to the brain's pleasure center, feeding it a trickle of power, keeping the full-grown newborn happy no matter what they do to her.

After the surgery is over—after the last bruise fades and the final scar is erased—the real Babette will download her mind into a liquid crystal analog in a clinic in Nice, which will then in turn be fed into the clone.

Babette will rise again—young, beautiful, and in better shape than she ever was.

It's a new technique, not without risks. Some patients suffer personality changes, memory loss, sometimes neuromuscular problems. But Babette will still have her original body, as long as it lasts, and if the technique works she'll have a brand new body and brand new career. There'll be two of her—no doubt her production company is already acquiring mother-and-daughter stories.

She could be a goddess forever.

Baca-Torrijos swabs away the drool from Babette's cheek. Everyone's ready.

Betrayed, Talbot thinks.

It's time to make the first cut. He picks up the knife, and out of the corner of one eye he sees the anaesthesiologist's cheek muscles twitch upward in an anticipatory smile …

My precious Babette. That's what Barrasa calls her.

"I want her to myself," he says. "A precious Babette for my very own."

At least Talbot doesn't have to worry about Babette's simulations being duplicated and sold by the tens of thousands. Barrasa doesn't need the money. Besides, he has principles.

"Filthy perverts touching my precious Babette," he says. "Doing atrocious things to her. Never!"

He has taken to calling Talbot at odd hours, usually after viewing another recording of Godolphin's murder. He appreciates the economy of Talbot's technique.

"I have myself killed," Barrasa says. "I know what is involved to murder in cold blood. You and I, we both believe in acting with precision. Once our minds are made up, nothing can stop us."

Talbot can only wish that were true. He can't think what to do except follow Barrasa's instructions.

Forget the two hundred million. Talbot's doing this for free, not counting the stock certificates that Cummings surrendered. He'd thrown the second bunch of certificates into the Caribbean, along with the dismembered parts of Godolphin's body in weighted plastic sacks. Back when he'd thought there was some wild hope he could evade Barrasa's dictates.

No way. Not once Talbot saw the recording, saw the cold, businesslike, intelligent, hyper-aware gleam in his own eyes as he hammered the probe home. Something tells him that a jury will not be sympathetic to this. Nor will the Prime Minister.

Barrasa wants the simulations. Every single one of them. And Talbot delivers.

Barrasa was born in Montevideo but went into orbit when young. He became an asteroid miner and made a fortune. It was said, however, that many of his most profitable claims were not his own, that his fortune was not built on successful pioneering, but on successful development of salvage claims after the previous inhabitants of the mining sites suffered mysterious decompression or fatal mining equipment failures. But after a while people stopped saying those sorts of things about Barrasa. He had became too wealthy, too powerful, and too dangerous for people to talk frankly about him at all. He owned several profitable asteroids, some of them towed into lunar orbit, as well as a small habitat of his own containing his smelters, offices, and about two thousand people. He was one of the class of people the screamsheets were now referring to as "Orbitals," people who had no terrestrial allegiances left, for whom Earth was a blue-white abstraction floating in the void.

But the Orbitals' indifference to Earth did not include disregard for the electronic media that reached through the vacuum and into their minds at the speed of light. Somewhere in his lonely life, in some hellish pressurized habitat, Barrasa had encountered Babette.

"I want to experience her purity," Barrasa says. "She has sinned, and she knows this, but in her inmost heart she is undefiled. It is the same with me. I have done bad things, but in my soul I am an innocent child."

In his soul, Talbot knows, Barrasa is deranged. The boy's been breathing vacuum too long. But Talbot can't think of a way to avoid contact with the man's insistent, purposeful dementia.

Talbot surrenders the recording of Babette's body, plus the recordings of all his rehearsals. He is told to enclose the data cube in a waterproof container, then hang it on a rope over the stern of his yacht overnight. Presumably a diver picked it up, because next morning it was gone.

He tries not to think about what Barrasa is doing with the recordings.

Meanwhile the goddess is built, day by day. Eye implants, breast implants, buttock lift, ischial implants, two ribs removed to narrow the waist. Wounds drain, bruises fade, scars are reduced with the laser. The clone, months old and already a wirehead jack-junkie, gazes up through it all with a simpering idiot smile. Talbot finds it difficult to concentrate. Whenever he sees Babette's insides, the meaty red grain of muscle or the semiliquid yellow gleam of fat, he begins to see Barrasa there, Barrasa feeling up Babette's insides with pathological devotion, or stooping to kiss or lick the wounds.

Once, with such a vision on his mind, Talbot seriously burns Baca-Torrijos' hand. He never lost control of the laser before.

He wishes the game were real, and not his life.

Sarai, after her initial fright, has grown bored with staying under guard on the island. She doesn't have many friends here, Talbot is either in the operating room or in the face all the time, and she wonders who those three A.M. phone calls are from. She begins to complain about his neglect.

The goddess nears readiness. Talbot is in awe of his own work: Babette is perfection, the fulfillment of his every professional dream. Whatever happens, he knows he will have created one true masterpiece.

After everything is complete the clone body will be scanned one more time, for Babette to voice her final approval and to have a record on file for any future operations, and then, assuming she approves, Babette will download her mind into her new flesh.

"Doctor Talbot," Alexandru says. "I must insist that you take a few days off. You're obviously working too hard."

"I'm a doctor," Talbot says. "I'm used to it."

They sit on the clinic's pleasant terrace under an umbrella of thatch. Alexandru has a piña colada, Talbot his gasless mineral water. Some of Talbot's other patients—minor celebrities, a famous race driver recuperating after a stupid accident with lighter fluid—are sitting to take the sun, or swim (scars encased in waterproof gel) in the pool below.

"I must insist," Alexandru says. "I have to think of Babette's safety. You had an accident the other day."

Anger spills through Talbot's mind. "How did you hear about that?" he demands.

"That doesn't matter. The point is that you are under extreme stress and I must insist that you take some time off."

"Absurd."

"Yes? Hold out your hand. See if it trembles."

"Don't be ridiculous." Talbot takes a firmer grip on his glass of mineral water.

"Three days, doctor. Take three days off. I should have realized when you brought your wife back under guard that …" Alexandru falls silent. He looks carefully at Talbot. "Was there some *reason* that you brought her back in such a panic? Has someone been making threats?"

"No. I just thought …" Talbot flails for words. "I feel better when she's here. It helps me work."

"Ah." Alexandru lets the syllable hang in the air. "You brought her back, but still you hardly see her."

"Mr. Alexandru. This is none of your business."

"So you say." He rather clearly disagrees.

Talbot feels sweat prickle on his nape. Alexandru knows something is wrong.

The calls from Barrasa keep coming. "My precious Babette's final recording," Barrasa says. "We should discuss the delivery."

"I want my own recording back," Talbot says. "The one of me and Godolphin."

"I can give you the cube with that recording," Barrasa says, "but how will you know I don't have a copy? There could be a thousand copies in existence by now."

"There had better not be," Talbot says.

"You'll have to trust me, I'm afraid. And why shouldn't you? I wish only to participate with you in the miracle of Babette. You must love her yourself, adore her, to have done these beautiful things to her. I am in awe of your skill."

Talbot forces himself to respond politely. "Thank you," he says.

"And you do these fine things for other celebrities, yes? Celebrities that people would want for their very own."

"No one like Babette," Talbot says. "No one at all important."

"But people would pay good money for these celebrities, yes? And why not give the simulations to them?"

"That would be highly unethical."

"For a doctor, yes. Not for a cold-blooded killer."

Talbot is appalled. "You want to share Babette with these people?" he demands.

Barrasa's answer is quick. "Not my precious Babette. Never her. But these others—whores, media trash, gossip mongers—all the people who will flock to you once it's known you worked on Babette—why not them?"

Talbot opens his mouth to reply, and then a realization comes to him. "Keep talking," he says.

And Barrasa comes back instantly, promoting his idea of Talbot selling his patients to every lunatic in the Earth system. Talbot barely listens.

Barrasa's answer was immediate. He's not off in orbit somewhere, because that would mean a time lag between one person's speech and another's. Barrasa's fairly close, and probably on Earth.

Talbot should have noticed this the first time Barrasa called.

But now that he is finally aware, Talbot knows exactly what to do.

The goddess lies, like Sleeping Beauty, awaiting the waking kiss of the electronics. She's perfect, as perfect as Talbot and all his skill can make her.

She's the most beautiful thing he's ever seen. Talbot examines the body with reverence and awe. His palate is dry, his pulse elevated.

He wills the eyes to open, to look into his. They remain shut.

Wires trail delicately out of the sockets on Babette's head. She lies on her own bed, in her own suite at the clinic. The room is filled with fresh-cut flowers. Dr. Garibaldi, from the clinic in Nice, has arrived to supervise the transfer.

There is a knock on the door. Talbot opens it and allows Babette's cosmetician to enter. Babette will awaken in a freshly made-up body.

Resentment hums in Talbot's thoughts. Why try to improve on perfection?

He leaves the room. He isn't needed for this part, and besides he has other things to do.

Talbot goes to his office, locks the door, tells the computer to refuse all calls. He puts the studs in his sockets and faces in and gives the computer his superuser passwords. His mind rolls into the processor. Talbot calls up software and uses his superuser status to monitor the phone banks. When the phone call comes he'll be ready.

Babette, he knows, is at an exclusive villa in the Italian piedmont. She's made several widely-publicized appearances in the last few weeks in order to draw off any attention from what's been going on at Talbot's clinic.

Babette, just that morning, had downloaded her brain into a vat of liquid crystal in Nice. And Nice is just waiting for the signal from Montserrat in order to transfer the program into the mind of Babette's clone.

Talbot waits, himself, for the same signal.

The signal comes. And Talbot triggers his own program.

Hello, Señor Barrasa. Surprised to see me?

What goes on in his own skull is difficult to define. Talbot's aware of things happening, of memories being triggered, reflexes being examined, scents rising unbidden … of something moving through his mind with an awesome, inexorable power. At the same time he's alert enough to monitor the progress of the massive electronic buffer he's set up, to make certain the program is performing as per schedule.

He's interfered with the process. The signal from Nice is arriving, yes, but not in the clone's mind. It's going to an electronic oblivion, a lightspeed shuttle to nowhere … Talbot's dumping it.

Instead it's his own mind that's going into Babette's clone. There's no certainty of this succeeding—there's only a decent chance of success if the minds match to begin with—but Talbot knows it's the only solution to his problems.

Señor Barrasa, we need to talk.

How many artists, he wonders, have the chance to inhabit, to physically inhabit, their own greatest work? Only those who alter their bodies, with body-building or implants or tattooing, and that work is crude compared to what Talbot has done.

He's going to incarnate himself in a divinity. He will be both a goddess and his own principal worshipper.

Babette, he thinks, is going to make some odd career moves. Buy a body sculpting clinic, get a license to practice. But why not? Personality changes and memory loss are a side effect of the clone transfer process. If she can't remember certain important details, certain important people, Babette can chalk it up to an incomplete transfer.

Instead of two Babettes, there will be two Talbots. The first one is a murderer and doesn't matter. It's the first Talbot, the unimportant one—the *mortal*—who has an important task to accomplish.

Barrasa has to be taken care of. Talbot is willing to bet that it's going to be easy.

He knows where Barrasa is. Once Talbot realized that he was in the neighborhood, he bought some satellite photographs and did some elementary research. There's been a yacht cruising in the channel between Montserrat and Antigua for the last several weeks, just turning lazy circles in the blue. A little checking confirmed it was owned by Barrasa's corporation.

Babette's earlier recordings had been picked up by a diver. Where had the diver come from but a boat?

Talbot should have realized it long ago.

Señor Barrasa, look what I brought. I thought I should bring it in person.

On the desk next to Talbot's hand is a surgical scalpel. The shaft is hard plastic contoured to his hand, and the blade under its plastic protector is the latest-generation ceramic. It won't set off a metal detector, and it will fit nicely, unobtrusively, delicately, in one of Talbot's ribbed socks.

Talbot will deliver Babette's last recording himself, motor straight to where Barrasa's yacht waits. He knows Barrasa will want to be alone when he gazes at his precious Babette. But he won't be alone, not if Talbot insists on pointing out some of the fine features of his work.

Let me explain something, Señor Barrasa. I want to show you a new procedure I performed just before the transfer. If you will just look over here? You'll have to crane your neck.

Talbot is willing to bet that he can slice Barrasa's throat before the man can call out or otherwise interfere. Talbot is also willing to bet that he can erase any incriminating recordings before the body is discovered.

And if he's discovered or thwarted or arrested afterwards or killed by the man's guards, so what? Talbot, the mortal, isn't the important one.

That Talbot can die.

Because the other Talbot, Talbot the goddess, will have risen.

Lights glow in Talbot's optical centers. The program has run its course.

Talbot faces out of the machine and removes the studs from his skull. His mouth is slightly dry, as are his palms. His pulse is only slightly elevated.

He knows he will do well. He needs only to know whether the transfer succeeded.

He puts the scalpel in his sock, rises from his chair, unlocks the door, walks to Babette's suite. Alexandru and other members of Babette's entourage are there.

"Is Babette all right?" Talbot asks.

Alexandru takes the smoked monocle out of his eye, wipes it with a handkerchief. "She was a bit confused, but that was only to be expected. She recognized me."

"That sounds promising. May I see her?"

"Dr. Garibaldi gave her a sedative. He wants her to rest."

"Ah."

Alexandru returns his monocle to his eye and looks at Talbot. "Babette had a message for you. She had a little difficulty talking, but she was very insistent. She said to tell you that everything had gone perfectly."

Cold joy tingles in Talbot's frame. He compels himself to nod graciously. "Thank you. That sets me at ease."

"Things have gone well so far."

"I think I'll spend the afternoon on the boat. Maybe go out for a ride."

Alexandru gives him a nod. "You deserve some relaxation, doctor, after all your work."

Talbot is already mentally rehearsing his lines. *Señor Barrasa, look what I have. Look what I have for you.*

He looks at Alexandru and thinks of the scalpel hidden in his sock.

"Perhaps I'll catch a big fish," he says.

And smiles.

The premise for this story popped into my head while I was speaking on a panel at Armadillocon, a science fiction convention in Austin, Texas. I and a number of other writers had just been granted a tour of MCC, the Austin research conglomerate, and we were describing our experiences for the fans.

One of the projects MCC was considering was a virtual operating theater, for use in training physicians. Surgeons would no longer have to practice appendix removal on an actual human being, but on a simulated virtual human existing only in a computer. As someone who has been operated on from time to time, and who still possessed an appendix that might yet go bad, I was greatly cheered by this innovation.

"But imagine what happens when this software gets out into the general population," I said. "People could learn to perform operations by themselves. Or they could learn how to do cosmetic surgery to keep themselves looking good. Or they could perform plastic surgery on virtual celebrities, like Liz Taylor, to see how they'd look with different modifications. Or if they didn't like Liz Taylor for some reason, they could perform the operation with a fire ax instead of a scalpel."

I became aware that the audience was staring at me in horror. I looked to my left, and saw the author Vernor Vinge scribbling in his notebook. I looked to my right, and there was Bruce Sterling likewise taking notes.

I better write this story *fast,* I said to myself.

"Erogenoscape" is set, for convenience, in the same future as "Solip:System," perhaps fifteen or twenty years earlier. Author/physician Sage Walker contributed greatly to the story's medical verisimilitude.

Foreign Devils

There is no longer anyone alive who knows her name.

She has always been known by her titles, titles related to the role she was expected to play. When she was sixteen and had been chosen as a minor concubine for the Son of Heaven, she had been called Lady Yehenara, because she was born in the Yehe tribe of the Nara clan of the great Manchu race. After she had given birth to an imperial heir, she had been called I Kuei-fei—Concubine of Feminine Virtue. Later, after her husband died and she assumed the regency for their son, she was given the title Tzu Hsi, Empress of the West, because she once lived in a pavilion on the western side of the Forbidden City.

But no one alive knows her real name, the milk-name her mother had given her almost sixty-five years ago, the name she had answered to when she was young and happy and free from care. Her real name is unimportant.

Only her position matters, and it is a lonely one.

She lives in a world of imperial yellow. The wall hangings are yellow, the carpets are yellow, and she wears a gown of crackling yellow brocade. She sleeps on yellow brocade sheets, and rests her head on pillows of yellow silk beneath embroidered yellow bed curtains.

Now Peking is on fire, and the hangings of yellow silk are stained with the red of burning.

She rises from her bed in the Hour of the Rat, a little after midnight. Her working day, and that of the Emperor, begins early.

A eunuch braids her hair while her ladies—all of them young, and all of them in gowns of blue—help her to dress. She wears a yellow satin gown embroidered with pink flowers, and a cape ornamented with four thousand pearls. The eunuch expertly twists her braided hair into a topknot, and fits over it a headdress made of jade adorned on either side with fresh flowers.

Gold sheaths protect the two long fingernails of her right hand, and jade sheaths protect the two long fingernails of her left. Her prize black lion dogs frolic around her feet.

The smell of burning floats into the room, detectable above the scent of her favorite Nine-Buddha Incense. The burning scent imparts a certain urgency to the proceedings, but her toilette cannot be completed in haste.

At last she is ready. She calls for her sedan chair and retinue—Li Lien-Ying, the Chief Eunuch, the Second Chief Eunuch, four Eunuchs of the Fifth Rank, twelve Eunuchs of the Sixth Rank, plus eight more eunuchs to carry the chair.

"Take me to the Emperor's apartments," she says.

The sedan chair swoops gently upward as the eunuchs lift it to their shoulders. As she leaves her pavilion, she hears the sound of the sentries saluting her as she passes.

They are not *her* sentries. These elite troops of the Tiger-Hunt Marksmen are not here to keep anyone *out*. They are in the employ of ambitious men, and the guards serve only to keep her a prisoner in her own palace.

Despite her titles, despite the blue-clad ladies and the eunuchs and the privileges, despite the silk and brocade and pearls, the Empress of the West is a captive. She can think of no way that she can escape.

The litter's yellow brocade curtains part for a moment, and the empress catches a brief glimpse of the sky. There is Mars, glowing high in the sky like a red lantern, and below it streaks a falling star, a beautiful ribbon of imperial yellow against the velvet night. It streaks east to west, and then is gone.

Perhaps, she thinks, it is a hopeful sign.

The audience room smells of burning. Yellow brocade crackles as the members of the Family Council perform their ritual kowtows before the Son of Heaven. Before they present their petitions to the Emperor they pause, as they realize from his flushed face and sudden intake of breath that he is having an orgasm as he sits in his dragon-embroidered robes upon his yellow-draped chair.

The Emperor Kuang Hsu is twenty-eight years old, and has suffered from severe health problems his entire life. Sometimes, in moments of tension, he succumbs to a sudden fit of orgasm. The doctors claim it is the result of a kidney malady, but no matter how many Kidney Rectifying Pills and gold-coated cinnabar the Emperor is made to swallow, his condition never improves.

The illness is sometimes embarrassing, but the family has become accustomed to it.

After the Emperor's breathing returns to normal, Prince Jung Lu presents his petition. "Your Majesty," he says, "for three days the Righteous Harmony Fists have rioted in the Tatar City and the Chinese City. There are no less than thirty thousand of these disreputable scoundrels in Peking. They have set fire to the home of Grand Secretary Hsu Tung and to many others. Grand Secretary Sun Chia-nai has been assaulted and robbed. As the Supreme Ones of the past safeguarded the tranquility of the realm by issuing edicts to suppress rebellion and disorder, and as the Righteous Harmony Fists have shown themselves violent, disorderly, and disrespectful of your majesty's servants, I hope that an edict from your majesty will soon be forthcoming that allows this unworthy person to use the Military Guards Army to suppress disorder."

Prince Tuan spits tobacco into his pocket spittoon. "I beg the favor of disagreeing with the esteemed prince," he says. Other officials, members of his Iron Hat Faction, murmur their agreement.

The Dowager Empress, sitting on her yellow cushion next to the Emperor, looks from one to the other, and feels only despair.

Jung Lu has been her friend from childhood. He is a moderate and sensible man, but the situation that envelopes them all is neither moderate nor sensible.

It is Prince Tuan, a younger man, bulky in his brocade court costume and with the famous Shangfang Sword strapped to his waist, who is in command of the situation. He and his allies—Tuan's brother Duke Lan, Prince Chuang of the Gendarmerie, the Grand Councillor Kang I, Chao Shu-chiao of the Board of Punishments—form the core of those Iron Hats who had seized power two years ago, at the end of the Hundred Days' Reform.

It is Tuan who has surrounded the Dragon Throne with his personal army of ten thousand Tiger-Hunt Marksmen. It is Tuan who controls the ferocious Muslim cavalry of General Tung, his ally, camped in the gardens south of the city. It is Tuan who extorted the honor of carrying the Shangfang Sword in the imperial presence, and with it the right to use the sword to execute anyone on the spot, for any reason. And it is Tuan's son, Pu Chun, who has been made heir to the throne.

It is Prince Tuan, and the others of his Iron Hat Faction, who have encouraged the thousands of martial artists and spirit warriors of the Righteous Harmony Fists to invade Peking, to attack Chinese Christians and others against whom they have a grudge, and who threaten to envelop China in a war with all the foreign powers at once.

The young Emperor, Kuang Hsu, opens his mouth but cannot say a word. He has a bad stammer, and in stressful situations he cannot speak at all.

Prince Tuan fills the silence. "I am certain that, should the Son of Heaven deign to address us, he would assure us of his confidence in the patriotism and loyalty of the Righteous Harmony Fists. His majesty knows that any disorders are incidental, and that the Righteous Harmony Fists are united in their desire to rid the Middle Kingdom of the Foreign Devils that oppress our nation.

"In the past," he continues, getting to his point—for in the Imperial Court, one always presents conclusions by invoking the past—"In the past, the great rulers of the Middle Kingdom established order in their dominions by calling upon their loyal subjects to do away with foreign influences and causes of disorder. If his majesty will only issue an edict to this effect, the Righteous Harmony Fists can use their martial powers and their invincible magic to sweep the Foreign Devils from our land."

The Emperor attempts again to speak and again fails. This time it is the Dowager Empress who fills the silence.

"Will such an edict not bring us to war with all the Foreign Devils at once? We have never been able to hold off even one foreign power at a time. The white ghosts of England and France, and even lately the dwarf-bandits of Japan, have all won concessions from us."

Prince Tuan scowls, and his hand tightens on the Shangfang Sword. "The Righteous Harmony Fists are not members of the imperial forces. They are merely righteous citizens stirred to anger by the actions of the Foreign Devils and the Secondary Foreign Devils, the Christian converts. The government cannot be held responsible for their actions. And besides—the Righteous Harmony Fists are invulnerable. You have seen yourself, a few weeks ago, when I brought one of their members into this room and fired a pistol straight at him. He was not harmed."

The Empress of the West falls silent as clouds of doubt enter her mind. She had seen the pistol fired, and the man had taken no hurt. It had been an impressive demonstration.

"I regret to report to the Throne," Jung Lu says, "of an unfortunate incident in the city. The German ambassador, von Ketteler, personally opened fire on a group of Righteous Harmony Fists peacefully exercising in the open. He killed seven and wounded many more."

"An outrage!" Prince Tuan cries.

"Truly," Jung Lu says, "but unfortunately the Righteous Harmony Fists proved somewhat less than invulnerable to von Ketteler's bullets. Perhaps their invincibility has been overstated."

Prince Tuan glares sullenly at Jung Lu. He bites his lip, then says, "It is the fault of wicked Chinese Christian women. The Secondary Foreign Devils flaunted their naked private parts through windows, and the Righteous Harmony Fists lost their strength."

There is a thoughtful pause as the others absorb this information. And then the Emperor opens his mouth again.

The Emperor has, for the moment, mastered his speech impediment, though his gaunt young face is strained with effort and there are long, breathy pauses between each word. "Our subjects depend on the Dragon Throne for their safety," he gasps. "Prince Jung Lu is ordered to restore order in the city and to stand between the foreign legations and the Righteous Harmony Fists ... to prevent further incidents."

Kuang Hsu falls back on his yellow cushions, exhausted from the effort to speak. "The Son of Heaven is wise," Jung Lu says.

"Truly," says Prince Tuan, his eyes narrowing.

Using appropriate formal language, and of course invoking the all-important precedents from the past, court scribes write the edict in Manchurian, then translate the words into Chinese. The Dowager Empress holds the Chinese translation to her failing eyes and reads it with care. As a female, she had not been judged worthy of education until she had been chosen as an imperial concubine. She has never learned more than a few hundred characters of Chinese, and is unable to read Manchurian at all.

But whether she can read and write or not, her position as Empress Dowager gives her the power of veto over any Imperial edict. It is important that she view any document personally.

"Everything is in order," she ventures to guess.

The Imperial Seal Eunuch inks the heavy Imperial Seal and presses it to the edict, and with ceremony the document is presented to Prince Jung Lu. Prince Tuan draws himself up and speaks. "This insignificant person must beg the Throne for permission to deal with this German, von Ketteler. This white ghost is killing Chinese at random, for his own amusement, and in the confused circumstances none can be blamed if there is an accident."

The Empress of the West and the Emperor exchange quick glances. Perhaps, thinks the Empress, it is best to let Prince Tuan win a point. It may assuage his blood lust for the moment.

And she very much doubts anyone will miss the German ambassador.

She tilts her head briefly, an affirmative gesture. The Emperor's eyes flicker as he absorbs her import.

"We leave it to you," he says. It is a ritual form of assent, the throne's formal permission for an action to take place.

"The Supreme One's brilliance and sagacity exceeds all measure," says Prince Tuan.

The family council ends. The royal princes make their kowtows and leave the chamber.

The Empress Dowager leaves her chair and approaches her nephew, the Emperor. He seems shrunken in his formal dragon robes—he has twenty-eight sets of robes altogether, one auspicious for each day of the lunar month. Tenderly the Dowager dabs sweat from his brow with a handkerchief. He reaches into his sleeve for a lighter and a packet of Turkish cigarets.

"We won't win, you know," he sighs. His stammer has disappeared along with his formidable, intimidating relations. "If we couldn't beat the Japanese dwarf-bandits, we can't beat anybody. We're just going to lose more territory to the Foreign Devils, just as we've already lost Burma, Nepal, Indochina, Taiwan, Korea, Hong Kong, all the treaty ports we've had to cede to Foreign Devils …"

'You don't believe the spirit fighters' magic will help us?"

The Emperor laughs and draws on his cigaret. "Cheap tricks to impress peasants. I have seen that bullet-catching trick done by conjurers."

"We must delay. Delay as long as possible. If we delay, the correct path may become clear."

The Emperor flicks cigaret ash off his yellow sleeve. His tone is bitter. "Delay is the only possible course for those who have no power. Very well. We will delay as long as possible. But delay the war or not, we will still lose."

Tears well in the old woman's eyes. It is all, she knows, her fault.

Her husband, the Emperor, had died of grief after losing the Second Opium War to the Foreign Devils. Their child was only an infant at the time. She did her best to bring up her son, engaging the most rigorous and moral of teachers, but after reigning for only a few years her son had died at the age of eighteen from exhaustion brought on by unending sexual dissipation.

Since then she has devoted her life to caring for her nephew, the new Emperor. She had rescued Kuang Hsu from her sister, who had beaten him savagely and starved him—one of his brothers had actually been starved to death—but she had erred again in choosing the young Emperor's companions. He had been so bullied by eunuchs, so plagued by ill health, and so intimidated by his tutors and the blustering royal princes, that he had remained shy, hesitant, and self-conscious. He had only acted decisively once, two years ago, during the Hundred Days' Reform, and that had ended badly, with the palace surrounded by Prince Tuan's Tiger-Hunt Marksmen and the Emperor held captive.

"I will leave your majesty to rest," she says. He looks at her, not un-kindly.

"Thank you, mother," he says.

Tears prickle the dowager's eyes. Even though she has betrayed him, still he calls her "mother" instead of "aunt."

She walks from the room, and with her twenty-four attending eunuchs returns to her palace.

Alone in the darkness of the litter, no one sees the tears that patter on the yellow brocade cushions.

"All the news is good," Prince Tuan says. "One of our soldiers, a Manchu bannerman named Enhai, has shot the German ambassador outside the Tsungli

Yamen. Admiral Seymour's Foreign Devils, marching up the railway line from
Tientsin, have turned back after a battle with the Righteous Harmony Fists."

"I had heard the Righteous Harmony Fists had all been killed," says
Jung Lu. "Where was their bullet-catching magic?"

"Their magic was sufficient to turn back Admiral Seymour," Prince Tuan
retorts.

"He may have just gone back for reinforcements. More and more foreign warships are appearing off Tientsin."

It is the Hour of the Ox, just before dawn. Several days have passed
since Prince Jung Lu was ordered to seal off the foreign legations. This has
reduced the number of incidents in the city, though the Foreign Devils continue their distressing habit of shooting any Chinese they see, sometimes using machine guns on crowds. Since no one is attacking them, the foreigners'
behavior is puzzling. Jung Lu sent several peace delegations to inquire their
reasons, but the delegates had all been shot down as soon as they appeared in
sight of the legations. Jung Lu has been forced to admit that the foreigners
may no longer be behaving rationally.

"In the past," Prince Tuan says, "Heaven made known its wishes through
the movements of the stars and planets and through portents displayed in the
skies. This unworthy servant reminds the Throne that this is a year with an
extra intercalary month, and therefore a year that promises unusual occurrences.
This is also a Kengtze year, which occurs only every ten years. Therefore the
Heavens demonstrate the extraordinary nature of this year, and require that all
inhabitants of the Earth assist Heaven in creating extraordinary happenings."

"I have not heard that Kengtze years were lucky for the Pure Dynasty,"
Jung Lu remarks. But Prince Tuan doesn't even slow down.

"There are other indications that war is at hand," he says. "The red planet
Mars is high in the Heavens, and the ancients spoke truly when they declared,
'When Mars is high, prepare for war and civil strife; when Mars sinks below
the horizon, send the soldiers home.'

"But there is another indication more decisive than any of these. Heaven
has declared its will by dropping meteors upon the Middle Kingdom. Three
falling stars have landed outside of Tientsin. Another three landed south of
the capital near Yungtsing. According to the office of Telegraph Sheng, three
have also landed in Shangtung, three more southwest of Shanghai, and three
near Kwangtung."

The Empress Dowager and the Emperor exchange glances. Several of
these falling meteors have been observed from the palace, and their significance discussed. But reports of meteors landing in threes throughout eastern
China are new.

"Heaven is declaring its will!" Prince Tuan says. "The meteors have all
landed near places where there are large concentrations of Foreign Devils!

Obviously Heaven wishes us to exterminate these vermin!"

Tuan gives a triumphant laugh, and draws the Shangfang Sword. The Emperor turns pale and shrinks into his heavy brocade robes.

"I demand an edict from the Dragon Throne!" Tuan shouts. "Let the Son of Heaven command that all Foreign Devils be killed!"

The Emperor tries to speak, but terror has plainly seized his tongue. Choosing her words carefully, the Empress Dowager speaks in his place. *Delay*, she thinks.

"We will consult the auspices and act wisely in accordance with their wishes."

Prince Tuan gives a roar of anger and brandishes the sword. "No more delay! Heaven has made its will clear! If you don't issue the edicts, I'll do it myself!"

There is a moment of horrified silence. The Emperor's face turns stony as he looks at Prince Tuan. Sweat pops onto his brow with the effort to control his tongue.

"W-w-why," he stammers, "don't you go k-k-k-kill yourself?"

There is another moment of silence. Prince Tuan coldly forces a smile onto his face.

"The Son of Heaven makes a very amusing witticism," he says.

And then, at swordpoint, he commands the Imperial Seal Eunuch to bring out the heavy seal that will confirm his edicts.

As she watches, the Empress Dowager's heart floods with sorrow.

It is the Hour of the Tiger, two days after Prince Tuan seized control. A red dawn provides a scarlet blush to the yellow hangings. Tuan and his allies confer before the Dragon Throne. Tuan has brought his son, the imperial heir Pu Chun, to watch his father as he commands the fate of China. The boy spends most of his time practicing martial arts, pretending to skewer Foreign Devils with his sword.

The Emperor, disgusted, smokes a cigaret behind a wall-hanging. No one bothers to ask his opinion of the edicts that are going out under his seal.

The Righteous Harmony Fists have all been drafted into the army and sent to reinforce General Nieh, standing between Tientsin and the capital. Governors have been ordered to defend their provinces against attack. Jung Lu's army has been ordered to wipe out the foreigners in the legation quarter, but so far he has found reason to delay.

Can China fight the whole world? the Empress Dowager wonders.

But she sits on her yellow cushion, and smokes her water pipe, and plays with her little lion dogs while she pretends unconcern. It is all she can do.

A messenger arrives and hands to Jung Lu a pair of messages from the office of Telegraph Sheng, and Jung Lu reads them with a puzzled expression. He approaches the Empress, leans close, and speaks in a low tone.

"The Foreign Devils off Tientsin have ordered our troops to evacuate the Taku Forts by midnight—that is midnight yesterday, so the ultimatum has already expired."

Anxiety grips the Empress's heart. "Can our troops hold the forts?"

Jung Lu frowns. "Their record is not good."

If the Taku Forts fall, the Empress knows, Tientsin will fall. And once Tientsin falls, it is but a short march from there to Peking. It has all happened before.

Sick at heart, the Empress remembers the headlong flight from the capital during the Second Opium War, how her happy, innocent little lion dogs had been thrown down wells rather than let the Foreign Devils capture them.

It is going to happen again, she thinks.

Prince Tuan marches toward them. Hearing his steps, Jung Lu's face turns to a mask. He hides the first message in his sleeve.

"This insignificant person hopes the mighty commander of the Military Guards Army will share his news," Tuan says.

Jung Lu hands Tuan the second of the two messages. "Confused news of fighting south of Tientsin. Some towns have been destroyed—the message says by monsters that rode to earth on meteors, but obviously the message was confused. Perhaps he meant to say that meteors have landed on some towns."

"Were they Christian towns?" Tuan asks. "Perhaps Heaven's vengeance is falling on the Secondary Foreign Devils. There are many Christians around Tientsin."

"The message does not say."

Prince Tuan looks at the message and spits into his pocket spittoon. "It probably doesn't matter," he says.

It is the Hour of the Snake. Bright morning sun blazes on the room's yellow hangings. A lengthy dispatch has arrived from the office of Telegraph Sheng. Prince Tuan reads it, then laughs and swaggers toward the captive Emperor.

"This miserable one regrets to report to the Throne that last night an allied force of Foreign Devils captured the forts at Taku," he says.

Then why are you smiling? the Empress wonders, and takes a slow, deliberate puff of smoke from her water pipe while she strives to control her alarm.

"Are steps being taken to rectify the situation?" asks the Emperor.

Tuan's smile broadens. "Heaven, which is just, has acted on behalf of the Son of Heaven. The Foreign Devils, their armies, and their fleets have been destroyed!"

The Empress exchanges glances with her nephew. The Emperor gives a puzzled frown as he absorbs the information. "Please tell us what has occurred," he says.

"The armies of the Foreign Devils were preparing to advance on Tientsin from Taku," Prince Tuan says, "when a force of metal giants appeared from the south. The Foreign Devils were obliterated! Their armies were destroyed by a blast of fire, and then their warships!"

"I fail to understand ..." the Empress begins.

"It's obvious!" Prince Tuan says. "The metal giants rode from Heaven to earth on meteors! The Jade Emperor must have sent them expressly to destroy the Foreign Devils."

"Perhaps our information is incomplete," Jung Lu says cautiously.

Prince Tuan laughs. "Read the dispatch yourself," he says, and carelessly shoves the long telegram into the older man's hands.

The Emperor looks from one to the other, suspicion plain on his face. He clearly does not know whether to believe the news, or whether he wants to believe.

"We will wait for confirmation," he says.

More dispatches arrive over the course of the day. The destruction of the foreign armies and fleets is confirmed. Confused news of fighting comes from other areas where meteors are known to have landed. Giants are mentioned, as are bronze tripods. Prince Tuan and other members of his Iron Hat Faction swagger in triumph, boasting of the destruction of all the Foreign Devils. Pu Chun, the imperial heir, skips about the room in delight, pretending he is a giant and kicking imaginary armies out of his path.

It is the Hour of the Monkey. Supper dishes have been brought into the audience chamber, and the council members eat as they view the dispatches.

"The report from Tientsin says that the city is on fire," Jung Lu reports. "The message is unfinished. Apparently something happened to the telegraph office, or perhaps the wires were cut."

Kuang Hou scowls. His face is etched with tension, and he speaks only with difficulty. "Tientsin is a city filled with our loyal subjects. If they are on our side, how is it that the Falling Star Giants are destroying a Chinese city?"

"There are many Foreign Devils in Tientsin," Prince Tuan says. "Perhaps it was necessary to destroy the entire city in order to eradicate the foreign influence."

A look of disgust passes across the Emperor's face at this casual attitude toward his subjects. He opens his mouth to speak, but then a spasm crosses his face. He flushes in shame.

The others in the room politely turn their gaze to the wall hangings while the Emperor has an orgasm.

Afterward he cannot speak at all. He fumbles with his soiled dragon robes as he walks behind the hangings in order to smoke a cigaret.

Despair fills the Dowager Empress as she watches his attempt to regain his dignity.

Over the next two days, messages continue to arrive. Telegraph offices in the major cities are destroyed, and soon the only available information comes from horsemen galloping to the capital from local commanders and provincial governors.

General Nieh's army, stationed between Peking and Tientsin, has been wiped out by Falling Star Giants, along with most of the Righteous Harmony Fists that had been sent as reinforcements. Their spirit magic has proved inadequate to the occasion. From the inadequate information available it would seem that Shanghai, Tsingtao, and Canton have been attacked and very possibly destroyed. Just south of Peking, in Hopeh, three Falling Star Giants have been causing unimaginable destruction in one of China's richest provinces, and Hopeh's governor has committed suicide after he admitted to the Throne his inability to control the situation.

The Empress Dowager notes that the Iron Hats' swaggering is noticeably reduced.

"Perhaps it is time," says Jung Lu, "to examine the possibility that the Falling Star Giants are just another kind of Foreign Devil, as rapacious as the first, and more powerful."

"Nonsense," says Prince Tuan automatically. "Heaven has sent the Falling Star Giants to aid us." But he looks uncertain as he says it.

It is the Hour of the Sheep. The midday sun beats down on the capital, turning even the shady gardens of the Forbidden City into broiling ovens.

The Emperor struggles with his tongue. "W-we desire that the august prince Jung Lu continue."

Jung Lu is happy to oblige. "This unworthy servant begs the Throne to recall that General Nieh and the Righteous Harmony Fists were neither Foreign Devils nor Christians, and they were destroyed. There are few Foreign Devils or Secondary Foreign Devils in Hopeh, but the massacres there have been terrible. And everywhere the Falling Star Giants appear, many more Chinese than Foreign Devils have been killed." Jung Lu looks solemn. "I regret the necessity to alert the Throne to a dangerous possibility. If the Falling Star Giants advance west up the railway line from Tientsin, and simultaneously march north from Hopeh, Peking will be caught between two forces. I must sadly recommend that we consider the defense of the capital."

The Empress Dowager glances at Prince Tuan, expecting him to contradict this suggestion, but instead the prince only gnaws his lip and looks uncertain.

A little flame of hope kindles in the Empress's heart.

The Emperor also sees Tuan's uncertainty, and presses his advantage while he can. "Has the commander of the Military Guards Army any suggestions to make?" he asks.

"From the reports available," Jung Lu says, "it would seem that the Falling Star Giants have two weapons. The first is a beam of heat that incinerates all that it touches. This we call the Fire of the Meteor, from the flame of a falling star, and it is used to defeat armies and fleets. The second weapon is a poison black smoke that is fired from rockets. This we call the Tail of the Meteor, from a falling star's smoky tail, and it is used against cities, smothering the entire population."

"These weapons are not new," says a new voice. It is old Kang I, the Grand Councillor.

Kang I is a relic of a former age. In his many years he has served four Emperors, and in his rigid adherence to tradition and hatred of foreigners has joined the Iron Hats from pure conviction.

Kang I spits into his pocket spittoon and speaks in a loud voice. "This worthless one begs the Throne to recall the Heng Ha Erh Chiang, the Door Gods. At the famous Battle of Mu between the Yin and the Chou, Marshal Cheng Lung was known as Heng the Snorter, because when he snorted, two beams of light shot from his nostrils and incinerated the enemy. Likewise, Marshal Ch'en Chi was known as Ha the Blower, because he was able to blow out clouds of poisonous yellow gas that smothered his foe.

"Thus it is clear," he concludes, "that these weapons were invented centuries ago in China, and must subsequently have been stolen by the Falling Star Giants, who are obviously a worthless and imitative people, like all foreigners." He falls silent, a superior smile ghosting across his face.

The Empress finds herself intrigued by this anecdote. "Does the esteemed councillor know if the historical records offer a method of defeating these weapons?"

"Indeed. Heng the Snorter was killed by a spear, and Ha the Blower by a magic heroar spar ar him by an ox spirit."

"We have many spears," Jung Lu says softly. "But this ignorant one confesses his bafflement concerning where a suitable ox-spirit may be obtained. Perhaps the esteemed Grand Councillor has a suggestion?"

The smile vanishes from Kang I's face. "All answers may be found in the annals," he says stonily.

The Emperor, admirably controlling any impulse to smile at the Iron Hat's discomfort, turns again to Jung Lu. "Does the illustrious prince have any suggestions?"

"We have only three forces near Peking," Jung Lu says. "Of these, my Military Guards Army is fully occupied in blockading the foreign legations here in Peking. General Tung's horsemen are already in a position to move eastward to Tientsin. This leaves our most modern and best-equipped force, the Tiger-Hunt Marksmen, admirably suited to march south to stand between the capital and the Falling Star Giants of Hopeh. May this insignificant one suggest that the Dragon Throne issue orders to the Tiger-Hunt Marksmen and to General Tung at once?"

The Empress, careful to keep her face impassive, watches Prince Tuan as Jung Lu makes his recommendations. The ten thousand Tiger-Hunt Marksmen and General Tung's Muslim cavalry are Prince Tuan's personal armies. All his political power derives from his military strength. To risk his forces in battle is to endanger his own standing.

"What of the Throne?" Tuan asks. "If the Tiger-Hunt Marksmen march south, who will guard His Majesty? The Imperial Guard are only a few hundred men—surely their numbers are inadequate."

"The Throne may best be guarded by defeating the Falling Star Giants," Jung Lu says.

"I must insist that half the Tiger-Hunt Marksmen be left in the capital to guard the person of the Son of Heaven," Tuan says.

The Empress and Emperor look at one another. Best to act now, the Empress thinks, before Prince Tuan regains his confidence. Half the Tiger-Hunt Marksmen are better than none.

Kuang Hsu turns back to the princes. "We leave it to you," he says.

In the still night the tramp of boots echoes from the high walls of the Forbidden City. Columns of Tiger-Hunt Marksmen, under the command of Tuan's brother Duke Lan, are marching off to meet the enemy.

In the Hour of the Dog, after nightfall, one of the Empress's blue-gowned maidens escorts Prince Jung Lu into her presence. He had avoided the Tiger-Hunt Marksmen by using the tunnels beneath the Forbidden City— they were designed to help servants move unobtrusively about their duties, but over the years they have been used for less licit purposes.

"We are pleased to express our gratitude," the Empress says, and takes from around her neck a necklace in which each pearl has been carved into the likeness of a stork. She places the necklace into the delighted hands of her maid.

Sad, she thinks, that it is necessary to bribe her own servants to encourage them to do what they should do unquestioningly, which is to obey and keep silent.

The darkness of the Empress's pavilion is broken only by starlight reflected from the yellow hangings. The odor of Nine-Buddha incense floats in the air.

"My friend," she tells Jung Lu, and reaches to touch his sleeve. "You must survive this upcoming battle. You and your army must live to rescue the

Emperor from the Iron Hats."

"My life is in the hands of Fate," Jung Lu murmurs. "I must fight along-side my army."

"I *order* you to survive!" the Empress demands. "His Majesty cannot spare you."

There is a moment of silence, and then the old man sighs.

"This unworthy one will obey Her Majesty," he says.

Irrational though it may be, the Empress begins to glimpse a tiny, feeble ray of hope.

Hot western winds buffet the city, and the sky turns yellow with loess, dust blown hundreds of *li*. It falls in the courtyards of the Forbidden City, on the shoulders of the black-clad eunuchs as they scurry madly through the court-yards with arms full of valuables or documents. Hundreds of carts jam the byways. The Imperial Guard, in full armor, stand in disciplined lines about the litters of the royal family. Prince Tuan stands in the yard, waving the Shangfang Sword and shouting orders. Nobody obeys him, least of all his own son, Pu Chun, the imperial heir who crouches in terror beneath a cart.

The court is fleeing the city. Yesterday, the Falling Star Giants finally made their advance on Peking. At first the news was all bad, horsemen riding into the city with stories of entire regiments being incinerated by the Fire of the Meteor.

After that it was worse, because there was no news at all.

In the early hours of the morning an order arrived from Jung Lu to evacu-ate the court to the Summer Palace north of the city. Since then, all has been madness.

It is the Hour of the Hare, early in the morning. The Empress's blue-clad maidservants huddle in knots, weeping. The Empress, however, is made of sterner stuff. She has been through this once before. She picks up one of her little lion dogs and thrusts it into the arms of one of her maids.

"Save my dogs!" she orders. She can't stand the idea of losing them again.

"Falling Star Giants seen from the city walls!" someone cries. There is no telling whether or not the report is true. Serving women dash heedlessly about the court, their gowns whipped by the strong west wind.

"Flee at once!" Prince Tuan shrieks. "The capital is lost!" He runs for his horse and gallops away. His son, screaming in terror, follows on foot, waving his arms.

The Emperor appears, a plain traveling cloak thrown over his shoul-ders. "Mother," he says, "it is time to go."

The Empress carries two of her favorite dogs to the litter. Her eunuchs hoist her to their shoulders, and the column begins to march for the Chienmen Gate. The western wind rattles the banners of the guard, but over the sound

of the wind the Empress can hear a strange wailing sound, like a demon calling out to its mate. And then a wail from another direction as the mate answers.

"Faster!" someone calls, and the litter begins to jounce. The guardsmen's
armor rattles as they begin to jog. The Empress braces herself against the sides
of the litter.

"Black smoke!" Another cry. "The Tail of the Meteor!"

Women scream as the escort breaks into a run. The Empress's lion dogs
whimper in fear. She clutches the curtains and peers anxiously past them. The
black smoke is plain to see, a tall column billowing out over the walls. As she
watches, another rocket falls, trailing black.

But the strong west wind catches the tops of the dark, billowing column, and tears the smoke away, bearing it to the east.

As the column flees to safety, loess covers the city in a soft blanket of
imperial yellow.

Much of the disorganized column, including most of the wagon train with its
documents and treasure, is caught in the black smoke and never escapes the
capital. Half the Tiger-Hunt Marksmen are dead or missing.

The terror and confusion make the Empress Dowager breathless, but it
is the many missing lion dogs that make her weep.

The column pauses north of the city at the Summer Palace only for a
few hours, to beat some order into the chaos, then sets out into the teeth of
the gale to Jehol on the Great Wall. In the distance the strange wailings of the
Falling Star Giants are sometimes heard, but streamers of yellow dust conceal
them.

By this time Prince Tuan has found his courage, his son, and his troops,
the few thousand Tiger-Hunt Marksmen to have survived the fall of the capital. He calls a family conference in a requisitioned mansion, and Tuan issues
edicts under the Imperial Seal calling for the extermination of all foreigners
and Chinese Christians.

"Who will obey you?" the Emperor shouts at him. His hopelessness has
made him fearless, has caused his stammer to disappear. "You have lost all
China!"

"Heaven will not permit us to fail," Tuan says.

"I command you to kill yourself!" cries the Emperor.

Tuan turns to the Emperor and laughs aloud. "Once again His Majesty
makes a witticism!"

But as news trickles in over the next few days, Tuan's belligerence turns
sullen. A few survivors from a Peking suburb tell of the city's being inundated
by black smoke after a second attack. Tuan's ally Prince Chuang is believed
dead in the city, and old Kang I was found stone dead in his cart in Jehol,

apparently having died unnoticed in the evacuation. Tuan's great ally General Tung has been killed along with his entire army. And his brother Duke Lan, after losing his entire division of Tiger-Hunt Marksmen to the Fire of the Meteor, committed suicide by drinking poison. There is no word from any of the great cities where meteors were known to have landed. No messages have come from Jung Lu, and he is believed dead.

"West!" Prince Tuan orders. His son Pu Chun stands by his side. "We will go west!"

"Kill yourself!" cries the Emperor. Pu Chun laughs.

"Somebody just farted," he sneers.

It is the Hour of the Horse, and the hot noon sun shortens tempers. The Empress Dowager holds her favorite lion dog for comfort. The dog whimpers, sensing the tension in the room.

"We will move tomorrow," Tuan says, and casts a cold look over his shoulder as he marches away from the imperial presence.

Kuang Hsu slumps defeated in his chair. The old lady rises, the lion dog still in her arms, and slowly walks to her nephew's side. Tears spill from her eyes onto his brocade sleeve.

"Please forgive me," she says.

"Don't cry, mother," he says. "It isn't your fault that Foreign Devils have learned to ride meteors."

"I don't mean that," the Empress says. "I mean two years ago, during the Hundred Days' Reform."

"Ahh," the Emperor sighs. He turns away. "Let us not speak of it."

"They frightened me, Prince Tuan and the others. They said your reforms were destroying the country. They said the Japanese were using you. They said the dwarf-bandits were plotting to kill us all. They said if I didn't come out of retirement, we would be destroyed."

"The Japanese modernized their country." Kuang Hsu speaks unwillingly. His eyes rise to gaze into the past, at his own dead hopes. "I asked for advice from Ito, who had written their constitution. That was all. There was no danger to anyone."

"The Japanese had just killed the Korean Empress! I was afraid they would kill me next!" The old woman clutches at the Emperor's hand. "I was old and afraid!" she says. "I betrayed you. Please forgive me for everything."

He turns to her and raises a hand to her cheek. His own eyes glitter with tears. "I understand, mother," he says. "Please don't cry."

"What can we do?"

He sighs again and turns away. "Ito told me that I could accomplish nothing as long as I was in the Forbidden City. That I could never truly be an Emperor with the eunuchs and the princes and the court in the way. Well—now the Forbidden City is no more. The eunuchs' power is gone, and there is no court. There are only a few of the princes left, and only one of those is important."

He wipes tears from his eyes with his sleeve, and the Empress sees cold determination cross his face. "I will wait," he says. "But when the opportunity comes, I will act. I *must* act."

The royal column continues its flight. There seems no purpose in its peregrinations, and the Empress of the West cannot tell if they are running away from something, or toward something else. Possibly they are doing both at once.

Apparently the Falling Star Giants have better things to do than pursue. Exhausted and with nowhere else to go, the royal family ends up in the governor's mansion in the provincial capital of Taiyuan. The courtyard is spattered with blood because the governor, Yu Hsien, had dozens of Christian missionaries killed here, along with their wives and children. Their eyeless foreign heads now decorate the city walls.

One afternoon the Empress looks out the window, and sees Pu Chun practicing martial arts in the court. In his hands is a bloodstained beheading sword given him by Governor Yu.

She never looks out the window again.

All messages from the east are of death and unimaginable suffering. Cities destroyed, armies wiped out, entire populations fleeing before the attackers in routs as directionless as that of the court.

There is no news whatever from the rest of the world. Apparently all the Foreign Devils have been afflicted by Foreign Devils of their own.

And then, in the Hour of the Rooster, word comes that Prince Jung Lu has arrived and requests an audience, and the Empress feels her heart leap. She had never permitted herself to hope, not once she heard of the total destruction of Peking.

At once she convenes a Family Council.

The horrors of war have clearly affected Jung Lu. He walks into the imperial presence with a weary tread, and painfully gets on his knees to perform the required kowtows.

"This worthless old man begs to report to the Throne that the Falling Star Giants are all dead."

There is a long, stunned silence. The Emperor, flushed with sudden excitement, tries to speak but trips over his own tongue.

Joy floods Tzu Hsi's heart. "How did this occur?" she asks. "Did we defeat them in battle?"

"They were not defeated," Jung Lu says. "I do not know how they died. Perhaps it was a disease. I stayed only to confirm the reports personally, and then I rode here at once with all the soldiers I could raise. Five thousand Manchu bannermen await the Imperial command outside the city walls."

The Empress strokes one of her lion dogs while she makes a careful calculation. Jung Lu's five thousand bannermen considerably outnumber Prince Tuan's remaining Tiger-Hunt Marksmen, but Tuan's men have modern weapons and the bannermen do not. And these bannermen are not likely to be brave, as they probably survived the Falling Star Giants only by fleeing at the very rumor of their arrival.

She sees the relieved smile on Prince Tuan's face. "Heaven is just!" he says.

All turn at a noise from the Emperor. Kuang Hsu's hands clutch the arms of his chair, and his face twists with the effort to speak. Then he gasps and has an orgasm.

An hour ago he was a ghost-Emperor, nothing he did mattered, and he spoke freely. Now that he is the Son of Heaven again, his stammer and his nervous condition have returned.

A few moments later he speaks, his head turned away in embarrassment.

"Tonight we will thank Heaven for its mercy and benevolence. Tomorrow, at the Hour of the Dragon, we will assemble again in celebration." He looks at Pu Chun, who stands near Prince Tuan. "I have observed the Heir practice wushu in the courtyard. I hope the Heir will favor us with a demonstration of his martial prowess."

Prince Tuan flushes with pleasure. He and his son fall to their knees and kowtow.

"We will obey the Imperial command with pleasure," Tuan says.

The Emperor turns his head away as he dismisses the company. At first the Empress thinks it is because he is shamed by his public orgasm, but then she sees the tight, merciless smile of triumph on the Emperor's lips, and a cold finger touches the back of her neck.

In the next hours the Empress of the West tries to smuggle a message to Jung Lu in hopes of seeing him privately, but the situation is so confusing that the messenger cannot find him. She decides to wait for a better time.

With the morning the Hour of the Dragon arrives, and the Family Council convenes. The remaining Iron Hats cluster together in pride and triumph. It is clearly their hour—the Falling Star Giants have abdicated, as it were, and left the nation to the mercies of the Iron Hats. As if in recognition of this fact, the Emperor awards Prince Tuan the office of Grand Councillor in place of the late Kang I.

Then Pu Chun is brought forward to perform wushu, and the Emperor calls the Imperial Guard into the room to watch. The imperial heir leaps about the room, shouting and waving the blood-encrusted sword given him by Governor Yu as he decapitates one imaginary Foreign Devil after another. The Empress has seen much better martial art in her time, but at the end of the performance, all are loud in their praise of the young heir, and the Emperor descends from his chair to congratulate him.

Fighting his tongue—the Emperor seems unusually tense today—he turns to the heir and says, "I wonder if the Heir has learned a sword technique called The Dragon in Flight from Low to High?"

Pu Chun is reluctant to admit that he is not a complete master of the sword, but with a bit of paternal prodding he admits that this technique seems to have escaped him.

Kuang Hsu's stammer is so bad he can barely get the words out. "Will the Heir permit me to teach?"

"Your Majesty honors us beyond all description," Prince Tuan says. Despite his lifelong ill health, the Emperor like every Manchu prince practiced wushu since he was a boy, and always received praise from his instructors.

The Emperor turns to Prince Tuan, his face red with the struggle to speak. "May ... I ... have the honor ... to use ... the Shangfang Sword?"

"The Son of Heaven does his unworthy servant too much honor!" Prince Tuan eagerly strips the long blade from its sheath and presents it on his knees to the Emperor.

The Emperor strikes a martial pose, sword cocked, and Pu Chun imitates him. Watching from her chair, the Empress feels her heart stop. Terror fills her. She knows what is about to happen.

The movement is too swift to follow, but the Shangfang Sword whistles as it hurtles through air, and its blade is sharp and true. Suddenly Prince Tuan's head rolls across the floor. Blood fountains from the headless trunk.

Fury blazes from Kuang Hsu's eyes, and his body, unlike his tongue, has no stammer. His second strike crushes the skull of Tuan's ally, Governor Yu. His third kills the president of the Board of Punishments. And his fourth— the Empress cries out to stop, but is too late—the fourth blow strikes the neck of the boy heir, Pu Chun, who is so stunned by the unexpected death of his father that he doesn't think to protect himself from the blade that kills him.

"Protect the Emperor!" Jung Lu cries to his guardsmen. "Kill the traitors!"

Those Iron Hats still breathing are finished off by the Imperial Guard. And then the Guard rounds up the Iron Hats' subordinate officers, and within minutes their heads are struck off.

The Emperor dictates an order to open the city gates, and the order is signed with the Imperial Seal. Jung Lu's loyal bannermen pour into the city and surround the throne with a wall of guns, swords, and spears.

Only then does the Emperor notice the old woman, still frozen in fear, who sits on her throne clutching her whimpering lion dogs.

Kuang Hsu approaches, and the Empress shrinks from the blood that soaks his dragon-embroidered robes.

"I am sorry, mother, that you had to watch this," he says.

The Empress manages to find words within the cloud of terror that fills her mind.

"It was necessary," she says.

"The Foreign Devils have been destroyed," the Emperor says, "and so have the Falling Star Giants. The Righteous Harmony Fists are no more, and neither are the Iron Hats. Now there is much suffering and loss of life, but China has survived such catastrophes before."

The Empress looks at the blood-spattered dragons on the Emperor's robes. "The Dragon has flown from Low to High," she says.

"Yes." The Emperor looks at the Shangfang Sword, still in his hand. "The Falling Star Giants have landed all over the world," he says. "For many years the Foreign Devils will be busy with their own affairs. While they are thus occupied we will take control of our own ports, our own laws, the railroads, industries, and telegraphs. By the time they are ready to deal with us again, the Middle Kingdom will be strong and united, and on its way to being as modern as any nation in the world."

Kuang Hsu looks up at the Empress of the West.

"Will you help me, mother?" he asks. "There will be need of reform—not just for a Hundred Days, but for all time. And I promise you—" His eyes harden, and for a moment she sees a dragon there, the animal that according to legend lives in every Emperor, and which has slumbered in Kuang Hsu till now. "I promise you that you will be safe. No one will be in a position to harm you."

"I am old," the Empress says, "but I will help however I can." She strokes the head of her lion dog. Her heart overflows. Tears of relief sting her eyes. "May the Hour of the Dragon last ten thousand years," she says.

"*Ten thousand years!*" the guards chorus, and to the cheers the Emperor walks across the blood-stained floor to the throne that awaits him.

So here's another voice on the phone. "I've sold an anthology," it said, "and I think you're going to *like* this one."

Oh yeah, right. Convince me.

"We're coming up on the hundredth anniversary of H. G. Wells' *War of the Worlds.* So I thought I'd edit an anthology consisting of stories set in the War of the Worlds, though not in England."

I controlled excessive salivation enough to say, "Can I have China?"

"You bet," said Kevin J. Anderson.

I was doubly fortunate as far as this story was concerned, because not only did I get China, but due to the reasoning (which I will spare you) that led Kevin to conclude that the War of the Worlds took place right at the turn of the century, I got China in 1900. 1900 was the year of the Boxer Rebellion, the greatest crisis of the late Manchu dynasty. The Righteous Harmony Fists—called "Boxers" in the West—were originally an anti-Manchu force of martial artists, magicians, and their disciples, but were turned by various court factions against the foreigners that had occupied parts of China. Against this background, it seemed only logical to add another group of foreigners—in this case Martians.

As I began my research, I looked forward to writing about Tzu Hsi, the Empress Dowager, who the world knows as an evil seductress who captured her husband's will through her astounding sexual prowess, had her rivals thrown down wells, murdered her own son in order to stay in power, had scads of lovers, and ruined the dynasty through her whimsical tyranny.

Once I began to research Tzu Hsi, I discovered that this vampire myth figure was constructed largely by Sir Edward Trelawny Backhouse, "the Hermit of Peking," a dissolute Western forger and con man, who pretended to have had access to the courts of the Forbidden City, and who sold his invented stories to journalists and historians. (Backhouse's deceptions survived their author by decades, until exposed by Hugh Trevor-Roper in *The Hermit of Peking,* but these inventions still find their way into legitimate histories.) Both the Western powers and anti-Manchu Chinese alike found Backhouse's lies useful in their campaigns against the Manchus, and until recently, no one has ever tried to correct the historical record.

The real Tzu Hsi, according to Sterling Seagrave's biography *Dragon Lady,* was rather a likeable lady, ill-educated and shy, who did her best to keep the Empire on course and out of trouble, and who had so little personal power that she lived as the pawn of one court faction or another.

By the way, every named person in "Foreign Devils," from Telegraph Sheng to Chief Eunuch Li, is an actual historical person, all behaving more or less as they did historically. The reader may well wonder whether the strange, yellow-clad world of the Forbidden City is more alien than that of Wells' fictional Martians.

At Worldcon 1997 in San Antonio, "Foreign Devils" was kindly given the Sidewise Award for alternate history.

Wall, Stone, Craft

One

She awoke, there in the common room of the inn, from a brief dream of roses and death. Once Mary came awake she recalled there were wild roses on her mother's grave, and wondered if her mother's spirit had visited her.

On her mother's grave, Mary's lover had first proposed their elopement. It was there the two of them had first made love.

Now she believed she was pregnant. Her lover was of the opinion that she was mistaken. That was about where it stood.

Mary concluded that it was best not to think about it. And so, blinking sleep from her eyes, she sat in the common room of the inn at Le Caillou and resolved to study her Italian grammar by candlelight.

Plurals. *La nascita, le nascite. La madre, le madri. Un bambino, i bambini ...*

Interruption: stampings, snortings, the rattle of harness, the barking of dogs. Four young Englishmen entered the inn, one in scarlet uniform coat, the others in fine traveling clothes. Raindrops dazzled on their shoulders. The innkeeper bustled out from the kitchen, smiled, proffered the register.

Mary, unimpressed by anything English, concentrated on the grammar.

"Let me sign, George," the redcoat said. "My hand needs the practice."

Mary glanced up at the comment.

"I say, George, here's a fellow signed in Greek!" The Englishman peered at yellowed pages of the inn's register, trying to make out the words in the dim light of the innkeeper's lamp. Mary smiled at the English officer's efforts.

"Perseus, I believe the name is. Perseus Busseus—d'ye suppose he means Bishop?—Kselleius. And he gives his occupation as *'te anthropou philou'*— that would make him a friendly fellow, eh?—" The officer looked over his shoulder and grinned, then returned to the register. "'*Kai atheos.*'"The officer scowled, then straightened. "Does that mean what I think it does, George?"

George—the pretty auburn-haired man in byrons—shook rain off his short cape, stepped to the register, examined the text. "Not 'friendly fellow,'" he said. "That would be '*anehr philos.*' '*Anthropos*' is mankind, not man." There was the faintest touch of Scotland in his speech.

"So it is," said the officer. "It comes back now."

George bent at his slim waist and looked carefully at the register. "What the fellow says is, 'Both friend of man and—'" He frowned, then looked at his friend. "You were right about the 'atheist,' I'm afraid."

The officer was indignant. "Ain't funny, George," he said.

George gave a cynical little half-smile. His voice changed, turned comical and fussy, became that of a high-pitched English schoolmaster. "Let us try to make out the name of this famous atheist." He bent over the register again. "Perseus—you had that right, Somerset. Busseus—how *very* irregular. Ksel-leius—Kelly? Shelley?" He smiled at his friend. His voice became very Irish. "Kelly, I imagine. An atheistical upstart Irish schoolmaster with a little Greek. But what the Busseus might be eludes me, unless his middle name is Omnibus."

Somerset chuckled. Mary rose from her place and walked quietly toward the pair. "The gentleman's name is Bysshe, sir," she said. "Percy Bysshe Shelley."

The two men turned in surprise. The officer—Somerset—bowed as he perceived a lady. Mary saw for the first time that he had one empty sleeve pinned across his tunic, which would account for the comment about the hand. The other—George, the man in byrons—swept off his hat and gave Mary a flourishing bow, one far too theatrical to be taken seriously. When he straightened, he gave Mary a little frown.

"Bysshe Shelley?" he said. "Any relation to Sir Bysshe, the baronet?"

"His grandson."

"Sir Bysshe is a protegé of old Norfolk." This an aside to his friends. Radical Whiggery was afoot, or so the tone implied. George returned his attention to Mary as the other Englishmen gathered about her. "An interesting family, no doubt," he said, and smiled at her. Mary wanted to flinch from the compelling way he looked at her, gazed upward, intently, from beneath his brows. "And are you of his party?"

"I am."

"And you are, I take it, Mrs. Shelley?"

Mary straightened and gazed defiantly into George's eyes. "Mrs. Shelley resides in England. My name is Godwin."

George's eyes widened, flickered a little. Low English murmurs came to Mary's ears. George bowed again. "Charmed to meet you, Miss Godwin."

George pointed to each of his companions with his hat. "Lord Fitzroy Somerset." The armless man bowed again. "Captain Harry Smith. Captain Austen of the Navy. Pásmány, my fencing master." Most of the party, Mary thought, were young, and all were handsome, George most of all. George turned to Mary again, a little smile of anticipation curling his lips. His burning look was almost insolent. "My name is Newstead."

Mortal embarrassment clutched at Mary's heart. She knew her cheeks were burning, but still she held George's eyes as she bobbed a curtsey.

George had not been Marquess Newstead for more than a few months. He had been famous for years as both an intimate of the Prince Regent and the most dashing of Wellington's cavalry officers, but it was his exploits on the field of Waterloo and his capture of Napoleon on the bridge at Genappe that had made him immortal. He was the talk of England and the Continent, though he had achieved his fame under another name.

Before the Prince Regent had given him the title of Newstead, auburn-haired, insolent-eyed George had been known as George Gordon Noël, the sixth Lord Byron.

Mary decided she was not going to be impressed by either his titles or his manner. She decided she would think of him as George.

"Pleased to meet you, my lord," Mary said. Pride steeled her as she realized her voice hadn't trembled.

She was spared further embarrassment when the door burst and a servant entered followed by a pack of muddy dogs—whippets—who showered them all with water, then howled and bounded about George, their master. Standing tall, his strong, well-formed legs in the famous side-laced boots that he had invented to show off his calf and ankle, George laughed as the dogs jumped up on his chest and bayed for attention. His lordship barked back at them and wrestled with them for a moment—not very lordlike, Mary thought—and then he told his dogs to be still. At first they ignored him, but eventually he got them down and silenced.

He looked up at Mary. "I can discipline men, Miss Godwin," he said, "but I'm afraid I'm not very good with animals."

"That shows you have a kind heart, I'm sure," Mary said.

The others laughed a bit at this—apparently kindheartedness was not one of George's better-known qualities—but George smiled indulgently.

"Have you and your companion supped, Miss Godwin? I would welcome the company of fellow English in this tiresome land of Brabant."

Mary was unable to resist an impertinence. "Even if one of them is an atheistical upstart Irish schoolmaster?"

"Miss Godwin, I would dine with Wolfe Tone himself." Still with that intent, under-eyed look, as if he was dissecting her.

Mary was relieved to turn away from George's gaze and look toward the back of the inn, in the direction of the kitchen. "Bysshe is in the kitchen giving instructions to the cook. I believe my sister is with him."

"Are there more in your party? "

"Only the three of us. And one rather elderly carriage horse."

"Forgive us if we do not invite the horse to table."

"Your ape, George," Somerset said dolefully, "will be quite enough."

Mary would have pursued this interesting remark, but at that moment Bysshe and Claire appeared from out of the kitchen passage. Both were laughing, as if at a shared secret, and Claire's black eyes glittered. Mary repressed a spasm of annoyance.

"Mary!" Bysshe said. "The cook told us a ghost story!" He was about to go on, but paused as he saw the visitors.

"We have an invitation to dinner," Mary said. "Lord Newstead has been kind enough—"

"Newstead!" said Claire. "*The* Lord Newstead?"

George turned his searching gaze on Claire. "I'm the only Newstead I know."

Mary felt a chill of alarm, for a moment seeing Claire as George doubtless saw her: black-haired, black-eyed, fatally indiscreet, and all of sixteen.

Sometimes the year's difference in age between Mary and Claire seemed a century.

"Lord Newstead!" Claire babbled. "I recognize you now! How exciting to meet you!"

Mary resigned herself to fate. "My lord," she said, "may I present my sister, Miss Jane—Claire, rather, Claire Clairmont, and Mr. Shelley."

"Overwhelmed and charmed, Miss Clairmont. Mr. Perseus Omnibus Kselleius, tí kánete?"

Bysshe blinked for a second or two, then grinned. "Thanmásia eùxaristô," returning politeness, "kaí eseîs?"

For a moment Mary gloried in Bysshe, in his big frame in his shabby clothes, his fair, disordered hair, his freckles, his large hands—and his absolute disinclination to be impressed by one of the most famous men on Earth.

George searched his mind for a moment. "Polú kalá, eùxaristô. Thá éthela ná—" He groped for words, then gave a laugh. "Hang the Greek!" he said. "It's been far too many years since Trinity. May I present my friend Somerset?"

Somerset gave the atheist a cold Christian eye. "How d'ye do?"

George finished his introductions. There was the snapping of coach whips outside, and the sound of more stamping horses. The dogs began barking again. At least two more coaches had arrived. George led the party into the dining room. Mary found herself sitting next to George, with Claire and Bysshe across the table.

"Damme, I quite forgot to register," Somerset said, rising from his bench. "What bed will you settle for, George?"

"Nothing less than Bonaparte's."

Somerset sighed. "I thought not," he said.

"Did Bonaparte sleep here in Le Caillou?" Claire asked.

"The night before Waterloo."

"How exciting! Is Waterloo nearby?" She looked at Bysshe. "Had we known, we could have asked for his room."

"Which we then would have had to surrender to my lord Newstead," Bysshe said tolerantly. "He has greater claim, after all, than we."

George gave Mary his intent look again. His voice was pitched low. "I would not deprive two lovely ladies of their bed for all the Bonapartes in Europe."

But rather join us in it, Mary thought. That look was clear enough.

The rest of George's party—servants, aides-de-camp, clerks, one black man in full Mameluke rig, turned-up slippers, ostrich plumes, scarlet turban and all—carried George's equipage from his carriages. In addition to an endless series of trunks and a large miscellany of weaponry there were more animals. Not only the promised ape—actually a large monkey, which seated itself on George's shoulder—but brightly-colored parrots in cages, a pair of greyhounds, some hooded hunting hawks, songbirds, two forlorn-looking kit foxes in cages, which set all the dogs howling and jumping in eagerness to get at them, and a half-grown panther in a jewelled collar, which the dogs knew better than to bark at. The innkeeper was loud in his complaint as he attempted to sort them all out and stay outside of the range of beaks, claws, and fangs.

Bysshe watched with bright eyes, enjoying the spectacle. George's friends looked as if they were weary of it.

"I hope we will sleep tonight," Mary said.

"If you sleep not," said George, playing with the monkey, "we shall contrive to keep you entertained."

How gracious to include your friends in the orgy, Mary thought. But once again kept silent.

Bysshe was still enjoying the parade of frolicking animals. He glanced at Mary. "Don't you think, Maie, this is the very image of philosophical anarchism?"

"You are welcome to it, sir," said Somerset, returning from the register. "George, your mastiff has injured the ostler's dog. He is loud in his complaint."

"I'll have Ferrante pay him off."

"See that you do. And have him pistol the brains out of that mastiff while he's at it."

"Injure poor Picton?" George was offended. "I'll have none of it."

"Poor Picton will have his fangs in the ostler next."

"He must have been teasing the poor beast."

"Picton will kill us all one day." Grudgingly.

"Forgive us, Somerset-laddie." Mary watched as George reached over to Somerset and tweaked his ear. Somerset reddened but seemed pleased.

"Mr. Shelley," said Captain Austen. "I wonder if you know what surprises the kitchen has in store for us."

Austen was a well-built man in a plain black coat, older than the others, with a lined and weathered naval face and a reserved manner unique in this company.

"Board 'em in the smoke! That's the Navy for you!" George said. "Straight to the business of eating, never mind the other nonsense."

"If you ate wormy biscuit for twenty years of war," said Harry Smith, "you'd care about the food as well."

Bysshe gave Austen a smile. "The provisions seem adequate enough for a country inn," he said. "And the rooms are clean, unlike most in this country. Claire and the Maie and I do not eat meat, so I had to tell the cook how to prepare our dinner. But if your taste runs to fowl or something in the cutlet line I daresay the cook can set you up."

"No meat!" George seemed enthralled by the concept. "Disciples of J. F. Newton, as I take it?"

"Among others," said Mary.

"But are you well? Do you not feel an enervation? Are you not feverish with lack of a proper diet?" George leaned very close and touched Mary's forehead with the back of one cool hand while he reached to find her pulse with the other. The monkey grimaced at her from his shoulder. Mary disengaged and placed her hands on the table.

"I'm quite well, I assure you," she said.

"The Maie's health is far better than when I met her," Bysshe said.

"Mine too," said Claire.

"I believe most diseases can be conquered by proper diet," said Bysshe. And then he added,

> "He slays the lamb that looks him in the face,
> And horribly devours his mangled flesh."

"Let's have some mangled flesh tonight, George," said Somerset gaily.

"Do let's," added Smith.

George's hand remained on Mary's forehead. His voice was very soft. "If eating flesh offend thee," he said, "I will eat but only greens."

Mary could feel her hackles rise. "Order what you please," she said. "I don't care one way or another."

"Brava, Miss Godwin!" said Smith thankfully. "Let it be mangled flesh for us all, and to perdition with all those little Low Country cabbages!"

"I don't like them, either," said Claire.

George removed his hand from Mary's forehead and tried to signal the innkeeper, who was still struggling to corral the dogs. George failed, frowned, and lowered his hand.

"I'm cheered to know you're familiar with the works of Newton," Bysshe said.

"I wouldn't say *familiar*," said George. He was still trying to signal the innkeeper. "I haven't read his books. But I know he wants me not to eat meat, and that's all I need to know."

Bysshe folded his big hands on the table. "Oh, there's much more than that. Abstaining from meat implies an entire new moral order, in which mankind is placed on an equal level with the animals."

"George in particular should appreciate that," said Harry Smith, and made a face at the monkey.

"I think I prefer being ranked above the animals," George said. "And above most people, too." He looked up at Bysshe. "Shall we avoid talk of food matters before we eat? My stomach's rumbling louder than a battery of Napoleon's daughters." He looked down at the monkey and assumed a high-pitched Scots dowager's voice. "An' sae is Jerome Bonaparte's, annit nae, Jerome?"

George finally succeeded in attracting the innkeeper's attention and the company ordered food and wine. Bread, cheese, and pickles were brought to tide them over in the meantime. Jerome Bonaparte was permitted off his master's lap to roam free along the table and eat what he wished.

George watched as Bysshe carved a piece of cheese for himself. "In addition to Newton, you would also be a follower of William Godwin?"

Bysshe gave Mary a glance, then nodded. "Ay. Godwin also."

"I thought I recognized that 'philosophical anarchism' of yours. Godwin was the rage when I was at Harrow. But not so much thought of now, eh? Excepting of course his lovely namesake." Turning his gaze to Mary.

Mary gave him a cold look. "Truth is ever in fashion, my lord," she said.

"Did you say *ever* or *never?*" Playfully. Mary said nothing, and George gave a shrug. "Truthful Master Godwin, then. And who else?"

"Ovid," Mary said. The officers looked a little serious at this. She smiled. "Come now—he's not as scandalous as he's been made out. Merely playful."

This did not reassure her audience. Bysshe offered Mary a private smile. "We've also been reading Mary Wollstonecraft."

"Ah!" George cried. "Heaven save us from intellectual women!"

"Mary Wollstonecraft," said Somerset thoughtfully. "She was a harlot in France, was she not?"

"I prefer to think of my mother," said Mary carefully, "as a political thinker and authoress."

There was sudden silence as Somerset turned white with mortification. Then George threw back his head and laughed.

"Sunburn me!" he said. "That answers as you deserve!"

Somerset visibly made an effort to collect his wits. "I am most sorry, Miss—" he began.

George laughed again. "By heaven, we'll watch our words hereafter!"

Claire tittered. "I was in suspense, wondering if there would be a mishap. And there was, there *was!*"

George turned to Mary and managed to compose his face into an attitude of solemnity, though the amusement that danced in his eyes denied it.

"I sincerely apologize on behalf of us all, Miss Godwin. We are soldiers and are accustomed to speaking rough among ourselves, and have been abroad and are doubtless ignorant of the true worth of any individual—" He searched his mind for a moment, trying to work out a graceful way to conclude. "—outside of our own little circle," he finished.

"Well said," said Mary, "and accepted." She had chosen more interesting ground on which to make her stand.

"Oh yes!" said Claire. "Well said indeed!"

"My mother is not much understood by the public," Mary continued. "But intellectual women, it would seem, are not much understood by *you.*"

George leaned away from Mary and scanned her with cold eyes. "On the contrary," he said. "I am married to an intellectual woman."

"And she, I imagine ..." Mary let the pause hang in the air for a moment, like a rapier before it strikes home. "... resides in England?"

George scowled. "She does."

"I'm sure she has her books to keep her company."

"And Francis Bacon," George said, his voice sour. "Annabella is an authority on Francis Bacon. And she is welcome to reform *him,* if she likes."

Mary smiled at him. "Who keeps *you* company, my lord?"

There was a stir among his friends. He gave her that insolent, under-eyed look again.

"I am not often lonely," he said.

"Tonight you will rest with the ghost of Napoleon," she said. "Which of you has better claim to that bed?"

George gave a cold little laugh. "I believe that was decided at Waterloo."

"The Duke's victory, or so I've heard."

George's friends were giving each other alarmed looks. Mary decided she had drawn enough Byron blood. She took a piece of cheese.

"Tell us about Waterloo!" Claire insisted. "Is it far from here?"

"The field is a mile or so north," said Somerset. He seemed relieved to turn to the subject of battles. "I had thought perhaps you were English tourists come to visit the site."

"Our arrival is coincidence," Bysshe said. He was looking at Mary narrow-eyed, as if he was trying to work something out. "I'm somewhat embarrassed for funds, and I'm in hope of finding a letter at Brussels from my—" He began to say "wife," but changed the word to "family."

"We're on our way to Vienna," Smith said.

"The long way 'round," said Somerset. "It's grown unsafe in Paris—too many old Bonapartists lurking with guns and bombs, and of course George is the laddie they hate most. So we're off to join the Duke as diplomats, but we plan to meet with his highness of Orange along the way. In Brussels, in two days' time."

"Good old Slender Billy!" said Smith. "I haven't seen him since the battle."

"The battle!" said Claire. "You said you would tell us!"

George gave her an irritated look. "Please, Miss Clairmont, I beg you. No battles before dinner." His stomach rumbled audibly.

"Bysshe," said Mary, "didn't you say the cook had told you a ghost story?"

"A good one, too," said Bysshe. "It happened in the house across the road, the one with the tile roof. A pair of old witches used to live there. Sisters." He looked up at George. "We may have ghosts before dinner, may we not?"

"For all of me, you may."

"They dealt in charms and curses and so on, and made a living supplying the, ah, the supernatural needs of the district. It so happened that two different men had fallen in love with the same girl, and each man applied to one of the weird sisters for a love charm—each to a different sister, you see. One of them used his spell first and won the heart of the maiden, and this drove the other suitor into a rage. So he went to the witch who had sold him his charm, and demanded she change the young lady's mind. When the witch insisted it was impossible, he drew his pistol and shot her dead."

"How very un-Belgian of him," drawled Smith.

Bysshe continued unperturbed. "So quick as a wink," he said, "the dead witch's sister seized a heavy kitchen cleaver and cut off the young man's head with a single stroke. The head fell to the floor and bounced out the porch steps. And ever since that night—" He leaned across the table toward Mary, his voice dropping dramatically. "—people in the house have sometimes heard a thumping noise, and seen the *suitor's head, dripping gore, bouncing down the steps!*"

Mary and Bysshe shared a delicious shiver. George gave Bysshe a thoughtful look.

"D'ye credit this sort of thing, Mr. Omnibus?"

Bysshe looked up. "Oh yes. I have a great belief in things supernatural."

George gave an insolent smile, and Mary's heart quickened as she recognized a trap.

"Then how can you be an atheist?" George asked.

Bysshe was startled. No one had ever asked him this question before. He gave a nervous laugh. "I am not so much opposed to God," he said, "as I am a worshipper of Galileo and Newton. And of course an enemy of the established Church."

"I see."

A little smile drifted across Bysshe's lips.

> *"Yes!"* he said, *"I have seen God's worshippers unsheathe*
> *The sword of his revenge, when grace descended,*
> *Confirming all unnatural impulses,*
> *To satisfy their desolating deeds;*
> *And frantic priests waved the ill-omened cross*
> *O'er the unhappy earth; then shone the sun*
> *On showers of gore from the upflashing steel*
> *Of safe assassin—"*

"And *have* you seen such?" George's look was piercing.

Bysshe blinked at him. "Beg pardon?"

"I asked if you *had* seen showers of gore, upflashing steel, all that sort of thing."

"Ah. No." He offered George a half-apologetic smile. "I do not hold warfare consonant with my principles."

"Yes." George's stomach rumbled once more. "It's rather more in my line than yours. So I think I am probably better qualified to judge it …" His lip twisted. "… *and* your principles."

Mary felt her hackles rise. "Surely you don't dispute that warfare is a great evil," she said. "And that the church blesses war and its outcome."

"The church—" He waved a hand. "The chaplains we had with us in Spain were fine men and did good work, from what I could see. Though we had damn few of them, as for the most part they preferred to judge war from their comfortable beds at home. And as for war—ay, it's evil. Yes. Among other things."

"Among other things!" Mary was outraged. "What other things?"

George looked at each of the officers in turn, then at Mary. "War is an abomination, I think we can all agree. But it is also an occasion for all that is great in mankind. Courage, comradeship, sacrifice. Heroism and nobility beyond the scope of imagination."

"Glory," said one-armed Somerset helpfully.

"Death!" snapped Mary. "Hideous, lingering death! Disease. Mutilation!" She realized she had stepped a little far, and bobbed her head toward Somerset, silently begging his pardon for bringing up his disfigurement. "Endless suffering among the starving widows and orphans," she went on. "Early this year Bysshe and Jane and I walked across the part of France that the armies had marched over. It was a desert, my lord. Whole villages without a single soul. Women, children, and cripples in rags. Many without a roof over their head."

"Ay," said Harry Smith. "We saw it in Spain, all of us."

"Miss Godwin," said George, "those poor French people have my sympathy as well as yours. But if a nation is going to murder its rightful king, elect a tyrant, and attack every other nation in the world, then it can but expect to receive that which it giveth. I reserve far greater sympathy for the poor orphans and widows of Spain, Portugal, and the Low Countries."

"And England," said Captain Austen.

"Ay," said George, "and England."

"I did not say that England has not suffered," said Mary. "Anyone with eyes can see the victims of the war. And the victims of the Corn Bill as well."

"Enough." George threw up his hands. "I heard enough debate on the Corn Bill in the House of Lords—I beg you, not here."

"People are starving, my lord," Mary said quietly.

"But thanks to Waterloo," George said, "they at least starve in peace."

"Here's our flesh!" said a relieved Harry Smith. Napkins flourished, silverware rattled, the dinner was laid down. Bysshe took a bite of his cheese pie, then sampled one of the little Brabant cabbages and gave a freckled smile— he had not, as had Mary, grown tired of them. Smith, Somerset, and George chatted about various Army acquaintances, and the others ate in silence. Somerset, Mary noticed, had come equipped with a combination knife-and-fork and managed his cutlet efficiently.

George, she noted, ate only a little, despite the grumblings of his stomach.

"Is it not to your taste, my lord?" she asked.

"My appetite is off." Shortly.

"That light cavalry figure don't come without sacrifice," said Smith. "I'm an infantryman, though," brandishing knife and fork, "and can tuck in to my vittles."

George gave him an irritated glance and sipped at his hock. "Cavalry, infantry, Senior Service, staff," he said, pointing at himself, Smith, Austen, and Somerset with his fork. The fork swung to Bysshe. "Do you, sir, have an occupation? Besides being atheistical, I mean."

Bysshe put down his knife and fork and answered deliberately. "I have been a scientist, and a reformer, and a sort of an engineer. I have now taken up poetry."

"I didn't know it was something to be *taken up,*" said George.

"Captain Austen's sister does something in the literary line, I believe," Harry Smith said.

Austen gave a little shake of his head. "Please, Harry. Not here."

"I know she publishes anonymously, but—"

"She doesn't want it known," firmly, "and I prefer her wishes be respected."

Smith gave Austen an apologetic look. "Sorry, Frank."

Mary watched Austen's distress with amusement. Austen had a spinster sister, she supposed—she could just imagine the type—who probably wrote ripe horrid gothic novels, all terror and dark battlements and cloaked sensuality, all to the constant mortification of the family.

Well, Mary thought. She should be charitable. Perhaps they were good.

She and Bysshe liked a good gothic, when they were in the mood. Bysshe had even written a couple, when he was fifteen or so.

George turned to Bysshe. "That was your own verse you quoted?"

"Yes."

"I thought perhaps it was, as I hadn't recognized it."

"Queen Mab," said Claire. "It's *very* good." She gave Bysshe a look of adoration that sent a weary despairing cry through Mary's nerves. "It's got all Bysshe's ideas in it," she said.

"And the publisher?"

"I published it myself," Bysshe said, "in an edition of seventy copies."

George raised an eyebrow. "A self-published phenomenon, forsooth. But why so few?"

"The poem is a political statement in accordance with Mr. Godwin's *Political Justice.* Were it widely circulated, the government might act to suppress it, and to prosecute the publisher." He gave a shudder. "With people like Lord Ellenborough in office, I think it best to take no chances."

"Lord Ellenborough is a great man," said Captain Austen firmly. Mary was surprised at his emphatic tone. "He led for Mr. Warren Hastings, do you know, during his trial, and that trial lasted seven years or more and ended in acquittal. Governor Hastings did me many a good turn in India—he was the making of me. I'm sure I owe Lord Ellenborough my purest gratitude."

Bysshe gave Austen a serious look. "Lord Ellenborough sent Daniel Eaton to prison for publishing Thomas Paine," he said. "And he sent Leigh Hunt to prison for publishing the truth about the Prince Regent."

"One an atheist," Austen scowled, "the other a pamphleteer."

"Why, so am I both," said Bysshe sweetly, and, smiling, sipped his spring water. Mary wanted to clap aloud.

"It is the duty of the Lord Chief Justice to guard the realm from subversion," said Somerset. "We were at war, you know."

"We are no longer at war," said Bysshe, "and Lord Ellenborough still sends good folk to prison."

"At least," said Mary, "he can no longer accuse reformers of being Jacobins. Not with France under the Bourbons again."

"Of course he can," Bysshe said. "Reform is an idea, and Jacobinism is an idea, and Ellenborough conceives them the same."

"But are they not?" George said.

Mary's temper flared. "Are you serious? Comparing those who seek to correct injustice with those who—"

"Who cut the heads off everyone with whom they disagreed?" George interrupted. "I'm perfectly serious. Robespierre was the very type of reformer—virtuous, sober, sedate, educated, a spotless private life. And how many thousands did he murder?" He jabbed his fork at Bysshe again, and Mary restrained the impulse to slap it out of his hand. "You may not like Ellenborough's sentencing, but a few hours in the pillory or a few months in prison ain't the same as beheading. And that's what reform in England would come to in the end—mobs and demagogues heaping up death, and then a dictator like Cromwell, or worse luck Bonaparte, to end liberty for a whole generation."

"I do not look to the French for a model," said Bysshe, "but rather to America."

"So did the French," said George, "and look what *they* got."

"If France had not desperately needed reform," Bysshe said, "there would have been nothing so violent as their revolution. If England reforms itself, there need be no violence."

"Ah. So if the government simply resigns, and frame-breakers and agitators and democratic philosophers and wandering poets take their place, then things shall be well in England."

"Things will be better in any case," Bysshe said quietly, "than they are now."

"Exactly!" Claire said.

George gave his companions a knowing look. *See how I humor this vagabond?* Mary read. Loathing stirred her heart.

Bysshe could read a look as well as Mary. His face darkened. "Please understand me," he said. "I do not look for immediate change, nor do I preach violent revolution. Mr. Godwin has corrected that error in my thought. There will be little amendment for years to come. But Ellenborough is old, and the King is old and mad, and the Regent and his loathsome brothers are not young ..." He smiled. "I will outlive them, will I not?"

George looked at him. "Will you outlive me, sir? I am not yet thirty."

"I am three-and-twenty." Mildly. "I believe the odds favor me."

Bysshe and the others laughed, while George looked cynical and dyspeptic. *Used to being the young cavalier,* Mary thought. *He's not so young any longer—how much longer will that pretty face last?*

"And of course advance of science may turn this debate irrelevant," Bysshe went on. "Mr. Godwin calculates that with the use of mechanical aids, people may reduce their daily labor to an hour or two, to the general benefit of all."

"But you oppose such machines, don't ye?" George said. "You support the Luddites, I assume?"

"Ay, but—"

"And the frame-breakers are destroying the machines that have taken their livelihood, aren't they? So where is your general benefit, then?"

Mary couldn't hold it in any longer. She slapped her hand down on the table, and George and Bysshe started. "The riots occur because the profits of the looms were not used to benefit the weavers, but to enrich the mill owners! Were the owners to share their profits with the weavers, there would have been no disorder."

George gave her a civil bow. "Your view of human nature is generous," he said, "if you expect a mill owner to support the families of those who are not even his employees."

"It would be for the good of all, wouldn't it?" Bysshe said. "If he does not want his mills threatened and frames broken."

"It sounds like extortion wrapped in pretty philosophy."

"The mill owners will pay one way or another," Mary pointed out. "They can pay taxes to the government to suppress the Luddites with militia and dragoons, or they can have the goodwill of the people, and let the swords and muskets rust."

"They will buy the swords every time," George said. "They are useful in ways other than suppressing disorder, such as securing trade routes and the safety of the nation." He put on a benevolent face. "You must forgive me, but your view of humanity is too benign. You do not account for the violence and passion that are in the very heart of man, and which institutions such as law and religion are intended to help control. And when science serves the passions, only tragedy can result—when I think of science, I think of the science of Dr. Guillotin."

"We are fallen," said Captain Austen. "Eden will never be within our grasp."

"The passions are a problem, but I think they can be turned to good," said Bysshe. "That is—" He gave an apologetic smile. "That is the aim of my current work. To use the means of poetry to channel the passions to a humane and beneficent aim."

"I offer you my very best wishes," condescendingly, "but I fear mankind will disappoint you. Passions are—" George gave Mary an insolent, knowing smile. "—are the downfall of many a fine young virtue."

Mary considered hitting him in the face. Bysshe seemed not to have noticed George's look, nor Mary's reaction. "Mr. Godwin ventured the thought that dreams are the source of many irrational passions," he mused. "He believes that should we ever find a way of doing without sleep, the passions would fall away."

"Ay!" barked George. "Through enervation, if nothing else."

The others laughed. Mary decided she had had enough, and rose.

"I shall withdraw," she said. "The journey has been fatiguing."

The gentlemen, Bysshe excepted, rose to their feet. "Good night, Maie," he said. "I will stay for a while, I think."

"As you like, Bysshe." Mary looked at her sister. "Jane? I mean Claire? Will you come with me?"

"Oh, no." Quickly. "I'm not at all tired."

Annoyance stiffened Mary's spine. "As you like," she said.

George bowed toward her, picked a candle off the table, and offered her an arm. "May I light you up the stair? I should like to apologize for my temerity in contradicting such a charming lady." He offered his brightest smile. "I think *my* poor virtue will extend that far, yes?"

She looked at him coldly—she couldn't think it customary, even in George's circles, to escort a woman to her bedroom.

Damn it anyway. "My lord," she said, and put her arm through his.

Jerome Bonaparte made a flying leap from the table and landed on George's shoulder. It clung to his long auburn hair, screamed, and made a face, and the others laughed. Mary considered the thought of being escorted up to bed by a lord and a monkey, and it improved her humor.

"Goodnight, gentlemen," Mary said. "Claire."

The gentlemen reseated themselves and George took Mary up the stairs. They were so narrow and steep that they couldn't go up abreast; George, with the candle, went first, and Mary, holding his hand, came up behind. Her door was the first up the stairs; she put her hand on the wooden door handle and turned to face her escort. The monkey leered at her from his shoulder.

"I thank you for your company, my lord," she said. "I fear your journey was a little short."

"I wished a word with you," softly, "a little apart from the others."

Mary stiffened. To her annoyance her heart gave a lurch. "What word is that?" she asked.

His expression was all affability. "I am sensible to the difficulties that you and your sister must be having. Without money in a foreign country, and with your only protector a man—" He hesitated. Jerome Bonaparte, jealous for his attention, tugged at his hair. "A charming man of noble ideals, surely, but without money."

"I thank you for your concern, but it is misplaced," Mary said. "Claire and I are perfectly well."

"Your health ain't my worry," he said. Was he deliberately misunderstanding? Mary wondered in fury. "I worry for your future—you are on an adventure with a man who cannot support you, cannot see you safe home, cannot marry you."

"Bysshe and I do not wish to marry." The words caught at her heart. "We are free."

"And the damage to your reputation in society—" he began, and came up short when she burst into laughter. He looked severe, while the monkey mocked him from his shoulder. "You may laugh now, Miss Godwin, but there are those who will use this adventure against you. Political enemies of your father at the very least."

"That isn't why I was laughing. I am the daughter of William Godwin and Mary Wollstonecraft—I *have* no reputation! It's like being the natural daughter of Lucifer and the Scarlet Woman of Babylon. Nothing is expected of us, nothing at all. Society has given us license to do as we please. We were dead to them from birth."

He gave her a narrow look. "But you have at least a little concern for the proprieties—why else travel pseudonymously?"

Mary looked at him in surprise. "What d'you mean?"

He smiled. "Give me a little credit, Miss Godwin. When you call your sister *Jane* half the time, and your protector calls you *May* ..."

Mary laughed again. "*The* Maie—Maie for short—is one of Bysshe's pet names for me. The other is Pecksie."

"Oh."

"And Jane is my sister's given name, which she has always hated. Last year she decided to call herself Clara or Claire—this week it is Claire."

Jerome Bonaparte began to yank at George's ear, and George made a face, pulled the monkey from his shoulder, and shook it with mock ferocity. Again he spoke in the cracked Scots dowager's voice. "Are ye sae donsie wicked, creeture? Tae Elba w'ye!"

Mary burst into laughter again. George gave her a careless grin, then returned the monkey to his shoulder. It sat and regarded Mary with bright, wise eyes.

"Miss Godwin, I am truly concerned for you, believe else of me what you will."

Mary's laughter died away. She took the candle from his hand. "Please, my lord. My sister and I are perfectly safe in Mr. Shelley's company."

"You will not accept my protection? I will freely give it."

"We do not need it. I thank you."

"Will you not take a loan, then? To see you safe across the Channel? Mr. Shelley may pay me back if he is ever in funds."

Mary shook her head.

A little of the old insolence returned to George's expression. "Well. I have done what I could."

"Good night, Lord Newstead."

"Good night."

Mary readied herself for bed and climbed atop the soft mattress. She tried to read her Italian grammar, but the sounds coming up the stairway were a distraction. There was loud conversation, and singing, and then Claire's fine voice, unaccompanied, rising clear and sweet up the narrow stair.

Torcere, Mary thought, looking fiercely at her book, *attorcere, rattorcere, scontorcere, torcere.*

Twist. Twist, twist, twist, twist.

Claire finished, and there was loud applause. Bysshe came in shortly afterwards. His eyes sparkled and his color was high. "We were singing," he said.

"I heard."

"I hope we didn't disturb you." He began to undress.

Mary frowned at her book. "You did."

"And I argued some more with Byron." He looked at her and smiled. "Imagine it—if we could convert Byron! Bring one of the most famous men in the world to our views."

She gave him a look. "I can think of nothing more disastrous to our cause than to have him lead it."

"Byron's famous. And he's a splendid man." He looked at her with a self-conscious grin. "I have a pair of byrons, you know, back home. I think I have a good turn of ankle, but the things are the very devil to lace. You really need servants for it."

"He's Newstead now. Not Byron. I wonder if they'll have to change the name of the boot?"

"Why would he change his name, d'you suppose? After he'd become famous with it."

"Wellington became famous as Wellesley."

"Wellington *had* to change his name. His brother was *already* Lord Wellesley." He approached the bed and smiled down at her. "He likes you."

"He likes any woman who crosses his path. Or so I understand."

Bysshe crawled into the bed and put his arm around her, the hand resting warmly on her belly. He smelled of the tobacco he'd been smoking with George. She put her hand atop his, feeling on the third finger the gold wedding ring he still wore. Dissatisfaction crackled through her. "You are free, you know." He spoke softly into her ear. "You can be with Byron if you wish."

Mary gave him an irritated look. "I don't *wish* to be with Byron. I want to be with you."

"But you *may,*" whispering, the hand stroking her belly, "be with Byron if you want."

Temper flared through Mary. "I don't *want* Byron!" she said. "And I don't want Mr. Thomas Jefferson Hogg, or any of your other friends!"

He seemed a little hurt. "Hogg's a splendid fellow."

"Hogg tried to seduce your wife, and he's tried to seduce me. And I don't understand how he remains your best friend."

"Because we agree on everything, and I hold him no malice where his intent was not malicious." Bysshe gave her a searching look. "I only want you to be free. If we're not free, our love is chained, chained absolutely, and all ruined. I can't live that way—I found that out with Harriet."

She sighed, put her arm around him, drew her fingers through his tangled hair. He rested his head on her shoulder and looked up into her eyes. "I want to be *free* to be with you," Mary told him. "Why will that not suit?"

"It suits." He kissed her cheek. "It suits very well." He looked up at her happily. "And if Harriet joins us in Brussels, with a little money, then all shall be perfect."

Mary gazed at him, utterly unable to understand how he could think his wife would join them, or why, for that matter, he thought it a good idea.

He misses his little boy, she thought. *He wants to be with him.*

The thought rang hollow in her mind.

He kissed her again, his hand moving along her belly, touching her lightly. "My golden-haired Maie." The hand cupped her breast. Her breath hissed inward.

"Careful," she said. "I'm very tender there."

"I will be nothing but tenderness." The kisses reached her lips. "I desire nothing but tenderness for you."

She turned to him, let his lips brush against hers, then press more firmly. Sensation, a little painful, flushed her breast. His tongue touched hers. Desire rose and she put her arms around him.

The door opened and Claire came in, chattering of George while she undressed. Mood broken, tenderness broken, there was nothing to do but sleep.

"Come and look," Mary said, "here's a cat eating roses; she'll turn into a woman, when beasts eat these roses they turn into men and women." But there was no one in the cottage, only the sound of the wind.

Fear touched her, cold on the back of her neck.

She stepped into the cottage, and suddenly there was something blocking the sun that came through the windows, an enormous figure, monstrous and black and hungry ...

Nausea and the sounds of swordplay woke her. A dog was barking maniacally. Mary rose from the bed swiftly and wrapped her shawl around herself. The room was hot and stuffy, and her gorge rose. She stepped to the window, trying not to vomit, and opened the pane to bring in fresh air.

Coolness touched her cheeks. Below in the courtyard of the inn was Pásmány, the fencing teacher, slashing madly at his pupil, Byron. Newstead. *George*, she reminded herself, she would remember he was *George*.

And serve him right.

She dragged welcome morning air into her lungs as the two battled below her. George was in his shirt, planted firmly on his strong, muscular legs, his pretty face set in an expression of intent calculation. Pásmány flung himself at the man, darting in and out, his sword almost fluid in its movement. They were using straight heavy sabers, dangerous even if unsharpened, and no protective equipment at all. A huge black dog, tied to the vermilion wheel of a big dark-blue barouche, barked at the both of them without cease.

Nausea swam over Mary; she closed her eyes and clutched the windowsill. The ringing of the swords suddenly seemed very far away.

"Are they fighting?" Claire's fingers clutched her shoulder. "Is it a duel? Oh, it's *Byron!*"

Mary abandoned the window and groped her way to the bed. Sweat beaded on her forehead. Bysshe blinked muzzily at her from his pillow.

"I must go down and watch," said Claire. She reached for her clothing and, hopping, managed to dress without missing a second of the action outside. She grabbed a hairbrush on her way out the door and was arranging her hair on the run even before the door slammed behind her.

"Whatever is happening?" Bysshe murmured. She reached blindly for his hand and clutched it.

"Bysshe," she gasped. "I am with child. I must be."

"I shouldn't think so." Calmly. "We've been using every precaution." He touched her cheek. His hand was cool. "It's the travel and excitement. Perhaps a bad egg."

Nausea blackened her vision and bent her double. Sweat fell in stately rhythm from her forehead to the floor. "This can't be a bad egg," she said. "Not day after day."

"Poor Maie." He nestled behind her, stroked her back and shoulders. "Perhaps there is a flaw in the theory," he said. "Time will tell."

No turning back, Mary thought. She had *wanted* there to be no turning back, to burn every bridge behind her, commit herself totally, as her mother had, to her beliefs. And now she'd succeeded—she and Bysshe were linked forever, linked by the child in her womb. Even if they parted, if—free, as they both wished to be—he abandoned this union, there would still be that link, those bridges burnt, her mother's defiant inheritance fulfilled …

Perhaps there is a flaw in the theory. She wanted to laugh and cry at once.

Bysshe stroked her, his thoughts his own, and outside the martial clangor went on and on.

It was some time before she could dress and go down to the common rooms. The sabre practice had ended, and Bysshe and Claire were already breaking their fast with Somerset, Smith, and Captain Austen. The thought of breakfast made Mary ill, so she wandered outside into the courtyard, where the two breathless swordsmen, towels draped around their necks, were sitting on a bench drinking water, with a tin dipper, from an old wooden bucket. The huge black dog barked, foaming, as she stepped out of the inn, and the two men, seeing her, rose.

"Please sit, gentlemen," she said, waving them back to their bench; she walked across the courtyard to the big open gate and stepped outside. She leaned against the whitewashed stone wall and took deep breaths of the country air. Sweet-smelling wildflowers grew in the verges of the highway. Prosperous-looking villagers nodded pleasantly as they passed about their errands.

"Looking for your haunted house, Miss Godwin?"

George's inevitable voice grated on her ears. She looked at him over her shoulder. "My intention was simply to enjoy the morning."

"I hope I'm not spoiling it."

Reluctant courtesy rescued him from her own riposting tongue. "How was the Emperor's bed?" she said finally.

He stepped out into the road. "I believe I slept better than he did, and longer." He smiled at her. "No ghosts walked."

"But you still fought a battle after your sleep."

"A far, far better one. Waterloo was not something I would care to experience more than once."

"I shouldn't care to experience it even the first time."

"Well. You're female, of course." All offhand, unaware of her rising hackles. He looked up and down the highway.

"D'ye know, this is the first time I've seen this road in peace. I first rode it north during the retreat from Quatre Bras, a miserable rainy night, and then there was the chase south after Boney the night of Waterloo, then later the advance with the army to Paris …" He shook his head. "It's a pleasant road, ain't it? Much better without the armies."

"Yes."

"We went along there." His hand sketched a line across the opposite horizon. "This road was choked with retreating French, so we went around them. With two squadrons of Vandeleur's lads, the 12th, the Prince of Wales's

Own, all I could find once the French gave way. I knew Boney would be running, and I knew it had to be along this road. I had to find him, make certain he would never trouble our peace. Find him for England." He dropped right fist into left palm.

"Boney'd left two battalions of the Guard to hold us, but I went around them. I knew the Prussians would be after him, too, and their mounts were fresher. So we drove on through the night, jumping fences, breaking down hedges, galloping like madmen, and then we found him at Genappe. The bridge was so crammed with refugees that he couldn't get his barouche across."

Mary watched carefully as George, uninvited, told the story that he must, by now, have told a hundred times, and wondered why he was telling it now to someone with such a clear distaste for things military. His color was high, and he was still breathing hard from his exercise; sweat gleamed on his immaculate forehead and matted his shirt; she could see the pulse throbbing in his throat. Perhaps the swordplay and sight of the road had brought the memory back; perhaps he was merely, after all, trying to impress her.

A female, of course. Damn the man.

"They'd brought a white Arab up for him to ride away," George went on. "His Chasseurs of the Guard were close around. I told each trooper to mark his enemy as we rode up—we came up at a slow trot, in silence, our weapons sheathed. In the dark the enemy took us for French—our uniforms were similar enough. I gave the signal—we drew pistols and carbines—half the French saddles were emptied in an instant. Some poor lad of a cornet tried to get in my way, and I cut him up through the teeth. Then there he was—the Emperor. With one foot in the stirrup, and Roustam the Mameluke ready to boost him into the saddle."

A tigerish, triumphant smile spread across George's face. His eyes were focused down the road, not seeing her at all. "I put my dripping point in his face, and for the life of me I couldn't think of any French to say except to tell him to sit down. *'Asseyez-vous!'* I ordered, and he gave me a sullen look and sat down, right down in the muddy roadway, with the carbines still cracking around us and bullets flying through the air. And I thought, He's finished. He's done. There's nothing left of him now. We finished off his bodyguard—they hadn't a chance after our first volley. The French soldiers around us thought we were the Prussian advance guard, and they were running as fast as their legs could carry them. Either they didn't know we had their Emperor or they didn't care. So we dragged Boney's barouche off the road, and dragged Boney with it, and ten minutes later the Prussians galloped up—the Death's Head Hussars under Gneisenau, all in black and silver, riding like devils. But the devils had lost the prize."

Looking at the wild glow in George's eyes Mary realized that she'd been wrong—the story was not for her at all, but for *him*. For George. He needed it somehow, this affirmation of himself, the enunciated remembrance of his moment of triumph.

But why? Why did he need it?

She realized his eyes were on her. "Would you like to see the coach, Miss Godwin?" he asked. The question surprised her.

"It's here?"

"I kept it." He laughed. "Why not? It was mine. What Captain Austen would call a fair prize of war." He offered her his arm. She took it, curious about what else she might discover.

The black mastiff began slavering at her the second she set foot inside the courtyard. Its howls filled the air. "Hush, Picton," George said, and walked straight to the big gold-trimmed blue coach with vermilion wheels. The door had the Byron arms and the Latin motto CREDE BYRON.

Should she believe him? Mary wondered. And if so, how much?

"This is Bonaparte's?" she said.

"Was, Miss Godwin. Till June 16th last. *Down,* Picton!" The dog lunged at him, and he wrestled with it, laughing, until it calmed down and began to fawn on him.

George stepped to the door and opened it. "The Imperial symbols are still on the lining, as you see." The door and couch were lined with rich purple, with golden bees and the letter *N* worked in heavy gold embroidery. "Fine Italian leatherwork," he said. "Drop-down secretaires so that the great man could write or dictate on the march. Holsters for pistols." He knocked on the coach's polished side. "Bulletproof. There are steel panels built in, just in case any of the Great Man's subjects decided to imitate Marcus Brutus." He smiled. "I was glad for that steel in Paris, I assure you, with Bonapartist assassins lurking under every tree." A mischievous gleam entered his eye. "And last, the best thing of all." He opened a compartment under one of the seats and withdrew a solid silver chamber pot. "You'll notice it still bears the imperial *N.*"

"Vanity in silver."

"Possibly. Or perhaps he was afraid one of his soldiers would steal it if he didn't mark it for his own."

Mary looked at the preposterous object and found herself laughing. George looked pleased and stowed the chamber pot in its little cabinet. He looked at her with his head cocked to one side. "You will not reconsider my offer?"

"No." Mary stiffened. "Please don't mention it again."

The mastiff Picton began to howl again, and George seized its collar and told it to behave itself. Mary turned to see Claire walking toward them.

"Won't you be joining us for breakfast, my lord?"

George straightened. "Perhaps a crust or two. I'm not much for breakfast."

Still fasting, Mary thought. "It would make such sense for you to give up meat, you know," she said. "Since you deprive yourself of food anyway."

"I prefer not to deny myself pleasure, even if the quantities are necessarily restricted."

"Your swordplay was magnificent."

"Thank you. Cavalry style, you know—all slash and dash. But I *am* good, for a' that."

"I know you're busy, but—" Claire bit her lip. "Will you take us to Waterloo?"

"Claire!" cried Mary.

Claire gave a nervous laugh. "Truly," she said. "I'm absolutely with child to see Waterloo."

George looked at her, his eyes intent. "Very well," he said. "We'll be driving through it in any case. And Captain Austen has expressed an interest."

Fury rose in Mary's heart. "Claire, how *dare* you impose—"

"Ha' ye nae pity for the puir lassie?" The Scots voice was mock-severe. "Ye shallnae keep her fra' her Waterloo."

Claire's Waterloo, Mary thought, was exactly what she wanted to keep her from.

George offered them his exaggerated, flourishing bow. "If you'll excuse me, ladies, I must give the necessary orders."

He strode through the door. Pásmány followed, the swords tucked under his arm. Claire gave a little joyous jump, her shoes scraping on cobbles. "I can hardly believe it," she said. "Byron showing us Waterloo!"

"I can't believe it either," Mary said. She sighed wearily and headed for the dining room.

Perhaps she would dare to sip a little milk.

They rode out in Napoleon's six-horse barouche, Claire, Mary, and Bysshe inside with George, and Smith, Somerset, and Captain Austen sharing the outside rear seat. The leather top with its bulletproof steel inserts had been folded away and the inside passengers could all enjoy the open air. The barouche wasn't driven by a coachman up top, but by three postboys who rode the right-hand horses, so there was nothing in front to interrupt the view. Bysshe's mule and little carriage, filled with bags and books, ate dust behind alone with the officers' baggage coaches, all driven by George's servants.

The men talked of war and Claire listened to them with shining eyes. Mary concentrated on enjoying the shape of the low hills with their whitewashed farmhouses and red tile roofs, the cut fields of golden rye stubble, the smell of wildflowers and the sound of birdsong. It was only when the carriage passed a walled farm, its whitewash marred by bullets and cannon shot, that her reverie was marred by the thought of what had happened here.

"La Haie Sainte," George remarked. "The King's German Legion held it throughout the battle, even after they'd run out of ammunition. I sent Mercer's horse guns to keep the French from the walls, else Lord knows what would have happened." He stood in the carriage, looked left and right, frowned. "These roads we're about to pass were sunken—an obstacle to both sides, but mainly to the French. They're filled in now. Mass graves."

"The French were cut down in heaps during their cavalry attack," Somerset added. "The piles were eight feet tall, men and horses."

"How gruesome!" laughed Claire.

"Turn right, Swinson," said George.

Homemade souvenir stands had been set up at the crossroads. Prosperous-looking rustics hawked torn uniforms, breastplates, swords, muskets, bayonets. Somerset scowled at them. "They must have made a fortune looting the dead."

"And the living," said Smith. "Some of our poor wounded weren't brought in till two days after the battle. Many had been stripped naked by the peasants."

A young man ran up alongside the coach, shouting in French. He explained he had been in the battle, a guide to the great Englishman Lord Byron, and would guide them over the field for a few guilders.

"Never heard of you," drawled George, and dismissed him. "Hey! Swinson! Pull up here."

The postboys pulled up their teams. George opened the door of the coach and strolled to one of the souvenir stands. When he returned it was with a French breastplate and helmet. Streaks of rust dribbled down the breastplate, and the helmet's horsehair plume smelled of mildew.

"I thought we could take a few shots at it," George said. "I'd like to see whether armor provides any protection at all against bullets—I suspect not. There's a movement afoot at Whitehall to give breastplates to the Household Brigade, and I suspect they ain't worth the weight. If I can shoot a few holes in this with my Mantons, I may be able to prove my point."

They drove down a rutted road of soft earth. It was lined with thorn hedges, but most of them had been broken down during the battle and there were long vistas of rye stubble, the gentle sloping ground, the pattern of plow and harvest. Occasionally the coach wheels grated on something, and Mary remembered they were moving along a mass grave, over the decaying flesh and whitening bones of hundreds of horses and men. A cloud passed across the sun, and she shivered.

"Can ye pull through the hedge, Swinson?" George asked. "I think the ground is firm enough to support us—no rain for a few days at least." The lead postboy studied the hedge with a practiced eye, then guided the lead team through a gap in it.

The barouche rocked over exposed roots and broken limbs, then ground onto a rutted sward of green grass, knee-high, that led gently down into the valley they'd just crossed. George stood again, his eyes scanning the ground. "Pull up over there," he said, pointing, and the coachman complied.

"Here you can see where the battle was won," George said. He tossed his clanging armor out onto the grass, opened the coach door and stepped out himself. The others followed, Mary reluctantly. George pointed with one elegant hand at the ridge running along the opposite end of the valley from their own, a half-mile opposite.

"Napoleon's grand battery," he said. "Eighty guns, many of them twelve-pounders—Boney called them his daughters. He was an artillerist, you know, and he always prepared his attacks with a massed bombardment. The guns fired for an hour and put our poor fellows through hell. Bylandt's Dutchmen were standing in the open, right where we are now, and the guns broke 'em entirely.

"Then the main attack came, about two o'clock. Count d'Erlon's corps, 16,000 strong, arrayed 25 men deep with heavy cavalry on the wings. They captured La Haye and Papelotte, those farms over there on the left, and rolled up this ridge with drums beating the *pas de charge ...* "

George turned. There was a smile on his face. Mary watched him closely—the pulse was beating like d'Erlon's drums in his throat, and his color was high. He was loving every second of this.

He went on, describing the action, and against her will Mary found herself seeing it, Picton's division lying in wait, prone on the reverse slope, George bringing the heavy cavalry up, the cannons banging away. Picton's men rising, firing their volleys, following with the bayonet. The Highlanders screaming in Gaelic, their plumes nodding as they drew their long broad-swords and plunged into the fight, the pipers playing "Johnnie Cope" amid all the screams and clatter. George leading the Household and Union Brigades against the enemy cavalry, the huge grain-fed English hunters driving back the chargers from Normandy. And then George falling on d'Erlon's flanks, driving the French in a frightened mob all the way back across the valley while the British horsemen slashed at their backs. The French gunners of the grand battery unable to fire for fear of hitting their own men, and then dying themselves under the British sabres.

Mary could sense as well the things George left out. The sound of steel grating on bone. Wails and moans of the wounded, the horrid challenging roars of the horses. And in the end, a valley filled with stillness, a carpet of bodies and pierced flesh ...

George gave a long sigh. "Our cavalry are brave, you know, far too brave for their own good. And the officers get their early training in steeplechases and the hunt, and their instinct is to ride straight at the objective at full gallop, which is absolutely the worst thing cavalry can ever do. After Slade led his command to disaster back in the Year Twelve, the Duke realized he could only commit cavalry at his peril. In Spain we finally trained the horse to maneuver and to make careful charges, but the Union and Household troops hadn't been in the Peninsula, and didn't know the drill. ... I drove myself mad in the weeks before the battle, trying to beat the recall orders into them." He laughed self-consciously. "My heart was in my mouth during the whole charge, I confess, less with fear of the enemy than with terror my own men would run mad. But they answered the trumpets, all but the Inniskillings, who wouldnae listen—the Irish blood was up—and while they ran off into the valley, the rest of us stayed in the grand battery. Sabred the gunners, drove off the limbers with the ready ammunition—and where we could we took the wheels off the guns, and rolled 'em back to our lines like boys with hoops. And the Inniskillings—" He shook his head. "They ran wild into the enemy lines, and Boney loosed his lancers at 'em, and they died almost to a man. I had to watch from the middle of the battery, with my officers begging to be let slip again and rescue their comrades, and I had to forbid it."

There were absolute tears in George's eyes. Mary watched in fascination and wondered if this was a part of the performance, or whether he was genuinely affected—but then she saw that Bysshe's eyes had misted over and Somerset was wiping his eyes with his one good sleeve. So, she thought, she *could* believe Byron, at least a little.

"Well." George cleared his throat, trying to control himself. "Well. We came back across the valley herding thousands of prisoners—and that charge proved the winning stroke. Boney attacked later, of course—all his heavy cavalry came knee-to-knee up the middle, between La Haie Sainte and Hougoumont," gesturing to the left with one arm, "we had great guns and squares of infantry to hold them, and my heavies to counterattack. The Prussians were pressing the French at Plancenoit and Papelotte. Boney's last throw of the dice sent the Old Guard across the valley after sunset, but our Guards under Maitland held them, and Colborne's 52nd and the Belgian Chasseurs got round their flanks, and after they broke I let the Household and Union troopers have their head—we swept 'em away. Sabred and trampled Boney's finest troops right in front of his eyes, all in revenge for the brave, mad Inniskillings—the only time his Guard ever failed in attack, and it marked the end of his reign. We were blown by the end of it, but Boney had nothing left to counterattack with. I knew he would flee. So I had a fresh horse brought up and went after him."

"So you won the battle of Waterloo!" said Claire.

George gave her a modest look that, to Mary, seemed false as the very devil. "I was privileged to have a decisive part. But 'twas the Duke that won the battle. We all fought at his direction."

"But you captured Napoleon and ended the Empire!"

He smiled. "That I did do, lassie, ay."

"Bravo!" Claire clapped her hands.

Harry Smith glanced up with bright eyes. "D'ye know, George," he said, "pleased as I am to hear this modest recitation of your accomplishments, I find precious little mention in your discourse of the *infantry*. I seem to remember fighting a few Frenchies myself, down Hougoumont way, with Reille's whole corps marching down on us, and I believe I can recollect in my dim footsoldier's mind that I stood all day under cannonshot and bursting mortar bombs, and that Kellerman's heavy cavalry came wave after wave all afternoon, with the Old Guard afterward as a lagniappe ..."

"I am pleased that you had some little part," George said, and bowed from his slim cavalry waist.

"Your lordship's condescension does you more credit than I can possibly express." Returning the bow.

George reached out and gave Smith's ear an affectionate tweak. "May I continue my tale? And then we may travel to Captain Harry's part of the battlefield, and he will remind us of whatever small role it was the footsoldiers played."

George went through the story of Napoleon's capture again. It was the same, sentiment for sentiment, almost word for word. Mary wandered away, the fat moist grass turning the hem of her skirt green. Skylarks danced through the air, trilling as they went. She wandered by the old broken thorn hedge and saw wild roses blossoming in it, and she remembered the wild roses planted on her mother's grave.

She thought of George Gordon Noël with tears in his eyes, and the way the others had wanted to weep—even Bysshe, who hadn't been there—and all for the loss of some Irishmen who, had they been crippled or out of uniform or begging for food or employment, these fine English officers would probably have turned into the street to starve ...

She looked up at the sound of footsteps. Harry Smith walked up and nodded pleasantly. "I believe I have heard George give this speech," he said.

"So have I. Does he give it often?"

"Oh yes." His voice dropped, imitated George's limpid dramatics. *"He's finished. He's done. There's nothing left of him now."* Mary covered amusement with her hand. "Though the tale has improved somewhat since the first time," Smith added. "In this poor infantryman's opinion."

Mary gave him a careful look. "Is he all he seems to think he is?"

Smith gave a thin smile. "Oh, ay. The greatest cavalryman of our time, to be sure. Without doubt a genius. *Chevalier sans peur et*—well, I won't say *sans reproche.* Not quite." His brow contracted as he gave careful thought to his next words. "He purchased his way up to colonel—that would be with Lady Newstead's money—but since then he's earned his spurs."

"He truly is talented, then."

"Truly. But of course he's lucky, too. If Le Marchant hadn't died at Salamanca, George wouldn't have been able to get his heavy brigade, and if poor General Cotton hadn't been shot by our own sentry George wouldn't have got all the cavalry in time for Vitoria, and of course if Uxbridge hadn't run off with Wellington's sister-in-law then George might not have got command at Waterloo. ... Young and without political influence as he is, he wouldn't have *kept* all those commands for long if he hadn't spent his every leave getting soused with that unspeakable hound the Prince of Wales. Ay, there's been luck involved. But who won't wish for luck in his life, eh?"

"What if his runs out?"

Smith gave this notion the same careful consideration. "I don't know," he said finally. "He's fortune's laddie, but that don't mean he's without character."

"You surprise me, speaking of him so frankly."

"We've been friends since Spain. And nothing I say will matter in any case." He smiled. "Besides, hardly anyone ever asks for *my* opinion."

The sound of Claire's laughter and applause carried across the sward. Smith cocked an eye at the other party. "Boney's at sword's point, if I'm not mistaken."

"Your turn for glory."

"Ay. If anyone will listen after George's already won the battle." He held out his arm and Mary took it. "You should meet my wife. Juanita—I met her in Spain at the storming of Badajoz. The troops were carrying away the loot, but I carried her away instead." He looked at her thoughtfully. "You have a certain spirit in common."

Mary felt flattered. "Thank you, Captain Smith. I'm honored by the comparison."

They moved to another part of the battlefield. There was a picnic overlooking the château of Hougoumont that lay red-roofed in its valley next to a well-tended orchard. Part of the chateau had been destroyed in the battle, Smith reported, but it had been rebuilt since.

Rebuilt, Mary thought, by owners enriched by battlefield loot.

George called for his pistols and moved the cuirass a distance away, propping it up on a small slope with the helmet sitting on top. A servant brought the Mantons and loaded them, and while the others stood and watched, George aimed and fired. Claire clapped her hands and laughed, though there was no discernible effect. White gunsmoke drifted on the morning breeze. George presented his second pistol, paused to aim, fired again. There was a whining sound and a scar appeared on the shoulder of the cuirass. The other men laughed.

"That cuirassier's got you for sure!" Harry Smith said.

"May I venture a shot?" Bysshe asked. George assented.

One of George's servants reloaded the pistols while George gave Bysshe instruction in shooting. "Hold the arm out straight and use the bead to aim."

"I like keeping the elbow bent a little," Bysshe said. "Not tucked in like a duellist, but not locked, either."

Bysshe took effortless aim—Mary's heart leaped at the grace of his movement—then Bysshe paused an instant and fired. There was a thunking sound and a hole appeared in the French breastplate, directly over the heart.

"Luck!" George said.

"Yes!" Claire said. "Purest luck!"

"Not so," Bysshe said easily. "Observe the plume holder." He presented the other pistol, took briefest aim, fired. With a little whine the helmet's metal plume holder took flight and whipped spinning through the air. Claire applauded and gave a cheer.

Mary smelled powder on the gentle morning wind.

Bysshe returned the pistols to George. "Fine weapons," he said, "though I prefer an octagonal barrel, as you can sight along the top."

George smiled thinly and said nothing.

"Mr. Shelley," said Somerset, "you have the makings of a soldier."

"I've always enjoyed a good shoot," Bysshe said, "though of course I won't fire at an animal. And as for soldiering, who knows what I might have been were I not exposed to Mr. Godwin's political thought?"

There was silence at this. Bysshe smiled at George. "You shouldn't lock the elbow out," he said. "That fashion, every little motion of the body transmits itself to the weapon. If you keep the elbow bent a bit, it forms a sort of a spring to absorb involuntary muscle tremors and you'll have better control." He looked at the others gaily. "It's not for nothing I was an engineer!"

George handed the pistols to his servant for loading. "We'll fire another volley," he said. His voice was curt.

Mary watched George as the Mantons were loaded, as he presented each pistol—straight-armed—and fired again. One knocked the helmet off its perch, the other struck the breastplate at an angle and bounced off. The others laughed, and Mary could see a little muscle twitching in George's cheek.

"My turn, George," said Harry Smith, and the pistols were recharged. His first shot threw up turf, but the second punched a hole in the cuirass. "There," Smith said, "that should satisfy the Horse Guards that armor ain't worth the weight."

Somerset took his turn, firing awkwardly with his one hand, and missed both shots.

"Another volley," George said.

There was something unpleasant in his tone, and the others took hushed notice. The pistols were reloaded. George presented the first pistol at the target, and Mary could see how he was vibrating with passion, so taut his knuckles were white on the pistol-grip. His shots missed clean.

"Bad luck, George," Somerset said. His voice was calming. "Probably the bullets were deformed and didn't fly right."

"Another volley," said George.

"We have an appointment in Brussels, George."

"It can wait."

The others drew aside and clustered together while George insisted on firing several more times. "What a troublesome fellow he is," Smith muttered. Eventually George put some holes in the cuirass, collected it, and stalked to the coach, where he had the servants strap it to the rear so that he could have it sent to the Prince of Wales.

Mary sat as far away from George as possible. George's air of defiant petulance hung over the company as they started north on the Brussels road. But then Bysshe asked Claire to sing, and Claire's high, sweet voice rose above the green countryside of Brabant, and by the end of the song everyone was smiling. Mary flashed Bysshe a look of gratitude.

The talk turned to war again, battles and sieges and the dead, a long line of uniformed shadows, young, brave men who fell to the French, to accident, to camp fever. Mary had little to say on the subject that she hadn't already offered, but she listened carefully, felt the soldiers' sadness at the death of comrades, the rejoicing at victory, the satisfaction of a deadly, intricate job done well. The feelings expressed seemed fine, passionate, even a little exalted. Bysshe listened and spoke little, but gradually Mary began to feel that he was somehow included in this circle of men and that she was not—perhaps his expert pistol shooting had made him a part of this company.

A female, of course. War was a fraternity only, though the suffering it caused made no distinction as to sex.

"May I offer an observation?" Mary said.

"Of course," said Captain Austen.

"I am struck by the passion you show when speaking of your comrades and your—shall I call it your craft?"

"Please, Miss Godwin," George said. "The enlisted men may have a *craft,* if you like. We are gentlemen, and have a *profession.*"

"I intended no offense. But still—I couldn't help but observe the fine feelings you show towards your comrades, and the attention you give to the details of your ... profession."

George seemed pleased. "Ay. Didn't I speak last night of war being full of its own kind of greatness?"

"Greatness perhaps the greater," Bysshe said, "by existing in contrast to war's wretchedness."

"Precisely," said George.

"Ay," Mary said, "but what struck me most was that you gentlemen showed such elevated passion when discussing war, such sensibility, high feeling, and utter conviction—more than I am accustomed to seeing from any … respectable males." Harry Smith gave an uncomfortable laugh at this characterization.

"Perhaps you gentlemen practice war," Mary went on, "because it allows free play to your passions. You are free to feel, to exist at the highest pitch of emotion. Society does not normally permit this to its members—perhaps it *must* in order to make war attractive."

Bysshe listened to her in admiration. "Brava!" he cried. "War as the sole refuge of the passions—I think you have struck the thing exactly."

Smith and Somerset frowned, working through the notion. It was impossible to read Austen's weathered countenance. But George shook his head wearily.

"Mere stuff, I'm afraid," he said. "Your analysis shows an admirable ingenuity, Miss Godwin, but I'm afraid there's no more place for passion on the battlefield than anywhere else. The poor Inniskillings had passion, but look what became of *them*." He paused, shook his head again. "No, it's drill and cold logic and a good eye for ground that wins the battles. In my line it's not only my own sensibility that must be mastered, but those of hundreds of men and horses."

"Drill is meant to master the passions," said Captain Austen. "For in a battle, the impulse, the overwhelming passion, is to run away. This impulse must be subdued."

Mary was incredulous. "You claim not to experience these elevated passions which you display so plainly?"

George gave her the insolent, under-eyed look again. "All passions have their place, Miss Godwin. I reserve mine for the appropriate time."

Resentment snarled up Mary's spine. "Weren't those tears I saw standing in your eyes when you described the death of the Inniskillings? Do you claim that's part of your drill?"

George's color brightened. "I didn't shed those tears during the battle. At the time I was too busy damning those cursed Irishmen for the wild fools they were, and wishing I'd flogged more of them when I'd the chance."

"But wasn't Bonaparte's great success on account of his ability to inspire his soldiers and his nation?" Bysshe asked. "To raise their passions to a great pitch and conquer the world?"

"And it was the uninspired, roguey English with their drill and discipline who put him back in his place," George said. "Bonaparte should have saved the speeches and put his faith in the drill-square."

Somerset gave an amused laugh. "This conversation begins to sound like one of Mrs. West's novels of Sense and Sensibility that were so popular in the Nineties," he said. "I suppose you're too young to recall them. *A Gossip's Story*, and *The Advantages of Education*. My governess made me read them both."

Harry Smith looked at Captain Austen with glittering eyes. "In *fact*—" he began.

Captain Austen interrupted. "One is not blind to the world of feeling," he said, "but surely Reason must rule the passions, else even a good heart can be led astray."

"I can't agree," Bysshe said. "Surely it is Reason that has led us to the world of law, and property, and equity, and kingship—and all the hypocrisy that comes with upholding these artificial formations, and denying our true nature, all that deprives us of life, of true and natural goodness."

"Absolutely!" said Claire.

"It is Reason," Mary said, "which makes you deny the evidence of my senses. I *saw* your emotion, gentlemen, when you discussed your dead comrades. And I applaud it."

"It does you credit," Bysshe added.

"Do you claim not to feel anything in battle?" Mary demanded. "Nothing at all?"

George paused a moment, then answered seriously. "My concentration is very great. It is an elevated sort of apprehension, very intent. I must be aware of so much, you see—I can't afford to miss a thing. My analytical faculty is always in play."

"And that's all?" cried Mary.

That condescending half-smile returned. "There isnae time for else, lass."

"At the height of a charge? In the midst of an engagement?"

"Then especially. An instant's break in my concentration and all could be lost."

"Lord Newstead," Mary said, "I cannot credit this."

George only maintained his slight smile, knowing and superior. Mary wanted to wipe it from his face, and considered reminding him of his fractious conduct over the pistols. *How's that for control and discipline,* she thought.

But no, she decided, it would be a long, unpleasant ride to Brussels if she upset George again.

Against her inclinations, she concluded to be English, and hypocritical, and say nothing.

Bysshe found neither wife nor money in Brussels, and George arranged lodgings for them that they couldn't afford. The only option Mary could think of was to make their way to a Channel port, then somehow try to talk their way to England with promise of payment once Bysshe had access to funds in London.

It was something for which she held little hope.

They couldn't afford any local diversions, and so spent their days in a graveyard, companionably reading.

And then, one morning two days after their arrival in Brussels, as Mary lay ill in their bed, Bysshe returned from an errand with money, coins clanking in a bag. "We're saved!" he said, and emptied the bag into her lap.

Mary looked at the silver lying on the comforter and felt her anxiety ease. They were old Spanish coins with the head of George III stamped over their original design, but they were real for all that. "A draft from Har ... from your wife?" she said.

"No." Bysshe sat on the bed, frowned. "It's a loan from Byron—Lord Newstead, I mean."

"Bysshe!" Mary sat up and set bedclothes and silver flying. "You took money from that man? Why?"

He put a paternal hand on hers. "Lord Newstead convinced me it would be in your interest, and Claire's. To see you safely to England."

"We'll do well enough without his money! It's not even his to give away, it's his wife's."

Bysshe seemed hurt. "It's a loan," he said. "I'll pay it back once I'm in London." He gave a little laugh. "I'm certain he doesn't expect repayment. He thinks we're vagabonds."

"He thinks worse of us than that." A wave of nausea took her and she doubled up with a little cry. She rolled away from him. Coins rang on the floor. Bysshe put a hand on her shoulder, stroked her back.

"Poor Pecksie," he said. "Some English cooking will do you good."

"Why don't you believe me?" Tears welled in her eyes. "I'm with child, Bysshe!"

He stroked her. "Perhaps. In a week or two we'll know for certain." His tone lightened. "He invited us to a ball tonight."

"Who?"

"Newstead. The ball's in his honor, he can invite whomever he pleases. The Prince of Orange will be there, and the English ambassador."

Mary had no inclination to be the subject of one of George's freaks. "We have no clothes fit for a ball," she said, "and I don't wish to go in any case."

"We have money now. We can buy clothes." He smiled. "And Lord Newstead said he would loan you and Claire some jewels."

"Lady Newstead's jewels," Mary reminded.

"All those powerful people! Imagine it! Perhaps we can effect a conversion."

Mary glared at him over her shoulder. "That money is for our passage to England. George wants only to display us, his tame Radicals, like his tame monkey or his tame panther. We're just a caprice of his—he doesn't take either us or our arguments seriously."

"That doesn't invalidate our arguments. We can still make them." Cheerfully. "Claire and I will go, then. She's quite set on it, and I hate to disappoint her."

"I think it will do us no good to be in his company for an instant longer. I think he is ..." She reached behind her back, took his hand, touched it. "Perhaps he is a little mad," she said.

"Byron? Really? He's *wrong*, of course, but ..."

Nausea twisted her insides. Mary spoke rapidly, desperate to convince Bysshe of her opinions. "He so craves glory and fame, Bysshe. The war gave expression to his passions, gave him the achievement he desired—but now the war's over and he can't have the worship he needs. That's why he's taken up with us—he wants even *our* admiration. There's no future for him now—he could follow Wellington into politics but he'd be in Wellington's shadow forever that way. He's got nowhere to go."

There was a moment's silence. "I see you've been giving him much thought," Bysshe said finally.

"His marriage is a failure—he can't go back to England. His relations with women will be irregular, and—"

"*Our* relations are irregular, Maie. And it's the better for it."

"I didn't mean that. I meant he cannot love. It's worship he wants, not love. And those pretty young men he travels with—there's something peculiar in that. Something unhealthy."

"Captain Austen is neither pretty nor young."

"He's along only by accident. Another of George's freaks."

"And if you think he's a pederast, well—we should be tolerant. Plato believed it a virtue. And George always asks after *you*."

"I do not wish to be in his thoughts."

"He is in yours." His voice was gentle. "And that is all right. You are free."

Mary's heart sank. "It is *your* child I have, Bysshe," she said.

Bysshe didn't answer. *Torcere,* she thought. *Attorcere, rattorcere.*

Claire's face glowed as she modelled her new ball gown, circling on the parlor carpet of the lodgings George had acquired for Bysshe's party. Lady Newstead's jewels glittered from Claire's fingers and throat. Bysshe, in a new coat, boots, and pantaloons, smiled approvingly from the corner.

"Very lovely, Miss Clairmont," George approved.

George was in full uniform, scarlet coat, blue facings, gold braid, and byrons laced tight. His cocked hat was laid carelessly on the mantel. George's eyes turned to Mary.

"I'm sorry you are ill, Miss Godwin," he said. "I wish you were able to accompany us."

Bysshe, Mary presumed, had told him this. Mary found no reason why she should support the lie.

"I'm not ill," she said mildly. "I simply do not wish to go—I have some pages I wish to finish. A story called *Hate.*"

George and Bysshe flushed alike. Mary, smiling, approached Claire, took her hand, admired gown and gems. She was surprised by the effect: the jewels, designed for an older woman, gave Claire a surprisingly mature look, older and more experienced than her sixteen years. Mary found herself growing uneasy.

"The seamstress was shocked when she was told I needed it tonight," Claire said. "She had to call in extra help to finish in time." She laughed. "But money mended everything!"

"For which we may thank Lord Newstead," Mary said, "and Lady Newstead to thank for the jewels." She looked up at George, who was still smouldering from her earlier shot. "I'm surprised, my lord, that she allows them to travel without her."

"Annabella has her own jewels," George said. "These are mine. I travel often without her, and as I move in the highest circles, I want to make certain that any lady who finds herself in my company can glitter with the best of them."

"How chivalrous." George cocked his head, frying to decide whether or not this was irony. Mary decided to let him wonder. She folded her hands and smiled sweetly.

"I believe it's time to leave," she said. "You don't want to keep his highness of Orange waiting."

Cloaks and hats were snatched; goodbyes were said. Mary managed to whisper to Claire as she helped with her cloak.

"Be careful, Jane," she said.

Resentment glittered in Claire's black eyes. "*You* have a man," she said. Mary looked at her. "So does Lady Newstead."

Claire glared hatred and swept out, fastening bonnet-strings. Bysshe kissed Mary's lips, George her hand. Mary prepared to settle by the fire with pen and manuscript, but before she could sit, there was a knock on the door and George rushed in.

"Forgot me hat," he said. But instead of taking it from the mantel, he walked to where Mary stood by her chair and simply looked at her. Mary's heart lurched at the intensity of his gaze.

"Your hat awaits you, my lord," she said.

"I hope you will reconsider," said George.

Mary merely looked at him, forced him to state his business. He took her hand in both of his, and she clenched her fist as his fingers touched hers.

"I ask you, Miss Godwin, to reconsider my offer to take you under my protection," George said.

Mary clenched her teeth. Her heart hammered. "I am perfectly safe with Mr. Shelley," she said.

"Perhaps not as safe as you think." She glared at him. George's eyes bored into hers. "I gave him money," he said, "and he told me you were free. Is that the act of a protector?"

Rage flamed through Mary. She snatched her hand back and came within an inch of slapping George's face.

"Do you think he's sold me to you?" she cried.

"I can conceive no other explanation," George said.

"You are mistaken and a fool." She turned away, trembling in anger, and leaned against the wall.

"I understand this may be a shock. To have trusted such a man, and then discovered—"

The wallpaper had little bees on it, Napoleon's emblem. "Can't you understand that Bysshe was perfectly literal!" she shouted. "I am free, he is free, Claire is free—free to go, or free to stay." She straightened her back, clenched her fists. "I will stay. Goodbye, Lord Newstead."

"I fear for you."

"Go away," she said, speaking to the wallpaper; and after a moment's silence she heard George turn, and take his hat from the mantel, and leave the building.

Mary collapsed into her chair. The only thing she could think was, *Poor Claire.*

Two

Mary was pregnant again. She folded her hands over her belly, stood on the end of the dock, and gazed up at the Alps.

Clouds sat low on the mountains, growling. The passes were closed with avalanche and unseasonal snow, the *vaudaire* storm wind tore white from the steep waves of the grey lake, and *Ariel* pitched madly at its buoy by the water-front, its mast-tip tracing wild figures against the sky.

The *vaudaire* had caused a "seiche"—the whole mass of the lake had shifted toward Montreux, and water levels had gone up six feet. The strange freshwater tide had cast up a line of dead fish and dead birds along the stony waterfront, all staring at Mary with brittle glass eyes.

"It doesn't look as if we'll be leaving tomorrow," Bysshe said. He and Mary stood by the waterfront, cloaked and sheltered by an umbrella. Water broke on the shore, leaped through the air, reaching for her, for Bysshe. ... It spattered at her feet.

She thought of Harriet, Bysshe's wife, hair drifting, clothes floating like seaweed. Staring eyes like dark glass. Her hands reaching for her husband from the water.

She had been missing for weeks before her drowned body was finally found.

The *vaudaire* was supposed to be a warm wind from Italy, but its warmth was lost on Mary. It felt like the burning touch of a glacier.

"Let's go back to the hotel," Mary said. "I'm feeling a little weak."

She would deliver around the New Year unless the baby was again premature.

A distant boom reached her, was echoed, again and again, by mountains. Another avalanche. She hoped it hadn't fallen on any of the brave Swiss who were trying to clear the roads.

She and Bysshe returned to the hotel through darkening streets. It was a fine place, rather expensive, though they could afford it now. Their circumstances had improved in the last year, though at cost.

Old Sir Bysshe had died, and left Bysshe a thousand pounds per year. Harriet Shelley had drowned, bricks in her pockets. Mary had given birth to a premature daughter who had lived only two weeks. She wondered about the child she carried—she had an intuition all was not well. Death, perhaps, was stalking her baby, was stalking them all.

In payment for what? Mary wondered. What sin had they committed?

She walked through Montreux's wet streets and thought of dead glass eyes, and grasping hands, and hair streaming like seaweed. Her daughter dying alone in her cradle at night, convulsing, twitching, eyes open and tiny red face torn with mortal terror.

When Mary had come to the cradle later to nurse the baby, she had thought it in an unusually deep sleep. She hadn't realized that death had come until after dawn, when the little corpse turned cold.

Death. She and Bysshe had kissed and coupled on her mother's grave, had shivered together at the gothic delights of *Vathek,* had whispered ghost stories to one another in the dead of night till Claire screamed with hysteria.

Somehow death had not really touched her before. She and Bysshe had crossed war-scarred France two years ago, sleeping in homes abandoned for fear of Cossacks, and somehow death had not intruded into their lives.

"Winter is coming," Bysshe said. "Do we wish to spend it in Geneva? I'd rather push on to Italy and be a happy salamander in the sun."

"I've had another letter from Mrs. Godwin."

Bysshe sighed. "England, then."

She sought his hand and squeezed it. Bysshe wanted the sun of Italy, but Bysshe was her sun, the blaze that kept her warm, kept her from despair. Death had not touched *him*. He flamed with life, with joy, with optimism.

She tried to stay in his radiance. Where his light banished the creeping shadows that followed her.

As they entered their hotel room they heard the wailing of an infant and found Claire trying to comfort her daughter Alba. "Where have you been?" Claire demanded. There were tears on her cheeks. "I fell asleep and dreamed you'd abandoned me! And then I cried out and woke the baby."

Bysshe moved to comfort her. Mary settled herself heavily onto a sofa.

In the small room in Montreux, with dark shadows creeping in the corners and the *vaudaire* driving against the shutters, Mary put her arms around her unborn child and willed the shade of death to keep away.

Bysshe stopped short in the midst of his afternoon promenade. "Great heavens," he said. His tone implied only mild surprise—he was so filled with life and certitude that he took most of life's shocks purely in stride.

When Mary looked up, she gasped and her heart gave a crash.

It was a barouche—*the* barouche. Vermilion wheels, liveried postboys wearing muddy slickers, armorial bearings on the door, the bulletproof top raised to keep out the storm. Baggage piled on platforms fore and aft.

Rolling past as Mary and Bysshe stood on the tidy Swiss sidewalk and stared.

CREDE BYRON, Mary thought viciously. As soon credit Lucifer.

The grey sky lowered as they watched the barouche grind past, steel-rimmed wheels thundering on the cobbles. And then a window dropped on its leather strap, and someone shouted something to the postboys. The words were lost in the *vaudaire*, but the postboys pulled the horses to a stop. The door opened and George appeared, jamming a round hat down over his auburn hair. His jacket was a little tight, and he appeared to have gained a stone or more since Mary had last seen him. He walked toward Bysshe and Mary, and Mary tried not to stiffen with fury at the sight of him.

"Mr. Omnibus! Tí kánete?"

"Very well, thank you."

"Miss Godwin." George bowed, clasped Mary's hand. She closed her fist, reminded herself that she hated him.

"I'm Mrs. Shelley now."

"My felicitations," George said.

George turned to Bysshe. "Are the roads clear to the west?" he asked. "I and my companion must push on to Geneva on a matter of urgency."

"The roads have been closed for three days," Bysshe said. "There have been both rockslides and avalanches near Chexbres."

"That's what they told me in Vevey. There was no lodging there, so I came here, even though it's out of our way." George pressed his lips together, a pale line. He looked over his shoulder at the coach, at the mountainside, at the dangerous weather. "We'll have to try to force our way through tomorrow," he said. "Though it will be damned hard."

"It shouldn't," Bysshe said. "Not in a heavy coach like that."

George looked grim. "It was unaccountably dangerous just getting here," he said.

"Stay till the weather is better," Bysshe said, smiling. "You can't be blamed if the weather holds you up."

Mary hated Bysshe for that smile, even though she knew he had reasons to be obliging.

Just as she had reasons for hating.

"Nay." George shook his head, and a little Scots fell out. "I cannae bide."

"You might make it on a mule."

"I have a lady with me." Shortly. "Mules are out of the question."

"A boat? ..."

"Perhaps if the lady is superfluous," Mary interrupted, "you could leave her behind, and carry out your errand on a mule, alone."

The picture was certainly an enjoyable one.

George looked at her, visibly mastered his unspoken reply, then shook his head.

"She must come."

"Lord Newstead," Mary went on, "would you like to see your daughter? She is not superfluous either, and she is here."

George glanced nervously at the coach, then back. "Is Claire here as well?"

"Yes."

George looked grim. "This is not ... a good time."

Bysshe summoned an unaccustomed gravity. "I think, my lord," Bysshe said, "there may never be a better time. You have not been within five hundred miles of your daughter since her birth. You are on an urgent errand and may not tarry—very well. But you must spend a night here, and can't press on till morning. There will never be a better moment."

George looked at him stony-eyed, then nodded. "What hotel?"

"La Royale."

He smiled. "Royal, eh? A pretty sentiment for the Genevan Republic."

"We're in Vaud, not Geneva."

"Still not over the border?" George gave another nervous glance over his shoulder. "I need to set a faster pace."

His long hair streamed in the wind as he stalked back to the coach. Mary could barely see a blonde head gazing cautiously from the window. She half-expected that the coach would drive on and she would never see George again, but instead the postboys turned the horses from the waterfront road into the town, toward the hotel.

Bysshe smiled purposefully and began to stride to the hotel. Mary followed, walking fast across the wet cobbles to keep up with him. "I can't but think that good will come of this," he said.

"I pray you're right."

Much pain, Mary thought, *however it turned out.*

George's new female was tall and blonde and pink-faced, though she walked hunched over as if embarrassed by her height, and took small, shy steps. She was perhaps in her middle twenties.

They met, embarrassingly, on the hotel's wide stair, Mary with Claire, Alba in Claire's arms. The tall blonde, lower lip outthrust haughtily, walked past them on the way to her room, her gaze passing blankly over them. Perhaps she hadn't been told who Alba's father was.

She had a maid with her and a pair of George's men, both of whom had pistols stuffed in their belts. For a wild moment Mary wondered if George had abducted her.

No, she decided, this was only George's theatricality. He didn't have his menagerie with him this time, no leopards or monkeys, so he dressed his postboys as bandits.

The woman passed. Mary felt Claire stiffen. "She looks like *you,*" Claire hissed.

Mary looked at the woman in astonishment. "She doesn't. Not at all."

"She does! Tall, blonde, fair eyes ..." Claire's own eyes filled with tears. "Why can't she be dark, like me?"

"Don't be absurd!" Mary seized her sister's hand, pulled her down the stairs. "Save the tears for later. They may be needed."

In the lobby Mary saw more of George's men carrying in luggage. Pásmány, the fencing master, had slung a carbine over one shoulder. Mary's mind whirled—perhaps this was an abduction after all.

Or perhaps the blonde's family—or husband—was in pursuit.

"This way." Bysshe's voice. He led them into one of the hotel's candlelit drawing rooms, closed the crystal-knobbed door behind them. A huge porcelain stove loomed over them.

George stood uncertain in the candlelight, elegant clothing over muddy boots. He looked at Claire and Alba stonily, then advanced, peered at the tiny form that Claire offered him.

"Your daughter Alba," Bysshe said, hovering at his shoulder.

George watched the child for a long, doubtful moment, his auburn hair hanging down his forehead. Then he straightened. "My offer rests, Miss Clairmont, on its previous terms."

Claire drew back, rested Alba on her shoulder. "Never," she said. She licked her lips. "It is too monstrous."

"Come, my lord," Bysshe said. He ventured to put a hand on George's shoulder. "Surely your demands are unreasonable."

"I offered to provide the child with means," George said, "to see that she is raised in a fine home, free from want, and among good people—friends of mine, who will offer her every advantage. I would take her myself but," hesitating, "my domestic conditions would not permit it."

Mary's heart flamed. "But at the cost of forbidding her the sight of her mother!" she said. "That is too cruel."

"The child's future will already be impaired by her irregular connections," George said. "Prolonging those connections could only do her further harm." His eyes flicked up to Claire. "Her mother can only lower her station, not raise it. She is best off with a proper family who can raise her with their own."

Claire's eyes flooded with tears. She turned away, clutching Alba to her. "I won't give her up!" she said. The child began to cry.

George folded his arms. "That settles matters. If you won't accept my offer, then there's an end." The baby's wails filled the air.

"Alba cries for her father," Bysshe said. "Can you not let her into your heart?"

A half-smile twitched across George's lips. "I have no absolute certainty that I *am* this child's father."

A keening sound came from Claire. For a wild, raging moment Mary looked for a weapon to plunge into George's breast. "Unnatural man!" she cried. "Can't you acknowledge the consequences of your own behavior?"

"On the contrary, I am willing to ignore the questionable situation in which I found Miss Clairmont and to care for the child completely. But only on my terms."

"I don't trust his promises!" Claire said. "He abandoned me in Munich without a penny!"

"We agreed to part," George said.

"If it hadn't been for Captain Austen's kindness, I would have starved."
She leaned on the door jamb for support, and Mary joined her and buoyed
her with an arm around her waist.

"You ran out into the night," George said. "You wouldn't take money."

"I'll tell her!" Claire drew away from Mary, dragged at the door, hauled
it open. "I'll tell your new woman!"

Fear leaped into George's eyes. "Claire!" He rushed to the door, seized
her arm as she tried to pass; Claire wrenched herself free and staggered into the
hotel lobby. Alba wailed in her arms. George's servants were long gone, but
hotel guests stared as if in tableaux, hats and walking-sticks half-raised. Fully
aware of the spectacle they were making, Mary, clumsy in pregnancy, inserted
herself between George and Claire. Claire broke for the stair, while George
danced around Mary like an awkward footballer. Mary rejoiced in the fact that
her pregnancy seemed only to make her more difficult to get around.

Bysshe put an end to it. He seized George's wrist in a firm grip. "You
can't stop us all, my lord," he said.

George glared at him, his look all fury and ice. "What d'ye want, then?"

Claire, panting and flushed, paused halfway up the stair. Alba's alarmed
shrieks echoed up the grand staircase.

Bysshe's answer was quick. "A competence for your daughter. Nothing
more."

"A thousand a year," George said flatly. "No more than that."

Mary's heart leaped at the figure that doubled the family's income.

Bysshe nodded. "That will do, my lord."

"I want nothing more to do with the girl than that. Nothing whatever."

"Call for pen and paper. And we can bring this to an end."

Two copies were made, and George signed and sealed them with his
signet before bidding them all a frigid good-night. The first payment was made
that night, one of George's men coming to the door carrying a valise that
clanked with gold. Mary gazed at it in amazement—why was George carrying so much?

"Have we done the right thing?" Bysshe wondered, looking at the valise
as Claire stuffed it under her bed. "This violence, this extortion?"

"We offered love," Mary said, "and he returned only finance. How else
could we deal with him?" She sighed. "And Alba will thank us."

Claire straightened and looked down at the bed. "I only wanted him to
pay," said Claire. "Any other considerations can go to the devil."

The *vaudaire* blew on, scarcely fainter than before. The water level was still
high. Dead fish still floated in the freshwater tide. "I would venture it," Bysshe
said, frowning as he watched the dancing *Ariel*, "but not with the children."

Children. Mary's smile was inward as she realized how real her new baby was to Bysshe. "We can afford to stay at the hotel a little longer," she said.

"Still—a reef in the mains'l would make it safe enough."

Mary paused a moment, perhaps to hear the cold summons of Harriet Shelley from beneath the water. There was no sound, but she shivered anyway. "No harm to wait another day."

Bysshe smiled at her hopefully. "Very well. Perhaps we'll have a chance to speak to George again."

"Bysshe, sometimes your optimism is ..." She shook her head. "Let us finish our walk."

They walked on through windswept morning streets. The bright sun glared off the white snow and deadly black ice that covered the surrounding high peaks. Soon the snow and ice would melt and threaten avalanche once more. "I am growing weary with this town," Bysshe said.

"Let's go back to our room and read *Chamouni,*" Mary suggested. Mr. Coleridge had been a guest of her father's, and his poem about the Alps a favorite of theirs now they were lodged in Switzerland.

Bysshe was working on writing another descriptive poem on the Vale of Chamouni—unlike Coleridge, he and Mary had actually seen the place—and as an homage to Coleridge, Bysshe was including some reworked lines from *Kubla Khan.*

The everlasting universe of things, she recited to herself, *flows through the mind.*

Lovely stuff. Bysshe's best by far.

On their return to the hotel they found one of George's servants waiting for them. "Lord Newstead would like to see you."

Ah, Mary thought. *He wants his gold back.*

Let him try to take it.

George waited in the same drawing room in which he'd made his previous night's concession. Despite the bright daylight the room was still lit by lamps—the heavy dark curtains were drawn against the *vaudaire.* George was standing straight as a whip in the center of the room, a dangerous light in his eyes. Mary wondered if this was how he looked in battle.

"Mr. Shelley," George said, and bowed, "I would like to hire your boat to take my party to Geneva."

Bysshe blinked. "I—" he began, then, "*Ariel* is small, only twenty-five feet. Your party is very large and—"

"The local commissaire visited me this morning," George interrupted. "He has forbidden me to depart Montreux. As it is vital for me to leave at once, I must find other means. And I am prepared to pay well for them."

Bysshe looked at Mary, then at George. Hesitated again. "I suppose it would be possible ..."

"Why is it," Mary demanded, "that you are forbidden to leave?"

George folded his arms, looked down at her. "I have broken no law. It is a ridiculous political matter."

Bysshe offered a smile. "If that's all, then …"

Mary interrupted. "If Mr. Shelley and I end up in jail as a result of this, I wonder how ridiculous it will seem."

Bysshe looked at her, shocked. "Mary!"

Mary kept her eyes on George. "Why should we help you?"

"Because …" He paused, ran a nervous hand through his hair. Nor used, Mary thought, to justifying himself.

"Because," he said finally, "I am assisting someone who is fleeing oppression."

"Fleeing a husband?"

"Husband?" George looked startled. "No—her husband is abroad and cannot protect her." He stepped forward, his color high, his nostrils flared like those of a warhorse. "She is fleeing the attentions of a seducer—a powerful man who has callously used her to gain wealth and influence. I intend to aid her in escaping his power."

Bysshe's eyes blazed. "Of *course* I will aid you!"

Mary watched this display of chivalry with a sinking heart. The masculine confraternity had excluded her, had lost her within its own rituals and condescension.

"I will pay you a further hundred—" George began.

"Please, my lord. I and my little boat are entirely at your service in this noble cause."

George stepped forward, clasped his hand. "Mr. Omnibus, I am in your debt."

The *vaudaire* wailed at the window. Mary wondered if it was Harriet's call, and her hands clenched into fists. She would resist the cry if she could.

Bysshe turned to Mary. "We must prepare." Heavy in her pregnancy, she followed him from the drawing room, up the stair, toward their own rooms. "I will deliver Lord Newstead and his lady to Geneva, and you and Claire can join me there when the roads are cleared. Or if weather is suitable I will return for you."

"I will go with you," Mary said. "Of course."

Bysshe seemed surprised that she would accompany him on this piece of masculine knight-errantry. "It may not be entirely safe on the lake," he said.

"I'll make it safer—you'll take fewer chances with me aboard. And if I'm with you, George is less likely to inspire you to run off to South America on some noble mission or other."

"I wouldn't do that." Mildly. "And I think you are being a little severe."

"What has George done for us that we should risk anything for him?"

"I do not serve him, but his lady."

"Of whom he has told you nothing. You don't even know her name. And in any case, you seem perfectly willing to risk *her* life on this venture."

Alba's cries sounded through the door of their room. Bysshe paused a moment, resignation plain in his eyes, then opened the door. "It's for Alba, really," he said. "The more contact between George and our little family, the better it may be for her. The better chance we will have to melt his heart."

He opened the door. Claire was holding her colicky child. Tears filled her black eyes. "Where have you been for so long? I was afraid you were gone forever!"

"You know better than that." Mary took the baby from her, the gesture so natural that sadness took a moment to come—the memory that she had held her own lost child this way, held it to her breast and felt the touch of its cold lips.

"And what is this about George?" Claire demanded.

"He wants me to take him down the lake," Bysshe said. "And Mary wishes to join us. You and Alba can remain here until the roads are clear."

Claire's voice rose to a shriek. *"No! Never!"* She lunged for Alba and snatched the girl from Mary's astonished arms. "You're going to abandon me— just like George! You're all going to Geneva to laugh at me!"

"Of course not," Bysshe said reasonably.

Mary stared at her sister, tried to speak, but Claire's cries trampled over her intentions.

"You're abandoning me! I'm useless to you—worthless! You'll soon have your own baby!"

Mary tried to comfort Claire, but it was hopeless. Claire screamed and shuddered and wept, convinced that she would be left forever in Montreux. In the end there was no choice but to take her along. Mary received mean satisfaction in watching Bysshe as he absorbed this reality, as his chivalrous, noble-minded expedition alongside the hero of Waterloo turned into a low family comedy, George and his old lover, his new lover, and his wailing bastard.

And ghosts. Harriet, lurking under the water. And their dead baby calling.

Ariel bucked like a horse on the white-topped waves as the *vaudaire* keened in the rigging. Frigid spray flew in Mary's face and her feet slid on slippery planking. Her heart thrashed into her throat. The boat seemed half-full of water. She gave a despairing look over her shoulder at the retreating rowboat they'd hired to bring them from the jetty to their craft.

"Bysshe!" she said. "This is hopeless."

"Better once we're under way. See that the cuddy will be comfortable for Claire and Alba."

"This is madness."

Bysshe licked joyfully at the freshwater spray that ran down his lips. "We'll be fine, I'm sure."

He was a much better sailor than she: she had to trust him. She opened the sliding hatch to the cuddy, the little cabin forward, and saw several inches of water sloshing in the bottom. The cushions on the little seats were soaked. Wearily, she looked up at Bysshe.

"We'll have to bail."

"Very well."

It took a quarter hour to bail out the boat, during which time Claire paced back and forth on the little jetty, Alba in her arms. She looked like a specter with her pale face peering out from her dark shawl.

Bysshe cast off the gaskets that reefed the mainsail to the boom, then jumped forward to the halyards and raised the sail on its gaff. The wind tore at the canvas with a sound like a cannonade, open-hand slaps against Mary's ears. The shrouds were taut as bowstrings. Bysshe reefed the sail down, hauled the halyards and topping lift again till the canvas was taut, lowered the lee-boards, then asked Mary to take the tiller while he cast *Ariel* off from its buoy.

Bysshe braced himself against the gunwale as he hauled on the mooring line, drawing *Ariel* up against the wind. When Bysshe cast off from the buoy the boat paid instantly off the wind and the sail filled with a rolling boom. Water surged under the boat's counter and suddenly, before Mary knew it, *Ariel* was flying fast. Fear closed a fist around her windpipe as the little boat heeled and the tiller almost yanked her arms from their sockets. She could hear Harriet's wails in the windsong. Mary dug her heels into the planks and hauled the tiller up to her chest, keeping *Ariel* up into the wind. Frigid water boiled up over the lee counter, pouring into the boat like a waterfall.

Bysshe leapt gracefully aft and released the mainsheet. The sail boomed out with a crash that rattled Mary's bones and the boat righted itself. Bysshe took the tiller from Mary, sheeted in, leaned out into the wind as the boat picked up speed. There was a grin on his face.

"Sorry!" he said. "I should have let the sheet go before we set out."

Bysshe tacked and brought *Ariel* into the wind near the jetty. The sail boomed like thunder as it spilled wind. Waves slammed the boat into the jetty. The mast swayed wildly. The stone jetty was at least four feet taller than the boat's deck. Mary helped Claire with the luggage—gold clanked heavily in one bag—then took Alba while Bysshe assisted Claire into the boat.

"It's *wet*," Claire said when she saw the cuddy.

"Take your heavy cloak out of your bags and sit on it," Mary said.

"This is *terrible*," Claire said, and lowered herself carefully into the cuddy.

"Go forrard," Bysshe said to Mary, "and push off from the jetty as hard as you can."

Forrard. Bysshe so enjoyed being nautical. Clumsy in skirts and pregnancy, Mary climbed atop the cuddy and did as she was asked. The booming sail filled, Mary snatched at the shrouds for balance, and *Ariel* leaped from the jetty like a stone from a child's catapult. Mary made her way across the tilting deck to the cockpit. Bysshe was leaning out to weather, his big hands controlling the tiller easily, his long fair hair streaming in the wind.

"I won't ask you to do that again," he said. "George should help from this point."

George and his lady would join the boat at another jetty—there was less chance that the authorities would intervene if they weren't seen where another Englishman was readying his boat.

Ariel raced across the waterfront, foam boiling under its counter. The second jetty—a wooden one—approached swiftly, with cloaked figures upon it. Bysshe rounded into the wind, canvas thundering, and brought *Ariel* neatly to the dock. George's men seized shrouds and a mooring line and held the boat in its place.

George's round hat was jammed down over his brows and the collar of his cloak was turned up, but any attempt at anonymity was wrecked by his famous laced boots. He seized a shroud and leaped easily into the boat, then turned to help his lady.

She had stepped back, frightened by the gunshot cracks of the luffing sail, the wild swings of the boom. Dressed in a blue silk dress, broad-brimmed bonnet, and heavy cloak, she frowned with her haughty lower lip, looking disdainfully at the little boat and its odd collection of passengers.

George reassured his companion. He and one of his men, the swordmaster Pásmány, helped her into the boat, held her arm as she ducked under the boom.

George grabbed the brim of his hat to keep the wind from carrying it away and performed hasty introductions. "Mr. and Mrs. Shelley. The Comtesse Laufenburg."

Mary strained her memory, trying to remember if she'd ever heard the name before. The comtesse smiled a superior smile and tried to be pleasant. "Enchanted to make cognizance of you," she said in French.

A baby wailed over the sound of flogging canvas. George straightened, his eyes a little wild.

"Claire is here?" he asked.

"She did not desire to be abandoned in Montreux," Mary said, trying to stress the word *abandoned.*

"My God!" George said. "I wish you had greater consideration of the … realities."

"Claire is free and may do as she wishes," Mary said.

George clenched his teeth. He took the comtesse by her arm and drew her toward the cuddy.

"The boat will be better balanced," Bysshe called after, "if the comtesse will sit on the weather side." *And perhaps,* Mary thought, *we won't capsize.*

George gave Bysshe a blank look. "The larboard side," Bysshe said helpfully. Another blank look.

"Hang it! The left."

"Very well."

George and the comtesse ducked down the hatchway. Mary would have liked to have eavesdropped on the comtesse's introduction to Claire, but the furious rattling sail obscured the phrases, if any. George came up, looking grim, and Pásmány began tossing luggage toward him. Other than a pair of valises, most of it was military: a familiar-looking pistol case, a pair of sabers, a brace of carbines. George stowed it all in the cuddy. Then Pásmány himself leaped into the boat, and George signaled all was ready. Bysshe placed George by the weather rail, and Pásmány squatted on the weather foredeck.

"If you gentlemen would push us off?" Bysshe said.

The sail filled and *Ariel* began to move fast, rising at each wave and thudding into the troughs. Spray rose at each impact. Bysshe trimmed the sail, the luff trembling just a little, the rest full and taut, then cleated the mainsheet down.

"A long reach down the length of the lake," Bysshe said with a smile. "Easy enough sailing, if a little hard on the ladies."

George peered out over the cuddy, his eyes searching the bank. The old castle of Chillon bulked ominously on the shore, just south of Montreux.

"When do we cross the border into Geneva?" George asked.

"Why does it matter?" Bysshe said. "Geneva joined the Swiss Confederation last year."

"But the administrations are not yet united. And the more jurisdictions that lie between the comtesse and her pursuers, the happier I will be."

George cast an uncomfortable look astern. With spray dotting his cloak, his hat clamped down on his head, his body disposed awkwardly on the weather side of the boat, George seemed thoroughly miserable and in an overwhelming flood of sudden understanding, Mary suddenly knew why. It was over for him. His noble birth, his fame, his entire life to this point—all was as naught Passion had claimed him for its own. His career had ended: there was no place for him in the army, in diplomatic circles, even in polite society. He'd thrown it all away in this mad impulse of passion.

He was an exile now, and the only people whom he could expect to associate with him were other exiles.

Like the exiles aboard *Ariel.*

Perhaps, Mary thought, he was only now realizing it. Poor George. She actually felt sorry for him.

The castle of Chillon fell astern, like a grand symbol of George's hopes, a world of possibility not realized.

"Beg pardon, my lord," she said, "but where do you intend to go?"

George frowned. "France, perhaps," he said. "The comtesse has ... some friends ... in France. England, if France won't suit, but we won't be able to stay there long. America, if necessary."

"Can the Prince Regent intervene on your behalf?"

George's smile was grim. "If he wishes. But he's subject to strange fits of morality, particularly if the sins in question remind him of his own. Prinny will *not* wish to be reminded of Mrs. Fitzherbert and Lady Hertford. He *does* wish to look upright in the eyes of the nation. And he has no loyalty to his friends, none at all." He gave a poised, slow-motion shrug. "Perhaps he will help, if the fit is on him. But I think not." He reached inside his greatcoat, patted an inside pocket. "Do you think I can light a cigar in this wind? If so, I hope it will not discomfort you, Mrs. Shelley."

He managed a spark in his strike-a-light, puffed madly till the tinder caught, then ignited his cigar and turned to Bysshe. "I found your poems, Mr. Omnibus. Your *Queen Mab* and *Alastor*. The latter of which I liked better, though I liked both well enough."

Bysshe looked at him in surprise. Wind whistled through the shrouds. "How did you find *Mab?* There were only seventy copies, and I'm certain I can account for each one."

George seemed pleased with himself. "There are few doors closed to me." Darkness clouded his face. "Or rather, *were.*" With a sigh. He wiped spray from his ear with the back of his hand.

"I'm surprised that you liked *Mab* at all," Bysshe said quickly, "as its ideas are so contrary to your own."

"You expressed them well enough. As a verse treatise of Mr. Godwin's political thought, I believed it done soundly—as soundly as such a thing *can* be done. And I think you can have it published properly now—it's hardly a threat to public order, Godwin's thought being so out of fashion even among radicals." He drew deliberately on his cigar, then waved it. The wind tore the cigar smoke from his mouth in little wisps. *"Alastor,* though better poetry, seemed in contrast to have little thought behind it. I never understood what that fellow was *doing* on the boat—was it a metaphor for life? I kept waiting for something to *happen.*"

Mary bristled at George's condescension. What are *you* doing on this little boat? she wanted to ask.

Bysshe, however, looked apologetic. "I'm writing better things now."

"He's writing *wonderful* things now," Mary said. "An ode to Mont Blanc. An essay on Christianity. A hymn to intellectual beauty."

George gave her an amused look. "Mrs. Shelley's tone implies that, to me, intellectual beauty is entirely a stranger, but she misunderstands my point. I found it remarkable that the same pen could produce both *Queen Mab* and *Alastor,* and have no doubt that so various a talent will produce very good work in the poetry line—provided," nodding to Bysshe, "that Mr. Shelley continues in it, and doesn't take up engineering again, or chemistry." He grinned. "Or become a sea captain."

"He is and remains a poet," Mary said firmly. She used a corner of her shawl to wipe spray from her cheek.

"Who else do you like, my lord?" Bysshe asked.

"Poets, you mean? Scott, above all. Shakespeare, who is sound on political matters as well as having a magnificent ... shall I call it a *stride?* Burns, the great poet of my country. And our Laureate."

"Mr. Southey was kind to me when we met," Bysshe said. "And Mrs. Southey made wonderful tea-cakes. But I wish I admired his work more." He looked up. "What do you think of Milton? The Maie and I read him constantly."

George shrugged. "Dour Puritan fellow. I'm surprised you can stand him at all."

"His verse is glorious. And he wasn't a Puritan, but an Independent, like Cromwell—his philosophy was quite unorthodox. He believed, for example, in plural marriage."

George's eyes glittered. "Did he now."

"Ay. And his Satan is a magnificent creation, far more interesting than any of his angels or his simpering pedantic Christ. That long, raging fall from grace, into darkness visible."

George's brows knit. Perhaps he was contemplating his own long fall from the Heaven of polite society. His eyes turned to Mary.

"And how is the originator of Mr. Shelley's political thought? How does your father, Mrs. Shelley?"

"He is working on a novel. An important work."

"I am pleased to hear it. Does he progress?"

Mary was going to answer simply "Very well," but Bysshe's answer came first. "Plagued by lack of money," he said. "We will be going to England to succor him after this, ah, errand is completed."

"Your generosity does you credit," George said, and then resentment entered his eyes and his lip curled. "Of course, you will be able to better afford it, now."

Bysshe's answer was mild. "Mr. Godwin lives partly with our support, but he will not speak to us since I eloped with his daughter. You will not acknowledge Alba, but at least you've been ... persuaded ... to do well by her."

George preferred not to rise to this, settled instead for clarification. "You support a man who won't acknowledge you?"

"It is not my father-in-law I support, but rather the author of *Political Justice.*"

"A nice discernment," George observed. "Perhaps over-nice."

"One does what goodness one can. And one hopes people will respond." Looking at George, who smiled cynically around his cigar.

"Your charity speaks well for you. But perhaps Mr. Godwin would have greater cause to finish his book if poverty were not being made so convenient for him."

Mary felt herself flushing red. But Bysshe's reply again was mild. "It isn't that simple. Mr. Godwin has dependents, and the public that once cerebrated his thought has, alas, forgotten him. His novel may retrieve matters. But a fine thing such as this work cannot be rushed—not if it is to have the impact it deserves."

"I will bow to your expertise in matters of literary production. But still ... to support someone who will not even speak to you—that is charity indeed. And it does not speak well for Mr. Godwin's gratitude."

"My father is a great man!" Mary knew she was speaking hotly, and she bit back on her anger. "But he judges by a ... a very high standard of morality. He will accept support from a sincere admirer, but he has not yet understood the depth of sentiment between Bysshe and myself, and believes that Bysshe has done my reputation harm—not," flaring again, "that I would care if he had."

Ariel thudded into a wave trough, and George winced at the impact. He adjusted his seat on the rail and nodded. "Mr. Godwin will accept money from an admirer, but not letters from an in-law. And Mr. Shelley will support the author of *Political Justice,* but not *his* in-laws."

"And you," Mary said, "will support a blackmailer, but not a daughter."

George's eyes turned to stone. Mary realized she had gone too far for this small boat and close company.

"Gentlemen, it's cold," she announced. "I will withdraw."

She made her way carefully into the cuddy. The tall comtesse was disposed uncomfortably, on wet cushions, by the hatch, the overhead planking brushing the top of her bonnet. Her gaze was mild, but her lip was haughty. There was a careful three inches between her and Claire, who was nursing Alba and, clearly enough, a grudge.

Mary walked past them to the peak, sat carefully on a wet cushion near Claire. Their knees collided every time *Ariel* fell down a wave. The cuddy smelled of wet stuffing and stale water. There was still water sluicing about on the bottom.

Mary looked at Claire's baby and felt sadness like an ache in her breast.

Claire regarded her resentfully. "The French bitch hates us," she whispered urgently. "Look at her expression."

Mary wished Claire had kept her voice down. Mary leaned out to look at the comtesse, managed a smile. *"Vous parlez anglais?"* she asked.

"Non. Je regrette. Parles-tu francais?" The comtesse had a peculiar accent. As, with a name like Laufenburg, one might expect.

Pleasant of her, though, to use the intimate *tu. "Je comprends un peu."* Claire's French was much better than hers, but Claire clearly had no interest in conversation.

The comtesse looked at the nursing baby. A shadow flitted across her face. "My own child," in French, "I was forced to leave behind."

"I'm sorry." For a moment Mary hated the comtesse for having a child to leave, that and for the abandonment itself.

No. Bysshe, she remembered, had left his own children. It did not make one unnatural. Sometimes there were circumstances.

Speech languished after this unpromising beginning. Mary leaned her head against the planking and tried to sleep, sadly aware of the cold seep of water up her skirts. The boat's movement was too violent to be restful, but she composed herself deliberately for sleep. Images floated through her mind: the great crumbling keep of Chillon, standing above the surging grey water like the setting of one of "Monk" Lewis's novels; a grey cat eating a blushing rose; a figure, massive and threatening, somehow both George and her father Godwin, flinging back the bed-curtains to reveal, in the bright light of morning, the comtesse Laufenburg's placid blonde face with its outthrust, Habsburg lip.

Habsburg. Mary sat up with a cry and banged her skull on the deckhead.

She cast a wild look at Claire and the comtesse, saw them both drowsing, Alba asleep in Claire's lap. The boat was rolling madly in a freshening breeze; there were ominous, threatening little shrieks of wind in the rigging. The cuddy stank badly.

Mary made her way out of the cuddy, clinging to the sides of the hatch as the boat sought to pitch her out. Bysshe was holding grimly to the tiller with one big hand, controlling the sheet with the other while spray soaked his coat; George and Pásmány were hanging to the shrouds to keep from sliding down the tilted deck.

Astern was Lausanne, north of the lake, and the Cornettes to the south; and Mont Billiat, looming over the valley of the Dranse to the south, was right abeam: they were smack in the middle of the lake, with the *vaudaire* wind funneling down the valley, stronger than ever with the mountain boundary out of the way.

Mary seized the rail; hauled herself up the tilting deck toward George. "I know your secret," she said. "I know who your woman is."

George's face ran with spray; his auburn hair was plastered to the back of his neck. He fixed her with eyes colder than the glaciers of Mont Blanc. "Indeed," he said.

"Marie-Louise of the house of Habsburg." Hot anger pulsed through her, burned against the cold spindrift on her face. "Former Empress of the French!"

Restlessly, George turned his eyes away. "Indeed," he said again.

Mary seized a shroud and dragged herself to the rail next to him. Bysshe watched in shock as Mary shouted into the wind. "Her husband abroad! Abroad, forsooth—all the way to St. Helena! Forced to leave her child behind, because her father would never let Napoleon's son out of his control for an instant. Even a Habsburg lip—my God!"

"Very clever, Miss Godwin. But I believe you have divined my sentiments on the subject of clever women." George gazed ahead, toward Geneva. "Now you see why I wish to be away."

"I see only vanity!" Mary raged. "Colossal vanity! You can't stop fighting Napoleon even now! Even when the battlefield is only a bed!"

George glared at her. "Is it my damned fault that Napoleon could never keep his women?"

"It's your damned fault that *you* keep her!"

George opened his mouth to spit out a reply and then the *vaudaire*, like a giant hand, took *Ariel's* mast in its grasp and slammed the frail boat over. Bysshe cried out and hauled the tiller to his chest and let the mainsheet go, all far too late. The deck pitched out from under Mary's heels and she clung to the shroud for dear life. Pásmány shouted in Hungarian. There was a roar as the sail hit the water. The lake foamed over the lee rail and the wind tore Mary's breath away. There were screams from the cuddy as water poured into the little cabin.

"Halyards and topping lift!" Bysshe gasped. He was clinging to the weather rail: a breaker exploded in his face and he gasped for air. "Let 'em go!"

If the sail filled with water all was lost. Mary let go of the shroud and palmed her way across the vertical deck. Freezing lakewater clutched at her ankles. Harriet Shelley shrieked her triumph in Mary's ears like the wind. Mary lurched forward to the mast, flung the halyard and topping lift off their cleats. The sail sagged free, empty of everything but the water that poured onto its canvas surface, turning it into a giant weight that would drag the boat over. Too late.

"Save the ladies, George!" Bysshe called. His face was dead-white but his voice was calm. "I can't swim!"

Water boiled up Mary's skirts. She could feel the dead weight dragging her down as she clutched at George's leg and hauled herself up the deck. She screamed as her unborn child protested, a gouging pain deep in her belly.

George raged wildly. "Damn it, Shelley, what can I *do?*" He had a leg over one of the shrouds; the other was Mary's support. The wind had taken his hat and his cloak rattled around him like wind-filled canvas.

"Cut the mast free!"

George turned to Mary. "My sword! Get it from the cabin!"

Mary looked down and into the terrified black eyes of Claire, half-out of the cuddy. She held a wailing Alba in her arms. "Take the baby!" she shrieked.

"Give me a sword!" Mary said. A wave broke over the boat, soaking them all in icy rain. Mary thought of Harriet smiling, her hair trailing like seaweed.

"Save my baby!"

"The *sword!* Byron's *sword! Give it!*" Mary clung to George's leg with one hand and thrust the crying babe away with the other.

"*I hate you!*" Claire shrieked, but she turned and fumbled for George's sword. She held it up out of the hatch, and Mary took the cut steel hilt in her hand and drew it rasping from the scabbard. She held it blindly above her head and felt George's firm hand close over hers and take the sabre away. The pain in her belly was like a knife. Through the boat and her spine she felt the thudding blows as George hacked at the shrouds, and then there was a rending as the mast splintered and *Ariel*, relieved of its top-hamper, swung suddenly upright.

Half the lake seemed to splash into the boat as it came off its beam-ends. George pitched over backwards as *Ariel* righted itself, but Mary clung to his leg and kept him from going into the lake while he dragged himself to safety over the rail.

Another wave crashed over them. Mary clutched at her belly and moaned. The pain was ebbing. The boat pirouetted on the lake as the wind took it, and then *Ariel* jerked to a halt. The wreckage of the mast was acting as a sea anchor, moderating the wave action, keeping the boat stable. Alba's screams floated high above *Ariel's* remains.

Wood floats, Mary remembered dully. And *Ariel* was wood, no matter how much water slopped about in her bottom.

Shelley staggered to his feet, shin-deep in lake water. "By God, George," he gasped. "You've saved us."

"By God," George answered, "so I have." Mary looked up from the deck to see George with the devil's light in his eyes, his color high and his sabre in his hand. So, she reckoned, he must have seemed to Napoleon at Genappe. George bent and peered into the cuddy.

"Are the ladies all right?"

"Je suis bien, merci." From the Austrian princess.

"Damn you to hell, George!" Claire cried. George only grinned.

"I see we are well," he said.

And then Mary felt the warm blood running down the insides of her legs, and knew that George was wrong.

Mary lay on a bed in the farmhouse sipping warm brandy. Reddening cloths were packed between her legs. The hemorrhage had not stopped, though at least there was no pain. Mary could feel the child moving within her, as if struggling in its terror. Over the click of knitting needles, she could hear the voices of the men in the kitchen, and smell George's cigar.

The large farm, sitting below its pastures that stretched up the Noirmont, was owned by a white-mustached old man named Fleury, a man who seemed incapable of surprise or confusion even when armed men arrived at his doorstep, carrying between them a bleeding woman and a sack filled with gold. He turned Mary over to his wife, hitched up his trousers, put his hat on, and went to St. Prex to find a doctor.

Madame Fleury, a large woman unflappable as her husband, tended Mary and made her drink a brandy toddy while she sat by Mary and did her knitting.

When Fleury returned, his news wasn't good. The local surgeon had gone up the road to set the bones of some workmen caught in an avalanche—perhaps there would be amputations—but he would return as soon as he could. The road west to Geneva was still blocked by the slide; the road east to Lausanne had been cleared. George seemed thoughtful at the news. His voice echoed in from the kitchen. "Perhaps the chase will simply go past," he said in English.

"What sort of pursuit do you anticipate?" Bysshe asked. "Surely you don't expect the Austrian Emperor to send his troops into Switzerland."

"Stranger things have happened," George said. "And it may not be the Emperor's own people after us—it might be Neipperg, acting on his own."

Mary knew she'd heard the name before, and tried to recall it. But Bysshe said, "The general? Why would he be concerned?"

There was cynical amusement in George's voice. "Because he's her highness's former lover! I don't imagine he'd like to see his fortune run away."

"Do you credit him with so base a motive?"

George laughed. "In order to prevent Marie-Louise from joining Bonaparte, Prince Metternich *ordered* von Neipperg to leave his wife and to seduce her highness—and that one-eyed scoundrel was only too happy to comply. His reward was to be the co-rulership of Parma, of which her highness was to be Duchess."

"Are you certain of this?"

"Metternich told me at his dinner table over a pipe of tobacco. And Neipperg *boasted* to me, sir!" A sigh, almost a snarl, came from George. "My heart wrung at his words, Mr. Shelley. For I had already met her highness and—" Words failed him for a moment. "I determined to rescue her from Neipperg's clutches, though all the Hungarian Grenadiers of the Empire stood in the way!"

"That was most admirable, my lord," Bysshe said quietly.

Claire's voice piped up. "Who is this Neipperg?"

"Adam von Neipperg is a cavalry officer who defeated Murat," Bysshe said. "That's all I know of him."

George's voice was thoughtful. "He's the best the Austrians have. Quite the *beau sabreur,* and a diplomat as well. He persuaded Crown Prince Bernadotte to switch sides before the battle of Leipzig. And yes, he defeated Murat on the field of Tolentino, a few weeks before Waterloo. Command of the Austrian army was another of Prince Metternich's rewards for his ... services."

Murat, Mary knew, was Napoleon's great cavalry general. Neipperg, the best Austrian cavalryman, had defeated Murat, and now Britain's greatest horseman had defeated Napoleon *and* Neipperg, one on the battlefield and both in bed.

Such a competitive little company of cavaliers, she thought. Madame Fleury's knitting needles clacked out a complicated pattern.

"You think he's going to come after you?" Bysshe asked.

"*I* would," simply. "And neither he nor I would care what the Swiss think about it. And he'll find enough officers who will want to fight for the, ah, *honor* of their royal family. And he certainly has scouts or agents among the Swiss looking for me—surely one of them visited the commissaire of Montreux."

"I see." Mary heard the sound of Bysshe rising from his seat. "I must see to Mary."

He stepped into the bedroom, sat on the edge of the bed, took her hand. Madame Fleury barely looked up from her knitting.

"Are you better, Pecksie?"

"Nothing has changed." *I'm still dying,* she thought.

Bysshe sighed. "I'm sorry," he said, "to have exposed you to such danger. And now I don't know what to do."

"And all for so little."

Bysshe was thoughtful. "Do you think liberty is so little? And Byron—the voice of monarchy and reaction—fighting for freedom! Think of it!"

My life is bleeding away, Mary thought incredulously, *and his child with it.* There was poison in her voice when she answered.

"This isn't about the freedom of a woman, it's about the freedom of one man to do what he wants."

Bysshe frowned at her.

"He can't love," Mary insisted. "He felt no love for his wife, or for Claire." Bysshe tried to hush her—her voice was probably perfectly audible in the kitchen. But it was pleasing for her not to give a damn.

"It's not love he feels for that poor woman in the cellar," she said. "His passions are entirely concerned with himself—and now that he can't exorcise them on the battlefield, he's got to find other means."

"Are you certain?"

"He's a mad whirlwind of destruction! Look what he did to Claire. And now he's wrecked *Ariel*, and he may yet involve us all in a battle—with Austrian cavalry, forsooth! He'll destroy us all if we let him."

"Perhaps it will not come to that."

George appeared in the door. He was wrapped in a blanket and carried a carbine, and if he was embarrassed by what he'd heard, he failed to display it. "With your permission, Mr. Shelley, I'm going to try to sink your boat. It sits on a rock just below our location, a pistol pointed at our head."

Bysshe looked at Mary. "Do as you wish."

"I'll give you privacy, then." And pointedly closed the door.

Mary heard his bootsteps march out, the outside door open and close. She put her hand on Bysshe's arm. *I am bleeding to death,* she thought. "Promise me you will take no part in anything," she said. "George will try to talk you into defending the princess—he knows you're a good shot."

"But what of Marie-Louise? To be dragged back to Austria by force of arms—what a prospect! An outrage, inhuman and degrading."

I am bleeding to death, Mary thought. But she composed a civil reply. "Her condition saddens me. But she was born a pawn and has lived a pawn her entire life. However this turns out, she will be a pawn either of George or of Metternich, and we cannot change that. It is the evil of monarchy and tyranny that has made her so. We may be thankful we were not born among her class."

There were tears in Bysshe's eyes. "Very well. If you think it best, I will not lift a hand in this."

Mary put her arms around him, held herself close to his warmth. She clenched trembling hands behind his back.

Soon, she thought, *I will lack the strength to do even this. And then I will die.*

There was a warm and spreading lake between her legs. She felt very drowsy as she held Bysshe, the effects of the brandy, and she closed her eyes and tried to rest. Bysshe stroked her cheek and hair. Mary, for a moment, dreamed.

She dreamed of pursuit, a towering, shrouded figure stalking her over the lake—but the lake was frozen, and as Mary fled across the ice she found other people standing there, people to whom she ran for help only to discover them all dead, frozen in their places and covered with frost. Terrified, she ran among them, seeing to her further horror that she knew them all: her mother and namesake; and Mr. Godwin; and George, looking at her insolently with eyes of black ice; and lastly the figure of Harriet Shelley, a woman she had never met in life but who Mary knew at once. Harriet stood rooted to a patch of ice and held in her arms the frost-swathed figure of a child. And despite the rime that covered the tiny face, Mary knew at once, and with agonized despair, just whose child Harriet carried so triumphantly in her arms.

She woke, terror pounding in her heart. There was a gunshot from outside. She felt Bysshe stiffen. Another shot. And then the sound of pounding feet.

"They're here, damn it!" George called. "And my shot missed!"

Gunfire and the sound of hammering swirled through Mary's perceptions. Furniture was shifted, doors barricaded, weapons laid ready. The shutters had already been closed against the *vaudaire*, so no one had to risk himself securing the windows. Claire and Alba came into Mary's room, the both of them screaming; and Mary, not giving a damn any longer, sent them both out. George put them in the cellar with the Austrian princess—Mary was amused that they seemed doomed to share quarters together. Bysshe, throughout, only sat on the bed and held Mary in his arms. He seemed calm, but his heart pounded against her ear. M. Fleury appeared, loading an old Charleville musket as he offhandedly explained that he had served in one of Louis XVI's mercenary Swiss regiments. His wife put down her knitting needles, poured buckshot into her apron pockets, and went off with him to serve as his loader. Afterwards Mary wondered if that particular episode, that vision of the old man with his gun and powder horn, had been a dream—but no, Madame Fleury was gone, her pockets filled with lead.

Eventually the noise died away. George came in with his Mantons stuffed in his belt, looking pleased with himself. "I think we stand well," he said. "This place is fine as a fort. At Waterloo we held Hougoumont and La Haye Sainte against worse—and Neipperg will have no artillery. The odds aren't bad—I counted only eight of them." He looked at Bysshe. "Unless you are willing to join us, Mr. Shelley, in defense of her highness's liberty."

Bysshe sat up. "I wish no man's blood on my hands." Mary rejoiced at the firmness in his voice.

"I will not argue against your conscience, but if you won't fight, then perhaps you can load for me?"

"What of Mary?" Bysshe asked.

Indeed, Mary thought. *What of me?*

"Can we arrange for her, and for Claire and Alba, to leave this house?"

George shook his head. "They don't dare risk letting you go—you'd just inform the Swiss authorities. I could negotiate a cease-fire to allow you to become their prisoners, but then you'd be living in the barn or the outdoors instead of more comfortably in here." He looked down at Mary. "I do not think we should move your lady in any case. Here in the house it is safe enough."

"But what if there's a battle? My God—there's already been shooting!"

"No one was hurt, you'll note—though if I'd had a Baker or a jäger rifle instead of my puisny little carbine, I daresay I'd have dropped one of them. No—what will happen now is that they'll either try an assault, which will take a while to organize, because they're all scattered out watching the house, and which will cost them dearly in the end ... or they'll wait. They don't know how many people we have in here, and they'll be cautious on that account. We're inside, with plenty of food and fuel and ammunition, and they're in the outdoors facing unseasonably cold weather. And the longer they wait, the more likely it will be that our local Swiss yeomen will discover them, and then ..." He gave a low laugh. "Austrian soldiers have never fared well in Switzerland, not since the days of William Tell. Our Austrian friends will be arrested and imprisoned."

"But the surgeon? Will they not let the surgeon pass?"

"I can't say."

Bysshe stared. "My God! Can't you speak to them?"

"I will ask if you like. But I don't know what a surgeon can do that we cannot."

Bysshe looked desperate. "There must be something that will stop the bleeding!"

Yes, Mary thought. *Death. Harriet has won.*

George gazed down at Mary with thoughtful eyes. "A Scotch midwife would sit her in a tub of icewater."

Bysshe stiffened like a dog on point. "Is there ice? Is there an ice cellar?" He rushed out of the room. Mary could hear him stammering out frantic questions in French, then Fleury's offhand reply. When Bysshe came back he looked stricken. "There is an icehouse, but it's out behind the barn."

"And in enemy hands." George sighed. "Well, I will ask if they will permit Madame Fleury to bring ice into the house, and pass the surgeon through when he comes."

George left the room and commenced a shouted conversation in French with someone outside. Mary winced at the volume of George's voice. The voice outside spoke French with a harsh accent.

No, she understood. They would not permit ice or a surgeon to enter a house.

"They suspect a plot, I suppose," George reported. He stood wearily in the doorway. "Or they think one of my men is wounded."

"They want to make you watch someone die," Mary said. "And hope it will make you surrender."

George looked at her. "Yes, you comprehend their intent," he said. "That is precisely what they want." Bysshe looked horrified.

George's look turned intent. "And what does Mistress Mary want?"

Mary closed her eyes. "Mistress Mary wants to live, and to hell with you all."

George laughed, a low and misanthropic chuckle. "Very well. Live you shall—and I believe I know the way."

He returned to the other room, and Mary heard his raised voice again. He was asking, in French, what the intruders wanted, and in passing comparing their actions to Napoleon's abduction of the Duc d'Enghien, justly abhorred by all nations.

"A telling hit," Mary said. "Good old George." She wrapped her two small pale hands around one of Bysshe's big ones.

The same voice answered, demanding that Her Highness the Duchess of Parma be surrendered. George returned that her highness was here of her own free will, and that she commanded that they withdraw to their own borders and trouble her no more. The emissary said his party was acting for the honor of Austria and the House of Habsburg. George announced that he felt free to doubt that their shameful actions were in any way honorable, and he was prepared to prove it, *corps-à-corps,* if *Feldmarschall-leutnant* von Neipperg was willing to oblige him.

"My God!" Bysshe said. "He's calling the blackguard out!"

Mary could only laugh. A duel, fought for an Austrian princess and Mary's bleeding womb.

The other asked for time to consider. George gave it.

"This neatly solves our dilemma, don't it?" he said after he returned. "If I beat Neipperg, the rest of those German puppies won't have direction— they'd be on the road back to Austria. Her royal highness and I will be able to make our way to a friendly country. No magistrates, no awkward questions, and a long head start." He smiled. "And all the ice in the world for Mistress Mary."

"And if you lose?" Bysshe asked.

"It ain't to be thought of. I'm a master of the sabre, I practice with Pásmány almost daily, and whatever Neipperg's other virtues I doubt he can compare with me in the art of the sword. The only question," he turned thoughtful, "is whether we can trust his offer. If there's treachery ..."

"Or if he insists on pistols!" Mary found she couldn't resist pointing this out. "You didn't precisely cover yourself with glory the last time I saw you shoot."

George only seemed amused. "Neipperg only has one eye—I doubt he's much of a shot, either. My second would have to insist on a sabre fight," and here he smiled, *"pour l'honneur de la cavalerie."*

Somehow Mary found this satisfying. "Go fight, George. I know you love your legend more than you ever loved that Austrian girl—and this will make a nice end to it."

George only chuckled again, while Bysshe looked shocked. "Truthful Mistress Mary," George said. "Never without your sting."

"I see no point in politeness from this position."

"You would have made a good soldier, Mrs. Shelley."

Longing fell upon Mary. "I would have made a better mother," she said, and felt tears sting her eyes.

"God, Maie!" Bysshe cried. "What I would not give!" He bent over her and began to weep.

It was, Mary considered, about time, and then reflected that death had made her satirical.

George watched for a long moment, then withdrew. Mary could hear his boots pacing back and forth in the kitchen, and then a different, younger voice called from outside.

The *Feldmarschall-leutnant* had agreed to the encounter. He, the new voice, was prepared to present himself as von Neipperg's second.

"A soldier all right," George commented. "Civilian clothes, but he's got that sprig of greenery that Austrian troops wear in their hats." His voice lifted. "That's far enough, laddie!" He switched to French and said that his second would be out shortly. Then his bootsteps returned to Mary's rooms and put a hand on Bysshe's shoulder.

"Mr. Shelley," he said, "I regret this intrusion, but I must ask—will you do me the honor of standing my second in this affaire?"

"Bysshe!" Mary cried. "Of course not!"

Bysshe blinked tear-dazzled eyes but managed to speak clearly enough. "I'm totally opposed to the practice. It's vicious and wasteful and utterly without moral foundation. It reeks of death and the dark ages and ruling-class affectation."

George's voice was gentle. "There are no other gentlemen here," he said. "Pásmány is a servant, and I can't see sending our worthy M. Fleury out to negotiate with those little noblemen. And—" He looked at Mary. "Your lady must have her ice and her surgeon."

Bysshe looked stricken. "I know nothing of how to manage these en-counters," he said. "I would not do well by you. If you were to fall as a result of my bungling, I should never forgive myself."

"I will tell you what to say, and if he doesn't agree, then bring negotia-tions to a close."

"Bysshe," Mary reminded, "you said you would have nothing to do with this."

Bysshe wiped tears from his eyes and looked thoughtful.

"Don't you see this is theater?" Mary demanded. "George is adding this scene to his legend—he doesn't give a damn for anyone here!"

George only seemed amused. "You are far from death, madam, I think, to show such spirit," he said. "Come, Mr. Shelley! Despite what Mary thinks, a fight with Neipperg is the only way we can escape without risking the ladies."

"No," Mary said.

Bysshe looked thoroughly unhappy. "Very well," he said. "For Mary's sake, I'll do as you ask, provided I do no violence myself. But I should say that I resent being placed in this ... *extraordinary* position in the first place."

Mary settled for glaring at Bysshe.

More negotiations were conducted through the window, and then Bysshe, after receiving a thorough briefing, straightened and brushed his jacket, brushed his knees, put on his hat, and said goodbye to Mary. He was very pale under his freckles.

"Don't forget to point out," George said, "that if von Neipperg attempts treachery, he will be instantly shot dead by my men firing from this house."

"Quite."

He left Mary in her bed. George went with him, to pull away the furni-ture barricade at the front door.

Mary realized she wasn't about to lie in bed while Bysshe was outside risking his neck. She threw off the covers and went to the window. Unbarred the shutter, pushed it open slightly.

Wet coursed down her legs.

Bysshe was holding a conversation with a stiff young man in an over-coat. After a few moments, Bysshe returned and reported to George. Mary, feeling like a guilty child, returned to her bed.

"Baron von Strickow—that's Neipperg's second—was taken with your notion of the swordfight *pour la cavalerie*, but insists the fight should be on horseback." He frowned. "They know, of course, that you haven't a horse with you."

"No doubt they'd offer me some nag or other." George thought for a moment. "Very well. I find the notion of a fight on horseback too piquant quite to ignore—tell them that if they insist on such a fight, they must bring forward six saddled horses, and that I will pick mine first, and Neipperg second."

"Very well."

Bysshe returned to the negotiations, and reported back that all had been settled. "With ill grace, as regards your last condition. But he conceded it was fair." Bysshe returned to Mary's room, speaking to George over his shoulder. "Just as well you're doing this on horseback. The yard is wet and slippery— poor footing for sword work."

"I'll try not to do any quick turns on horseback, either." George stepped into the room, gave Mary a glance, then looked at Bysshe. "Your appreciation of our opponents?"

"The Baron was tired and mud-covered. He's been riding hard. I don't imagine the rest of them are any fresher." Bysshe sat by Mary and took her hand. "He wouldn't shake my hand until he found out my father was a baronet. And then I wouldn't shake his."

"Good fellow!"

Bysshe gave a self-congratulatory look. "I believe it put him out of countenance."

George was amused. "These kraut-eaters make me look positively democratic." He left to give Pásmány his carbine and pistols—"the better to keep Neipperg honest."

"What of the princess?" Mary wondered. "Do you suppose he will bother to tell her of these efforts on her behalf?"

Shortly thereafter came the sound of the kitchen trap being thrown open, and George's bootheels descending to the cellar. Distant French tones, the sound of female protest, George's calm insistence. Claire's furious shrieks. George's abrupt reply, and then his return to the kitchen.

George appeared in the door, clanking in spurs and with a sword in his hand. Marie-Louise, looking pale, hovered behind him.

Mary looked up at Bysshe. "You won't have to participate in this any longer, will you?"

George answered for him. "I'd be obliged if Mr. Shelley would help me select my horse. Then you can withdraw to the porch—but if there's treachery, be prepared to barricade the door again."

Bysshe nodded. "Very well." He rose and looked out the window. "The horses are coming, along with the Baron and a one-eyed man."

George gave a cursory look out the window. "That's the fellow. He lost the eye at Neerwinden—French sabre cut." His voice turned inward. "I'll try to attack from his blind side—perhaps he'll be weaker there."

Bysshe was more interested in the animals. "There are three white horses. What are they?"

"Lipizzaners of the royal stud," George said. "The Roman Caesars rode 'em, or so the Austrians claim. Small horses by the standard of our English hunters, but strong and very sturdy. Bred and trained for war." He flashed a smile. "They'll do for me, I think."

He stripped off his coat and began to walk toward the door, but recollected, at the last second, the cause of the fight and returned to Marie-Louise. He put his arms around her, murmured something, and kissed her cheek. Then, with a smile, he walked into the other room. Bysshe, deeply unhappy, followed. And then Mary, ignoring the questioning eyes of the Austrian princess, worked her way out of bed and went to the window.

From the window Mary watched as George took his time with the horses, examining each minutely, discoursing on their virtues with Bysshe, checking their shoes and eyes as if he were buying them. The Austrians looked stiff and disapproving. Neipperg was a tall, bull-chested man, handsome despite the eyepatch, with a well-tended halo of hair.

Perhaps George dragged the business out in order to nettle his opponent.

George mounted one of the white horses and trotted it round the yard for a brief while, then repeated the experiment with a second Lipizzaner. Then he went back to the first and declared himself satisfied.

Neipperg, seeming even more rigid than before, took the second horse, the one George had rejected. Perhaps it was his own, Mary thought.

Bysshe retreated to the front porch of the farmhouse, Strickow to the barn, and the two horsemen to opposite ends of the yard. Both handled their horses expertly. Bysshe asked each if he were ready, and received a curt nod.

Mary's legs trembled. She hoped she wouldn't fall. She had to see it. *"Un,"* Strickow called out in a loud voice. *"Deux. Trois!"* Mary had expected the combatants to dash at each other, but they were too cautious, too professional—instead each goaded his beast into a slow trot and held his sabre with the hilt high, the blade dropping across the body, carefully on guard. Mary noticed that George was approaching on his opponent's blind right side. As they came together there were sudden flashes of silver, too fast for the eye to follow, and the sound of ringing steel.

Then they were past. But Neipperg, as he spurred on, delivered a vicious blind swipe at George's back. Mary cried out, but there was another clang—George had dropped his point behind his back to guard against just that attack.

"Foul blow!" Bysshe cried, from the porch, then clapped his hands. "Good work, George!"

George turned with an intent smile on his face, as if he had the measure of his opponent. There was a cry from elsewhere in the farmhouse, and Claire came running, terror in her eyes. "Are they fighting?" she wailed, and pushed past Mary to get to the window.

Mary tried to pull her back and failed. Her head swam. "You don't want to watch this," she said.

Alba began to cry from the cellar. Claire pushed the shutters wide and thrust her head out.

"Kill him, George!" she shouted. "Kill him!"

George gave no sign of having heard—he and Neipperg were trotting at each other again, and George was crouched down over his horse's neck, his attention wholly on his opponent.

Mary watched over Claire's shoulder as the two approached, as blades flashed and clanged—once, twice—and then George thrust to Neipperg's throat and Mary gasped, not just at the pitilessness of it, but at its strange physical consummation, at the way horse and rider and arm and sword, the dart of the blade and momentum of the horse and rider, merged for an instant in an awesome moment of perfection ...

Neipperg rode on for a few seconds while blood poured like a tide down his white shirtfront, and then he slumped and fell off his animal like a sack. Mary shivered, knowing she'd just seen a man killed, killed with absolute forethought and deliberation. And George, that intent look still on his face as he watched Neipperg over his shoulder, lowered his scarlet-tipped sword and gave a careless tug of the reins to turn his horse around ...

Too careless. The horse balked, then turned too suddenly. Its hind legs slid out from under it on the slick grass. George's arms windmilled as he tried to regain his balance, and the horse, with an almost-human cry, fell heavily on George's right leg.

Claire and Mary cried out. The Lipizzaner's legs flailed in the air as he rolled over on George. Bysshe launched himself off the porch in a run. George began to scream, a sound that raised the hair on Mary's neck.

And, while Adam von Neipperg twitched away his life on the grass, Marie-Louise of Austria, France, and Parma, hearing George's cries of agony, bolted hysterically for the door and ran out onto the yard and into the arms of her countrymen.

"No!" George insisted. "No surgeons!" Not a word, Mary noted, for the lost Marie-Louise. She watched from the doorway as his friends carried him in and laid him on the kitchen table. The impassive M. Fleury cut the boot away with a pair of shears and tore the leather away with a suddenness that made George gasp. Bysshe peeled away the bloody stocking, and bit his lip at the sight of protruding bone.

"We *must* show this to the surgeon, George," Bysshe said. "The foot and ankle are shattered."

"No!" Sweat beaded on George's forehead. "I've seen surgeons at their work. My God—" There was horror in his eyes. "I'll be a *cripple!*"

M. Fleury said nothing, only looked down at the shattered ankle with his knowing veteran's eyes. He hitched up his trousers, took a bucket from under the cutting board, and left to get ice for Mary.

The Austrians were long gone, ridden off with their blonde trophy. Their fallen paladin was still in the yard—he'd only slow down their escape.

George was pale and his skin was clammy. Claire choked back tears as she looked down at him. "Does it hurt very much?"

"Yes," George confessed, "it does. Perhaps Madame Fleury would oblige me with a glass of brandy."

Madame Fleury fetched the jug and some glasses. Pásmány stood in the corner exuding dark Hungarian gloom. George looked up at Mary, seemed surprised to find her out of bed.

"I seem to be unlucky for your little family," he said. "I hope you will forgive me."

"If I can," said Mary.

George smiled. "Truthful Miss Mary. How fine you are." A spasm of pain took him and he gasped. Madame Fleury put some brandy in his hand and he gulped it.

"Mary!" Bysshe rushed to her. "You should not be seeing this. Go back to your bed."

"What difference does it make?" Mary said, feeling the blood streaking her legs; but she allowed herself to be put to bed.

Soon the tub of icewater was ready. It was too big to get through the door into Mary's room, so she had to join George in the kitchen after all. She sat in the cold wet, and Bysshe propped her back with pillows, and they both watched as the water turned red.

George was pale, gulping brandy from the bottle. He looked at Bysshe.

"Perhaps you could take our mind off things," he said. "Perhaps you could tell me one of your ghost stories."

Bysshe could not speak. Tears were running down his face. So to calm him, and to occupy her time when dying, Mary began to tell a story. It was about an empty man, a Swiss baron who was a genius but who lacked any quality of soul. His name, in English, meant the Franked Stone—the stone whose noble birth had paid its way, but which was still a stone, and being a stone unable to know love.

And the baron had a wasting disease, one that caused his limbs to wither and die. And he knew he would soon be a cripple.

Being a genius the baron thought he knew the answer. Out of protoplasm and electricity and parts stolen from the graveyard he built another man. He called this man a monster, and held him prisoner. And every time one of the baron's limbs began to wither, he'd arrange for his assistants to cut off one of the monster's limbs, and use it to replace the baron's withered part. The monster's own limb was replaced by one from the graveyard. And the monster went through enormous pain, one hideous surgical procedure after another, but the baron didn't care, because he was whole again and the monster was only a monster, a thing he had created.

But then the monster escaped. He educated himself and grew in understanding and apprehension and he spied on the baron and his family. In revenge the monster killed everyone the baron knew, and the baron was angered not because he loved his family but because the killings were an offense to his pride. So the baron swore revenge on the monster and began to pursue him.

The pursuit took the baron all over the world, but it never ended. At the end the baron pursued the monster to the Arctic, and disappeared forever into the ice and mist, into the heart of the white desert of the Pole.

Mary meant the monster to be Soul, of course, and the baron Reason. Because unless the two could unite in sympathy, all was lost in ice and desolation.

It took Mary a long time to tell her story, and she couldn't tell whether George understood her meaning or not. By the time she finished the day was almost over, and her own bleeding had stopped. George had drunk himself nearly insensible, and a diffident notary had arrived from St. Prex to take everyone's testimony.

Mary went back to bed, clean sheets and warmth and the arms of her lover. She and her child would live.

The surgeon came with them, took one look at George's foot, and announced it had to come off.

The surgery was performed on the kitchen table, and George's screams rang for a long time in Mary's dreams.

In a few days Mary had largely recovered. She and Bysshe thanked the Fleurys and sailed to Geneva on a beautiful autumn day in their hired boat. George and Claire—for Claire was George's again—remained behind to sort out George's legal problems. Mary didn't think their friendship would last beyond George's immediate recovery, and she hoped that Claire would not return to England heavy with another child.

After another week's recovery in Geneva, Bysshe and Mary headed for England and the financial rescue of Mr. Godwin. Mary had bought a pocketbook and was already filling its pages with her story of the Franked Stone. Bysshe knew any number of publishers, and assured her it would find a home with one of them.

Frankenstein was an immediate success. At one point there were over twenty stage productions going on at once. Though she received no money from the stage adaptations, the book proved a very good seller, and was never out of print. The royalties proved useful in supporting Bysshe and Mary and Claire—once she returned to them, once more with child—during years of wandering, chiefly in Switzerland and Italy.

George's promised thousand pounds a year never materialized.

And the monster, the poor abused charnel creature that was Mary's settlement with death, now stalked through the hearts of all the world.

George went to South America to sell his sword to the revolutionary cause. Mary and Bysshe, reading of his exploits in tattered newspapers sent from England, found it somehow satisfying that he was, at last and however reluctantly, fighting for liberty.

They never saw him again, but Mary thought of him often—the great, famed figure, limping painfully through battle after battle, crippled, ever-restless, and in his breast the arctic waste of the soul, the franked and steely creator with his heart of stone.

First of all, I would like to thank my wife Kathy Hedges for this story's splendid title.

"Wall, Stone, Craft" is part of a series of stories, so far incomplete, to which I have given the totally uncommercial name "Dead Romantics." Each of these science fiction stories features an author as its protagonist. The first, "No Spot of Ground," chronicled the Civil War adventures of Brigadier General Edgar A. Poe, CSA. Stories planned, yet not written, will involve Mark Twain and Ambrose Bierce. "Red Elvis," seen elsewhere in this volume, isn't quite a part of the Dead Romantics series, but is perhaps a first cousin.

The Dead Romantics stories are purely self-indulgence. I write them entirely for the pleasure of the act, and because I am interested in certain types of creative minds in certain types of situations. I don't necessarily expect anyone else to understand them. They are pet projects, written only when the stories are fully matured in my thoughts, which is one reason why the series has taken so long to complete.

It may be surprising that "Wall, Stone, Craft" started as a story about Jane Austen. What would happen, I originally wondered, if the author of such propriety-obsessed novels as Mansfield Park were to have a blazing and highly public affaire with Lord Byron, the Regency's original bad boy?

A glance at the encyclopedia showed that this intriguing notion wouldn't hold water. About the time that Byron was cutting his first swath through London society, Jane Austen was dying of Bright's disease in a seaside resort. The generations were just too far apart chronologically.

Miss Jane, though not present in the story, remains represented by her brother Frank, a sterling naval officer who ended his life as Admiral of the Fleet. And Byron is forced to keep company, more or less, mostly with the people who kept company with him historically.

"Wall, Stone, Craft," in its final version, is composed of two interlinked ideas. First an idea that Byron himself advanced, that had he not been born with a clubfoot he would have become a military man. Second, the notion, popularized by Brian Aldiss among others, that *Frankenstein* was the first and most paradigmatic science fiction novel. Would a different Byron, a military Byron, have resulted in Mary Shelley's creating a different Baron Frankenstein, and thus a different paradigm for science fiction?

I also wanted to write what I suspect is the first fictional treatment of Mary Shelley and Byron in which they *didn't* go to bed with one another.

As with others of my historicals, all named characters, with the exception of the sturdy Swiss farmer Fleury, existed historically, including the remarkable Adam von Neipperg, a dashing adventurer who really was entrusted by the Allied governments with the delicate task of seducing the Empress Marie-Louise.

I was very pleased when "Wall, Stone, Craft," my little self-indulgence that I expected no one else to understand, was nominated for the Nebula, Hugo, and World Fantasy awards.

Acknowledgments

Every NESFA Press book is the result of a combined effort on the part of many people whose only aim is to share their favorite stories by their favorite authors with other fans. The editor wishes to gratefully acknowledge the efforts of this mighty cadre of proofreaders: Bonnie Atwood, Nomi Burstein, Michael Feldhusen, Paul Giguere, Mark Hertel, Rick Katze, and Joe Rico. Thanks to Paul Giguere and Mark Olson for editorial suggestions. Groveling, effusive thanks to my wife, Ann A. Broomhead, for her thorough proofing and unlimited patience. Thanks also to NESFA's Proofreader Emeritus, George Flynn for his complete proofing of this volume, to Lisa Hertel for her work on the cover design and layout, and to NESFA's Publications Czar Tony Lewis. My eternal gratitude to the artist, Omar Rayyan, for his wonderful cover art, cover design, and delightful interior illustrations. Thanks to The Writer for his good humor and cooperation. Lastly, I acknowledge Michael A. Burstein for no particular reason.

Timothy P. Szczesuil
Wayland, MA
December 1997

Colophon

The text of this book was scanned using a venerable HP Scanjet 3P (B&W), spell checked and proofed in Microsoft Word 95, and typeset using Adobe PageMaker 6.5 in our favorite font: Adobe Garamond 11 on 12, and in the story afterwards in Arial 10 on 11.

Current Titles from the NESFA Press

The Essential Hal Clement Series

Trio for Slide Rule and Typewriter:
The Essential Hal Clement, Vol. 1 .... $25
Music of Many Spheres:
The Essential Hal Clement, Vol. 2 .... $25
Variations on a Theme by Sir Isaac Newton:
The Essential Hal Clement, Vol. 3 .... $25

Major Ingredients by Eric Frank Russell $29
Moon Dogs by Michael Swanwick
(The Boskone 37 Book) $25
Rings by Charles Harness $25
Double Feature by Emma Bull & Will Shetterly
(Trade Paperback) $13
Dreamweaver's Dilemma by Lois McMaster Bujold
(Trade Paperback) $12

The Cordwainer Smith Series

The Rediscovery of Man: The Complete Short Science
Fiction of Cordwainer Smith $25
Norstrilia by Cordwainer Smith $22
Concordance to Cordwainer Smith by Anthony Lewis
(Trade Paperback) $13

All titles are hardback unless otherwise noted, and printed on long-life acid-free paper. NESFA Press accepts payment by mail by check, Mastercard or Visa. Please add $2 postage ($4 for multiple books) for each order ($4/$8 out of US). Massachusetts residents please add 5% sales tax. Write for our complete catalog. You can also receive our catalog by email; for more information direct your Internet web browser to www.nesfa.org.

Write to: NESFA Press
                 PO Box 809
                 Framingham, MA 01701

FAX (Visa/MC orders): 617-776-3243
Orders take about 3 weeks to arrive.